CW01024941

FAMILY ROUNDABOUT

Persephone Book N°24
Published by Persephone Books Ltd 2001

First published 1948 by Hutchinson

Endpapers taken from 'Roundabout', a cotton and rayon tissue designed by Albert Swindells for Warners in 1946. Reproduced by courtesy of Warner Fabrics Archive.

Typeset in ITC Baskerville by Keystroke,
Jacaranda Lodge, Wolverhampton

Colour by Cheney & Sons Ltd, Banbury

Printed and bound by Biddles Ltd,
Guildford and King's Lynn

ISBN 1 903155 134

Persephone Books Ltd
28 Great Sutton Street
London EC1V 0DS
020 7253 5454

www. persephonebooks.co.uk

FAMILY ROUNDABOUT

by

RICHMAL CROMPTON

with a new preface by

JULIET AYKROYD

PERSEPHONE BOOKS
LONDON

PREFACE

Richmal Crompton is not well known for her novels. She is famously the creatrix of William: scruffy, pugnacious anti-hero of 345 stories for children. William was a success from his debut in Newnes' *Home* Magazine in 1919. Here was the David-and-Goliath story refreshingly recast with an indomitable 11-year-old pitted against a world of obtuse relatives, foolish vicars, maiden ladies, pseuds, wimps, churls and curly-haired cads. By 1969 – the year Crompton died – 30 collections of *William* stories had sold over 8 million copies. Though some of his behaviour has been censured (and censored) for incorrectness, the stories are still very funny; and their shelf life goes on, with reprints in 1999 of 20 collections, radio and television spin-offs, a website, translations into 28 languages including Icelandic, an annual William conference and a society of devotees, the Outlaws Club, whose members include politicians and film stars. An icon of comic subversion, with appeal to boys and girls of all ages, William sits scowlingly enthroned.

Crompton once hinted ruefully that her 'Frankenstein's monster' had ambushed recognition she would have welcomed for her serious fiction. Between 1923 and 1960 she published

9 volumes of short stories and 41 novels. These sold steadily, attracted warm reviews and a faithful readership, but were not best sellers. After launching 12 of them, the chairman of Hodder suggested structural changes which, he claimed, would boost sales of her future work into the best-selling class. She promptly changed publishers. Her novels drew on sensitive personal experience, and could not be written to anyone's formula. She did not need to make money. The William stories brought her in a good income from the start – enough to build herself a house near Bromley in Kent and contribute with characteristic generosity to the support of her mother and siblings all her life. Much as she enjoyed writing the best of her children's stories, in her view they were potboilers: the novels were much more important to her.

Her favoured form is the family saga, an excellent vehicle for a gifted story-teller. In *Portrait of a Family* (1931), *There are Four Seasons* (1937), *Weatherley Parade* (1944) and *The Ridleys* (1947) she adroitly handles a large cast over several generations. *Family Roundabout* (1948) deals with two widowed matriarchs, each with five children and several grandchildren, and takes us from 1920 to 1939.

These were years of upheaval for women. In the wake of the Great War came emancipation and accelerating social change. To be married and have children was no longer a woman's only acceptable destiny (Crompton herself did not marry). Divorce was fraught, but not the hushed calamity it had been once. And in the aftermath of Freud and Jung, the right psychological climate for the upbringing of children was being anxiously discussed as never before, with the work of liberal innovators like Montessori and Piaget in opposition to the views of behaviourists and child 'trainers' like Truby-King. A fervent awareness of these matters is at the heart of *Family Roundabout*.

The title has many resonances. It is an apt image of the up-and-down fortunes of the Fowlers and Willoughbys, who are entwined by the marriage of Helen Fowler and Max Willoughby. Roundabouts exert centrifugal as well as cohesive forces, and a favourite theme of Crompton's is how families can entrap as well as sustain: its members must strike a balance between responsibility and personal freedom. Because of Judy's dependence on her, Mrs. Fowler is powerless to go on the travels she longs for. Those who make a half-hearted attempt to abandon the carousel, Oliver Willoughby for example, are left dangling. Those who leap right off, like Judy and Peter Fowler, hurt others as well as themselves.

The two clans spin around the pivotal figures of the two matriarchs, who embody opposite kinds of mothering. *Family Roundabout* could be described as a novel-length debate on the subject of what makes a good mother, and in the course of it there is plenty to entertain us in the polarised portraits of Mrs. Fowler and Mrs. Willoughby. There is a whiff of class difference, very much of its time: the Fowlers are down-at-heel gentry, the Willoughbys are rich 'trade': but the distinction is no more than a background wash for more interesting contrasts.

At first our sympathies are swung a little unevenly towards Mrs. Fowler. She has about her (as her daughter Judy puts it) 'this suggestion of loving, uncritical understanding. She was never inquisitive about one's affairs. She was content to give all and demand nothing in return.' Mrs. Willoughby, contrariwise, 'expected – and received – implicit obedience' from everybody. Mrs. Fowler is diffident to the point of self-effacement: 'She shrank from bringing pressure to bear on (her children) in any way, or obtruding on their privacy, and so, she suspected, she often failed them.' Mrs. Willoughby is bossy and interfering, and so blinkered that the downtrodden Cynthia is the only child she deems 'really satisfactory'. Mrs. Fowler is bookish; Langley Place looks out over a lawn and flower garden to a park and hills beyond. Mrs. Willoughby is a philistine of the 'no-novels-before-tea' school, and The Beeches seems to have no outlook at all, physical or spiritual. We feel comfortable with Mrs. Fowler's whimsical charm, her beautiful threadbare furnishings and sweet-smelling flowers. Mrs. Willoughby keeps us at a distance with her 'massive, solid, expensive and ugly' house and her 'uncompromising expression.' Her barometrical eagle's-beak nose has a cartoon-like clarity; Mrs. Fowler's features are misty. Mrs. Willoughby is decisive. Mrs. Fowler is vague, sometimes wilfully; and we enjoy her inner altercations between Milly and Millicent; Mrs. Willoughby rarely lets us into her thoughts.

In a nice symbolic touch, we first meet Mrs. Fowler lounging on her terrace in 'a shabby chair, with stray bits of wicker protruding from arms and legs.' At the same moment the upright Mrs. Willoughby is arranging her expensive mahogany drawing-room chairs in a large semi-circle, 'a symbol of the family unity.' For Sunday tea Mrs. Fowler's family has cucumber sandwiches, strawberries and cream and 'the iced cake for which Cook was famous.' Mrs. Willoughby with her own hands prepares a lavish buffet like a picture from Mrs. Beeton of 'cold chickens, cold ham, pattees, galantines, prawns in aspic, jellies, creams, trifles, blancmanges, biscuits and cakes of every kind.' Which meal, we are invited to consider, would we rather be offered?

Being a good novelist, Crompton does not come up with answers, and the mothering debate is not tidily resolved. Mrs. Fowler's hands-off approach is on the face of it more appealing than Mrs. Willoughby's repressive autocracy, but in the end we are left pondering. What *is* a successful mother, or, come to that, a successful child? If a happy marriage is a measure of success, the Fowler children are disasters (apart from Helen whose marriage is humdrum.) They all become entangled in dismal problems. Not one of them seems equipped to make wise choices. Mrs. Fowler's self-effacement begins to look like timorousness, or indolence, even a kind of opting-out. Perhaps her suspicions were right, and she *has* failed them. Two thirds of the way through the book she takes up her tapestry work

> . . . then let it fall on her lap and sat motionless. . . . Matthew, Peter, Helen, Anice, Judy. . . . The shadows seemed to be closing round all of them. And I can't do anything to help them, she thought. . . . All I can do is to sit here and worry.

Mrs. Willoughby also shifts in our estimation. Her nurturing is to say the least unimaginative, but 'tempered by genuine kindness.' She is formidable but never malicious. She begins to topple in Chapter Fourteen, when she is defied by her granddaughter Jessica. In this forceful scene the reader's feelings are cleverly engaged on the child's side as she gulps and quivers with terror; the outburst comes with shock and release:

> 'I *won't* go,' she said. 'If you drag me there, I'll fight all the way. I'll scratch and kick and bite you. I *hate* you. When I'm grown up I'll go right away from you and never speak to you or see you again. You're a horrid, cruel old woman.' (Beneath her rage stirred a sudden feeling of exultation. I'm not frightened of her any more. I shall never be frightened of her again.) 'I wish I had someone else for a grandmother. I wish I had – someone kind like Mrs. Fowler.'

This is a turning point in the novel, and the blow couldn't be worse for Mrs. Willoughby. Up to now she has been 'omnipotent and aloof.' Here is the first 'crack in the foundation of her house.' She is undermined by feelings she is not self-perceptive enough to analyse, but from now on her colourless offspring struggle to regain the vitality she has sapped from them and slip one by one from her control, leaving her lonely and rheumatic. Because she has enfeebled their emotional capacities and demands, her sons and daughters ironically end up happier by a fraction than the Fowler children. And when Jessica's threat proves prophetic and she goes off to Spain with her Communist, the inference is that by the 1930s the family roundabout is beginning to lose its concentric power, and each subsequent generation will find it easier to spin off and away.

In retrospect, Mrs. Fowler's Sunday tea at the beginning was a little too dainty. Mrs. Willoughby's massive repast offered substance, but was too cold, too glutinous. When Mrs. Fowler is for once forced to take some positive action, and decide what to do about Gillian's party frock (one of the novel's best episodes), she has to metamorphose:

> 'Perhaps if I pretend to be Mrs. Willoughby, it will come to me, thought Mrs. Fowler. . . . She stood in the middle of her bedroom and pretended to be Mrs. Willoughby . . . thinking herself with desperate intensity into that brisk, efficient personality. She glanced at the mirror on the wall, half expecting to see an eagle's beak in place of her own nose. She didn't, but in that moment she knew what Mrs. Willoughby would have done. . . . '

The final word on the mothering question is probably Mrs. Fowler's: '*I'd be better if I had more of her in me*. A little smile twitched her lips. *And perhaps she'd be better if she had more of me in her. . . .*' But the very last poignant frame of the two old ladies broadly reconciled, cutting and dealing a pack of cards, seems to absolve both of ultimate responsibility for their children's lives: no one has control over the hand dealt to them by fate.

The tale of the two matriarchs is the hub of the story; the subplots are woven around it artfully, like teams on an old-time roundabout, with characters thematically coupled in lights and shades: sophisticated Judy with immature Cynthia, smug Helen with shrewish Anice, brazen Belle with quiet Rachel, feckless Martin with sturdy Max, sensitive Peter with blockish Matthew, unproductive Oliver with over-productive Arnold. The Peter-Belle-Matthew-Rachel drama packs the most punch, with its surprising reversals and painful, understated climax. Sex and adultery are not glamorised in Crompton's books, and divorce is generally bitter and best avoided (she supported her own sister Gwen through unpleasant divorce proceedings). However, she offers one hopeful outcome here in another strand of the good-mothering theme: the touching survival of Gillian, rescued by events from the appalling Belle. Gillian is one of many convincing unsickly child-portrayals in Crompton's novels, and Belle is an acutely-observed casebook neurotic; Rachel in *Portrait of a Family*, and Lilian in *The Old Man's Birthday* (1934) are earlier versions of Belle.

The male characters revolve somewhat woodenly on the edge of the roundabout, as they tend to in other women's novels of the period. Crompton is recounting the lives of women, not the history of men; Hitler is marginalised in one sentence (and anonymously) by Mrs. Willoughby as a 'common little German upstart'. The foolish Max and the fussy Oliver are close to caricature. Men are characterised by facial distinctions: Peter Fowler's smile is 'rather a lighting up of his thin, sensitive face than an actual movement of his lips', and, whether consciously or not, Crompton equates unattractiveness with niceness; the unfortunate but kindly Martin's mouth 'was the ugliest [Anice] had ever seen – his teeth so over-crowded and irregular that it seemed his lips could only just close over them.' There are interesting tensions in the strikingly handsome Arnold, the one really dislikeable person in the book, and the sexually-queasy Judy-Arnold relationship. Arnold's awfulness as a person and a novelist is thrust hard at us. The description in Chapter Twenty-Three of a standard Arnold novel ('Arnold liked his heroes and heroines to meet first in childhood, to cherish the memory of each other . . . then to meet again by chance . . . One of them was generally married, which provided the . . . drama necessary to draw out the story to the requisite three hundred pages.') is disconcertingly close to the plot of one of Crompton's own early novels, and implies some fierce, possibly subliminal exercise in satirical self-deprecation.

Family Roundabout is the work of a mature writer. It avoids sentimentality and melodrama, is unflaggingly readable and the pared-down style makes for some deadpan comic effects:

> There was a short silence, in which Aunt Bessie could be heard saying earnestly to Max:
>
> 'And there's always senna, Josiah. I've never known senna to fail.'
>
> 'Let's go in to supper,' said Mrs. Willoughby abruptly.

The dialogue owes something to Ivy Compton-Burnett, whom Crompton admired, also to the terseness of film-speak. And radio is an important influence: by 1948 she had been turning the *William* stories into radio scripts for four years. The conversation between Mrs. Willoughby and Helen as they prepare for Clarissa's party could be an extract from a radio play:

> 'I think that's enough bread-and-butter, don't you? They won't eat much with all these jellies and trifles and things. . . . Shall we start on the sandwiches now? Gillian sent an acceptance, very badly worded and spelt abominably. You'd have thought that Belle would have helped her with it.'
>
> 'They must begin with bread-and-butter, but – yes, perhaps this is enough. . . . I don't listen to rumours of that sort as a rule, but people are talking a good deal about your sister-in-law.'
>
> 'And Tony Westerham,' said Helen. 'I know . . . I've got the tomatoes here ready sliced. . . . And they're saying that Matthew drinks and knocks her about.'
>
> 'There's no truth in that, of course. . . . Don't make them too thin.'

Had she been born later, with her good ear for natural speech and her idiosyncratic visual sense Richmal Crompton could surely have written excellent TV serials.

Overall, the novel is more sombre than its predecessors, as if tinged by the austerity and isolation of England during the war years, the need for reticence, the battening-down on spontaneity. It may also be coloured by personal memories. Crompton's mother, Clara Lamburn, died in 1939, the year in which *Family Roundabout* ends. She lived with Richmal as companion, housekeeper, proof-reader and business manager for 22 years. In 1923 she nursed her 33-year-old daughter through an attack of polio which left her partially disabled; later both women suffered from breast cancer. Clara was a powerful person: self-confident, extrovert, a founder of the Bromley Common W.I., and a great maker of jam. She held court every Saturday at Medhurst's in Bromley, and expected all her family to attend, exactly as Mrs. Willoughby demands that her family turn up at Crofton's in Bellington. Her granddaughter Margaret Disher described her as 'majestic, beautiful, kind and sympathetic' though 'not exactly cuddly. . . . ' Her nurturing may well have been on the overwhelming side. At the risk of descending to what Dorothy L. Sayers dismissed as 'a slovenly sub-department of morbid psychology', one might hazard a guess that the two *Family Roundabout* matriarchs are a composite representation of Clara, and reflect some at least of her daughter's retrospective filial feelings.

For all its crepuscular mood, there are some sparkling pleasures in the novel. Sewing is a *leitmotif*, signifying stability and usefulness – the essence of female-ness. (Mrs. Brown's therapeutic sock-mending is a running gag in the *William* stories). In *Family Roundabout* different women sew different things; Mrs. Willoughby is a mender; Helen embroiders; Florence knits; Cynthia stitches name-tapes; Mrs. Fowler reluctantly does tapestry (Crompton herself used to sit sewing tapestry in the evenings with Clara). Clothes are given metaphorical meanings: the interchangeable Florence and Gertrude, for instance, wear 'dresses of foulard silk of the same pattern, except that Gertrude's had a blue ground and Florence's a beige.' Among the 'crow-like assembly' of poor relations the maverick Miss Hatton shines out in her pink tulle bow. Belle plans her appearance – with her baby as matching accessory – in red and white, the colours of her own hysteria. Particularly well-observed are the family-gathering set-pieces: the tea parties, the wedding at Langley Place, the christening and the literary evening are alive with details picked out and animated as if through the eye of a film camera.

Sometimes the writer's impish sense of the absurd bubbles up unchecked. When Oliver pontificates on Max and Helen's wedding he might have dropped in from a *William* story:

> Why this senseless parade of fashion and snobbery to mark the mating of a couple of animals? (A rather daring sentiment that he hoped to develop later into a piece of *vers libre* and send to one of the more advanced literary weeklies.) The sight of all these smug bourgeois nonentities swilling champagne was enough to make one feel sick – especially when one thought of the unemployed with barely enough to keep body and soul together.
>
> He seized a glass of champagne from a passing tray and a caviar sandwich from another and continued his meditations. . . .

Richmal Crompton once told an interviewer that in William she had 'released all her criminal tendencies.' In *Anne Morrison* (1925) the eponymous heroine is seized by 'a spirit of elfin mischief':

> She would join suddenly in the 'ragging' of . . . some inefficient mistress or monitress, grow more and more daring and fey with excitement, till she was taking the lead and the rest were following her with delight. Those irresponsible moments won her great popularity.

Anne Morrison has autobiographical elements, and here perhaps is a glimpse of the 'William' part of Richmal Crompton: intoxicated with creative power, scornful of stupidity, defiant of tyranny in all shapes, dogged, shatteringly honest. We might regret that she did not release more 'criminal tendencies' into her grown-up fiction, take more risks, push the boundaries of decorum and acceptability a little further. If her novels are (as she said of them herself with her usual modesty) among 'the second ranks of literature', William stands accused of syphoning off inspirational energy that might well have turned her into that rare phenomenon: a great and lasting comic novelist.

As it is, in *Family Roundabout* the criminal-William tendencies are transmuted into something extremely likeable: gleeful humour, acute observation of human silliness, compassion for the disempowered, and – a tribute to her Derbyshire background – a robust, no-nonsense approach to the business of everyday living. There is no pretension. On the other hand, there is stoicism – perhaps derived from personal affliction, and also from the Greek literature which she taught as a young woman, and loved all her life. The up-beat sense of continuity in *Family Roundabout* is beyond the scope of a formulaic *William* story. It is well expressed by a character in *Quartet* (1935):

There is no greater mistake than to take a too gloomy view of life. Life has its prisons, yes, but it has also its releases from prisons . . . As one grows older one becomes more optimistic. The great thing to remember about life is that it is wholly unexpected.

Juliet Aykroyd
London, 2001

FAMILY ROUNDABOUT

CHAPTER ONE

One Sunday afternoon in the July of 1920 Mrs. Fowler was sitting in her wicker chair under the lime tree at the end of the terrace. It was a shabby chair, with stray bits of wicker protruding from arms and legs, but it was comfortable and Mrs. Fowler preferred it to a deck-chair. She said that she always got entangled in deck-chairs when she tried to put them up herself, and, when they were finally put up by someone else, she never felt quite safe.

From where she sat she could see the green sweep of the lawn, merging into the darker green of the park, where cattle sheltered from the heat in the shade of the elm trees, and beyond that the blue haze of the distant hills. Over everything lay the stillness of the midsummer afternoon, and Mrs. Fowler, sitting there, slight and grey-haired, her hands in her lap, her eyes fixed on the distance, seemed to be part of the stillness.

Her thoughts had gone back into the past. On this day, thirty years ago, she had come to Langley Place as a bride. She had stood here on the terrace with Henry, looking out over lawn and parkland and meadow to the misty slopes of the hills. Henry, inarticulate, undemonstrative, had taken her hand in his, and she had known by the tightening of his clasp how deeply moved he was. Somehow the Henry of those early years – tall, handsome, virile, with the slight pomposity of manner that masked his secret shyness – was more real to her than the aging Henry of the later years.

He had been ten years her senior, and she had fallen in love with him at their first meeting, realizing even then how unlike she was to the wife he wanted. He wanted, she knew, a 'little woman', clinging, adoring, self-effacing, ready to accept and defer to his judgment – a replica, in short, of his mother. And deliberately, determinedly, she had set to work to make herself that woman, becoming, for love of him, stupid and docile, hiding her intelligence as though it were some secret vice. Stupidity is not an easy quality to assume, and there had been times when her real self had broken through the barricade, and she had startled and hurt him by what he called her 'oddness', but on the whole they had been happy. She had known the price she must pay for his love and she had been willing to pay it.

Her name was Millicent, but Henry, who liked diminutives, had called her Milly. She always thought of the quick-witted, quick-tempered girl who still existed somewhere within her as Millicent and Henry's wife as Milly. 'Now, Millicent . . .' she would say to herself warningly, as she bit back some trenchant comment, some shrewd rejoinder.

When her first passion for him cooled she had learnt to love him for his honesty and sincerity, for the sheer simple goodness and kindliness that underlay his narrowness and prejudice. And things were easier, of course, when the children came. The five of them absorbed her time and energies, so that she had perforce to become the quiet, beneficent ruler of the household that Henry had always believed her to be.

When he died, six years ago, she did not, as she had thought she would, resume the individuality she had cast off. The children took for granted in her the character she had shown ever since they could remember, and instinctively she continued to act her part. She remained where Henry had put her, where the children expected to find her, tranquil and unchanging, in the background of their lives. . . . Milly, Henry's wife. . . . Less and less often she had to say, 'Now, Millicent . . .'

* * *

She was glad to have this hour of quiet before the children arrived. (She still thought of them as the children, though Matthew, the eldest, was twenty-eight, Peter twenty-six, Anice twenty-four, Helen twenty-two and Judy, the baby, sixteen.) The anniversary of her first coming to Langley Place meant more to her even than the anniversary of her wedding, was a more precious and intimate memory than the memory of the crowded church, the noisy reception, the apologetic clumsiness of Henry's embraces. . . . She had stood just there at the top of the terrace steps, wearing a grey travelling dress and a small grey hat with wings. Nothing in the scene around had altered since then but everything was different. Then she had been a stranger looking at it shyly and a little apprehensively. It had seemed suspicious and remote, even faintly hostile. Now it was familiar and beloved. They belonged to each other, were on terms of comfortable intimacy, knew the best and worst of each other. Hardly a tree, hardly an inch of ground but held its memories.

It was only from this side of the house that the view remained unchanged. Langley Place had been the 'big house' of Hurstmede, a small village about three miles distant from the country town of Bellington, and between the two, along a lane where the branches of the trees on either side met overhead, had plied an ancient horse-drawn wagonette, whose times of stopping and starting were as erratic as its driver. Now neat little villas took the place of fields and hedges, the lane had been widened and macadamized, and a reliable service of motor-buses had supplanted the wagonette.

These changes had saddened Henry, but it was the Willoughbys' paper-mill that had seemed to him the final affront. The little villas were hidden by trees from the garden of Langley Place. Once within the big iron gates, he could pretend that they did not exist.

But the Willoughbys' mill was a monstrosity. Massive, barrack-like, it towered above the trees, dominating not only Bellington but the surrounding countryside.

The Willoughbys – as dominating as the mill they owned – lived on the outskirts of Bellington. Henry had always been scrupulously polite when he came in contact with them, but the orbits of the two families had lain far apart.

Those were the days of rigid class distinctions, and the Fowlers were of the county, while the Willoughbys were of the town. They sat on the same committees, attended the same public functions, but did not visit each other. Mrs. Fowler suspected that the Willoughbys felt the same contempt for Henry as Henry, half unconsciously, felt for them. Henry was in their eyes a useless member of the community, while the Willoughbys were the community itself. They were its mayors, its town councillors, its Guardians of the Poor. They organized its Christmas treats, its Poor Children's Holidays, its Old People's Parties. And it was Mrs. Willoughby, eagle-eyed, eagle-beaked, built on the formidable lines of a dreadnought, who was the ruling spirit of the clan. . . .

After the deaths of Henry and Mr. Willoughby (they had died the same year) the families had drawn closer together. Helen had joined the Bellington Tennis Club and had become acquainted with Max Willoughby – an acquaintance that had quickly ripened into friendship. Judy went to Bellington High School and had discovered in Cynthia Willoughby the complete identity of taste and outlook that schoolgirls of sixteen are apt to discover in each other.

Both Max and Cynthia were coming to tea today.

* * *

Mrs. Fowler roused herself reluctantly at the sound of Helen's voice. Helen and Anice always went for a walk together on Sunday afternoons, setting off punctually at three o'clock and returning at four. Sometimes Mrs. Fowler suspected that Anice would have been glad to drop the custom but dared not suggest it. Their relations were still the relations of their childhood. Anice sulked and grumbled but did not rebel.

Helen's voice, clear and incisive, cut sharply through the sleepy summer air. Anice's voice in answer was low and indistinct. It lacked the resonant timbre that belonged to Helen's, just as her character lacked the decision of Helen's. Mrs. Fowler sighed and sat upright in her chair, bracing herself to meet the impact of Helen's forcefulness.

'Well, darling,' said Helen, 'had a nice rest?'

She spoke kindly, but her tone implied that neither Mrs. Fowler nor anyone else needed a rest in the middle of the day.

Helen was a strikingly handsome girl, with fair hair, blue eyes, a well-formed mouth and a nose that was one straight line from brow to tip. She was generously proportioned, and about both physique and personality was a forthrightness that some people found a little intimidating. Shyness and wistfulness and wonder had never touched Helen's youth. Anice, too, was fair, but her features were indeterminate, her cheeks pale and her eyes more grey than blue. Beside Helen she looked colourless and insignificant.

'Tea not ready?' continued Helen briskly.

'It's not tea-time, is it?' said Mrs. Fowler, knowing quite well that it was.

'It's after four,' said Helen.

'We had lunch late, dear.'

'We did,' said Helen meaningly. 'At least half an hour late. And even then the meat was underdone. I can't think why you keep Cook, Mother.'

'Well, dear, we've had her for fifteen years,' said Mrs. Fowler.

'Is that any reason for keeping her another fifteen?' said Helen.

'Surely it is, dear,' said Mrs. Fowler.

Mrs. Fowler had learnt to take refuge from Helen's attacks in an intensification of her Milly-ishness. It nonplussed Helen, who did not know how to deal with it.

'The others will be here in a minute, and then everything will be a scramble,' said Helen. 'I suppose Peter and Belle are coming?'

'I hope so, dear,' said Mrs. Fowler.

At that moment Thompson, the housemaid, came out and began to set up the deck-chairs that were stacked against the side of the house. Helen stood and watched her, issuing orders and giving advice. Thompson obeyed in silence, her lips compressed into a thin line. Helen was not popular with the servants. When Thompson had gone Helen set Anice to work, rearranging the chairs and moving them further into the shade. Then she stood gazing at the house, her brows drawn into a frown.

'Those curtains look simply shocking from here, Mother,' she said.

Mrs. Fowler glanced at the tall narrow windows of the drawing-room, outlined in climbing honeysuckle. The sashes were flung up as far as they would go. Curtains of delicate blue damask hung there, faded to grey stripes where the folds met the sunshine.

'I think they look rather nice,' she said mildly. 'So did your father.'

Helen had begun her attempts at reorganizing the

household before she left school. She had even invaded Henry's 'study' – a euphemistic term for the room in which he dozed after meals – and suggested that the lovely, faded Persian carpet, worn and threadbare, should be replaced by a 'nice new Axminster'. Henry, who disliked change of any kind, had been outraged by the suggestion. When she left school she had made determined efforts to take the housekeeping out of Mrs. Fowler's hands, and Mrs. Fowler had resisted her – not because she liked housekeeping, but because she knew that once she began to give in to Helen there would be no end to it. She had her own methods of resistance – methods of gentle obstinacy and stupidity – which had so far served her well.

'Oh, come on,' said Anice impatiently. 'I want to have a wash before people arrive.'

It was characteristic of Anice that, though the sight of Helen's aggressive generalship irritated her, she could not just go away by herself and leave Helen to it. Sometimes it seemed as if she could not do anything without Helen.

'All right,' said Helen. She threw another glance around. 'I hope Thompson will remember to bring out the cushions.'

'She generally does,' said Mrs. Fowler with a hint of Millicent in her voice.

The two girls went towards the house, Helen turning to watch Thompson as she came out with an armful of garden cushions and put them on the deck-chairs.

'There are some more in the summer-house, Thompson,' called Helen.

'I know, Miss. I was just going to fetch them.'

'Well, be quick,' said Helen, vanishing through the open French window of the drawing-room.

Mistress and maid exchanged a covert glance of sympathy, then Thompson set off, a little more slowly than she would otherwise have done – for Helen had that effect on people – towards the summer-house.

Left alone, Mrs. Fowler would have liked to surrender again to the drowsy peace of the afternoon, but the circle of empty deck-chairs, with their silent reminder of the guests who would shortly be arriving, prevented her.

Sunday tea at Langley Place was an informal and very elastic affair. The children invited their friends. Neighbours dropped in. Sometimes so many people came that they had to sit on the balustrade and the steps of the terrace. Since Peter married he had seldom failed to join the party, either alone or with Belle. Lately Max Willoughby had been a regular attendant, and for the last few Sundays Martin Newbolt, a shy, plain youth who seemed to have attached himself to Anice, had hovered on the edge of the group.

She remembered that she had brought out the newspaper, meaning to read it before the guests arrived. She wasn't really interested in politics, and now that she hadn't Henry to keep her up to the mark (Henry had considered it his duty as a citizen to read *The Times* from end to end every day) frequently left her newspaper unread. But occasionally a sense of duty to Henry's memory would drive her to read it – leading articles, financial news and all – however dull it was. She picked it up now from the ground by her feet and scanned the headlines . . . Fresh Irish Atrocities . . . Home Rule

Proposals . . . Bolshevist Menace . . . Pound Sterling Drops Below Four Dollars . . . Then she laid it down again and sat upright in her chair.

Max Willoughby was making his way towards her across the terrace.

CHAPTER TWO

Max Willoughby was a large, blond, well-groomed man of about twenty-seven. He looked, as he was, prosperous, monied, assured. His father's death had left him owner of the Willoughby mill at an early age, and, though it was common knowledge that Mrs. Willoughby still kept the reins of the business in her hands, Max was a figure of local importance, and held a position that many older men envied him.

He greeted Mrs. Fowler with an air of modest deference and took the chair next to hers, smiling as he leant towards her to enquire solicitously after her health. His smile displayed a row of teeth that were just not too white and regular. There was a small, fair moustache on his upper lip. Mrs. Fowler found his largeness and nearness a little overpowering and checked an impulse to move her chair further away.

Reassured as to her health, he leant back and surveyed the empty chairs.

'I hope I'm not too early,' he said.

'Of course not. Helen and Anice will be down in a minute. They're just home from their walk.'

'I believe my young sister's here already.'

'Yes.' Mrs. Fowler glanced up at the open window of Judy's

bedroom, from which a burst of laughter suddenly rang out. 'She's with Judy.'

It had been Henry's idea to send Judy to Bellington High School. He had looked upon it as a democratic gesture, but Mrs. Fowler suspected that he was, perhaps subconsciously, influenced by the staggering sum that had appeared under the heading, 'Extras', on the bills of the expensive boarding school to which he had sent Helen and Anice.

'Got some joke up there,' said Max, smiling indulgently.

The Willoughbys were what is known as 'clannish', and Max was fond of his young sister, mitigating for her, as far as he could, the strictness of his mother's discipline.

'They're doing their homework, I believe,' said Mrs. Fowler. 'Essays or something.'

'Sounds a jolly essay,' said Max. He raised his voice and called, 'Hello, you two!'

Through the open window two heads appeared – Judy's dark, Cynthia's red-gold. They were still laughing.

'Hello,' said Judy; 'we're just coming down. I say, do you know what Cyn's just said? She said – '

The two dissolved into laughter again.

'Tidy your hair before you come down, Judy,' said Mrs. Fowler.

The two heads withdrew to the accompaniment of a fresh burst of giggles. A smile of satisfaction lingered on Max's lips. He had done all he could to encourage the friendship between his sister and Judy. It made the Fowlers less unapproachable, formed a ladder that might lead him to Helen.

'I took a short cut through the rose garden,' he said. 'Your roses are magnificent.'

‘Yes, I’m rather pleased with them,’ she said. ‘I look after them myself, you know, once Grimes has dug them over in the spring.’

‘They’re *splendid*!’ he said earnestly. ‘You evidently put a tremendous amount of work into them. . . . You mustn’t overdo it. Gardening’s very tiring.’

The proprietary tone of his voice startled her. I suppose he’s in love with Helen, she thought. I wonder what she feels about it. . . .

* * *

Then she saw Peter and Belle coming up the terrace steps, and, as she rose to meet them, glanced quickly, anxiously at Peter’s face. It was by Peter’s face, not Belle’s, that you gauged Belle’s mood. Belle always looked radiant and serene. Only the over-bright glancing eyes gave a clue to the neurotic restlessness that drove her. And at sight of Peter’s thin, dark face Mrs. Fowler’s heart sank. He looked worn and tired, the furrows in his cheeks deeply graven. It was evidently one of Belle’s bad days.

‘I don’t know how you can keep so cool,’ said Belle. ‘I find this heat ghastly. I’ve been moving trunks about all morning and I’m worn out.’

‘Moving trunks, dear?’ said Mrs. Fowler.

‘Yes. In the box-room. I wanted to have one side clear for the store cupboard, and it meant moving everything.’

There was no complaint in her voice. Her smile was sweet and untroubled.

‘Surely Peter could have helped you,’ said Mrs. Fowler.

Belle gave a short laugh.

'Oh, Peter! Peter was playing golf.'

'I didn't know she was going to do it,' said Peter.

Mrs. Fowler understood what had happened. Belle resented every interest of Peter's that she did not share, so, to punish him for going to golf, she had spent the morning moving trunks. In any case, when Belle was in a 'mood' she had to do some irksome and wholly unnecessary piece of work in order to add fuel to her resentment.

'I'd told you I wanted it done, darling,' she said.

'I didn't think there was any hurry.'

Belle shrugged eloquently.

'You were a silly child to do it,' said Mrs. Fowler, trying to speak playfully and affectionately. 'There were the maids. Or Miss Horsham would have done it for you.'

'The maids were busy, and – as for Miss Horsham!'

Belle shrugged still more eloquently, and Peter's mouth tightened. So there had been trouble about Miss Horsham, too, thought Mrs. Fowler.

Miss Horsham was a trained children's nurse, whom Belle had recently engaged to look after the two-year-old Gillian. At first Belle had been delighted with her, but Mrs. Fowler had noticed that lately she had been silent when the girl was mentioned. Miss Horsham was pretty and capable and devoted to Gillian, and perhaps Peter had, unwisely, praised her. Praise of any other woman was, in Belle's eyes, a direct insult to herself.

'I'd hoped you'd bring Gillian,' said Mrs. Fowler.

'Belle said she was starting a cold,' said Peter shortly.

Again Mrs. Fowler glanced quickly from one to the other.

Belle used Gillian shamelessly in the intermittent warfare she waged with her husband. She knew that Peter loved bringing Gillian to visit his old home. . . .

'Oh, well,' said Mrs. Fowler lightly, 'come and sit down.'

Belle joined the group on the terrace, sitting down slowly and gracefully, spreading out the skirts of her shell-pink georgette dress. The broad-brimmed hat threw a soft shadow over the lovely heart-shaped face and deepened the blue of her eyes.

'Isn't the scent of the honeysuckle delicious?' said Peter, relaxing wearily in his chair.

Belle wrinkled her small, slightly *retroussé* nose.

'I think it's horrible,' she said. 'So sickly.'

A sudden anger surged over Mrs. Fowler. She might at least let him enjoy the honeysuckle. . . .

Then Thompson brought out the tea – cucumber sandwiches, strawberries and cream, and the iced cake for which Cook was famous – and Anice and Helen came down. They sat together next to Max, and Max and Helen began to discuss a recent tennis tournament in a breezy, impersonal but slightly self-conscious fashion. It was as if they were uncomfortably aware that everyone suspected an 'understanding' between them and were determined to prove that there was none.

Anice joined in the conversation absently. She was bitterly ashamed of the jealousy of Helen that filled her heart. She had always been a little jealous of her, but since they had left school her jealousy had grown so strong that sometimes – just for a fleeting second – she almost hated her. Helen, eighteen months younger, so much prettier, so much more capable, so much more attractive. . . . They went everywhere together as a matter of course, and everywhere Anice found herself overshadowed by the younger sister. If it hadn't been for Helen she, Anice, would have been quite good-looking, but Helen's beauty was like strong sunlight, killing the small flame of Anice's homely prettiness. And because Helen gave her opinion promptly and uncompromisingly on every question that came up no-one ever wanted to hear Anice's.

It occurred to her, as she sat listening to Helen's description of the perfect back hander, how typical it was of the difference between them that Helen should attract a man like Max Willoughby and that she should attract Martin Newbolt – plain, awkward, with neither money nor charm. He had just arrived, and the familiar wave of irritation surged over her as she watched him. He hadn't even the sense to come across and join the group where she was. He smiled at her shyly and sat down in the empty chair next to Belle's.

She studied him covertly. . . . His eyes were beautiful (it was his eyes she had first noticed), but his mouth was the ugliest she had ever seen – his teeth so over-crowded and irregular that it seemed his lips could only just close over them. Whenever she looked at his teeth she thought, Someone ought to have done something about it. . . .

But no one had ever bothered to do anything about Martin. His parents had died when he was a child, and he had grown up anyhow in his uncle's house, one of the tall dark houses in the centre of Bellington in which the aristocracy used to live and which, as the aristocracy moved out towards the country, were becoming, for the most part, lodging-houses or tenements. Martin's uncle kept a bookshop in the Market Square – a dignified family business that, in the time of Martin's grandfather, had been one of the intellectual centres of the town.

It had been a prosperous business in those days, stretching its tentacles into all the surrounding villages. There had generally been a long line of carriages and pony-traps outside Newbolt's. . . . But both Martin and his uncle were vague and impractical, and since W. H. Smith's had opened a branch on the opposite side of the Square, displaying an alluring assortment of fancy goods as well as the latest books, Newbolt's had gone rapidly downhill. . . . She still watched him as he rose to greet a fresh batch of visitors, greeting them with the slight hesitation that marred his speech.

Despite his awkwardness, there was an air of breeding about him that Max, for all his good looks and assurance, lacked. Anice drew comfort from the thought that the Newbolts were people of culture and good family. Martin's uncle was a scholar of Christ Church, and, although he seemed to take so little interest in Martin that he never even knew whether he was at home or not, had sent him to Oxford. If only Martin had been more ambitious! If only he had not been so ready to take his place in the shop when he came down from Oxford! And he appeared to be quite content with it even now – pottering about in the dark little room at the back, studying catalogues, discussing books in a leisurely fashion with old customers who spent more time than money there, neglecting to ingratiate himself with new and wealthier ones.

She had first come to know him in the shop, going to buy books for birthday presents and Christmas presents, finding excuses, as time went on, to make small purchases that she did not really need. She had fought against the attraction. She had always had vague dreams of startling everyone by a brilliant marriage that should redeem her insignificance and put Helen once and for all in the shade. She didn't want to fall in love with Martin Newbolt, but she couldn't help herself. . . . And she had known from the beginning that he was in love with her.

Oddly enough, it was Peter, not Anice, who had first brought him to Langley Place. Peter, who was a partner in an old-established firm of architects in Bellington, had discovered by chance when buying a book on architecture at Newbolt's that he and Martin had several friends in common at Oxford and had asked him to dinner.

Belle, of course, had not liked him. She despised him for working in a shop, and she was piqued because he did not respond to her charm. But once Peter had taken him to Langley Place he continued to attend the Sunday teas there, and Anice continued to call at the shop during the week for packets of envelopes and sheets of brown paper, deciding on each occasion that it must be the last. . . . I shall have to make up my mind soon, she was thinking now, as she watched him. Do I want to marry him? I don't know. . . . I should hate to be poor and live in a poky little house, but I couldn't bear never to see him again. . . . I suppose I do love him. . . . Then she met his eyes, and a wave of happiness surged over her, so deep and strong that there was no room in her heart for anything else.

* * *

'Heard from Matthew lately?' Peter was saying.

'Yes, I had a letter yesterday,' said Mrs. Fowler. 'I'll show it to you after tea. He caught one of those monkeys that keep pulling up his rose trees, but he didn't know what to do with it, so he let it go.'

Peter smiled. His smile was rather a lighting up of his thin, sensitive face than an actual movement of the lips. The two brothers had always been friends, and Peter had missed Matthew more than any of them when he went out to Kenya. Matthew had done well in Kenya, but he was still homesick and was now talking of returning to England. *I don't regret coming here*, he had written in his last letter; *in fact, I wouldn't have missed it for worlds, but if I stay much longer I shall settle down here for good, and I don't want to do that.*

Mrs. Fowler thought of Matthew as he had been when he went away from her – fair, stocky, with a round, pleasant, boyish face – and wondered what the intervening years had done to him.

'He's still thinking of coming back,' she went on.

'Good!' said Peter.

'Back *here*?' said Belle, a note of acid surprise underlying the sweetness of her voice.

Both Peter and Mrs. Fowler realized suddenly that Belle was feeling neglected. Martin Newbolt, who sat next to her, was watching Anice as if Belle did not exist, and it was torture to Belle to be treated as if she did not exist.

'Come and sit near me, dear,' said Mrs. Fowler hastily. 'I've been wanting to talk to you all afternoon.'

But when Belle moved her chair nearer the tea-table Mrs. Fowler couldn't think of anything to say. What Belle wanted, of course, was flattery – she had a diseased appetite for it – and, though Mrs. Fowler often tried to supply it, her native sincerity prevented her. Milly, of course, was insincere up to a point but not to the point required by Belle. . . .

'How charming Helen looks!' said Belle graciously.

'Yes,' agreed Mrs. Fowler. 'She's had that blue linen dress for two or three years, but I always like her in it. Have some more tea, dear?'

'Thank you. It's delicious tea.'

'I got it from Bantram's. I always used to get my tea at Harwood's, you know, but I think I like this better. . . . Mr. Bantram was saying that his wife's taken over the girls' club for the Parish Church. She's been running it for several weeks now.'

'How *does* she find the time?'

'I don't know, but I suppose one can always find time for anything one's keen on. She's certainly a wonderful little woman. She runs the house and the shop and does a hundred and one jobs outside them.'

A harmless enough conversation, thought Mrs. Fowler with satisfaction. Only Peter knew that on Belle's bad days no conversation was harmless. . . .

Mrs. Fowler glanced around.

'Where *are* those two children?' she said.

* * *

Upstairs Judy stood at the dressing-table, drawing a comb through her dark hair.

'It'll be too marvellous if she really does take us up to *Henry the Fifth*,' she said.

Cynthia was sitting on the bed, her elbows on her knees, her chin on her hands, gazing into space.

'She took last year's Sixth to *Henry the Fifth* and *Richard the Second*,' she said, 'and she took Camilla Perkins and Frances Block to the Lakes for a week.'

'I'd be terrified of that,' said Judy. 'It would be heavenly, but I'd be terrified all the time of – disappointing her, somehow. . . .'

'She's so wonderful, isn't she?' said Cynthia.

They both turned to look at a photograph that stood on the mantelpiece, depicting a somewhat horse-like face, with prominent features, a soulful expression and severely dressed hair. It was balanced on the other side of the mantelpiece by the photograph of a good-looking middle-aged man in riding kit. Mr. Somers, Judy's godfather, was her ideal of masculine perfection, as Miss Cavendish, the Senior English mistress at Bellington High School, was her ideal of feminine perfection.

'It doesn't really do her justice, you know,' said Cynthia. Her pale freckled face, in its frame of untidy red hair, was tense and earnest. 'She's much more beautiful than that. I don't mean beautiful in a chocolate-boxy way. I mean – well, her real self is beautiful, and you can't see her real self in a photograph.'

'You see her real self when she's reading poetry aloud, don't you?' said Judy. 'It makes you feel you want to live a better life, but somehow' – she gave a cynical little laugh – 'you never do.'

‘I nearly cried when she read that bit out of *King Lear* on Tuesday,’ said Cynthia complacently.

‘I quite cried when she read *Kim*,’ said Judy. ‘At least,’ she added honestly, ‘I had a funny feeling in my throat. . . . Do you remember when she said that no one could call themselves cultured who hadn’t read *Paradise Lost*?’

‘Yes.’

‘Well, I started reading it on Friday.’

‘Did you get far?’

‘Not very,’ admitted Judy.

‘I tried to get Byron from the Free Library, but it was out. He must have been fascinating. Wicked, but fascinating. I don’t think I could have resisted him, could you?’

‘I don’t know,’ said Judy. ‘We ought to have, you know, because he was married.’

‘She was very unsympathetic. She didn’t make him happy. There was a lot of excuse for him. Miss Cavendish once said that we should never judge others, however much appearances might be against them.’

‘I wonder if Miss Cavendish would have resisted him . . .’

‘Of course she would. She has terribly high principles. Anyway, I don’t think she’d like us to be talking about it like this. . . . It’s her birthday in August, you know. What are we going to give her?’

‘Let’s try and think of something original. Camilla Perkins gave her a copy of Boswell’s *Life of Johnson* last year, specially bound with her initials on the cover. She was awfully pleased with it.’

‘I once tried to read Rasselas, but I don’t think I was

mentally developed enough. I'm going to try again some day. What about an ornament for her room?'

'She didn't like that china cat that Pamela gave her last year. She was very polite about it, but you could see that she didn't like it.'

'Well, there was something a bit vulgar about the way it was smiling.'

'What about a paper-weight – the sort that you turn upside down and a snowstorm comes?'

'They're not easy to get. And, anyway, aren't they rather childish?'

'Yes, but sort of intellectually childish. . . . Look out of the window and tell me who's there.'

Cynthia thrust her head out of the window, and Judy practised expressions in her mirror, trying to see what she looked like with her lashes lowered on to her cheeks and finding it difficult, because, to see it properly, she had to open her eyes. She hated the round childishness of her face and the dimples that peeped out on her smooth pale cheeks, and, with the aid of her hand-mirror, had discovered several angles from which she looked interesting and world-weary and disillusioned. There was one angle – a sort of quarter view – that she could only just catch with her head turned right away, from which she looked almost tragic, but there again she suspected that closing her eyes improved it, and then she couldn't see it properly.

'Who's there?' she said absently.

'I can see Helen,' said Cynthia, leaning further out.

'What's she doing? Bossing about, I suppose, as usual.'

'She's talking to Max.'

'Poor Max!'

'He looks as if he liked it.'

'He hasn't to live with her. She's as terrible as an army with banners. Where does that come from?'

'I don't know.'

'Neither do I, but it must come from somewhere. I couldn't have made it up.'

'Belle's there, too. She looks lovely.'

'She always does. Who's she talking to?'

'No-one at present.'

'Perhaps it's one of the days when she's her own worst enemy.'

'What does that mean? I've never really understood.'

'It's a polite way of saying that people are bad-tempered.'

'She doesn't look bad-tempered.'

'No, that sort doesn't.'

'And I can see Anice and Martin Newbolt and the Vicar and the Vicaress and a few odds and ends.'

'We ought to be going down. Tidy your hair. It looks awful.'

Cynthia joined Judy at the dressing-table and smoothed back her hair, studying the two reflections with a thoughtful frown.

'I wish I knew whether I was pretty,' she said. 'There's no doubt about you, but I'm not sure about myself.'

'You look *interesting*,' said Judy.

'Well, anyway,' said Cynthia, 'if I'm not pretty, I'm definitely plain, and I'd rather be plain than just vague.' She turned her face away so that Judy could not see it. 'Judy. . . .'

‘Yes.’

‘I’ve been trying to tell you all afternoon. I’ve done something dreadful.’

‘How do you mean, dreadful?’

‘I don’t know. . . . Fast.’

‘Oh, Cynthia, you *couldn’t* have.’

‘Will you promise on your honour not to breathe a word to a soul?’

‘Promise on my honour.’

‘Well, you know that book we both loved so – *Summer Heritage*, by Arnold Palmer? You remember we both cried over it?’

‘Yes.’

‘Well, I *wrote* to him. I didn’t dare to tell you, but I wrote to him to tell him how beautiful it was.’

‘Perhaps he knew,’ said Judy, with a twinkle of mischief in her dark eyes.

‘Oh, Judy, don’t make fun of it, because I had the most *heavenly* letter back from him. Here it is.’

She drew a letter from her pocket and the two heads bent over it.

‘It’s lovely, isn’t it?’

‘Yes, it is.’

‘Do you think I dare write again?’

‘Why not?’

‘Will you sign it, too, if I do?’

‘No, that would be silly. But do write again.’

‘I wonder if he thought it frightful cheek.’

‘Of course he didn’t. He wouldn’t have answered if he had.

Oh, bother! I must change my stockings. I've got a hole that shows from miles away.'

Judy sat on the edge of her bed and peeled off her stockings with swift, deft movements.

'Throw me a pair out of that drawer. . . . I say, Cyn.'

'Yes?'

'We'll always be friends, won't we, even if I marry and you marry?'

'Oh, Judy, of course.'

'Well, I'm ready now. Come on. Let's hurry or there'll be nothing left.'

* * *

'I'm afraid I must be going now,' said Martin. 'Thank you so much, Mrs. Fowler.'

He rose awkwardly and spoke in his usual diffident, tentative fashion as if expecting to be contradicted.

'Come round by the stables,' said Anice, 'and I'll show you Vicky's puppies.'

Irritation showed in her voice and manner. He had come to see her, but he had lacked the wit to get her to himself. All afternoon he had sat there at the other end of the circle, making little effort to entertain his neighbours, watching her with that unconcealed adoration that partly thrilled, partly exasperated her. Even now it was she who had to find the excuse to be alone with him. . . .

They went round the side of the house and across the courtyard to the big stables, which were used chiefly as a store-room for lumber. There were bicycles, packing-cases, old pieces of furniture, a wheel-less wheelbarrow, a rusted mowing machine, the derelict tricycle on which Henry's mother used to patrol the village. . . . A saddle, oozing its stuffing, hung on the wall next to a broken scythe.

Vicky, a liver-and-salt spaniel, who had originally been bought by Henry as a gun-dog but had degenerated into a household pet, was in a straw-filled box behind the door, surrounded by her puppies. Martin stooped down and picked one up, holding it on a level with his eyes. Anice noticed how gently his long sensitive fingers held the fat little creature, noticed the tenderness of his ugly mouth as he smiled at it.

'You're a grand little chap,' he said, 'but your mother's getting anxious.'

He replaced the puppy in the box, stroking Vicky reassuringly. Then he and Anice stood and looked at each other. . . . Neither of them spoke. The sunlight poured through the open door in a golden shaft, bright with dancing motes, but it was cool and dim in the corner where they stood. Again that feeling of happiness swept over Anice, so intense that she could hardly bear it. It was like something from another world. She thought, Whatever happens, I shall always remember this. I shall see that old scythe hanging on the wall and that basket and that saddle. . . . I shall see them all plainly till the day I die. . . . And suddenly she was in his arms, his lips pressed against hers. Minutes passed before either of them spoke, and it was he who broke the silence.

'I can't believe it,' he said.

She said nothing, holding his face between her hands,

gazing at it intently, loving every line of it, even the ugliness of the mouth that marred it.

'Anice . . .'

'Don't talk,' she said dreamily. 'Not now. . . . Not yet.'

But later, as they walked across the park together, they discussed the practical side of the situation. He hadn't meant to ask her yet, he said – he hadn't the right to ask her – but he had loved her ever since he first saw her. He would have a talk with his uncle tonight. They couldn't marry on the salary his uncle paid him at present, and often his uncle forgot to pay him at all. He would ask his uncle about a partnership. He didn't even know what profit the shop made. Anice, listening, felt none of the irritation that his vagueness and ineptitude usually roused in her. Instead, she was conscious of a deep, all-pervading peace, an utter contentment.

'It doesn't matter, Martin,' she said. 'None of – that matters.'

He smiled crookedly.

'It's funny that I should be the practical one,' he said, 'but you see, you're used to – '

She interrupted him.

'I'm not used to anything. I mean, we live in a big house, but we're poor. Martin, don't let's fuss and worry. We love each other, and other things don't matter.'

A cold, warning voice seemed to tell her that other things did matter, that she would awake from this dream to find how much they mattered . . . but she silenced it, surrendering again to the happiness that drenched her. The whole earth seemed to be re-created. The fresh green grass around, starred with buttercups, was part of the miracle. When a thrush burst suddenly into song in the tree above them it was her own heart singing. . . .

CHAPTER THREE

Peter and Belle lived in a small, compact Georgian house halfway between Hurstmede and Bellington. Curving balustrades flanked the steps that led up to the green-painted front door, and an exquisite tracery of wrought iron formed the fanlight above. The garden at the back was enclosed by a high brick wall and over-shadowed by trees. An air of peace and mellow age hung over it.

They had walked home from Langley Place, and Peter lingered in the front garden, looking at the beds of antirrhinums that still drooped from the afternoon heat.

'We shall have to start watering if we don't get some rain soon,' said he.

'I suppose we shall,' said Belle.

Her voice was smooth and pleasant as ever, but Peter, glancing at her covertly, noticed the strained lines of her mouth in the shade of the broad-brimmed hat. He had hoped that the afternoon would have restored her precarious serenity. Evidently it had not done so. . . . Sometimes her moods blew over, but more often they worked up into hysterical outbursts to which in all these years of marriage he had never been able to accustom himself. He was the wrong husband for Belle, of course. He was too sensitive, too sympathetic, too ready to be hurt by her and to suffer with her. He could never ignore her moods or laugh them off.

He opened the front door, and she passed before him into the cool fragrant hall. A bowl of roses was reflected on the polished surface of a semicircular table that stood against the wall. Through the open door he could see the drawing-room, with its pale green panelling, Adam mantelpiece and the long curtains of oyster-coloured velvet. When they had moved into this house, four years ago, Belle had given endless care to the furnishing and arrangements, haunting sale-rooms and antique shops till she discovered, one by one, the pieces of furniture that she considered just right, herself working tapestry seats for chairs and fire-stool. He had never known her so happy and full of zest and eagerness as she had been in those days. She had good taste, and there was in her a strain of artistic creativeness to which her natural indolence had always denied outlet. But even then each success had been followed by the inevitable reaction, and the loveliest pieces of furniture in his home were connected in Peter's mind with the most outrageous scenes.

She went in silence towards the staircase. Peter hesitated for a few moments, then followed. He was, as usual, torn between his innate horror of a scene and a love that could not endure to leave her alone to her self-torment.

In the bedroom, she sat down in front of the dressing-table and took off her hat, frowningly intent on the process. Peter stood at the window, hands in pockets, looking down at the garden.

‘What were you and your mother talking about when she took you to see the roses?’ said Belle suddenly, in an elaborately casual voice.

So she had been tormenting herself about that – among other things – had suspected them of discussing her, criticizing her.

‘Roses, chiefly,’ he said. ‘They do so much better at Langley Place than here. They get more sun, of course.’

‘Yes . . . This is a very dark, depressing house. I often wish we hadn’t come here, but you would take it.’

He forbore to remind her that it was she who had discovered the house, and that she had given him no peace till he had signed the agreement. She loved it, he knew, as much as he did, but in these moods of hers she always tried to hurt him by disparaging the things and people he cared for most.

‘I often envy the women who live in those new little houses on the Bellington Road,’ she went on. ‘They look so bright and cheerful.’

‘We could move into one, if you like.’

‘Yes, and have you reproaching me for the rest of my life. How you love to put me in the wrong!’

She had taken off her hat and was running the comb through the soft waves of her hair. He turned round from the window.

‘Why don’t you lie down till dinner-time, Belle? You’re tired.’

‘Naturally I’m tired, after carting those trunks about all morning. You refuse to help me and then complain because I’m tired.’

His irritation rose despite himself.

'Don't be so foolish. I didn't refuse to help you.'

'And why not call me bad-tempered straight out instead of tired? It's what you mean, isn't it? You've already called me a fool and a liar.'

'I haven't called you either.'

She seemed not to hear him. She was examining her reflection in the glass, her delicate brows drawn together.

'I hadn't realized how unsuitable this dress was till your mother pointed it out.'

'My dear Belle – ' he began wearily, but she interrupted him.

'Didn't you hear her call me over-dressed?'

'No.'

'She said how much she liked that old cotton dress of Helen's and never even mentioned mine. It was quite obvious what she meant. And that wasn't all. . . . She criticized me for not giving all my time to social work and neglecting my home like Mrs. Bantram, and she even found fault with the tea I gave her when she came here. She's generally pretty rude to me, but I don't think she's ever been quite so offensive as she was this afternoon. And as for Judy – !'

'Well? What about Judy?'

'She and that little beast Cynthia Willoughby sniggering at me and making fun of me . . .'

His lips tightened. Judy was his favourite sister. From her babyhood he had felt a half paternal tenderness for her.

'I'm quite sure that neither Judy nor Cynthia was making fun of you.'

‘That’s right,’ she said, her voice rising. ‘Take her part against me. You always do and you always will. I ought to be used to it by now. Your whole family can insult me and sneer at me to their heart’s content and – and you let them do it. You encourage them. You – ’

No, the storm wasn’t going to blow over this time. It gathered strength and swept on. She would never go to Langley Place again to be insulted. She would never speak to any of his family again. She was sick of being treated like dirt. If he was half a man he’d put a stop to it. She hated them all. She wished she’d never met him. She wished she’d never married him. She was miserable. . . . She flung herself on her bed in a tempest of sobs and lay there, her whole body heaving convulsively. He looked at her helplessly. He never knew how to deal with her in these outbursts. And they affected him like some physical oppression, gave him a feeling of suffocation, set his heart pounding in his chest.

He sat on the edge of the bed.

‘Belle,’ he said, laying a hand on her shoulder.

She shook it off.

‘Go away . . . go *away*!’

‘Listen, Belle.’

‘Don’t touch me. . . . I *hate* you. . . . Go *away*!’

Her voice rose to a scream. He stood and looked down at her for a moment, then turned and went from the room. Outside he paused irresolutely. From the nursery on the half-landing he heard the sound of Gillian’s voice. He went down the steps and opened the door.

* * *

Gillian was sitting on Miss Horsham's knee in her nightdress. Her delicate, expressive little face lit up with pleasure as Peter entered, and, slipping to the ground, she ran across the room to him with outstretched arms. He caught her up and held her closely.

'It's after her bed-time,' said Miss Horsham apologetically, 'but it's so hot that she couldn't sleep. I was telling her a story.'

Still holding Gillian, Peter sat down in the armchair by the fireplace. Gillian turned earnest blue eyes to Miss Horsham.

'Go on, Nanny,' she said.

Miss Horsham smiled at Peter.

'Shall I?' she said. 'It's nearly finished.'

He nodded, relaxing in his chair. Gillian's head, with its mop of silky golden curls, rested on his shoulder. He strained his ears but could hear no sound from Belle's room. Perhaps she had stopped crying when he left her. The more detatched part of him realized that Belle liked an audience. . . . He looked across at Miss Horsham. She must have heard Belle's outburst. The whole house must have heard it. He wondered what she made of it all. Her face was a pale oval, her mouth long but very beautiful, with humour and serenity lurking in the corners of it. She reminded him of Boltraffio's Madonna, a copy of which hung in his mother's bedroom at Langley Place.

Since her arrival Gillian had been placid and amenable. Belle could discourse eloquently on the responsibilities of motherhood, but so variable were her moods that on her good days the child could do no wrong and on her bad days no right. In her charge Gillian became nervy and difficult.

The previous nurse had been a young, impressionable girl who had played the parts in turn of Belle's bosom friend and arch enemy, and who had been expected to act always as Belle's personal maid. This had not been good for Gillian, and Peter had been glad when she gave notice after one of their recurrent scenes. It was he who had suggested engaging a trained children's nurse, and Belle had welcomed the idea, chiefly because she felt that it would raise her prestige among her friends. He had realized from the beginning that the situation would involve difficulties, but so far things had gone fairly smoothly. Miss Horsham had resisted Belle's attempts to use her as a personal maid and to form an intimate friendship with her, and had resisted them with such tact that even Belle could not take offence.

And Gillian expanded like a flower in the new atmosphere of affection and understanding, losing her petulance and fretfulness, together with her pallor and the shadows beneath her eyes. She was devoted to Miss Horsham and that, till now, had been the only source of trouble, for Belle had begun of late to resent it. 'If she comes between Gillian and me,' she said, 'she'll have to go, of course.'

He sat there, his arm about Gillian, gazing absently at the fireplace, soothed by the girl's gentle voice. She was telling the story as naturally as if he were not there. And, to her, he suspected, he was not there. She had always politely ignored the rest of the household, concentrating all her care and attention on Gillian, treating the others as shadows, becoming a shadow herself when with them. . . .

His thoughts went back over the scene with Belle, and the

familiar weight of anxiety and apprehension fastened on his heart. He did not notice that the story had ended till Gillian recalled him to the present by sitting up straight on his knee and saying, 'More, Nanny! *Please*, Nanny!' He turned his head and met the girl's eyes. They were fixed on him with a curious impersonal compassion in their depths. She showed no embarassment at meeting his eyes and seemed to move hers almost reluctantly to Gillian.

'No, darling,' she said. 'You must go to bed now.'

Her voice was slow and musical and he realized suddenly how seldom he heard it, how silent she was except when with Gillian.

'Come, darling,' she said, holding her arms out to the child.

Gillian allowed herself to be lifted from Peter's knee.

'Say good night to Daddy.'

'Good night, Daddy.'

'Good night, Gilly.'

They went through the connecting door into the night-nursery, but the atmosphere of gentleness and comfort remained. He was glad to think of Gillian enclosed by that atmosphere, protected by it from fear and unhappiness. Feeling suddenly curious about the girl, he went across to the bookcase that held her books. . . . *The Blue Fairy Book*, *The Red Fairy Book*, Hans Andersen, Edwar0d Lear, *Alice in Wonderland*, Kipling, Lamb's *Essays*, the *Oxford Book of English Verse*. . . . He took down *The Red Fairy Book* and opened it. *Rachel Horsham on her tenth birthday, June 7, 1911, with love from Mother*. So she was only nineteen. Rachel . . . It suited her somehow. . . .

He replaced the book and took out the *Oxford Book of English Verse*. Certain names had been ticked in the index . . . Herrick, Herbert, Crashaw, Vaughan, Blake, Emily Brontë, Christina Rosetti. Still holding the book, he bent to look at the framed photographs that stood on the bookcase. One showed a man with a thin, keen, pleasant face, sitting in a pony-trap, holding the reins. That must be her father. He had been, Peter knew, a country doctor and both he and his wife had died fairly recently. Then there was a family group – the same man, a woman with Rachel's grave, oval face, and Rachel (odd how naturally he thought of her as Rachel, though he had only learnt her name a few moments ago) as a leggy and awkward child in a cotton frock with long black stockings and pigtails.

The door opened, and he turned to see her standing in the doorway. She looked at him with that faint smile that began in the dark eyes and barely touched the long, mobile lips.

'I hope you don't think me very impertinent,' he said.

'No. . . . It's nice of you to be interested.'

She spoke simply and without self-consciousness.

'We have the same favourites,' he said. He turned over the pages of the book and read:

My soul, there is a country
Far beyond the stars,
Where stands a wingèd sentry
All skilful in the wars.

'Yes, I love Vaughan,' she said.

A new eagerness sounded in her voice, making her seem suddenly poignantly young. He thought how lonely she must have been in this house all these weeks, with only Gillian for her companion. It couldn't have been an easy life – eluding Belle's attempts at intimacy, countering her unreasonable demands, keeping on good terms with the maids, who, he knew, resented the presence of a 'lady' in the nursery. And, though little more than a child, she had managed it, continuing on her quiet way with the curious remoteness that formed her defence.

She had taken the book from his hands.

'I like this, don't you?' she said.

> Brave flowers – that I could gallant it like you,
> And be as little vain!
> You come abroad, and make a harmless show,
> And to your beds of earth again.
> You are not proud; you know your birth;
> For your embroidered garments are from earth.

'Yes,' he smiled. 'Those seventeenth-century poets could write about flowers without getting sentimental. Like this one of Marvell's.' Again he turned the pages.

> See how the flowers, as at parade,
> Under their colours stand displayed;
> Each regiment in order grows,
> That of the tulip, pink and rose.

'We've lost the knack. . . .'

She took the book from him and he watched her as she read, noticing how her dark lashes swept her pale cheeks. . . . Then she closed the book and they looked at each other in silence. Again he was aware of the absence of constraint between them . . . Suddenly he remembered Belle. It was incredible that he should have forgotten her for so long – Belle, whom he had left sobbing on her bed in an abandon of hysterical distress. And with the thought of Belle came self-consciousness.

'Well, I mustn't take up any more of your time,' he said awkwardly. 'I expect you're busy. Or does time drag?'

'No . . . I read a lot. And there's always sewing.'

Reading and sewing. . . . Her armour against the demons of loneliness that must always be lying in wait for her in this alien household. Reluctantly he turned to the door. Leaving this room for Belle's bedroom was like leaving a cool dim wood for a sun-scorched meadow.

* * *

He stood for a moment outside the door of the bedroom, listening. Then, bracing himself for whatever lay before him, he entered. The first thing he noticed was that the air was heavy with Belle's favourite perfume.

She lay on her bed, but no longer in an attitude of despair. She had made up her face again, tidied her hair and changed into a *neglig*é of rose-coloured ninon. She lay on her back, her hands behind her head. Her eyes were bright and dewy, her cheeks softly flushed. There was a sort of bloom about her, deepening and enriching her beauty. He had often noticed how the scenes that left him so exhausted seemed to refresh and revivify her. Her gaze followed him languorously as he crossed the room.

'Where have you been?' she said, motioning him to a seat on the bed.

'In the nursery.'

'Was Miss Horsham there?'

'Yes.'

'You poor boy!'

'What do you mean?'

'I think she's quite the stupidest girl I've ever met in my life.'

He was silent for a moment. Often his loyalty had to contend with his love of peace, and often, to his secret shame, he let pass unfair criticism of his friends and family rather than rouse her anger by defending them . . . but he could not let this pass.

'I don't think she's stupid,' he said slowly.

Belle smiled.

'You hate me running anyone down, don't you? . . . Oh, well, she looks after Gillian, and that's what she's here for.'

'Gillian's been much better lately.'

'Oh, she's always been a normal, healthy child. . . . Peter . . .'

'Yes?'

'I've been thinking . . . I'd like to give a bridge party at the end of the month. Shall we get Fawkner's to do the catering? It's less trouble, and they do it very well. Moyna had them for her bridge party. She only had nine tables. I'll have twelve. . . .'

Her mind seemed wholly intent on her bridge party. That was typical of her. She could make the most devastating scenes and forget all about them in a few minutes as completely as if they had never taken place. Not always, of course. . . . Sometimes, after an outburst, her temper would smoulder for days.

'Well?' she said, as he did not speak.

'Oh yes . . . just as you like,' he said absently.

'I'll ask Helen to help me. She's very capable. She plays a good hand of bridge, too. . . . You know, Peter, she won't be doing too badly for herself, marrying young Willoughby. They're nobodies, but they're rolling in money.'

'Is she going to marry him?'

'He's obviously in love with her. . . . And Anice will be a fool if she marries Martin Newbolt. She hasn't much in the way of looks, of course, but she ought to do better than that. Your mother should have put her foot down right at the beginning. She's too slack about that sort of thing. And she ought to be looking round for someone for Judy. You can't begin too soon. . . . I'm sorry I was horrid about them, darling.' She took his hand in hers. 'I was tired and had a headache. I didn't know what I was saying. I don't remember even now what I said. They *are* a bit casual with me, and I suppose I'm over-sensitive and – imagine things. I can't help it. . . .'

She looked up at him with an expression of childlike contrition. In the dim room her loveliness seemed to glow and blossom. The passion she could always rouse surged over him.

'Anyway, let's forget your family,' she went on in a voice that was hardly more than a whisper. 'I don't care about them. . . . I only care about you, Peter. . . .'

She put up her arms and drew his head down to hers.

CHAPTER FOUR

Whereas the Fowler family made Sunday afternoon the occasion of a family gathering at Langley Place, the Willoughby clan assembled for supper on Sunday evenings at The Beeches. It was a cold supper (so that the maids could go to church), and Mrs. Willoughby herself prepared most of the dishes that covered the massive mahogany dining-table. Everything in the Willoughby house was massive and solid and expensive, and, judged by modern standards, ugly.

Mrs. Willoughby herself might be said to be massive, solid, expensive and ugly. She was a tall woman with a fine presence and an uncompromising expression. Her features were all pronounced, but the most pronounced was her nose. It dominated her face and seemed, in some odd fashion, to vary in size according to the intensity of her feelings, assuming, when she was angry or on her dignity, the proportions of an eagle's beak, becoming again, when she was placid and contented, just a large nose.

Though her children were all grown up, except Cynthia, she still expected – and received – implicit obedience from them, even from Gertrude and Florence, who were married, and from Max, who was the head of the Willoughby business.

She ruled her grandchildren as autocratically as she ruled her children. 'We'll have to ask Grandma,' Gertrude and Florence would say, when their children wanted anything.

She stood now in the centre of the drawing-room, wearing one of those dresses of rich dark silk that she always wore on Sundays, casting a keen eye around to make sure that everything was just as it should be. The chairs were arranged in a large semi-circle. Mrs. Willoughby liked chairs to be arranged in a large semi-circle. It was, in her eyes, a symbol of the family unity. She disliked groups and cliques and *têtes-à-têtes*. . . . Apart from its rosewood and mahogany, the drawing-room seemed to be furnished principally with photographs. They stood massed in silver frames on mantelpiece, piano and occasional tables. The Willoughbys were frequently photographed, and it was one of the family traditions that no photograph should ever be discarded. The two-years-old Max beamed from his pram at one end of the mantelpiece, while at the other the nine-months-old Oliver, inadequately clothed in a vest, reposed on a sheepskin rug, and in the middle the three-years-old Cynthia danced an eternal hornpipe in a sailor-suit. Over the mantelpiece hung a large portrait of Mrs. Willoughby's husband, Josiah, wearing his mayoral robes and chain.

Just as Mrs. Willoughby was straightening a sofa that showed a tendency to form a clique with a couple of armchairs she heard the sound of voices in the hall, and Florence and Gertrude entered.

Florence and Gertrude had inherited their mother's features, with slightly less prominent noses and without the suggestion of authority that informed Mrs. Willoughby's whole countenance. Like their mother, they ignored the art of make-up. Like their mother, they wore 'sensible' clothes, avoiding any fashion that had come in during the current year. They had been 'nice' girls, pleasant, docile and industrious, and now they were 'nice' women, looking after their homes and husbands and children with the same pleasantness, docility and industry they had shown throughout their girlhood.

'Are we the first?' said Gertrude unnecessarily as they entered the room, which was empty except for Mrs. Willoughby.

Ignoring the question, Mrs. Willoughby offered each of them her cheek, which they kissed dutifully and then sat down side by side on the settee.

'Where's James?' said Mrs. Willoughby.

Florence looked uncomfortable.

'He's going to try to look in later,' she said evasively.

'And George is busy with his sermon,' put in Gertrude, answering the question before it was asked. 'He told me to tell you that he was sorry he couldn't come along.'

Mrs. Willoughby's sons-in-law had a way of shirking these Sunday evening gatherings at The Beeches. Mrs. Willoughby gave them a little rope but not much. When next she met Gertrude's husband, she would say, 'I shall expect you on Sunday, George,' and next Sunday he would be there. James was more elusive, but he always came to heel in the end. Gertrude had married the Vicar of Bellington Parish Church and Florence had married Bellington's Town Clerk. Through them Mrs. Willoughby could keep her finger on the pulse of the town. From the beginning she had quashed George's leanings towards ritual, and through James she managed to keep in check the more extravagant members of the Council who wanted to squander the ratepayers' money on exotic shrubs in the public gardens and unnecessary amenities in the workhouse.

Florence and Gertrude, who had been brought up never to tempt Satan by a display of idle hands and at the same time to limit Sunday needlework to the 'useful', had already set to work, Gertrude darning socks and Florence knitting a jersey for her small son, Bobby.

'I'm glad you've come early,' said Mrs. Willoughby. 'I wanted to have a little chat with you before the others arrived. Have you had the children's half-term reports?'

Florence and Gertrude dived into their handbags and brought out the reports. Mrs. Willoughby read them in silence, watched anxiously by her daughters. Mrs. Willoughby paid the children's school fees, as indeed she paid for most other things in connection with them. George, whose stipend was small, was glad of this, but James occasionally made futile and always unsuccessful attempts at independence.

'Timothy must have some coaching in Latin next holidays,' she said shortly to Gertrude as she handed back the reports. 'He'd better come and have it here. I'll get Mr. Laxton from the County School. He's always glad of a little holiday coaching. . . . Peggy seems to be improving, I'm glad to see.' She turned to Florence. 'Bobby's is excellent, as usual, but Jessica's is not at all satisfactory.'

'Yes,' sighed Florence. 'She's very naughty at home, too. James got simply furious with her last night.'

'I don't suppose that improved matters,' said Mrs. Willoughby tartly. (Mrs. Willoughby resented any interference from her sons-in-law in her training of her grandchildren.) 'She only does it to attract attention to herself. The best thing is to ignore her.'

'I'll try that,' said Florence uncertainly.

She remembered the nightmare feeling of not existing at all that she had had in her childhood on the occasions when Mrs. Willoughby had magnificently ignored her as punishment for some misdemeanour, but she doubted whether the same treatment would have the same effect in the case of Jessica and herself. . . .

'Perhaps I'd better speak to her on Saturday,' said Mrs. Willoughby, who secretly shared Florence's doubts.

On Saturday afternoons all the Willoughby grandchildren came to tea at The Beeches, and no excuses for absence were accepted. Actually few were offered, for Mrs. Willoughby always gave them a good tea and saw to it that they enjoyed themselves.

'Yes, Mother,' said Florence, 'I'd be glad if you would.'

* * *

Oliver, Mrs. Willoughby's younger son, entered the room in a casual lounging fashion that drew his mother's brows together in a quick frown, greeted his sisters without enthusiasm and took his seat in a corner of the room as if dissociating himself from the family group by the fireplace. He was a dark, slightly built youth, with a sensitive, intelligent face, set generally in lines of sombre discontent. He had recently joined the family business under Max and made no secret of his dislike of it. Mrs. Willoughby believed this to be partly her fault. He had won an Exhibition from school to Cambridge and she had weakly agreed to his taking it up. She had thought at the time that it could do him no harm, but she considered now that it had done him a great deal of harm. He had got in with what she called a 'bad set', meaning a literary and artistic set.

These interests took his mind off his work, and anything that took one's mind off one's work was, in Mrs. Willoughby's eyes, wholly bad. So far she had ignored his discontent and restlessness, telling herself that he would settle down in time, but he wasn't settling down, and the situation worried her, as far as Mrs. Willoughby allowed any situation to worry her. She saw that she would have to come to grips with it sooner or later. . . . It never occurred to her to consider his leaving the business. She held the purse strings and had no doubts of the final issue, but it was tiresome of him to behave like this. He had always been a tiresome child. . . .

He lit a cigarette and lay back in his chair, drumming his long, sensitive fingers on the arm of it and watching his mother and sisters with a faintly sardonic smile. Gertrude was telling Mrs. Willoughby that Peggy needed a new frock, and Mrs. Willoughby was arranging to meet her and Betty in the juvenile outfitting department of Crofton's (the big draper's in the Market Square just opposite Newbolt's) next Saturday morning in order to buy it. I don't believe those two girls have ever bought a mousetrap even, thought Oliver, without taking the old lady along with them to help choose it. They seem to like knuckling under. I wish to heaven I did. . . .

He looked at the firm, uncompromising lines of his mother's face and his mind went again to the drudgery of his work at the mill. He wished that Max and the old lady would come out into the open. He didn't know where he was with them. When he complained to his mother she appeared not to understand what he was talking about. She never had been a nagger, of course. She either ignored you or turned on you the full and blasting force of her authority. He almost wished she'd try the latter, though he hated rows of any kind.

Max's technique was different, hut equally effective. To all Oliver's complaints he opposed a bluff, hearty cheerfulness. 'That's all right, old chap. You're bound to feel a bit strange at first. You'll settle down all right. You're shaping quite well.'

As if he wanted to settle down and shape well! Their obtuseness gave him a feeling of helplessness and would, he knew, have ended by wearing him down, if it hadn't been for the fact that – only last week – he had had one of his stories accepted by a literary review of good standing. He hadn't told any of his family about that. (They didn't even know that he wrote stories.) He regarded it as a weapon to be kept in reserve for the final battle.

His father had left everything to his mother, but surely, Oliver thought, he had a right to a share of it. She must be rolling in money. He wouldn't need much to live in London till he got on his feet, and then he'd keep himself by writing. He longed to know people who had the same interests as himself. He hated the smugness and narrowness of this small provincial town. He threw the end of his cigarette into the fireplace with an impatient gesture.

'Pick that up, Oliver,' said Mrs. Willoughby sharply. 'I won't have the hearth littered like that.'

He obeyed instinctively and without resentment. Mrs. Willoughby issued orders to all her children – even Max – in that peremptory tone, and they were so much accustomed to it that they never even noticed it.

'And about your raspberry jam, Florence,' went on Mrs. Willoughby. 'I'll have half a dozen pounds sent from Harolds' on Thursday, and I'll come along in the afternoon and give you a hand.'

Oliver took a copy of the *Illustrated London News* from a table near his chair and turned over the pages, listening idly to Mrs. Willoughby's instructions on the making of Florence's jam, the training of Gertrude's maid, the treatment of Bobby's cough and the lengthening of Jessica's coat. Though Mrs. Willoughby never looked at him directly, she was aware of every impatient movement, every disdainful curl of his lip – and aware of them with rising irritation. The boy was becoming impossible. She must talk to Max about him. . . .

'Where are Max and Cynthia?' said Oliver, throwing the *Illustrated London News* on to the floor and picking it up before Mrs. Willoughby could tell him to.

'They've gone to tea to Langley Place,' said Mrs. Willoughby. 'They should be back soon.'

'Oh,' said Oliver.

He had a sudden vision of the terrace at Langley Place . . . of Mrs. Fowler in her wicker chair, behind the tea-table . . . the lovely, shabby old house in the background, the atmosphere of peace and leisure and – civilization. His own family he considered utterly uncivilized. They not only lacked culture and tolerance and graciousness, but they distrusted these things as forces that would undermine the world of complacency and materialism in which they lived. He wished he had had the courage to go to Langley Place this afternoon. Mrs. Fowler had given him a general invitation to go there, but he was always too shy to go unless specially invited. The last occasion on which he had been there stood out vividly in his memory. As he sat on the terrace the tension of his nerves had relaxed and a sense of release had stolen over him, as though he had been a prisoner set free. Judy had sat next to him in the dappled shade of the lime tree, her eyes dark and dewy in her pale face. Her laughter had been light and gay like the song of birds, and the dimples coming and going in her smooth cheeks had made him think of running water. In his mood of receptivity there had seemed to be a poignant quality of grace and freshness about her youth. . . . And yet she was the schoolgirl friend of his schoolgirl sister – a creature who played hockey and did 'gym' and got her sums wrong and had a 'pash' on Miss Cavendish. He didn't try to reconcile the two pictures. They existed independently and apart in his mind. He hadn't seen Judy since that day. Perhaps Cynthia would bring her back to supper tonight. . . .

'Max has been going over there a good deal lately, hasn't he?' said Gertrude.

Mrs. Willoughby gave a faint shrug. She had no great opinion of the Fowlers, considering them spineless and happy-go-lucky and lacking in the solid civic virtues. All they ever seemed to do for the community was to hold a fête in aid of the Conservative Party in their garden each summer, an occasion that was, in Mrs. Willoughby's opinion, more a display of their roses and sweet peas than of their public spirit.

* * *

The odds and ends of the family were arriving. The Willoughbys were not only clannish but devoid of snobbishness. None of their poor relations had been dropped in their upward climb, and all were welcome at every family gathering. Shabby old ladies who were great-aunts or second cousins once removed drifted into the drawing-room with a mixture of timidity and pride. It was all so grand, but it was Josiah who had achieved the grandeur and Josiah's wife who now reigned over it.

They gazed reverently at the portrait of Josiah in his robe and chain and remembered how they had prophesied success for him even when he was a little boy. He had won a prize for something (they'd forgotten what) in his first term at school. . . . He had always put his Saturday penny into his money-box.

Mrs. Willoughby tackled the problem of the poor relations in the same practical spirit in which she tackled all her problems. Those who were not too proud to accept money were given money – openly or in payment for some (not too strenuous) service.

Aunt Flo, a grey little shadow of a woman, came every Friday and took home a bag full of Willoughby socks to darn. Every week she found ten shillings in one of the toes. Aunt Bessie, a vague old woman on the verge of senility, who mistook Max for Josiah and had an embarrassing habit of discussing with him the constipation from which Josiah had evidently suffered, received regular weekly deliveries of groceries. Cousin Effie, who was incredibly fat and wore a lifetime's accumulation of jewellery on her enormous bosom, came to do household mending at The Beeches three times a week. Often there was little or no mending to be done, but Cousin Effie got a good mid-day meal and a fire to sit by. Cousin Maggie was a dressmaker (not a very good one), and Mrs. Willoughby's sense of family loyalty was so strong that she had some of her own dresses and all her daughters' made by her. Gertrude and Florence had endured this without protest, but Cynthia was beginning to show signs of restiveness.

The presence of this crow-like assembly (they all dressed in rusty black) exasperated Oliver, but Max, who had inherited the clannish spirit of his family, liked to see the drawing-room full of his dependents. They treated him with deference and admiration, making him feel like a Prince of the Blood Royal. . . .

As they drifted in, one by one, Mrs. Willoughby greeted them with a majesty that was tempered by genuine kindliness, then continued her conversation with Gertrude.

'Tell George that he must let me have the surplices on Tuesday without fail,' she said, 'otherwise I can't get them properly laundered and mended in time.'

‘He says you really needn’t trouble,’ said Gertrude, uncomfortably remembering the spirit of unchristian resentment with which George accepted his mother-in-law’s co-operation in his parochial duties. ‘He says he could easily send them to the laundry.’

‘Nonsense!’ said Mrs. Willoughby. ‘The laundry would ruin them. And I’d better see about buying some new ones for the smaller boys. I simply don’t know how they manage to get them in such a state. And there was some ink on George’s the last time I washed it. It took me hours to get it out. Tell him to be more careful in future.’

‘Yes, Mother,’ murmured Gertrude meekly.

‘Oh, and another thing,’ went on Mrs. Willoughby. ‘I don’t know who was supposed to be doing the brasses last month, but they were shocking. The lectern hadn’t been touched.’

‘It was Mrs. Meutier.’

‘Will you speak to her or shall I?’

‘Perhaps I’d better,’ said Gertrude, knowing quite well that she would not speak to Mrs. Meutier, but that she would give the lectern a good rub-up herself on Saturday evening. Better that than subject Mrs. Meutier to one of Mother’s talking-to’s. Gertrude herself was used to them, but Mrs. Meutier might take offence and stop putting five-pound notes into the Easter collection.

There was an old woman called Meutier, [said Oliver]
Whose lectern got dirtier and dirtier,
Till the Willoughby clan

On the warpath all ran,
Getting shirtier and shirtier and shirtier.

Mrs. Willoughby threw him a glance of heavy displeasure.

'That's neither clever nor funny, Oliver,' she said shortly.

'It wasn't meant to be,' said Oliver. 'It was merely an example of what my English master at school used to call my fatal facility.'

Cynthia entered the room, greeted the visitors and flopped on to a chair.

'Didn't Max come back with you?' said Mrs. Willoughby.

'No . . . Judy and I came away first. Judy walked to the end of the road with me.'

'Why didn't you bring her in?' said Oliver carelessly, appearing to give his whole attention to a picture of some Egyptian excavations on the middle page of the *Illustrated London News*.

'She had her essay to finish for tomorrow.'

'I suppose you spent the time making sheep's eyes at Miss Cavendish's photograph.'

Cynthia flushed. She hated being teased by Oliver.

'Miss Cavendish has a great-uncle,' she said with dignity, 'who once met Dickens.'

'And that, of course,' said Oliver, 'is proof of the outstanding quality of Miss Cavendish's intellect.'

He was disappointed that Judy hadn't come. . . .

'You can be as sarcastic as you like,' said Cynthia hotly, 'but – '

'Don't sit there idling, Cynthia,' put in Mrs. Willoughby.

'Get one of these mats I'm doing for the Sale of Work and start hemming it. . . . Max is late. I wonder where he is.'

* * *

Max and Helen were walking slowly across the park. Recently Helen had formed the habit of going home with Max to the Willoughby supper on Sunday evenings, but this evening, she knew, was different from any of the previous ones. Before we reach The Beeches, she said to herself, he'll have asked me to marry him, and I'll have said yes. . . . She felt quite calm and detached about it. She had considered the matter from every angle before she made up her mind. She liked Max and she thought she would be able to manage him. Already she had put her power to the test in several small ways, and the results had been encouraging, had indeed given her a thrill that she had never experienced before. It was strange, she thought, that she and Anice should get engaged the same day. Anice had said nothing when she came back from her walk with Martin (some guests still lingered round Mrs. Fowler), but she looked so radiant and glowing that Helen guessed what had happened. Poor Anice! Martin would never make much money. . . . Still, she, Helen, would always be there to keep an eye on them. Mentally Helen shouldered Anice and Martin along with her other new responsibilities.

Max was silent – usually he kept up a flow of breezy small talk – and, glancing at him sideways, she saw that he was very pale. She supposed that they would kiss each other when they became engaged and wondered how she would like it. She hated kissing, as a rule. . . .

They walked down the road between tall hedges a-foam with Queen Anne's Lace, till they reached the brick wall that enclosed the kitchen garden of The Beeches. Max opened the green-painted door and followed her down the small box-edged path that led past the greenhouses.

'You must see the carnations,' he said. 'They're wonderful this year.'

They entered the enclosed colourful little world and stood there, surrounded by the tall blooms – red, white, pink, salmon – with their green curling leaves. The air was moist and warm.

I suppose he's going to ask me now, thought Helen.

His pallor had increased.

'Helen,' he said unsteadily, 'I wonder if you know what I'm going to say to you.'

'I think I do,' she said.

Her blue eyes met his calmly and without embarrassment.

He looked a little taken aback, and she suspected with faint amusement that he would have preferred her to assume a Victorian coyness.

'Will you marry me?'

'Yes.'

Her voice was as steady and casual as if she had been replying to a comment on the weather.

He took her in his arms and she raised her lips submissively . . . then a sudden faintness came over her and she closed her eyes. When he released her she was trembling, and her cheeks were as pale as his. She looked round at the massed colours, seeing them through a sort of mist. Her heart was beating unevenly.

'You do love me, don't you, Helen?' he said hoarsely.

'Yes . . . ' She spoke, with an effort, in her usual voice. She felt shaken and a little aghast at the violence of the forces that had seized her. 'Let's go into the house now, shall we?'

They walked side by side down the narrow path. He tried to slip an arm round her waist, but she stiffened and he withdrew it.

'They'll be thrilled to death when they know,' he said.

She shared his mental picture of a crowd of laughing, congratulating Willoughbys and shrank from it. Not yet . . . not till she had erected her defences again and could receive the congratulations with the cool detachment on which she prided herself. How she had always despised these blushing, tremulous, engaged girls! It humiliated her to think that she was in no way superior to them.

'Max . . . '

'Yes?'

'Don't tell them yet.' She hesitated, trying to find a convincing reason for the delay, then went on: 'Mother doesn't know yet, and she ought to know first. You can tell your mother when they've all gone, but don't let's tell them all together now.'

'All right,' he said. 'I understand, darling.'

He wanted to loiter with her along the path and talk over the various stages of their acquaintance . . . asking her just when she first began to love him . . . reminding her of the time when . . . but she walked on with her usual quick, purposeful step, her blue eyes looking straight ahead, answering in monosyllables.

‘Darling,’ he said, ‘let’s be married soon. There’s really nothing to wait for, is there?’

‘No,’ she said, yielding just a little to the lingering sweetness of that moment in the carnation house. ‘No, there isn’t. . . .’

* * *

As they entered, the whole room seemed to draw a breath of relief, as if it had been waiting all evening – as, indeed, it had – for Max’s coming. All the old ladies bridled and beamed as he went round the circle, kissing each of them and enquiring about their little concerns. He remembered Aunt Flo’s cat and Aunt Bessie’s canary and Cousin Effie’s rheumatism, and those tiresome neighbours of Miss Hatton’s who would play the concertina late at night.

Miss Hatton was so distant a relation that no one could decide exactly what the relationship was. She kept a small school of which she was the sole staff and to which Mrs. Willoughby had sent all her children to learn their alphabet and tables. She was old and lame and her school afforded her the scantiest livelihood, but there was something gallant and unconquerable about her. Whereas the others all wore black velvet ribbons round their yellowing necks, Miss Hatton wore a length of black tulle, tied into a coquettish bow under one ear.

‘Prince Charming,’ murmured Aunt Flo, watching Max as he greeted them, one by one, with his welcoming smile and solicitous enquiries.

‘The very expression that had occured to me,’ said Oliver.

'You needn't be beastly about Max,' said Cynthia under her breath. 'He's awfully decent to you. You fool about in the business and he puts up with it all. Not many brothers would.'

'And from which of our amiable relatives have you heard those sentiments, my child?' said Oliver.

She looked at him uncertainly, afraid of his sarcasm and of the anger that could flare up in him so suddenly. He smiled at her reassuringly.

'All right, I won't spar with you,' he said, 'but don't talk of things you know nothing about. Actually I work hard at the business though I loathe it like hell. So confine yourself to your own affairs – your essays on "Is Spring Preferable to Autumn?", and your super woman, Miss Cavendish, and your grubby little school friends with ink all over their fingers.'

'You needn't be beastly about Judy, either,' said Cynthia, for Judy had once come to The Beeches straight from school, where she had mopped up an overturned inkwell with an inadequate supply of blotting-paper. 'She tried to get it off, but there wasn't any pumice stone.'

'I haven't seen her lately, by the way.'

'She's coming to tea on Wednesday.'

Oliver nodded, secretly pleased by the news. He wanted to see her again, because he wanted to see her as a grubby little schoolgirl, *gauche* and giggling, wanted to dispel the absurd impression he had carried away from his last visit to Langley Place. It made him feel a fool in his own eyes, and he didn't like feeling a fool in his own eyes.

'We must remember to provide pumice stone,' he said.

'Oh, you're *hateful*!' said Cynthia, taking up her needlework.

'Yes, get on with your hemming like a good little girl,' said Oliver.

His tone though mocking was kindly, and she gave him a faint smile as she broke off a length of cotton. She was fond of Oliver, but she never knew what to make of him. Nobody did. . . .

* * *

Helen was listening to Mrs. Willoughby's account of a new scheme for taking down the worst of Bellington's slums and building model workmen's flats in their place. It appeared that Mrs. Willoughby was on the committee, and, knowing that, you felt that the scheme would very soon be put into action, that she would give no one any peace till the flats were erected. Helen listened with interest and approval. She liked the atmosphere of driving energy that the Willoughbys carried about with them – an atmosphere noticeably absent in her own family.

Her own family would have been interested in the scheme in a detached, impersonal kind of way, but they would probably have considered the slum picturesque, found bits of interesting architecture all over it and regretted its disappearance. In any case, it would never have occurred to them to do anything about it themselves.

'Whole families live in the basements,' said Mrs. Willoughby. 'They're overrun with rats and the walls are dripping.'

'Dreadful,' murmured Helen.

'I think the pattern's wrong,' said Florence, holding up her half knitted jersey.

'Bring it here,' said Mrs. Willoughby.

Helen leant back in her chair and looked round the room. The memory of the trembling girl in the carnation house was fading. It was the first time she had allowed her emotions to get the better of her. She mustn't let it happen again. She met Max's eyes, eager and ardent, across the room and returned his gaze coolly, with a sense of relief and triumph. She was completely mistress of herself now. . . . Yes, he would be easy enough to manage. . . . Her eyes wandered round the room again. Everything was bright and new and shining. Nothing here was allowed to grow shabby or faded, as it was at Langley Place.

'Has George managed to fix up his holidays for August, Gertrude?' said Mrs. Willoughby, still busy with Florence's jersey.

Mrs. Willoughby always took a large furnished house at Herne Bay for the summer and expected the family to join her in relays. Both George and James had frequently tried to get out of this arrangement, but neither had yet succeeded.

'He's not *quite* sure that he'll be able to,' said Gertrude, then, as Mrs. Willoughby's nose seemed to grow larger, added hastily, 'but I dare say he will.'

Mrs. Willoughby's nose returned to its normal size, and she handed the jersey back to Florence.

'You'll have to undo it down to where I've put the pin,' she said. 'You've missed out four rows of the pattern. I was sure the book couldn't be wrong.'

'Thank you,' said Florence dispiritedly.

'You shouldn't attempt those complicated patterns,' said Mrs. Willoughby. 'You only get them wrong.'

There was a short silence, in which Aunt Bessie could be heard saying earnestly to Max:

'And there's always senna, Josiah. I've never known senna to fail.'

'Let's go in to supper,' said Mrs. Willoughby abruptly.

* * *

The lavishness of the cold buffet that formed the Willoughby Sunday evening supper always impressed Helen. There were cold chickens, cold ham, pattees, galantines, prawns in aspic, jellies, creams, trifles, blancmanges, biscuits and cakes of every kind. The standard of comfort at The Beeches was high. Though Mrs. Willoughby scrutinized every halfpenny and every ounce, she was a liberal provider. She kept a 'good table' for her family and her maids, and the tradesmen took for granted that the first of every new delicacy in season must be delivered without delay to The Beeches. What was left over from the Sunday evening supper was not wasted. In the hall stood a row of baskets, in which the poor relations brought their needlework and house shoes – baskets that seemed much too large for the roll of knitting and the pair of shoes – and, when they went home at night, each basket was found filled with remains of the supper, neatly covered by a table napkin, a transaction never referred to on either side.

'Now set to work handing things round,' said Mrs. Willoughby briskly. 'I'll go and see to the coffee.'

She went into the empty kitchen and busied herself at the old-fashioned range. It was an understood thing that

Mrs. Willoughby preferred to make the coffee herself, but this evening, at a sign from her, Max followed her into the kitchen, closing the door behind him.

'You'll have to speak seriously to Oliver, Max,' she said as she took the boiling kettle from the range. 'We've given him long enough to settle down. He's making no effort at all.'

Max leant against the white scrubbed table, his hands in his pockets.

'I don't know,' he said meditatively. 'Might be a good plan to give him a bit more rope. . . .'

He wasn't sure of his ground with Oliver and shrank from joining issues with him, aware that in any argument he would probably have the worst of it and that his position as head of the family carried little weight in Oliver's eyes. He suspected that his mother credited him with a forcefulness of character which in reality he lacked – a lack that he liked to conceal by keeping on good terms with people and following the line of least resistance. Actually Mrs. Willoughby had few illusions about him, but she had found that if you persistently credited people with a quality they often ended by acquiring it . . . and it suited her to delegate part of her own authority to Max, even though he only acted as a puppet government.

'As you like,' she said, 'but it mustn't go on too long. Pass me that tray.'

Pouring the coffee into the jug and seeming to be wholly intent on the process, she said casually:

'I gather that you and Helen Fowler are engaged.'

'Well, yes,' he said, taken aback. 'She wanted to tell her mother first. I was going to tell you as soon as they'd all gone.'

'Will you carry the tray in for me? Mind that jug. It's rather full. . . . I'm glad you're going to marry her. I don't care for her family, but I think she'll make you a good wife.'

CHAPTER FIVE

Max and Helen stood side by side under the cedar tree. Max was flushed with perspiration and emotion, but Helen looked cool and fresh as ever, despite the heat. Her wedding dress of white satin showed up the healthy clearness of her skin and the blue of her eyes. Her hair shone golden through the meshes of the veil. Bobby and Tim were her pages. Tim had already tired of the rôle and wandered off among the crowd, but Bobby, who took his responsibilities seriously, was sitting cross-legged on the grass by the train of Brussels lace, guarding it with jealous care.

Helen was greeting friends and relations with poise and self-possession, infusing into her manner to each the exact shade of cordiality that was due. Those who approached her with the intention of making some joke about her newly married state went away without making it. Mrs. Max Willoughby was already a woman with whom you did not take liberties even though you had known her from babyhood.

Though apparently intent on receiving the long queue of guests, she missed nothing of what went on around her. She approved of Max's general appearance – she had insisted on his going to a Savile Row tailor for his suit – but not of his manner. He smiled too much, was too uniformly friendly. I must tell him not to fidget with his watch-chain, too. It isn't just that he's nervous. I've noticed it before. . . . I'll wear the white *crêpe-de-Chine* nightdress tonight. . . . She thought of her bridal night without either shrinking or excitement. It was simply part of the business of getting married, and to her the least important part – much less important than the striped silk curtains for the drawing-room or the embossed wallpaper for the hall. One wanted children, of course, so one just went through with it. . . .

The poor relations were coming up to her in a body. They wore their best black dresses and their black velvet neck ribbons – except Miss Hatton, who had bought a length of pink tulle and tied it in a large bow under one ear to mark the festive nature of the occasion. Helen greeted them with special graciousness. Already in the dim eyes she saw something of the subjects' loyalty to their queen. Having paid their homage, they withdrew and stood in a little cluster apart on the lawn . . . talking about Max, his cleverness, his kindness, his generosity.

Miss Hatton told them how quickly he had learnt his alphabet and how he knew all the kings of England before he was seven. She had often told them this before, but she liked to impress upon them her superior status as official instructress to the young Willoughbys. It seemed to justify the pink tulle bow, of which she could see they disapproved. She patted it a little defiantly as she spoke.

Helen's gaze wandered round, noting that the Fowlers and the Willoughbys were not mixing very well, were in fact showing a tendency to gather in groups and eye each other distrustfully. Mrs. Fowler and Mrs. Willoughby were talking together in the middle of the lawn, but they suggested a couple of generals conducting a parley during an armed truce rather than heads of a united family. Helen had only been married to Max for an hour or so, but already it was the Willoughby group to which she felt she belonged.

'This is Sir Ernest and Lady Oxted, Max.'

'How do you do? I've heard my wife speak of you, of course. It's a great pleasure to meet you.'

Yes, he must learn not to be so effusive. . . . She glanced down at Bobby, who still sat on the grass at her feet. The sun had made him sleepy, and he was resting his elbow on the train.

'Be careful, Bobby,' she said in the kindly, authoritative voice she always used to children. 'Don't put your elbow on the lace like that.'

'Sorry,' said Bobby contritely, sitting up straight. She smiled at him and he looked up at her adoringly. He thought she was the most beautiful person he had ever seen in his life. He wanted to fight someone for her. . . . Reverently he straightened the lace veil where his elbow had rumpled it.

Helen's eyes passed on to where the bridesmaids stood clustered together like a bunch of flowers in their ankle-length dresses of delphinium-blue chiffon – Judy, Anice, Cynthia and a dim cousin of the Willoughbys' called Emmy. Judy's dark eyes shone with excitement, her cheeks held their creamy pallor even in the hot sunshine, her hair under the velvet cap had the sheen of a raven's wing. Helen looked at her with sudden interest. Till now her relations with Judy had been simple. As the eldest of the sisters she had snubbed her whenever the opportunity offered, and otherwise ignored her. It was something of a shock to realize that Judy was nearly grown-up and that she was extremely pretty. I must take her in hand, she thought. She mustn't be allowed to – drift like Anice.

Anice stood apart from the others, not talking or listening to them. She looked pale and, as usual, a little sulky. Martin Newbolt – vague, shabby and untidy – crossed the lawn in his usual awkward fashion. Irritation seized Helen as he approached her, though the smile with which she greeted him gave no sign of it. She must do something about Martin, too – take him in hand, smarten him up. . . . He must be rescued from that dreadful shop and given a job in Willoughbys'. She had spoken to Anice about it last night and Anice had been more reasonable than she had expected.

Peter was talking to the Willoughby grandchildren, and Helen's eyes rested with approval on his tall figure and thin, dark, pleasant face. He had given her away in church and had been very sweet to her throughout the day, doing all he could to take his father's place. His protective tenderness had touched even Helen, who was seldom touched by that sort of thing and who didn't really need anyone's protective tenderness. He was laughing now at something Jessica had just said. He loved children and always got on well with them.

A pity he only had Gillian, thought Helen, but Belle had made it clear that she wasn't going through *that* again. . . . Gillian was there in her pram with Miss Horsham. The poor relations had gathered round her, nodding their old heads and smiling. Gillian stared at them in solemn wonder. . . . Belle's rather shrill laugh cut through the air. She was sitting in a deck-chair next to her best friend, Moyna Pollard.

Moyna was a vivacious little woman, with hennaed hair and a pale, ferret-like face, who owed her popularity chiefly to her extensive knowledge of local scandal and a rather cruel gift of mimicry. There was something essentially second-rate about her, but Belle gravitated naturally to the second-rate. She had to shine at all costs, and it was easier to shine among the second-rate than among those whose standards were higher. Moyna was amusing Belle now by making fun of the guests. There was an undercurrent of malice in her mockery, for she suspected, with reason, that Mrs. Fowler would have liked to exclude her name from the list of invitations and had only included it at Belle's request. Attracted by Moyna's *gamin* vivacity, a small court gathered round the two, and Belle, who loved to be the centre of a noisy crowd, sparkled into radiant good-humour.

Everyone was drifting towards the buffet and waiters were beginning to move about with laden trays. Miss Hatton, looking self-conscious and a little defiant, seized a glass of champagne from a passing tray, to the consternation of the other poor relations, who were preparing to drink Max's and Helen's health in pale china tea.

Helen turned to Max. His eyes were fixed on her ardently . . . and, because she was young and wholesome and beautiful and more in love with him than she realized, her pulses leapt and a flush crept into her cheeks.

* * *

Mrs. Willoughby, having withdrawn to her own camp, was watching Mrs. Fowler covertly across the lawn. She felt puzzled and slightly disconcerted by the events of the last few weeks. It had seemed clear to her from the beginning that Mrs. Fowler was not bestirring herself sufficiently about this wedding. A function as important as this (and it would be the most important function Bellington had known for years) needed careful and detailed organization. Caterers and tradesmen must be chivvied and kept up to the mark. Lists must be made of things to be done. Lists and lists and more lists – for Mrs. Willoughby was a great believer in lists. Everyone must be set to work at some task or other. . . . So she had approached Mrs. Fowler soon after the date of the wedding was fixed.

Mrs. Fowler's vagueness at that first interview had assured her that she had not been a moment too soon. No, Mrs. Fowler said, she hadn't seen to this, hadn't done anything about that. There was plenty of time. . . .

Mrs. Willoughby always distrusted people who said there was plenty of time. In her opinion there was never plenty of time. So she had offered to relieve Mrs. Fowler of the more exacting duties connected with the preparations. And Mrs. Fowler had professed gratitude, had been pleasant and friendly and – maddeningly elusive.

Mrs. Willoughby, champing to get the thing under way, had been frustrated at every turn by Mrs. Fowler's elusiveness. As there weren't any lists, she could never find out just what Mrs. Fowler had done or even intended to do. 'Oh, I think that will be all right,' Mrs. Fowler would say. 'Don't trouble about that, Mrs. Willoughby. . . . No, I haven't done anything about it yet. There's plenty of time.'

Mrs. Willoughby would go home from Langley Place under the impression that Mrs. Fowler had agreed to all her suggestions and then find that quite different arrangements had been made – in so far as Mrs. Fowler's sketchy understandings with people could be called arrangements. She never seemed to give orders. She just seemed to expect people to know what she wanted, and – oddly and maddeningly – they generally did. Mrs. Willoughby quite thought they had arranged to hold the reception on the front lawn and at the last minute found that it was being prepared here on the smaller lawn at the foot of the terrace steps. And the marquee. . . . The marquee had been to Mrs. Willoughby the most infuriating part of the whole affair.

At any function out of doors Mrs. Willoughby always insisted on a marquee, because, whatever the weather was like, even on the morning of the day, you could never be sure that it would last. Both Florence and Gertrude had had marquees at their weddings though the sky had been cloudless. She had mentioned the marquee quite early on in the affair, and Mrs. Fowler had murmured: 'Yes, of course, what a splendid idea! We'll see what the weather's like nearer the time.' Even as late as yesterday she had asked Mrs. Fowler if she had remembered the marquee (the eagle's beak had figured largely in that interview), and Mrs. Fowler had said vaguely, 'Oh, I think it's going to be fine,' and gone on to talk of something else.

'The thing will be a complete failure,' Mrs. Willoughby had said grimly to Gertrude last night.

And, though it ought to have been, it wasn't. . . . Without lists, without bustling, without organization, the thing was going like clockwork. Mrs. Fowler didn't even seem to realize her responsibilities as a hostess. Vague and quiet, in her cool grey dress, she seemed to wander aimlessly about, talking to her friends as though she had no thought in her mind but the person she was talking to. And yet everyone was apparently happy and satisfied.

Mrs. Fowler, meeting Mrs. Willoughby's eyes across the lawn, looked away quickly with a mischievous brightening of her own. She was aware that Millicent had deliberately foiled and baffled Mrs. Willoughby all these weeks, ignoring Milly, who would have been glad to accept her suggestions and follow her lead. Millicent had behaved outrageously over the marquee, risking an influx of dripping guests into the house merely in order to baffle Mrs. Willoughby. 'You've been luckier than you deserve,' said Mrs. Fowler severely to Millicent, looking up at the cloudless sky.

'How lovely Helen looks!' said one of the guests who had just joined the group.

It was the hundredth time Mrs. Fowler had had to reply to the comment that afternoon, but she sounded as pleased and flattered as if she were hearing it for the first time.

'Yes, she does look rather sweet, doesn't she? She was so pleased with the decanter you sent her.'

Mrs. Fowler never made lists, but she could remember things when she wanted to. . . .

* * *

Oliver Willoughby leant over the terraced balustrade, watching the affair with his usual expression of morose cynicism. He had planned to come in a tweed suit, as a testimony to his recent conversion to Socialism, but at the last minute his courage had failed him, and he had donned the conventional morning coat, striped trousers and top hat. He had, however, taken off his top hat and allowed a carefully cultivated lock of hair to fall over his forehead. He could see his mother watching him disapprovingly. He had got into trouble with her last week for wearing a low collar and flowing tie. Her displeasure had been so uncompromising that he had not repeated the offence, contenting himself with a carefully careless arrangement of his hair and a vaguely Bohemian colourfulness of socks that she had not yet noticed.

A ridiculous affair, he commented to himself as he watched the crowd. Why this senseless parade of fashion and snobbery to mark the mating of a couple of animals? (A rather daring sentiment that he hoped to develop later into a piece of *vers libre* and send to one of the more advanced literary weeklies.) The sight of all these smug bourgeois nonentities swilling champagne was enough to make one feel sick – especially when one thought of the unemployed with barely enough to keep body and soul together.

He seized a glass of champagne from a passing tray and a caviar sandwich from another and continued his meditations. Probably he was the only man here with intelligence and imagination to see the thing for what it was – a pagan orgy masquerading as a Christian sacrament. Bloated capitalists, smug materialists, tyrants who worked men to death in mills and factories. . . . In all this hum of conversation, had one single word been said worth recording, one sentiment conceived that was not utterly banal and commonplace? Barring his own, he was sure there had not been.

He thought of Milton and Shakespeare and Burns. Those were his kinsmen, not this crowd of posturing provincial monkeys. . . . And all the time he was trying to keep his eyes from straying to Judy. She had come to tea with Cynthia last week straight from a hockey match – giggling and grubby, in a creased gym tunic – and he had believed his shameful infatuation to be killed for ever.

But here she was, so lovely in her ankle-length bridesmaid's dress that, whenever he looked at her, his heart quickened. She was moving across the lawn now with a grace that would have seemed unimaginable in the long-legged, black-stockinged schoolgirl of a week ago.

And then, before he could escape, Emmy joined him. He had always disliked Emmy, and she had always pursued him. Throughout his childhood, at birthday parties, Christmas parties, picnics, pantomimes, she had insisted on sitting next to him and thrusting her hot, sticky hand into his. She was a pale, freckled girl, with sandy hair, light eyelashes, a long nose and a receding chin. Usually she was shy and diffident, fully conscious of her lack of charm, but today the delphinium-blue dress seemed to have inspired her with a new assurance.

'Well, Oliver,' she said, 'this *is* nice! We haven't met since Gertrude's birthday, have we? . . . Well, well, *what* an event this is! Another of the family married! I wonder who the next will be?'

Oliver tried to think of some sarcastic rejoinder, but, 'Why should it be anyone?' was the best he could manage.

Emmy laughed coquettishly.

'Oh, Oliver, it's *got* to be someone. They always say that one marriage makes another. We don't *all* want to be old maids and bachelors.'

'Don't we?' he said with a sardonic smile.

'Helen's a lucky girl. Max will make her a good husband. There's a tradition in Bellington, you know, Oliver, that the Willoughbys make good husbands.'

'Is there?' said Oliver, looking around him with studied indifference.

'I've never been here before, you know,' said Emmy. 'I'd like to see over the garden while I'm here. Let's explore a little, shall we?'

Oliver was just going to excuse himself, murmuring something vague and unconvincing about Max's needing him, when he saw Judy and a tall, handsome, middle-aged man disappearing between two yew hedges down a path that led to the rose garden.

'Very well,' he said, and strode after them, Emmy keeping pace with him as best she could in her high-heeled blue velvet shoes.

* * *

'I'm going to have a wedding just like this when I'm grown-up,' said Peggy, perching on the end of the garden seat and looking down complacently at her white kid shoes and white silk socks. She had inherited Mrs. Willoughby's features in a modified form, and at present had that precarious infantile prettiness that so often vanishes before its owner reaches her teens.

'I'm not,' said Jessica, giving an angry little kick at the leg of the garden seat to mark her resentment of the whole affair. 'I'm not going to marry at all. I think it's silly.'

She was a slender, graceful child, with tawny eyes and reddish curls – unlike any of the other Willoughbys. She held her leghorn hat by its elastic, swinging it to and fro.

'You ought to put your hat on, Jessica,' said Peggy reprovingly. 'You've been naughty enough about it already.'

'I don't want to wear it,' said Jessica. 'I don't like it. It's uncomfortable.'

Jessica had been what Florence called 'awkward' all day. She didn't want to wear her new leghorn hat. She wanted to wear her old sunbonnet. When told that people did not wear sunbonnets at weddings, she demanded reasons, demolishing all that were given till Florence took refuge in, 'Do as you're told and don't argue.' She then complained that the hat elastic was too tight and, when a longer piece was stitched on in place of the original one, complained that it was too loose. When a knot was tied in it she said that it was too tight again, and, when the knot was loosened, that it was too loose . . . till finally Florence shook her, rammed the hat on her head and pulled her out to the waiting car, where Bobby was already sitting, resplendent in his white satin suit.

'Tim's being naughty, too,' said Jessica with satisfaction, looking at the rhododendron bush behind which Tim was skulking in his page's costume. He was bitterly ashamed of the white satin suit and felt the rest of his life, however long he lived, would be insufficient to expunge the memory. When a photograph of the wedding group was taken he had shut his eyes and screwed up his face with a vague idea of concealing his identity, but the group would be exhibited in Ransom's window and, despite the screwed-up face, his enemies would recognize him and triumph, while his friends would feel the secret amusement that even friends could not help feeling at the sight of a boy in a white satin suit.

'I know,' said Peggy. 'He's being *very* naughty, but Bobby and I are both being good.'

'That's all right, then,' said Jessica airily. 'One good one and one bad one in each family. It makes it even.'

Helen passed them, her hand on Max's arm, Bobby still holding her train.

'She's pretty, isn't she?' said Peggy.

'She's bossy,' said Jessica, 'and we've got enough bossers in our family.'

'*Jessica!*' gasped Peggy. 'How *can* you say that with Uncle Peter here? He's her brother, you know.'

Peter, who was standing near, looked down at them with a smile. 'It's all right,' he said. 'She *is* a bit bossy, but she's nice. You'll like her.'

'I think it's silly calling you Uncle Peter when you aren't an uncle,' said Jessica dispassionately. 'I'd rather call you Mr. Fowler, or Peter.'

'Call me Peter,' he said.

'You'll get into a frightful row if you do,' Peggy warned her.

'He said I could, so I'm going to,' said Jessica. 'I can't get into a row for doing something that a grown-up's told me to do.'

'You will if Grandma hears you.'

Peter saw Miss Horsham wheeling the pram across the lawn towards the drive and went to meet her.

Florence came up to Jessica.

'Put your hat on, Jessica.'

'I can't. It's uncomfortable.'

'Nonsense!'

'The elastic's too tight. . . . Anyway, Uncle Oliver isn't wearing his.'

'He's grown-up, and grown-ups can do what they like.'

'Why do you always have to do what Grandma tells you, then?'

Florence looked at her helplessly.

'Jessica, if you don't put your hat on at once I'll smack you.'

She realized that it was a mistake as soon as she'd said it. Jessica knew quite well that she wouldn't carry out the threat.

'All right,' challenged Jessica, looking up at her under silky golden lashes, 'smack me.'

Gertrude had joined the group.

'Really, Florence,' she said, 'you'll have to be firm with that child.'

She spoke complacently. There was an unacknowledged rivalry between the two families, and, though the sisters loved each other, each viewed the misbehaviour of the other's children with secret satisfaction.

'Where's Tim?' she went on, looking round.

Tim crept further into the refuge of the rhododendron bush.

Florence had flushed with humiliation. Jessica always seemed to behave worse than usual when Gertrude was there.

'Jessica,' she said, 'put on your hat, or I'll fetch Grandma to you.'

Jessica hesitated a few seconds then put on her hat. She put it on at a deliberately foolish angle, but she put it on. She knew when she was beaten.

'Tim's under the rhododendron bush, Mother,' said Peggy.

Tim emerged, scowling, his white satin suit stained with earth.

'Sneak!' he said to Peggy.

Florence's face had cleared.

'You'll have to be firm with him, Gertrude,' she said.

CHAPTER SIX

Peter and Rachel walked over the grass towards the drive.

'I'm taking Gilly home to tea now,' said Rachel. 'These affairs are a little over-exciting for her.'

He had joined her on an impulse. . . . Over and over again of late he had told himself that he must try to keep away from her . . . but he couldn't. At first he had gone to her for the peace she seemed able to give him, but now that peace itself was threatened by her. Helplessly he accepted the fact that he was in love with her. . . .

Last week Belle had arranged for him to take her, Rachel, Gillian and a neighbour's child for a picnic in the car, but at the last minute she had been invited to a bridge party and had told them to go without her. Peter had demurred and suggested that the expedition should be put off to another day, but Belle had insisted that the children must not be disappointed. He suspected that she regretted the impulse on which she had arranged the picnic – a form of entertainment that did not really appeal to her – and was glad of an excuse for not going with them. So he had surrendered to fate, sitting with Rachel on a slope of the thyme-covered downs, while the children played around them and the afternoon passed on golden wings.

They had talked of trivial things – the countryside, books, music, her childhood – but all the time a radiance of happiness had possessed him, and the day was akin to those dreams of his boyhood whose memory vanished as he awoke, but which left a lingering ecstasy behind.

Always, as they talked, they discovered fresh tastes in common. His spirit, starved by the barren years with Belle, seemed to hold out its hands to the warmth of her understanding and companionship. He could talk of his work, which Belle never allowed him to do. ('Oh, for heaven's sake, Peter,' she would say, 'don't talk shop. It's too boring for words.') He had found, he knew, the friend he had always wanted – if only it could stop at that. But, of course, it couldn't. . . .

For a few days after the picnic he had avoided her, and she, he suspected, had avoided him, but the life of the household inevitably threw them together, and the sense of intimacy of which he had been conscious from the first meeting had struck its roots so deeply into his being that she seemed to be with him, an unseen companion, as he went about his daily work, sharing his interests, his thoughts, his emotions. And yet they had said nothing to each other that might not have been said by the most casual acquaintances.

They stopped by tacit consent where the lawn joined the broad gravelled drive.

'I hope that someone's looked after you and that you've had some tea,' he said.

'Yes, thank you.'

'I did try to find you, but there was such a crowd.'

'It's been a great success, hasn't it?' she said, speaking

quickly and not quite steadily. 'Mrs. Max looked lovely. I hope your mother won't be too tired.'

Peter smiled.

'She takes this sort of thing in her stride, you know. She has a technique of her own. She never seems to make any trouble of anything, but it always goes with a swing from beginning to end. I've never discovered how she does it.'

He was talking simply to keep her there. His eyes were fixed on the wistful curves of her lips.

'I must go,' she said, still in that quick, unsteady voice. 'Gillian's tired.'

'Not tired,' said Gillian indignantly.

'Yes, you are, darling. Say good-bye to your mother and thank her for me, will you, Mr. Fowler? She's talking to someone, and I don't want to interrupt her.'

'Let me help you with the pram,' said Peter, and took the handle to lower it down from the grass verge to the gravel. As he did so his hand touched hers. He withdrew his quickly and looked at her. A faint flush tinged her cheeks and she turned her head away sharply.

'Good-bye,' she said, and set off down the drive.

* * *

He met his mother coming away from the buffet tables.

'Gillian's just gone,' he said. 'Miss Horsham asked me to say good-bye for her and thank you.'

'She's a nice girl,' said Mrs. Fowler. She took a cable out of her bag and handed it to him. 'Helen's just had this. I was looking for you to show it you.'

He read, *Love and best wishes, darling. Matthew.*

'I wish he could have been here,' he said.

The thought of Matthew brought a strange comfort with it. Throughout his boyhood Peter had always felt that nothing could go wrong so long as Matthew was there. . . .

A departing guest seized his mother, and he passed on.

'Hallo, Peter,' Belle hailed him gaily, and he went to where she sat, surrounded by her friends. She was still in radiant good-humour.

'Saw you shooing off the infant and the heavy Miss Horsham, darling,' she said. 'Sweet of you. I was just feeling that I ought to do it myself.' She turned to the others. 'Miss Horsham's our lady nurse, you know. Such a lady, in fact, that one can hardly get a word out of her. She bores me to tears, but Peter always has the patience of a saint with these people.'

It would never occur to Belle, of course, to be jealous of Miss Horsham. Miss Horsham lacked all those arts of deliberate allure that Belle used to attract men.

'Sit down, Peter darling,' she went on. 'We've been simply *screaming* at the Willoughbys. *Aren't* they a set of frumps! *Look* at all those old women they've brought with them. My dear, *do* watch the one with a pink bow. I'm sure she's tight. And Mrs. Willoughby! She looks like a funeral horse with all those black feathers in her hat. And that wretched little boy who was a page – all covered in mud! Still, they're rolling in money, and Helen isn't marrying the family. She can drop the worst specimens. She didn't sound a bit nervous, did she, Peter? Do you remember our wedding, darling? I was so nervous that my "I will" sounded like a mouse's squeak, and you were so nervous that you upset a glass of champagne over my wedding dress.'

'Yes,' said Peter. 'I remember. . . .'

* * *

'Have you spoken to your uncle yet?' said Anice.

She had taken Martin to the little summer-house overlooking the park. She wanted to be somewhere where she couldn't see Helen, beautiful and triumphant, enveloped already in that atmosphere of wealth and prosperity and adulation that would accompany her through life. As she walked across the lawn with Martin she had imagined that everyone was comparing her lot with Helen's. . . . Martin with Max. . . . She felt raw and angry – angry both on her own account and Martin's. If only they knew what he was really like – how staunchly honest and kind and sincere, how incapable of the slightest meanness of thought or action. But, of course, they didn't know. He was just young Newbolt, who served in his uncle's shop and was so absentminded that, more often than not, he gave you the wrong change.

He didn't answer, so she repeated rather sharply:

'Have you spoken to your uncle yet?'

That was one of his most irritating habits – to be so much absorbed by his own thoughts that he didn't hear what was said to him.

'Yes,' he said with a start. 'Yes, but it's difficult to tie him down to anything. It's not that he means to be unhelpful. It's just that he's – vague. And he's always shirked the business side – accounts and things. He's in a complete fog about it. Arranging a partnership would mean going into all that, and it bores him.'

She was silent. She had been to tea with Martin last week in the tall dark house where he lived with his uncle, and the visit had shocked and distressed her. The furniture was untended, the rooms stuffy and airless; over everything hung a smell of old books and dust. The atmosphere was concentrated in the old man's study. His desk was piled high with catalogues and papers. Books in old bindings, tattered, dust-covered, overflowed from the shelves on to chairs and tables and stood in untidy heaps about the floor.

Somehow, though she tried not to, Anice couldn't help liking Martin's uncle. He was a thin, stooping old man, with a straggling grey beard and eyes that peered at her through thick steel spectacles under bushy eyebrows . . . and he had treated her throughout the visit with a formal old-fashioned courtesy that she found disarming. But the old house-keeper, slatternly and none too clean, who brought in the plate of dry grocer's cake and pot of tepid tea, had filled her with revulsion. She had tried to instil something of her horror into Martin, for what chiefly distressed her was that to Martin this background seemed normal and natural.

'Martin, it's all so *dreadful*! Couldn't you get rid of that frightful old woman and find someone who'd keep the place clean?'

'Mrs. Porter?' said Martin mildly. 'Oh, she's all right. We've always had her. Uncle wouldn't know what to do without her.'

'But his room, Martin! Knee-deep in books and thick with dust! It can't have been turned out for years.'

Martin laughed.

'He'd kill anyone who tried to turn it out. . . . You know, when someone gets bitten by that "first edition" bug it's impossible to cure them.' He paused and added: 'And, of course, it *is* fascinating. He got hold of a first edition of Rowlandson's *Johnny Quae Genus* the other day. He was so bucked that he almost forgot to go down to the shop.'

'The shop's his job.'

'I know . . . but he hasn't really much use for modern books.'

Her depression deepened. . . . The problem was more complicated than she had realized at first. She wanted to rescue him, but he didn't seem to realize that he needed rescuing. She looked at him critically, then gave vent to the grievance she had been harbouring all afternoon.

'Martin,' she said, 'haven't you any better clothes than those?'

He looked down at the creased, rather shapeless suit.

'I haven't got a morning suit,' he said. 'Perhaps I ought to have bought one.'

He was humble and a little bewildered. It was difficult to go on – resenting him.

'You needn't have bought anything,' she said, 'but surely you've got something tidier than that.'

'It's not very old,' he said deprecatingly. 'It's my best.'

'Doesn't Mrs. Porter ever brush it?'

'I don't think so.'

‘Well, tell her to. Or brush it yourself. I suppose’ – with a touch of sarcasm – ‘you’ve got a clothes-brush.’

‘Oh yes,’ he said vaguely. ‘I think there’s one about.’

Her irritation rose afresh and with it that dragging pity for him that she could never conquer. His air of neglect tore at her heart and at the same time infuriated her.

‘After all, Martin,’ she said a little tartly, ‘you aren’t a child. You ought to be able to look after yourself.’ She was silent for a few moments, then said, ‘Martin . . .’

‘Yes?’

‘There’s something I want to discuss with you. I didn’t mean to discuss it today but, after all, there’s no reason why I shouldn’t. Do you think that the bookshop will ever bring in enough for you to keep a wife and family?’

‘I don’t know,’ he said. ‘I’ll have another shot at the old man. . . . I did try again last night, but he’d just got a new catalogue, and I found at the end that he hadn’t heard a word I’d said.’

‘Well, frankly, I don’t think it will. I don’t want to have to live as you and your uncle live, and you’ve no right to expect me to.’ She could see that she had hurt him, but she hardened her heart. ‘Helen was talking to me yesterday. She and Max had been discussing the question and he’s willing to offer you a job in Willoughbys’ with a salary that will at any rate keep us in comfort.’

His face seemed to stiffen.

‘It’s kind of him,’ he said, ‘but I shouldn’t dream of accepting, so it’s no use discussing it.’

She looked at him in surprise. There was a note of resolution in his voice that she had never heard in it before.

'Why not?' she challenged.

'I couldn't do any job in Willoughbys' that would be worth any salary at all – much less the sort of salary your brother-in-law suggests.'

'That's for him to decide, isn't it?'

'No, it's for me.'

'Listen, Martin,' she urged. 'It would simplify everything. You'd be independent of your uncle. We could get married, and – '

He interrupted her.

'I'm not going to be a hanger-on at Willoughbys' for any consideration whatever.'

'Your pride means more to you than your love for me, then?'

'They're the same thing,' he said slowly. 'I mean, I couldn't love you without my pride. Don't you understand?'

'No.'

There was another long silence, then he spoke stumblingly as if feeling for words.

'Look here, Anice. I'm no good to you. I never shall be. From the beginning I knew I'd no right to ask you. . . . Would you like to call it all off before it's too late?'

'Don't you love me?' said Anice. Her throat was dry and she saw the sunny park through a sort of mist.

He turned his eyes to her – the eyes that redeemed the plainness of his face.

'You know how much I love you,' he said.

'That's all that matters then, Martin. . . . I think I'm glad really that you don't want to go into Willoughbys'.

I'd hate to be a hanger-on, too. Let's not fuss and worry any more. . . .'

She slipped her hand into his and they sat there in silence . . . while the turmoil of her spirit died away and tranquillity stole over her, a tranquillity so deep that she forgot even her jealousy of Helen. . . .

* * *

Judy was walking towards the rose garden with Mr. Somers. As her godfather and a friend of her father's, he had taken her out at intervals during her childhood – to pantomimes, to Lord's, to the circus – and, though she had enjoyed the expeditions, she had always felt shy and nervous and inadequate, afraid of disgracing his magnificence, of failing to reach the high standard of manners and deportment that was his obvious due.

He was a strikingly handsome man, carrying with him something of the elegance of a bygone age, and Judy had always thrilled to his good looks and the careless ease with which he seemed to move in the world of fashion and luxury. As she walked beside him now, the old childish paralysis of shyness held her in its grip. . . . Only very very gradually did she begin to notice a subtle difference in his manner. The usual patronizing, jocular note was missing. He kept stealing covert glances at her face, round and smooth and dimpled, with the violet dark eyes and lovely childish lips, at the outlines of the slender figure beneath the graceful folds of the long blue dress. He gave a short laugh.

'I didn't realize, my dear,' he said. 'You're grown-up. Let me see . . . how old?'

'Seventeen,' said Judy, with her timid, little-girl smile.

'We must fix up another outing. . . . Or is it too dull these days coming out with an old man?'

The idea took away Judy's breath.

'Oh *no*!' she gasped.

'What shall it be?'

'Oh, anything. . . . Whatever you like.'

'Whatever *you* like,' he corrected. 'Attractive young women must have their own way. . . . What about Ranelagh? Would your mother let me take you there?'

'Why shouldn't she?' said Judy, her eyes opening wide in surprise. 'It would be a lovely treat.'

'A lovely treat for the old fogey! Or is he too much of an old fogey? Shall I get some young people to help out – or could you endure it with just me?'

They had reached the stone steps that led to the rose garden, and he slipped his hand under her arm to guide her down them, keeping it there for a few paces after they had reached the bottom, letting his long thin fingers linger on the satin-smooth skin of her forearm as he released her. She looked at him in faint wonder, and he met her gaze with a smile that was ingratiating and just a little foolish – so unlike his usual smile of weary amusement that for a moment he was almost unrecognizable.

'Or a theatre?' he said. '*My* treat, you know, would be just to be with you.'

His voice held that new ingratiating note. And suddenly

all his magnificence dropped from him. The spell was broken. The glamour was gone. He was no longer a potentate bestowing favours. He was a slave imploring them. And with the realization a sense of power – heady, intoxicating – swept over Judy.

She laughed – a gay and rather cruel little laugh.

'Oh, we'll have to see,' she said. 'We're rather full up just now, with Helen's wedding and Anice's engagement.'

'And you'll be the next, I suppose,' he said. 'I hope it won't be too soon. We don't want to lose you yet, you know.'

'Why not?' she challenged.

I'm flirting, she thought in amazed delight. I'm flirting, just like someone in a book. And with Mr. Somers . . . Mr. *Somers*. . . . Exaltation seized her. She seemed to be swept off her feet . . . to be soaring through the air.

'Don't fish for compliments,' he said with mock severity. 'You have a mirror, haven't you? Do you expect us to *want* to give you to a jealous young man, who'll keep you in order and hardly let you out of his sight?'

She tilted her head.

'When I marry, I'll do the keeping in order.'

He laughed.

'Well, let's make hay while the sun shines. He hasn't appeared yet, has he? When may I take you out? Next week?'

'That's rather soon, isn't it?'

'It will seem years. A purgatory of waiting.'

'Oh, I couldn't inflict that on you.'

'It would be worth it.'

Suddenly she was bored with him. She wanted to extend

her empire, to practice her new weapons on someone else. . . . A small group stood on the other side of the rose garden, with Emmy and Oliver in the centre. Taking her glance for invitation, they approached her, and suddenly, as it seemed, she found herself alone with Oliver.

'Enjoying it?' he said.

'Frightfully. Are you?'

'No.'

'That's not very complimentary.'

'I didn't mean that. . . . I've been trying to get near you all afternoon.'

'You can't have tried very hard. . . . I saw you picking a rose for Emmy. It looked quite romantic.'

He flushed.

'She asked me to.'

'Still more romantic.'

'May I pick one for you?'

'Are you picking roses for every girl you meet?'

'No. . . . Only for you.'

'And Emmy. I'd rather have some of Mrs. Simpkins pinks. They're just there, through that archway.'

She caught her breath. She'd gone too far – ordering Cynthia's grown-up brother about as if he were a little boy. He obeyed her, however, humbly, eagerly, making at last no secret of his enslavement.

But the mood of fey excitement that had upheld her was fading. Her exaltation ebbed like water from a broken bottle. She was suddenly afraid of this strange new world into which she had wandered. She wanted the known, the tested, the familiar. Without waiting for Oliver's return or looking at Mr. Somers, who had been cornered by Emmy, she ran swiftly along the path to the lawn where her mother was moving about among the guests.

'Why, Judy darling,' said Mrs. Fowler taking the flushed face between her cool white hands, 'you look dazzled and dazzling. What's happened to you?'

Judy laughed.

'I think it's the dress,' she said, slipping an arm round her mother's waist.

She was a little girl again, sheltered, happy, beloved.

* * *

Helen and Max had set off for their honeymoon, which was to be spent in Italy. The last of the guests had departed. Anice and Judy had gone to a party at the Willoughbys' from which Mrs. Fowler had excused herself on the grounds of having so much to see to at home. She stood now on the terrace, her hands resting on the stone balustrade, watching maids and waiters clearing up the débris on the lawn. Millicent and Milly were holding one of their usual altercations in her mind.

'I shall miss Helen terribly,' said Milly.

'No, you won't,' said Millicent. 'Right down at the bottom you're looking forward to being without her.'

Milly ignored this.

'I hope Max will be good to my little girl,' she said.

'It's Max who'll need protecting,' said Millicent drily, 'not your little girl.'

At this point Mrs. Fowler gave up the argument and turned her thoughts to the others. . . . Peter, quietly helpful at every turn throughout the day . . . Anice, her sulkiness lit by a thin precarious flame of happiness . . . Judy, flashing from little-girlhood into a delicious fleeting maturity. 'She's my baby,' said Milly, 'I don't want to lose her.' Millicent was just about to make some crushing rejoinder to this piece of smug possessiveness, when the caterer's foreman came up the terrace steps.

'I think that's everything, Madam,' he said, touching his cap. 'We'll go now, if that's all right.'

'Oh yes,' said Mrs. Fowler. 'Thank you so much. Everything was perfect.'

She tipped him – too generously, for she had royal standards of tipping that her husband had tried vainly to lower – then turned her thoughts to practical matters. There was a pile of letters of congratulation on her desk that she ought to answer. . . . There was the silver that had been used this afternoon to be checked. . . . There were the wedding presents to be put away. . . . There were the accounts to be gone through. . . . Having come to the conclusion that there was so much to do that she didn't know where to start, Mrs. Fowler decided not to start at all. She went to the library, took *Diary of a Nobody* from the shelves and, returning to her wicker chair under the lime tree, settled down to waste what precious hours still remained of the day.

CHAPTER SEVEN

Bellington always wore a gala air on Saturday morning. Shoppers, accompanied by prams, children and dogs, thronged the narrow pavements, gathering in groups to exchange news and gossip, so that pedestrians had to invade the streets, already full of cars and bicycles, with here and there an old-fashioned pony-trap. Most of the shops were long-established family businesses, and the owners would come down on Saturday morning and take up their position in the centre of their shops, greeting their customers (many of whom they had known from childhood and whose grandfathers had dealt with their grandfathers) and enquiring after their concerns with sympathetic interest, for in those days the relationship of tradesman and customer often implied a sincere and tested friendship.

Helen and Anice threaded their way through the crowd of shoppers in High Street, stopping occasionally to speak to friends. Helen was still the centre of local interest. She and Max had returned from their honeymoon a fortnight ago and were now settling into Cobham Lodge, a large square house of the same type as The Beeches, furnished according to the Willoughby standards of taste and comfort.

As Helen had foreseen, the management of Max had turned out to be child's play and already she had considerably tempered his natural exuberance. He was so much in love with her that, to please her, he would have assumed any character she assigned him. House-keeping, too, in the new house presented few difficulties. Her kind, impersonal, authoritative manner reduced maids to the automata she wished them to be, and the routine of the household moved already with the clockwork regularity that she had tried in vain to impose upon Langley Place.

Mrs. Fowler had seen little of her daughter since her return for Helen had been engulfed by the Willoughbys – proposed on to the Willoughby committees, entrusted with Willoughby stalls at bazaars, asked out to tea by Willoughby friends and relations. She even called Mrs. Willoughby 'mother', relegating Mrs. Fowler a little selfconsciously to 'mater'. 'You don't mind, do you, darling?' she had said. 'They all call her mother, and I'm there so much.' Already, to the mild discomfiture of Florence and Gertrude, she had become Mrs. Willoughby's lieutenant. It was Helen who had suggested boarding school for Jessica, Helen and Mrs. Willoughby together who had selected the school. Florence had been a little taken aback when informed of their decision. She had gone so far as to say to Gertrude:

'When they told me they'd fixed on the school and everything, I thought, well!' but she had raised no serious objection and had gone with Mrs. Willoughby to interview the head-mistress, or rather to listen to Mrs. Willoughby interviewing the head-mistress. 'She's like one of those cardinals in history,' said Cynthia to Judy, 'raised to power by the king. They generally had downfalls, but I don't think Helen's the sort to have a downfall.'

And now Helen had taken Anice's affairs in hand.

'Do you really mean to say that after all this time Martin hasn't made any definite arrangement with his uncle?' she said.

'Well,' hedged Anice, 'you know what the old man is. We thought we'd wait till the end of the next month, when the accountant goes through the figures.'

'Nonsense, Anice! You'll put it off for ever at this rate. It's extremely foolish of you, you know, not to let Max give Martin a job in the business.'

'It's no use discussing that. I feel just as Martin does about it.'

'Then you must insist on his uncle's coming to the point. If he won't take any notice of Martin, you must tackle him yourself.'

'I couldn't, Helen.'

'Then I will.'

'You *mustn't*. . . .'

'I will, and I'll do it now. He'll be in the shop, won't he? . . . Bother! Here's Belle.'

* * *

They could tell at once by Belle's face that something was wrong. She was pale, and the rosebud mouth was ominously set. It curved into a smile of mechanical sweetness, however, as the sisters approached her.

‘Good morning, my dears, and how’s the bride?’ she said.

Helen, who disliked being referred to as the bride, said nothing, so Anice replied:

‘She’s quite well, thank you, Belle. How are you?’

‘I’ve got one of my splitting headaches,’ said Belle.

‘Why did you come out, then?’ said Helen unsympathetically.

‘Someone has to do the shopping.’

‘Couldn’t Peter have done it on his way to the office?’

‘Oh, *Peter*!’ said Belle, and by the tone of her voice they knew that the trouble, whatever it was, involved Peter. ‘He’s a perfect fool about shopping. Why, when I asked him to call at Forresters’ for – ’

‘My dear Belle,’ interrupted Helen, ‘that was years ago, and we’ve heard the story so often. Why didn’t you send Miss Horsham, then?’

The rosebud mouth tightened again.

‘Miss Horsham! I wouldn’t trust that woman with half a crown.’

‘I don’t know her very well, of course,’ said Helen, ‘but I’m sure she isn’t dishonest.’

‘I’ve given her a month’s notice, anyway.’

‘Why?’

‘She was insolent to me.’

‘Miss Horsham?’ said Helen incredulously.

Belle shrugged.

‘Oh, don’t let’s talk about *my* troubles. How are you getting on at Cobham Lodge? All very grand, I’ve heard.’

'Have you?' said Helen, with raised eyebrows and the light of battle in her eye.

'Well, dear, my cook's a friend of your housemaid, you know, and she's told me all about the two extra bathrooms you've had put in. The black-and-green one sounds most odd.'

'I hope you'll come to my At Home next week,' said Helen suavely, 'then you can see it all for yourself instead of being dependent on your cook's account. Servants' gossip is often unreliable.'

'Really, Helen!' said Belle, with a toss of her head.

'Judy went to tea there last week,' put in Anice hastily, 'and she was so thrilled by the black-and-green bathroom that she insisted on having a bath then and there.'

'Oh, that reminds me,' said Belle, 'I saw Judy and Cynthia cycling down Monks' Hill the other day in gym tunics with hockey sticks. I thought they'd left school.'

'They have,' said Helen, 'but they belong to the Old Girls' Hockey Club.'

'Well, the wind was blowing their tunics right up above their knees. It looked disgusting. Someone ought to speak to them about it.'

'There's nothing to stop your speaking to them about it if you want to,' said Helen.

'Well, of course, Helen, if you've no objection to that sort of thing. . . . As to Cynthia, one can hardly be surprised. People like the Willoughbys have their own standards, and now that you're one of them it's perhaps wise of you to accept their standards.' She gave a shrill, mirthless little laugh and went on, 'And when are we going to be able to order our daily paper from Anice?'

'If you mean, when are Anice and Martin going to be married – '

'Yes, I did, dear. It was just my little joke. Though, of course, we do get our *Times* from Newbolt's.'

'I've no doubt Anice will allow you to continue to get it there. And – *Tit Bits*, isn't it?'

'I get that for the servants,' said Belle with dignity.

'How careless they are with it,' said Helen, 'always leaving it about the drawing-room!'

Belle looked at her watch and gave a simulated start of surprise.

'I'd no idea it was so late. I haven't nearly finished my shopping. So nice to have seen you, darlings. Good-bye.'

'Good-bye, Belle. Hope your head will soon be better.'

The two sisters walked on.

'She gets more insufferable every day,' said Helen.

'Yes, but you shouldn't bait her, Helen. She only takes it out of Peter.'

'I wonder what it was this time.'

* * *

Belle had awakened that morning to an unusual sense of well-being. The room was flooded with sunshine, and a blackbird was singing on a tree just outside her window. She remembered that it was Saturday. Bellington would be full of shoppers in their best summer clothes, for Bellington on Saturday mornings always partook of the nature of a fashion parade. Lying back against her pillows as she ate her breakfast (for Belle considered herself delicate and always breakfasted in bed), she planned her own costume for the morning's shopping.

She would wear her new white linen dress, with a red belt and the red hat she had bought at Crofton's last week. Then she remembered that at the same time, passing through the baby linen department on her way to the millinery, she had seen a little white organdie frock, smocked in red, and had bought it for Gillian. She would take Gillian into Bellington wearing the organdie frock. It would be an attractive finish to her own toilet. In imagination she saw the pair of them – herself pushing the pram in the white linen dress with the red hat and belt, and Gillian sitting under the white canopy wearing the red-and-white organdie frock, her golden curls shining in the sun. A complacent little smile curved her lips as she contemplated the picture.

She got up, dressed very carefully, choosing a shade of rouge and lipstick that matched the red hat, then went to the nursery. Rachel was just coming out, holding Gillian's hand.

'Put Gillian's new frock on, Miss Horsham,' said Belle. 'I'm going to take her with me into Bellington.'

She spoke in the rather distant voice she always used when speaking to Rachel in order to remind her that, though a 'lady', she was nevertheless Belle's paid employee.

'Yes, Mrs. Fowler,' said Rachel.

Belle lifted Gillian up and kissed her.

'Isn't that a lovely treat for you, darling?' she said. 'You're coming out with Mummy.'

Gillian drew back.

'Want to go with Nanny,' she said.

'But you love Mummy, darling,' protested Belle.

Gillian shook her curls.

'No. Love Nanny,' she said.

Belle put her down abruptly.

'She's only teasing you, Mrs. Fowler,' said Rachel. '*Of course* you love Mummy best, Gillian.'

'Don't love Mummy best. Love Nanny,' said Gillian, stretching out her hand to touch a tall *cloisonné* vase that stood on the landing and whose coloured surface always fascinated her.

Belle seized the hand and slapped it smartly.

'Leave that alone, you naughty girl.'

Gillian began to sob, and Rachel's face flushed as she stooped down to gather the child into her arms.

'There was no need for you to do that, Mrs. Fowler,' she said steadily. 'If you want Gillian to go into Bellington with you of course she'll go.'

Dull red blotches appeared in Belle's neck and spread upwards till they covered her cheeks.

'How *dare* you speak to me like that?' she said. 'You can take a month's notice.'

'Very well, Mrs. Fowler,' said Rachel, and withdrew to the nursery with Gillian, closing the door.

Belle went downstairs to the dining-room. Peter, who was having his breakfast, his paper propped against the coffee-pot, looked up with a frown as she entered.

'What on earth's the rumpus about?' he said.

'Miss Horsham's been insolent to me, and I've given her notice,' said Belle.

She was still breathing noisily and the red blotches still showed in her cheeks.

'What do you mean?' said Peter after a pause.

'You heard me, didn't you? I've never put up with insolence from a servant, and I'm not going to start now.'

'She's hardly a servant,' said Peter, 'and I can't believe that she was insolent.'

Belle's voice rose shrilly.

'That's right. Take her part against me. Humiliate me in front of the whole house. If you want to know what I think of her, I think she's a sly, underhand, conceited, double-faced – '

She heard Rachel's step on the stairs and went out into the hall.

'What time would you like me to have Gillian ready, Mrs. Fowler?'

'I'm not taking her. I thought I'd made that quite clear. I hope I made it equally clear that I'd given you notice.'

'You did, Mrs. Fowler.'

The hint of contempt in the quiet voice broke down what was left of Belle's self-control.

In the middle of the stream of abuse that followed, the dining-room door opened and Peter appeared. He was pale and the muscles of his face were taut.

'I won't have you speaking like that to anyone in this house, Belle, d'you hear?' he said.

There was a sudden silence. Rachel turned and went into

the kitchen. Belle stood there, her eyes, bright with anger, fixed on Peter.

'So that's the way the wind blows, is it?' she said slowly at last. 'How blind I've been all this time!'

But Peter had snatched his hat from the hat-stand and gone out, slamming the door.

Belle's mind went over the morning's events as she walked along High Street, and dwelt with lingering relish on the scene with Rachel. She'd given the girl a good dressing down . . . got some things off her chest that she'd been wanting to get off for a long time . . . taught her a lesson she wouldn't forget in a hurry. As to Peter, she'd teach him a lesson, too. Throwing his weight about! Interfering in her dealings with the servants! She didn't for a moment believe that there was anything between Peter and the girl – she was too sure of her power over him for that – but it would be a useful weapon. A rather cruel little smile touched her lips as she began to plan her punitive campaign. She'd make him pay – and pay dearly – for his revolt. She enjoyed quarrelling with Peter. And she could always forgive him when she'd had enough. She could never drive Peter so far from her that she couldn't get him back when she wanted him.

Then her thoughts turned to her conversation with Helen and Anice, and she went over that, too, altering a word here and a word there, giving herself all the best lines and taking out all Helen's good ones, till the honours of the whole encounter lay with her. So much absorbed was she by this process that she did not see Moyna Pollard till she felt herself grabbed by the arm.

'Hello, darling. How adorable you look! Come on. You're just in time for coffee with the crowd. We're going to the Tea Caddy.'

The Tea Caddy was a new tea-shop that had just been opened in High Street. It had orange curtains at the windows, spindly little tables covered with striped table-cloths, chairs so crowded together that it was almost impossible to move, and a display of 'Arts and Crafts' for sale at exorbitant prices. Belle's friends were already assembled and hailed her with screams of delight. Taking her seat among them, she gave the revised account of her scene with Rachel (she omitted Peter's share in it. That would be confided separately to each one under oath of secrecy) and of her encounter with Helen and Anice. They screamed applause and congratulation. Then the conversation drifted off to local scandal . . . and Belle gradually became silent.

'Wake up, darling,' said Moyna. 'What are you thinking of?'

Belle roused herself with a start.

'Nothing. . . .'

But there was a far-away look in her eyes. It had occurred to her suddenly that perhaps, after all, there might be something between Peter and Miss Horsham. She didn't think really there was, but she'd keep her eyes well open till the woman went.

* * *

Newbolt's bookshop – a dark, old-fashioned shop, divided into bays, marked Poetry, History, Fiction, *Belles Lettres* and

Miscellaneous – held its usual Saturday morning crowd, but it lacked the air of bustling activity that pervaded the other shops. The crowd here was a leisurely one, giving the impression of having all day before it. It browsed among the bookshelves. It took down books and read them shamelessly. Schoolgirls boasted of having read whole novels in Newbolt's by Saturday morning instalments. No-one ever bothered them or asked what they wanted. Some of the customers disliked this atmosphere. They preferred the shops where young men sprang forward obsequiously as soon as they entered the door. 'Really,' they said, 'one has to simply *insist* on being served at Newbolt's. It's too tiresome.'

As Helen and Anice entered, they saw Judy and Cynthia standing by a table of books in the middle of the shop talking together in the earnest conspiratorial fashion that marked their discussion of the most trivial matters. 'When they aren't giggling,' said Oliver, 'they're behaving like a couple of international spies.' The door into the inner office was open, and they could see Martin's uncle deep in conversation with the Vicar of St. Giles, a tall, gaunt clergyman in a threadbare overcoat, who shared his enthusiasm for first editions. The table was strewn with catalogues and papers, and the floor piled with books.

'What does he *do* with all those dreadful old books?' Anice had asked Martin impatiently. 'He's always buying them, and he never sells any of them.'

'Well, he means to sell them,' said Martin apologetically, 'but, of course, he never does. He's just got the bug for buying them.'

‘It doesn’t do the business any good.’

‘I’m afraid it doesn’t,’ Martin had agreed mildly.

Judy turned round from the table as Helen approached.

‘Hello, Helen.’

‘Hello. We’ve just seen Belle. She doesn’t like your knees.’

‘Why not?’

‘I don’t know. She saw them when you were cycling down Monks’ Hill, and it upset her.’

Judy grinned.

‘I’m so glad. . . . Anice, I wish you’d speak very strongly to Martin. He’s gone and sold *White Roses*, and Cynthia and I were in the middle of it.’

‘You can complain to him yourself, can’t you?’

‘We have done. He’s terribly sorry. He’s getting some more copies in next week, he says, but Cynthia and I wanted to finish it today. He doesn’t even know how it ends. It’s maddening.’

‘I’ve got a sort of idea how it ends,’ said Cynthia. ‘They’ve been through so much that I’m sure it ends by them getting married, but I want to know *how*. He’d heard that she’d got married to someone else last Saturday, but I’m sure it was a misunderstanding. . . .’ She glanced round the shop and continued dispassionately: ‘Do look at Oliver. Doesn’t he look frightful?’

Oliver was standing in the Poetry bay, intent, as it seemed, on a small thin volume that he had just taken down from the shelves. He was hatless, one carefully careless lock of hair fell over his brow and he was wearing orange socks. Though apparently oblivious of the near presence of his family, he was in reality acutely aware of it. Now, feeling the four pairs of eyes fixed on him, he flung back the lock in such a way that it fell over his brow again almost immediately and pretended to be more than ever absorbed in his book. He had been aware of Judy ever since she came into the shop. . . . They had avoided each other since the day of Helen's wedding. To Judy the scene in the rose garden was like the memory of a fantastic dream. She couldn't believe that it had ever really happened. She had only met him once since then – in Cynthia's home with all the family around – and they seemed to have slipped back into their old relations, Oliver belonging to the grown-up camp and Judy a schoolgirl friend of Cynthia's. The only difference, as far as Judy was concerned, was an odd sense of disquiet whenever Oliver was near her.

'What have you come for, Helen?' she said, anxious to turn the conversation from Oliver and to hide all traces of her self-consciousness. 'You're not going to read a book, surely?'

'Don't be cheeky,' said Helen. 'We've come to speak to Martin.'

Martin stood behind the counter, serving a master from the Grammar School, who was ordering text-books. Two women whom he had just served passed Helen and Anice.

'My goodness, isn't young Newbolt slow!' one of them was saying.

'Yes, but he's rather nice,' said the other.

'Come on, Anice. He is free now,' said Helen.

Anice hung back. Once Helen took charge of your affairs it was like being swept along by a whirlwind.

'Do let's wait till the accountant's been through the books.'

'Nonsense! You've waited long enough.'

But by the time they reached the counter another woman had seized on Martin. She wanted to order a book, but she wasn't sure of the author or title or publisher. Patiently Martin turned over the pages of his catalogue till he discovered the book she wanted, then wrote down the title in his order book, turning with a smile to Helen and Anice as the customer went away.

'I'm sorry to interrupt you on a busy morning, Martin,' said Helen briskly, 'but I want to get things settled. If you can't come to some satisfactory arrangement with your uncle about your salary and prospects, I'd like to speak to him myself.'

'Oh yes,' said Martin vaguely. 'Well, as a matter of fact the old man's getting out of it altogether. He told me so last night.'

'Getting out of it?'

'Yes. Retiring.'

'So the business will be yours?'

'Yes.'

Helen's sharp glance swept round the shop.

'There are a good many improvements long overdue,' she said. 'It should have larger windows. Those aren't any good for light or display. And the whole place wants doing up. It's in a shocking state. I'd have all those bays taken down if I were you . . . but we can go into all that later. . . . Now about the wedding itself. I should say the early autumn. That should give us time to make all the preparations. It will be from Langley Place, of course, but Mother and I will see to things. Mater finds these affairs a little tiring. When can you both come and talk it over with me? I'll get Mother to come in at the same time.' They looked at her helplessly. 'Next Wednesday? It's early-closing day, so Martin will be free. . . . Well, I'll expect you both to tea on Wednesday. Max will have to go to London on business, so the four of us can really get down to things.' She glanced at her watch. 'Half past eleven.' She turned her eyes to the clock on the wall, whose fingers stood at a quarter past. 'You ought to have that clock seen to, Martin. Nothing gives such an appearance of inefficiency as a clock that doesn't keep time. Well, I must go now. I'm meeting the family for coffee at Crofton's.'

Every Saturday morning at eleven a large table was reserved in Crofton's restaurant for the Willoughbys. Florence and Gertrude were always there with their children and, on rare occasions, their husbands. Sometimes Cynthia took Judy there, and a smattering of poor relations generally turned up.

Oliver was still standing in the Poetry bay when Helen went back through the shop.

'Coming to coffee, Oliver?' she said.

Oliver saw in imagination the solid phalanx of Willoughbys massed round the table in Crofton's restaurant and shuddered.

'God forbid!' he said. 'I mean, no, thank you.'

Helen went on towards the door.

'What about you, Cynthia?' she said, as she passed the centre table.

'Yes, I'll be there in a few minutes,' said Cynthia, who still had a schoolgirl's healthy appetite for 'elevenses'. 'Tell them to order whatever's going for me.'

Helen crossed the Market Square to Crofton's and went up the broad old-fashioned carpeted staircase to the restaurant.

It was a sombre room, panelled in dark wood, with solid mahogany tables, an abundance of spotless white damask and gleaming ranks of cutlery. The Willoughbys' table was already full except for a seat that Mrs. Willoughby had kept vacant at her right hand.

'Come and sit here, my dear,' she said, motioning Helen to it. 'Well, have you seen Anice?'

'Yes, it's all right about the business. Martin's uncle's retiring.'

'That's a good thing. Pick up your cap, Tim. Don't do it for him, Gertrude. Let him do it himself. Now about the wedding – '

Mr. Crofton, in cut-away coat and striped trousers, entered the restaurant and shook hands with Mrs. Willoughby, greeting each member of the family and enquiring solicitously after their health. He did this every Saturday morning, sunning himself complacently in the Willoughby patronage. Other people might set up art-and-crafty little tea-rooms in High Street with orange curtains and striped table-cloths, but, as long as the Willoughbys came to Crofton's, then Crofton's was the place to come to. . . .

* * *

When Helen had gone, Cynthia resumed her conspiratorial expression and, glancing round the shop, took a letter from her pocket.

'Here it is, Judy . . . I couldn't show it to you while Helen was here. What *shall* I do? I'm in the most frightful jam. . . . You see, I've written the most awful things to him. I mean, I've told him how wonderful I think his books are and how wonderful I think he must be. And, you know, Judy, it's quite true. He *is* wonderful. He seems to understand everything even before you tell him. He's so kind and understanding. And *terribly* handsome. You remember that photograph we found in *Books and Readers* – the one I cut out. . . . He's written me the most wonderful letters. You needn't read the whole letter. It's just the postscript. . . .'

Judy read the postscript. *I am coming to Bellington in September to lecture to the Literary Society. I hope we shall meet there.*

'Well, that's all right, isn't it?' said Judy. 'You can go to it and meet him. Oliver's the secretary. He'll take you.'

'But, Judy,' gasped Cynthia, 'don't you *see*? No one knows I know him. No one knows I've been writing to him. I shall get into the most *frightful* row if they find out. I must go to hear him lecture because I couldn't bear not to, but he'll mention the letters when he meets me, and then the whole thing will come out. I hardly slept all last night worrying over it.'

Judy saw that Cynthia was deriving as much excitement from the situation as if it were an illicit love affair in danger of discovery. A few months ago she would have been as deeply thrilled as Cynthia, but now it seemed trivial and schoolgirlish. Cynthia's perturbation, with its undercurrent of unconscious delight, irritated her.

'Why don't you just write and ask him to pretend not to know you till you're introduced. Explain that you don't want people to know that you've been writing to him.'

'Perhaps that would be best,' said Cynthia with a sigh. 'Life gets terribly complicated as one grows older, doesn't it? Of course, I don't want to do anything to spoil our friendship, because, though we've never met and he's so much older than I am, I feel that we have a tremendous amount in common. I don't want him to think me deceitful. He has very high ideals.'

'I'm sure he wouldn't think you deceitful. . . . Oh, look, Cynthia! There's that woman who talks to herself.'

But Cynthia, having begun to discuss the problem that had occupied her dreams and waking hours for two whole days and nights, was not to be so easily diverted from it.

'I've wondered once or twice whether to confide in Miss Cavendish, but I can't help thinking that she might be a little shocked. I mean, she might think it forward of me to have written at all. She has such high ideals of womanhood. . . . I say, Judy, you are going to tea with her on Wednesday, aren't you? She's only asked the two of us. I think it's so sweet of her to say that she wants us to be her friends now we've left school.'

'I'm not sure that I can manage it,' said Judy evasively.

She was ashamed to admit to Cynthia – she was ashamed to admit even to herself – that the glamour was fading from Miss Cavendish, that, at their last meeting, she had been bored by Miss Cavendish's high-flown sentiments and earnest Cult of the Best, that she had studied Miss Cavendish's horse-like face dispassionately and found it repellently plain. Cynthia, in spite of her other pre-occupations, still worshipped at the shrine. Perhaps I'm fickle, thought Judy with interest. . . .

'Oh, Judy, you must come,' said Cynthia. 'It won't be any fun without you. It never is.'

'I'll come if I can,' said Judy.

She gave a sweeping glance round the shop, a glance calculated to pass carelessly over the ceiling of the Poetry bay and yet to ascertain whether Oliver were still there. But the Poetry bay was empty.

* * *

'I don't know how we're going to stand it, Martin,' said Anice.

'It'll be pretty grim,' agreed Martin.

'Helen and the Willoughbys running the whole thing! A sort of imitation Helen's wedding, with everyone thinking how much prettier she was and what a much better marriage she was making.'

'I'm sorry, darling. I'm afraid that part's true. I mean, you're prettier than Helen, but there's no doubt that she made a better marriage.'

'Oh, Martin, I *want* to marry you, but I don't want the whole thing to be stage-managed by Helen and the Willoughbys.'

'Couldn't your mother assert herself?'

'No. She got so bored by the whole situation when Helen was married that she'll just let things slide. It isn't that she *can't* fight, it's that she can't be bothered to. And the Willoughbys amuse her. She likes to see them in action. She'd put a few spokes in their wheel just for the fun of the thing, but not enough.'

She stood aside to allow him to serve a customer, watching him tie up the parcel with his slow, deliberate movements. Then:

'Anice,' he said.

'Yes?'

'Let's get married on our own, without anyone knowing.'

'How could we?'

'Easily. I could get a licence. We could be married in London. No one here need know. . . . Would your mother mind terribly?'

'I don't think she'd mind at all. But Helen and the Willoughbys would be furious.'

'They don't matter, do they?'

'No. . . . Oh, Martin, it would be heavenly!'

'I'll go to London and fix it up tomorrow. I think you leave suitcases somewhere. I'll find out.'

Martin's uncle came out of his office with the shabby clergyman.

'Mr. Bretton wants to show you his first edition of *Humphrey Clinker*, Martin,' he said.

Martin took the book and opened it, his face alight with interest.

'It's the first issue, too,' he said. 'It's got the misprint on the title page.'

Anice saw that they had all forgotten her. She smiled to herself and went out into the sunny street.

CHAPTER EIGHT

The path in the wood wound tortuously among the trees through an undergrowth of bracken that would later be a sea of gold and that showed already faintly russet in the sunshine. A stream, spanned by a couple of planks, cut across the path, flowing crystal-clear between mossy banks.

Peter walked slowly, his gaze wandering around the familiar landmarks. The place had been a favourite spot for picnics in his childhood. They had sailed boats in the stream, played hide-and-seek, climbed the trees. Matthew had climbed them fearlessly, swinging himself from branch to branch, from one precarious foothold to another. . . . Peter had tried to emulate him, shutting his eyes every now and then to prevent himself from looking down through the branches at the sickening drop beneath. Often his heart would knock against his ribs as he followed Matthew's carelessly flung directions . . . 'Now the branch just above. You can reach it with your hand. . . . Swing yourself up. . . . Help yourself with a foot against the trunk. . . .'

A word of commendation from Matthew was in those days the highest prize that life had to offer, and to win it he would undergo any ordeal, anxious only to hide his fears from Matthew . . . and his fears were numerous and shameful. He was afraid of the dark, of the big black dog at the farm, of the cricket balls that Matthew threw with such deadly swiftness, of the white rats that Matthew kept as pets. Matthew was kind, teasing him in friendly, patronizing elder brother fashion, encouraging his efforts, praising his successes, tactfully ignoring the occasional failure of his attempts at manliness. 'He's not really a cissie,' he would say. 'He's got guts. . . .'

He seemed to see Matthew now – sturdy and stocky, his fair hair gleaming in the sunshine, his blue eyes screwed up against the light, his face set and earnest. Matthew was always so entire – given up to the interest of the moment, that nothing else existed for him.

He had reached the planks that led over the stream, and he stood in the middle, looking down at the water. The pebbles at the bottom shone like jewels. Tiny ferns grew in the moss on the banks. He had stood just there as a small boy, enraptured by the beauty of it . . . then Matthew had come, and, ashamed of his emotion, he had pretended to be looking for tiddlers, though Matthew had thought even that rather babyish. Slowly he walked over the bridge. It had seemed a perilous passage in his childhood. . . .

On the other side of the stream the path wound out of sight. Beyond the bend was a fallen log on which his mother used to sit and read when she brought them here for picnics. They preferred it when their mother brought them rather than Miss Cromer, the governess, who was bright and vivacious and insisted on joining in their games. Mrs. Fowler would sit on the log, reading, completely forgetful of them, till Helen reminded her that it was time to go home, and then she would close her book, look at them with a dreamy smile and say: 'Is it? So it is. What a pity!'

He had been to a 'job' beyond the village this afternoon, and, while engaged on it, so vivid a memory had come to him of his mother sitting there, her head bent over a book, as they played around her, that he had decided on a sudden impulse to re-visit the spot and try to capture something of the tranquillity that had always invested the scene in his mind.

He and Rachel had barely spoken to each other since the morning of Belle's outburst. Belle had been at her worst that night and the following day, but her anger and self-pity had affected him little.

He had played his part mechanically in the succession of scenes that she had forced on him, hardly answering her accusations, refusing to enter into the long emotional discussions she loved. Only when she turned the venom of her tongue on Rachel did a hot wave of anger surge over him. But even then he had contained himself and remained silent. She had concentrated her efforts during the next week on what she called 'winning back Gillian', taking the child about with her everywhere, buying her presents, feeding her with unwholesome food, keeping her up late at night, till the dark hollows began to return to Gillian's eyes, the fretful edge to her voice.

Belle, however, had soon tired of the process. A series of invitations to bridge parties had engrossed her attention, and

Gillian had returned to Rachel and a normal nursery existence. Peter had noticed that Belle watched him and Rachel closely at first, then, seeing nothing to feed her never very strong suspicions, had turned her mind to other matters.

The end of the month was drawing near, and Belle had not made any effort to engage another nurse. Having worked off her anger against Rachel by inflicting a hundred small humiliations on her during the past weeks, she was beginning to feel more tolerant towards her. The girl had her points, she said. She was a good nurse, she never objected to changing her free afternoon, she didn't make trouble with the maids. She only needed teaching her place occasionally. The streak of indolence in Belle made her shrink from the effort of altering her household arrangements.

'I've half a mind to let her stay on,' she had said casually to Peter last night.

He had turned away from her and pretended to busy himself at his chest of drawers, so that she could not see his face.

'Perhaps she's got another job,' he had said, trying to speak in his normal casual voice.

'She can't have,' said Belle. 'She hasn't asked me for a reference.'

'You said you wouldn't give her one,' he reminded her.

She shrugged.

'Oh, well . . . people always say that it's a mistake to withdraw a notice. A girl of that type would only take advantage of it. I'll call at the registry office tomorrow morning. Or Mrs. Drew may be getting rid of her nurse now that Rosemary's going to school. I'll see about it. . . . She's a nice girl, and I think she'd be more help to me than this Horsham woman's been. She'd do my mending and washing and that sort of thing. I shall certainly never get a lady again. It was a ridiculous idea of yours.'

* * *

As he turned the bend in the path beneath the trees his heart leapt, and just at first it seemed that he had strayed back into the world of his childhood and that the slight figure seated on the log, her head bent over a book, was his mother. Then she looked up and he saw that it was Rachel. For a few moments neither of them spoke. A faint flush had crept into the milky pallor of her cheeks.

'I was taking a short cut through the wood,' he said. 'Or, rather, I suppose it's a long cut. . . .'

'It's lovely, isn't it?' she said. 'I often come here on my free afternoons.'

He sat down by her.

'We used to picnic here when we were children,' he said. 'My mother used to sit on that log . . . reading . . .'

'Yes,' she said dreamily, 'somehow I can imagine it. . . . I shall miss the woods when I go.'

'You've made arrangements about – going?'

'Yes. To a place in Sussex. Someone my aunt knows.'

He sat there silent, his frowning gaze fixed on the ground. Then he spoke as if with an effort:

'I'm afraid you haven't been happy here.'

She turned her head away.

‘I’ve been – terribly happy but – ’

She stopped, and he saw that her lips were tightly set. Something quickened in the silence between them.

‘Rachel . . .’

Clasped in his arms, she clung to him, sobbing.

‘Oh, why had it to happen like this? And there’s no way out.’

‘There’s the obvious way out,’ he said slowly.

She freed herself and shook her head.

‘Not for us. Not that way. . . . There’s – Gillian, your family – everything.’

‘I know. . . . ’

‘It happened so gradually. At first I thought you were – just a friend. Then – that Sunday night when you came into the nursery, you looked so tired and unhappy it nearly broke my heart. I think it began then.’

‘I think I loved you from the moment I saw you.’

‘Everything I saw or heard or did or said was part of you.’

‘Yes . . . it was like that with me, too.’

‘Oh, Peter. . . . At any rate I’ve not gone without – knowing, without calling you by your name.’

‘Must you go? It could be – managed, somehow.’

‘No, I must go. You know I must really, don’t you?’

‘I suppose so. . . .’

‘Let’s make an end of it here and now. Kiss me again. . . . No, we mustn’t even do that. . . . Anyone might come and then – Oh, isn’t it hateful to have to feel like this about it . . . to have to be ashamed . . . to have to be careful? If only it hadn’t happened – this way!’

'I know.'

She gave him a tremulous smile.

'I shall remember this afternoon all the rest of my life. I shall remember that leaf lying on the moss and that robin on the branch. When I've forgotten everything else, I shall remember this . . . and your eyes and your face and your hands. . . .' She took one of his hands and raised it to her lips.

'Don't, my dear,' he breathed.

'Let's go now. I can't bear it any longer.'

'No. Stay here a little. Just for a few minutes. We won't talk. We'll just – be together.'

He drew her head against his shoulder, and they sat there in silence, his arm about her. Her eyes were closed, her lashes wet upon her cheeks. He held her tightly, his eyes fixed unseeingly on the ground in front of him, the muscles of his face set and taut.

* * *

They walked through the park to the main road that passed the gates of Langley Place. Peter generally called there on his way back from that particular 'job', and he knew that his mother would be expecting him. At the gates he stopped.

'Come in with me, Rachel.'

She shook her head.

'I'd rather not. It might be better, anyway, if we didn't go back together.'

Into both their minds came a feeling of shame and bitterness at this fresh realization that their love must be one of subterfuge and stealth, that they could not even walk openly together.

'I suppose so,' he said, 'but, Rachel, I must see you again before you go. Bring Gillian to the wood tomorrow – no, that wouldn't do.'

Gillian, of course, would chatter to Belle of the meeting, and they couldn't risk that.

'Never mind if we can't manage it, Peter,' she said. 'Even if we never see each other again, we shall have this afternoon to remember.'

'That's not enough for me. Is it enough for you? I must – see you again.'

'You see me every day.'

'That's worse than not seeing you at all. I'll come to the nursery tonight when Gillian's gone to bed.'

'No, Peter, not that . . .'

'In the wood, then?'

'Very well. Just once. Just to say good-bye. Now go, Peter. And – thank you. I shall be so happy.'

'And so unhappy.'

'Yes, both. How did you know? But, of course, you know.'

He stood at the iron gates and watched her till she disappeared down the tree-shadowed road.

Mrs. Fowler was sitting in her armchair by the fireplace working at a square of tapestry. She disliked most types of needlework, but found the rhythmic motions of tapestry work soothing, and took a childish pleasure in watching the picture grow before her eyes. She laid it aside as Peter entered.

'I'm so glad you've come, dear,' she said. 'I was hoping you would.'

She always gives you that feeling of warm welcome, thought Peter, as if she'd been looking forward all day to your coming. . . . He bent down to kiss her.

'Where are the others?' he said.

'Anice has gone to London with Martin, and Judy is at the Willoughbys'. They're having some novelist or other to dinner. I've forgotten his name. He's speaking to the Literary Society. Oliver's the secretary, you know.'

He nodded absently, and she realized that his thoughts were far away. He got up, moved restlessly about the room, then stood at the window, looking out, his hands in his pockets. Mrs. Fowler took up her tapestry work again, and there was silence for some moments. Then she said:

'Peter . . .'

'Yes?'

'I'm not a busybody, you know, but I was up in the blue room, and I happened to look out of the window. Was it Miss Horsham who was walking down with you through the park?'

'Yes.'

'Be careful, Peter. You know what people are in a small place like this. You know what Belle is. Even though there's nothing in it, they'll – talk, and Belle will make trouble.'

He was silent for so long that she thought he was going to ignore her warning. Then, without turning round, he said:

'There is something in it.'

'You mean . . . ?'

'I mean, we love each other.'

'Oh, Peter, I'm sorry.'

He turned round and met her eyes. There was no horror or disapproval in them – only a depth of love and pity. He was conscious of a sudden overwhelming sense of relief. He need not have been afraid of her knowing. She understood, as she had always understood. . . .

'What's to come of it, my dear?' she said.

He crossed the room and sat by her, his elbows on his knees, his frowning gaze fixed on the floor.

'Nothing, I suppose,' he said.

'You're not . . . ?'

'No. We're agreed on that. There's – Gillian, and other things.'

She laid a hand gently on his arm.

'I can only say it again. I'm sorry, my dear. If there's anything I can ever do to help, you must tell me.'

He gave her a twisted smile.

'Go on being yourself. That helps more than anything.'

'I can promise that. She's leaving Belle, isn't she?'

'Yes. At the end of the month. She's got a job in Sussex. You see – '

He stopped. There was the sound of voices in the hall, and Helen and Max entered.

* * *

Over Max there lay a sort of bloom of prosperity and success. He had a flourishing business, an expensive house, a good-looking, capable wife. Moreover, he and Helen had won the mixed doubles in the Bellington Tennis Tournament, and he had won the Golfing Tournament cup for the third year running. There was hardly a cloud to mar the serenity of his skies. Helen, too, wore an air of satisfaction, but it lacked the complacency that enveloped Max, for Helen was always, in her placid, masterful fashion, at grips with something. Even when her own affairs were going smoothly, the affairs of other people generally needed attention.

'Hello, Mater,' she said, kissing Mrs. Fowler. 'You all right? Hello, Peter.'

'Why the "mater" after all these years?' said Peter, irritated by the interruption and the air of rather smug content that hung over the couple.

'I've already explained that, Peter,' said Helen, speaking kindly and patiently.

'If one of us has to be Latinized,' said Mrs. Fowler, 'it's right that it should be I. After all, Mrs. Willoughby is so essentially Anglo-Saxon.'

Peter grunted, and Max stared at her uncomprehendingly.

'We were on our way to tennis at the Merridrews,' said Helen, 'so we thought we'd just look in.'

'They've got one of those new hard courts,' said Max. 'We've fixed up to have one made at Cobham Lodge.'

'They're terribly expensive, aren't they?' said Mrs. Fowler.

Max shrugged.

'Oh, well . . .' he said, and the complacency of his smile increased.

'We're having it done as cheaply as possible,' said Helen, 'and, of course, there isn't the same expense of upkeep as there is with a grass one. You get a better game, too.'

Spending for spending's sake never appealed to Helen. Determinedly and at every point she checked Max's love of ostentation, quashing his suggestions of a fountain, an ornamental pond, a second Daimler.

'Well, I'd better be getting on,' said Peter, rising jerkily from his chair.

'Peter seemed a bit on edge, didn't he?' said Helen, when he had gone. 'What's the matter with him?'

'He seemed just as usual to me,' said Mrs. Fowler.

Helen dismissed Peter from her mind.

'Now about Anice's wedding,' she said. 'Where is she, by the way?'

'She's gone to London for the day with Martin.'

'I should have thought they were both too busy to go jaunting off to London,' said Helen.

'All the more reason why they should, don't you think?' said Mrs. Fowler.

'Well . . . about the wedding,' said Helen, deciding that Mater was in one of her difficult moods. 'Who are to be the bridesmaids?'

'We haven't really decided yet,' said Mrs. Fowler.

'I don't see why we shouldn't have the same ones as I had,' said Helen, 'with another to take Anice's place, of course. They've got the dresses, so it wouldn't mean any more expense. Judy's hardly worn hers at all, has she?'

'I'll ask Anice if she'd mind.'

'I don't see why she should mind. They were lovely dresses and cost a lot of money. We could make them look different by rose-coloured sashes and caps. . . . And Mother was saying that she thought it would be better to let Fawkners' do the catering. They do it more cheaply and just as well.'

'We've always had Roberts'. . . .'

'That's no reason why you should go on having them.'

'Well, let's leave that for the present, shall we, dear? There's plenty of time. . . . What else is there to arrange?'

Helen brought a small strip of paper out of her bag. She had already acquired Mrs. Willoughby's habit of lists. She ticked off 'Bridesmaids' and put a question-mark against 'Fawkners'.

'Now the invitations . . . the same as mine, I suppose. Martin must give us his list as soon as possible. . . . Church decorations. . . . Mother and I will see to that. . . . Service, hymns . . . the same as mine, I suppose. Now – '

'You haven't told Mater what we really came to tell her,' put in Max.

'Oh yes . . . I'd forgotten for the moment. I'm so anxious to get this business of Anice's wedding fixed up. I'm going to have a baby, Mater.'

Max beamed uxoriously, and Mrs. Fowler caught her breath with delight.

'Oh, darling, I'm so glad,' she said, drawing Helen to her and kissing her. 'It's wonderful. . . .'

'It's hardly wonderful,' said Helen, smiling indulgently. 'I mean, we're both young and healthy and perfectly normal and we always intended to have children. We're going to have five – or six – with two years' interval between each.'

'Are you, dear?' said Mrs. Fowler, awed by this incursion of Helen's organizing power into the realms of nature and wondering if she would tick each one off a list as it appeared.

'I should like the first one to be a boy, of course,' said Helen, 'but I don't really mind. I'm having the bedroom on the second floor, overlooking the lawn, turned into a nursery.'

'When is it to be, dear?'

'Oh, not till February. It gives me plenty of time to get things ready.'

Mrs. Fowler looked at her helplessly. There was no softening of the pleasant, good-looking, rather hard young face. Not for Helen the joy and miracle of child-bearing. It was, in her eyes, just part of the routine of house-keeping.

'I'll make something,' offered Mrs. Fowler impulsively.

'I shouldn't bother, Mater dear,' said Helen kindly. 'Mother will see to all that. She's always glad to find something for the relations to do. Cousin Effie's a beautiful needlewoman, and, of course, Mother pays her, and she's glad to have the money.'

'Well, I'm not much of a needlewoman,' admitted Mrs. Fowler, 'but I'll knit a shawl.'

'Very well,' agreed Helen indulgently, and added (for Mrs. Fowler's knitting was notoriously erratic): 'I'll find you a simple pattern.'

* * *

Then Anice and Martin burst in – an Anice and Martin whom Mrs. Fowler had never seen before, Anice starry-eyed and beautiful, Martin glowing and confident. Helen looked at them a little disapprovingly and wondered if they had been drinking.

'Oh, there you are, Anice,' she said. 'I just came to talk over the details of your wedding with Mater.'

Anice took off her hat and shook back her hair with a gesture of glad defiance.

'You needn't trouble,' she said. 'We're married.'

'Married?' repeated Helen.

'Yes. We were married in London this afternoon.'

'By Jove!' said Max, grinning. 'Were you really? Good for you! Let's celebrate.'

They ignored him.

'Rather a foolish thing to do, wasn't it?' said Helen dispassionately.

'Why foolish?'

'Hasty weddings always cause talk.'

'I'm not going to have a baby, if that's what you mean. Time will clear me of that particular aspersion, at any rate.'

Max guffawed and was silenced by a glance from Helen.

'We've saved you a lot of trouble, you know, Helen,' said Martin. 'You needn't bother any longer about marquees and the rest of it.'

Helen's brows came together in a frown.

'But I can't understand why you did it,' she said. 'It seems so – unnecessary.'

'The nicest things are,' said Mrs. Fowler.

Helen shrugged.

'Oh, well . . . congratulations, anyway, dear. . . . And you, too, Martin.' She kissed them both. 'What's done can't be undone. We must just make the best of things. Where are you thinking of living?'

'We haven't thought of anything beyond today, have we, Martin?' said Anice.

'I bet you haven't,' said Max, giving another guffaw and checking it mid-way at another glance from Helen.

'I'll call at Polham's tomorrow morning and see what he's got,' said Helen. 'I think he's the best agent. Not too big, of course, and within easy reach of both Mater and me.'

Anice sighed. She hadn't, after all, escaped the far-reaching domination of Helen.

'Or Peter might know of something,' went on Helen. 'I'll try to get something fixed up for you, anyway.'

* * *

'How did you know, darling?' said Anice, when Helen, having completed the furnishing of Anice's house, had departed, with Max grinning amiably in the rear.

'I didn't exactly *know*,' said Mrs. Fowler, 'I only guessed. There was something so – shining about you. I just slipped it into your bag, in case. . . .'

'I wore it in my buttonhole.'

For Mrs. Fowler had taken a spray of the artificial orange-blossom from her own wedding wreath, wrapped it in tissue paper, and slipped it into the inner pocket of Anice's handbag before she set out for London.

'Did you feel hurt that I didn't tell you?' said Anice.

'No,' said Mrs. Fowler. 'I'm rather glad you didn't. I should have felt – responsible if I'd known. It was much more fun not knowing.'

'You're a sport, Mrs. Fowler,' said Martin. 'I'll do my damnedest to make Anice happy.'

'You can call her "mother",' said Anice, 'unless you prefer

“mater”, of course, and probably we shan’t either of us be happy, but all that matters just now is that we’re happy just now.’

They sat there in silence – Mrs. Fowler in her armchair, drawing her needle in and out of her tapestry work, Anice and Martin on the settee, hands clasped, heads resting on the cushions. A lethargy of content stole over them.

At last Martin stirred.

‘I ought to go now.’

‘No need to go, Martin,’ said Mrs. Fowler. ‘I’ve got the blue room ready.’

CHAPTER NINE

'All I can say is that it's most unfortunate,' said Mrs. Willoughby. 'I'm surprised your mother allowed it.'

'She didn't exactly allow it,' said Helen. 'She didn't know about it.'

'If any daughter of mine had been contemplating a secret marriage I'd have known about it,' said Mrs. Willoughby. 'It does a girl's reputation no good. It's a bad start. . . .'

'I pointed that out,' said Helen. 'I haven't told anyone but you yet.'

'Well, don't tell the others tonight. Not with Mr. Palmer here. The whole town will be talking about it tomorrow. It won't be very pleasant for your mother.'

'That sort of thing never bothers Mater,' said Helen. 'She just isn't interested.'

Mrs. Willoughby gave a sigh of exasperation. There were times when she made conscientious efforts to understand Mrs. Fowler, but she always gave it up in despair.

'Put the cups on the tray, my dear, will you?'

Helen and Mrs. Willoughby were making the coffee in the little pantry that opened off the kitchen. Mrs. Willoughby wore her best afternoon dress of black moiré silk, made in her usual old-fashioned style and secured at the neck by a large gold brooch. Only an occasion of the utmost importance could drive Mrs. Willoughby into her 'evening dress' of black taffeta whose small V neck was discreetly filled in with black lace – certainly not this family dinner in honour of Arnold Palmer, who was going to speak to the Literary Society afterwards.

Mrs. Willoughby had no great opinion of novelists. She recognized few gradations among them. They were people who wasted their time writing novels so that other people might waste their time reading them. She had imposed on her children the rule that had been imposed in her own childhood, 'No novels before tea' . . . and even after tea she felt (and let them know she felt) that their time might be better employed. But if a novelist *was* coming to speak at Bellington it was only right that the Willoughbys should give him dinner, especially as George was the President of the Literary Society and Oliver the Secretary.

The guests had been limited to the family connections, but when the Willoughby family connection mustered in force they made a formidable party in themselves. Of the poor relations only Miss Hatton, as representing the intellectual element, had been invited. She had spent the afternoon browsing over a dictionary of quotations called *Flowers from the Garden of Wisdom*, given to her by her father on her twenty-first birthday, in the hope that she might be able to introduce one or two of them into her conversation. She had already introduced several, none of them particularly relevant to the subject that was being discussed.

Emmy was there, looking pale and insignificant in the rather crude shade of blue that she mistakenly imagined to match her eyes. Her gaze had followed Oliver wistfully all evening. One of George's curates, who always saw her home after Sunday-school, where she taught the mixed infants, had told her last night that she was his ideal of womanhood, but she didn't want to be his ideal of womanhood. She wanted to be Oliver's. . . . James was the only member of the family who was not present, and Florence had given various conflicting reasons for his absence.

Dinner was now over, the guests had returned to the drawing-room, and Mrs. Willoughby, according to her custom, was seeing to the coffee, assisted by Helen. She had tied an apron over her dress, and, through the open door of the pantry, was keeping an eye on the maids in the kitchen. Aware of the eye, the maids bustled about, collecting the used dishes, stacking them in the sink, talking in undertones. They'll have something to talk about tomorrow, thought Mrs. Willoughby grimly. Really, these Fowlers!

Max entered, smiling expansively.

'Anything I can do to help?'

'I thought you were supposed to be entertaining the guests,' said Helen.

'They seem to be getting on quite well without me.'

Helen looked lovely tonight in a dress the colour of amber with a square low neck that just showed the beginnings of the firm white mounds of her breasts. Though her pregnancy had not as yet altered the lines of her figure, it had shed a sort of glow over her, deepening the blue of her eyes and the peach-like bloom of her skin. Max would have liked to slip an arm round her waist and kiss her, but she discouraged embraces in public and was chary of them even in private.

Mrs. Willoughby had watched the marriage with growing approbation. Max, like all men, needed managing, and Helen could manage him. In that, Mrs. Willoughby considered, lay all the essentials of a happy marriage.

She took off her apron, folded it up and put it away in a drawer.

'Carry in the tray, Max,' she said shortly, 'and I hope you won't mention this foolish marriage of Anice's to anyone tonight. They'll know about it soon enough. . . . Take the milk off the tray, Helen. He's sure to spill it if you don't.'

* * *

The guest of honour was standing on the hearthrug with George, discussing the literary figures of the day. Arnold Palmer seemed to have met them all. He was generously appreciative of their work and charmingly modest about his own.

Oliver brought Judy a cup of coffee and sat down by her near the french windows.

'Don't you want to talk to him?' said Judy.

'No, I can't stand his stuff. It's tripe.'

'Is it? Cynthia and I used to adore it. Cynthia still does.'

'It's tripe with a revolting veneer of literary virtuosity.'

'Aren't you mixing your metaphors? Can you have a veneer on tripe?'

He laughed.

'Let's go out into the garden.'

'Will they mind?'

It seemed somehow rather a daring thing to do at The Beeches, though it would have been quite natural at Langley Place.

'Let them mind,' said Oliver.

They stepped out into the cool shady garden and walked down the grass path between the flower borders. The air was sweet with the scent of white phlox and heliotrope, and the massed bloom of the Paul Scarlet roses at the end of the border seemed almost too heavy for their supports.

'Let's go to the summer-house,' said Oliver.

'It's sure to be earwiggy.'

'Do you dislike earwigs?'

'No. Not since I found out that the aim of their lives isn't to get into your ear and work their way to your brain. We believed that when we were children. Did you?'

'Yes. And I believed that those wax figures in the window of Crofton's Juvenile outfitting department were dead children that old Crofton caught and killed himself. A boy told me that and I never for a moment doubted it. I always used to run past the shop in case he came out and grabbed me.'

'Isn't it odd, the dreadful things you believe when you're a child? And they really don't worry you – much. We once had a nurse who told us that we'd bleed to death if we put our fingers in our noses.'

'That's nothing to some of the things we were told. . . . Here we are. I don't see any earwigs.'

‘It doesn’t look a bit like a summer-house. It’s so clean. Even the windows. . . .’

‘Damnable, isn’t it? Cleanliness should be confined to the house. It’s indecent when it invades the garden.’

‘Ours is all cobwebs and dirt, and everything in it seems to be broken.’

‘That’s how it should be.’

It was funny, she thought, how easy it was to talk to Oliver now. All the shyness and self-consciousness had gone. Instead, she had a quiet happy feeling when she was with him. They had stopped showing off to each other. They were just themselves. They talked of anything or nothing, and the time slipped by so quickly that it always amazed her to find how long they had been together.

‘You’re going to the infirmary dance, aren’t you?’ he said.

‘I think so. We generally do.’

‘Will you give me every dance?’

The dimples peeped out in her smooth cheeks.

‘Of course I can’t.’

‘Every other then?’

‘No, Oliver. You know I can’t.’

‘Every third?’

‘I’ll see.’

He looked at her in silence. There was something deliciously heart-rendingly immature about her as she sat there beside him in her white frock. Her eyes were soft and shadowed, her lips solemn and wistful like a sleeping child’s. He longed to kiss her, but felt that some spell would be broken if he did. Perhaps, at the dance . . .

'Oliver!' called Mrs. Willoughby sharply from the french window.

He muttered 'Blast!' under his breath and answered, 'Yes?'

'Come here.'

He muttered 'Damn!' and rose, walking slowly across the lawn with Judy beside him.

'Yes?' he said again as he entered the drawing-room.

'Get those snapshots you took at Saltholme last summer,' said Mrs. Willoughby. 'Emmy would like to see them.'

Mrs. Willoughby had decided that she didn't want another Fowler in the family. Helen, of course, was all right. Helen had never been a Fowler in anything but name. Over Judy, however, there hung a soft charm, an exquisite waywardness, a vague delicate grace that reminded one of her mother. She probably didn't even know how to boil an egg. . . . Emmy had been taught to cook and house-keep from her childhood. She could patch and darn as well as Mrs. Willoughby herself. She might lack charm, but Mrs. Willoughby had always distrusted charm, and as to waywardness, Oliver had enough for two. . . .

A tall thin young man, with prominent teeth – a Willoughby second cousin once removed – attached himself to Judy and gave her a harrowing description of his latest attack of influenza. Judy did not hear a word of it. Her cheeks were hot with anger. Ordering him about like that in front of everyone as if he were a small boy! How *dared* she!

* * *

Florence and Gertrude were sitting on the settee talking in undertones. Florence was in the throes of one of those family crises of which, it seemed to her in her darker moments, her life chiefly consisted. They began with something quite small and went on and on. . . . This one had begun with a table-runner.

James, knowing that she wanted a new runner for the dining-table, had himself called at Crofton's the day before yesterday and bought one. It was a colourful affair of black and pink and he had been very pleased with it. Yesterday afternoon Mrs. Willoughby had happened to call to see Florence, had inspected the runner, decided that it clashed with the curtains and had taken it back to Crofton's then and there to exchange it for a plain green one. When James came home last night he had been furious. . . .

'Absolutely *furious*,' she was saying to Gertrude. 'He said he was sick and tired of her interference and she'd no right to go altering things in his house just because she didn't like them. He wouldn't have minded, of course, if it had been me that didn't like it.'

'Did you like it?' said Gertrude.

'I didn't mind it,' said Florence, and added simply: 'I never mind anything. Not for myself, I mean. . . . That's why he wouldn't come tonight, because of the runner. He says he's going to take it back to Crofton's first thing tomorrow morning and get the black-and-pink one again. It makes things very difficult for me. I didn't sleep a wink last night worrying about it and wondering what to do.'

'I don't see what you *can* do,' said Gertrude.

'Well, I can't do much, of course. . . . I might go down to Crofton's and buy the green one again and slip it on when I knew Mother was coming.'

'One never does know when Mother's coming.'

'I know. That's what makes things so difficult. They'll both be furious whatever I do, and sometimes it lasts for weeks. James went on and *on* last night. He said some things about her that I really oughtn't to have listened to, but he was shouting so loud that I couldn't help listening. You know . . .'

'Yes?'

'I've been wondering whether to consult Helen about it.'

They looked at Helen in silence. She was pouring out the coffee with her usual air of being equal to any emergency. Her position as Mrs. Willoughby's right-hand was now secure, and Florence had had cause to think, 'Well,' many times in the last weeks. So deep was the sisters' sense of family loyalty, however, that they never gave expression to their resentment, and the resentment itself was gradually dying.

'Yes,' said Gertrude. 'She might be able to suggest something.'

'It's funny,' said Florence, 'how Mother will listen to her when she won't to us.'

'After all,' said Gertrude, a little shocked by the implied criticism, 'she's Max's wife.'

'Yes, I know,' said Florence absently, wondering what would happen if Mother took the black-and-pink runner back again to Crofton's and changed it for the green one again after James had changed it for the black-and-pink one, and indulging in a wild daydream in which a fire broke out in Crofton's linen department and destroyed the whole lot. . . .

George came up with two cups of coffee.

'James not here?' he said to Florence.

'No, he's got one of his rheumatic turns,' said Florence.

'You told Mother he'd got one of his colds,' Gertrude reminded her.

'He's got both,' snapped Florence.

* * *

Miraculously, and as if in direct answer to prayer, Cynthia found herself isolated with Arnold Palmer in the small recess by the fireplace. She was trembling with excitement, and her voice was a breathless undertone.

'Thank you so much for not giving me away,' she said.

He smiled at her. . . . His eyes were grey and deep-set, his temples hollowed and blue-veined, his hair just beginning to turn grey, his nose straight and shapely, his lips mobile and humorous, his dress suit so perfectly cut that it reminded Cynthia of the 'immaculate tailoring' of one of his own heroes. There was a faint cleft in his well-formed chin. As if all this were not enough, he was tall and slim and elegant. . . .

'Or myself,' he said. 'We're both in this, you know.'

'When George introduced you to me I was terrified he'd guess something.'

He looked down at her with a twinkle.

'That's the worst of having a bad conscience, isn't it?'

She flushed.

'Did you – did you think it dreadful of me to write to you?'

‘Considering what you wrote, you could hardly expect me to disapprove. I’m only human, you know. I see all the defects of my own work, but I hate other people to see them, too.’

‘Defects?’ she gasped. ‘Oh, but there aren’t any. Everything you write is – perfect. You must know it is.’

His long white fingers flicked the ash from his cigarette into the fireplace. The smile in his grey eyes deepened. The corners of his shapely mouth twitched.

‘How I wish the critics shared your illusions!’

‘But you have *wonderful* reviews. The one in the *Meteor* last week – ’

‘A sting in the tail of every sentence, my child. Cunningly concealed but unmistakable to those with eyes to see.’

‘I don’t believe it. He *couldn’t*. . . . Oh, there are so many things I want to ask you, I don’t know where to begin. It’s so wonderful to meet you, to speak to you like this. I’ve thought of you so much and there’s so little time.’

He took a flat gold watch, secured by a thin gold chain, from his trouser pocket. Everything he did raised him above the ruck of ordinary people. None of the Willoughbys had evening watches. . . .

‘There are about fifteen minutes before we need start, I am told, for the Central Hall. Now, fire away. I’ll give you a minute to ask each question and I’ll take a minute answering it. That gives us time for seven and a half.’

‘You’re laughing at me.’

‘Am I? I only laugh at people I like, you know. Now fire away!’

'Well . . . I did want to ask you which is your favourite book.'

'Always the one I'm going to write next. The one I haven't started yet.'

'I loved *Dead Embers* . . . but then I loved them all.'

'Next question, please.'

She laughed.

'Oh, don't! You're making it like an exam. Why, in *Red Dawn*, didn't you let Margot marry Roger? I cried my eyes out over it.'

He threw the end of his cigarette into the fireplace, took a gold case from his pocket, selected another cigarette and lit it before he answered.

'I'm going into that question in my talk tonight. As a general principle, I mean. I don't mean that I'm going to inflict a dissertation on my own plots upon my audience.'

'It must be wonderful to be able to – speak. I suppose you're never nervous. . . .'

'I wouldn't admit it to everyone – only to someone understanding like yourself – but, as a matter of fact, I'm feeling horribly nervous. I always do before I speak.'

'I can't tell you how I'm looking forward to it. I've been just living for it ever since I heard of it. . . . Oh, I did want to tell you how I loved that bit in *Green Arches* where Gavin and Althea meet on the bridge.'

'I hope you cried your eyes out over it.'

'You're laughing at me again, but I did.'

'Now don't you think that we've talked about my books quite long enough? Tell me who all these people are. I've been introduced to them but I've lost count. Who's that pretty girl over there by the table?'

'That's Judy. Her sister married my brother, so I suppose she's my sister-in-law, but she and I have been friends for years. . . . That's Helen, her sister, in the yellow dress. And that's Max, my elder brother, who's her husband, talking to George over there. George married Gertrude, my eldest sister. And that's Oliver, my other brother, showing snapshots to Emmy. Emmy's – '

'That's quite enough. You're bringing too many characters into the first chapter. It's a weakness of mine, too. I've never been able to cure myself of it. Let's stop at Judy and Helen and Max and you. All delightful people, good-looking, and full of possibilities. Anything might happen to any of you before the end of the book.'

'Nothing more exciting than this could ever happen to me.'

'Are you and Judy the same age?'

'About. We were at school together. We used to read your books in prep and write notes to each other telling each other how far we'd got and how wonderful it was.'

'Discriminating critics, indeed!' he commented a little dryly, his eyes still fixed on Judy.

Judy was watching Cynthia, thinking that she had never before seen her like this, eager and alive, as if a light were shining within her. Then her eyes went on to Mr. Palmer. He reminded her of Mr. Somers. Mr. Somers, too, had been tall and elegant and grey-haired. He had died last year, leaving Judy a Sèvres tea service, and Judy had been shocked to find that her pleasure at receiving the Sèvres tea service outweighed her grief at Mr. Somers' death. In her mind he was less a real person than a sort of bridge by which she had passed from childhood to young womanhood on the day of Helen's wedding.

'Penny for your thoughts,' said Mr. Palmer suddenly to Cynthia.

'It's something I'm trying *not* to think of,' said Cynthia, smiling tremulously.

'What is it?'

'Well, it sounds silly, but I've suddenly realized that it's the day I've been living for all these weeks, and now it's come and – there's nothing left to look forward to. I shall never see you again.'

'Don't be too sure,' he said. 'I should hate to think that, too, you know.'

'But – '

Then George came up and began to talk to the guest, and Cynthia stood by, dazed and enraptured, not listening to their conversation, till she heard Mr. Palmer say, with the slight drawl that matched so well his general elegance:

'I'd no idea that the country round here was so delightful. I've been looking out vaguely for a country cottage for some time. I really think I couldn't do better than to fix on this part of the world.'

'Yes,' said George, 'some of the villages round Bellington are charming. And quite unspoilt still. I'll put you in touch with one or two of the local agents, if you like.'

'Thank you,' said Mr. Palmer. He turned to Cynthia with a smile. 'So you may see quite a lot of me, after all.'

Cynthia's heart leapt then raced madly.

George took out his watch.

'And now,' he said, 'I really think we ought to be making our way to the Central Hall. We don't want to be late.'

'Procrastination,' said Miss Hatton triumphantly, 'is the thief of time.'

CHAPTER TEN

Peter drove his small two-seater slowly down the Sussex lane towards the inn where he had arranged to meet Rachel for tea. It was a warm afternoon in May. On either side of the lane the hawthorn hedges were breaking into tiny white rosettes of blossom; in the distant woods an azure haze showed the drifts of bluebells, while here and there on the banks by the roadside clusters of pale golden primroses still lingered. Cottage gardens were gay with tulips and wallflowers, lilac and laburnum. . . .

So absorbed was Peter in his own thoughts that he was blind to the beauty around him. His face above the steering-wheel was set and tense, his frowning gaze was fixed on the empty stretch of road. . . . He was thinking over the course of his love for Rachel – a love now that dominated his whole existence, so that he felt maimed and incomplete without her – trying to discern where the tortuous darkening path of it must end.

He had come down here to see her the first time on an impulse, telling himself that, if he saw her once more, he would be able to put her out of his life for ever, knowing in his heart that he was coming simply because he could not keep away. After that he had come again . . . and again. . . . Both of them had fought unavailingly against the force that drove them. Once Rachel had refused to meet him, but the despairing letter she had written afterwards brought him down to her the next day. Gradually their love was becoming the affair of stolen meetings against which they had once so firmly set their faces.

A bend in the lane brought the inn into sight – a picturesque, old-fashioned posting inn, set back from the road behind a chestnut tree in full bloom. It looks old and wise and – a little tired, thought Peter, as he drove the car into the courtyard. It isn't interested any longer in the passions of men and women. It's seen too many of them setting out to 'tread a maze that never shall have end'.

A group of young people, wearing shorts and heavy walking boots, came out of the doorway laughing and talking. There was about them a suggestion of gallant youth, a swagger of gay courage not yet put to the test that made Peter watch them wistfully. Suddenly he saw Rachel coming down the road. She looked pale, and there were shadows beneath her eyes, but her lips curved into a smile as he approached.

'Oh, Peter,' she said, 'I was so terribly afraid that something would happen to stop you coming.'

'Nothing would have stopped me coming,' said Peter.

They passed beneath the chestnut tree, where the young people were still laughing and talking as they adjusted their knapsacks, and entered the inn. The lounge was long and low and rather dark, with oak beams and an open brick fireplace. Peter and Rachel sat down on a settee in a corner of the room.

Rachel drew off her gloves and placed her hand on the seat between them. Peter's closed over it.

'How are things?'

'All right. . . . Mrs. Cooper's kind and the children are darlings. I ought to be happy.'

'But you're not. . . .'

'I am now. I was terrified all morning that she'd ask me to change my afternoon and that I couldn't let you know in time.'

'She doesn't know you were coming to meet me?'

'No. She isn't inquisitive. She never tries to – find things out. That's what makes me feel hateful sometimes, because –' She turned her head away sharply then looked at him with a smile that was not quite steady. 'Oh, well, don't let's think about that part of it. It's so lovely to be here with you . . . How's the family, Peter? Has Helen's baby come yet?'

'Yes. Yesterday. A magnificent specimen. Max in miniature, I gather.'

'How is she?'

'Splendid. Can you imagine her being anything else? She's already organizing the christening party.'

The corners of his lips flickered into a smile of affectionate amusement. Rachel knew that his love for his family was an essential part of him. The thought that she must remain for ever outside the interests that made up his daily life was a bitter one.

'And Gillian?' she said with something of an effort.

The mention of Gillian always brought with it a constraint that neither of them quite understood.

'Oh, Gillian's fine,' he said.

He spoke with rather over-done heartiness in his efforts to break down the constraint. A waiter brought up a table and took their order. Peter waited till he had gone, then said:

'She still misses you, you know. She's made me go on with that story you started, the one about the frog with the umbrella. . . .'

'Is the new nurse all right?'

'I think so. More or less. Gilly wouldn't have anything to do with her at first but she's gradually becoming reconciled. She's very much excited now at the thought of Matthew's coming home.'

'When is he coming?'

'In July, I think.'

'You'll be glad to have him home, won't you?' said Rachel, wondering for the hundredth time why it hurt so much to talk of his family.

'Yes. It'll be grand. Now tell me about yourself. . . .'

Entering the enclosed world she shared with him, talking of the interests they had in common, she let down her defences, becoming happy and natural, glowing with a radiance that only visited her when she was with Peter. He was laughing at something she had said when he saw her face grow rigid. She laid a hand on his arm and spoke in a quick, urgent whisper.

'Don't turn round, Peter, but – that friend of Belle's. The one with red hair – '

'Moyna Pollard?'

'Yes. She's just come in with another woman. They're

ordering tea. I don't think she's seen you. Keep your head turned this way.'

'What about you?'

'I'm in the shadow. She may not recognize me. Let's go on talking.'

Realizing the pass to which their love had brought them – skulking in corners, shrinking from discovery, afraid of every chance contact – she seemed to feel her whole body ablaze with shame. They went on talking mechanically, keeping their voices lowered, their heads turned away. Rachel began to pour out a cup of tea, but her hand trembled so much that she gave up the attempt.

'They're going, Peter. She's just paying the bill. I'm sure they haven't seen us. . . . They've gone now.'

Peter looked at her. His face was white and drawn.

'I can't stand this any longer, Rachel, can you?'

'No . . . we must – stop seeing each other.'

'We can't do that.'

'What can we do, then?'

'I'll ask Belle to divorce me.'

She drew in her breath so sharply that it sounded like a sob.

'*Peter!* You can't! . . . You mustn't. . . . There's your family . . . Gillian.'

'They mean nothing to me compared with you, not even Gillian.'

'Are you *sure*, Peter? Isn't it just an – impulse, just because that woman came in this afternoon?'

He shook his head.

‘No. . . . I’ve known for some time that it couldn’t go on and that I couldn’t give you up.’

‘I can’t believe it,’ she said unsteadily. ‘I never thought . . .’

He gave her a twisted smile.

‘My dear, it’s not going to be easy. For you, especially.’

‘I don’t mind, Peter. I don’t mind anything if it means being with you always. But – I want to be *sure*. Not about myself. I’m sure about myself. About you. . . . Perhaps it’s because I haven’t any family myself that I understand so well what yours means to you. Your mother . . . Judy . . . Gillian . . .’

His face seemed to stiffen for a moment then relaxed into a faint smile.

‘I’ve told you. They mean nothing compared with you.’

‘But you’ll miss them,’ she persisted. ‘Oh, please don’t think that I’m going to go on digging things up by the roots like this, but – I must be sure. Once I’m sure, I won’t – worry you. You see, Peter, when we’ve – got used to being together and the first thrill of it’s over, you might – begin to want them and to regret what you’ve done.’

‘I shall never regret it.’

She took his hand in both hers and held it tightly.

‘You’ll be giving up so much more for me than I’m giving up for you.’

‘You’ll be giving up a lot, Rachel,’ he said gravely. ‘Perhaps more than you realize now. But let’s not be tragic about it. We needn’t go too far away. We could stay within reach of Bellington.’

‘I couldn’t bear that, Peter,’ she said in a low, breathless voice. 'To be – near them, near' – she brought out the name with an effort – 'Belle.'

'After all, my work's there,' he reminded her gently.

'You could get work somewhere else. I could get work, too. I couldn't bear to be – near them.'

'All right, darling.'

'You do understand, don't you?'

'Of course I do. And – Rachel.'

'Yes?'

'Things may not be straightforward. Belle may refuse to divorce me. Would you mind?'

'Mind? Peter, of course not. You're all I want. Nothing else in the whole world matters. And . . .' She hesitated.

'Yes?'

'You'd – belong to me more that way. Or – oughtn't I to feel like that? Is it selfish?'

'I don't think so.'

They were silent for some moments. Then she said:

'Peter . . .'

'Yes?'

'When are you going to tell Belle?'

'Tonight.'

'No . . . don't tell her till tomorrow morning.'

'Why?'

'I want you to – sleep on it. I don't want to feel that you've decided on an impulse because of this afternoon. And if you decide – not to, after all, I shall understand. I shall never mention it again. We can – go on as we are.'

'It's settled. Nothing will make me change my mind now.'

'Peter darling, she'll be so foul and you hate rows so.'

'It'll soon be over. . . . She's no happier with me than I am with her. She may just – accept the situation.'

Even as he said it he knew that it was not true. Belle would never accept the situation. He tried to conquer the fear that was like a physical oppression – fear less of Belle herself than of the shrill strident anger against which he had never learnt to arm himself. Rachel looked at him, her heart heavy with compassion.

'Darling,' she said, and moved closer to him, resting her shoulder against his as if to give him comfort by the contact.

'Don't worry,' he said. 'I shan't.'

'And you promise not to tell her till tomorrow?'

'If you insist.'

'I do. You might wake up tomorrow and think you'd been mad to suggest it.'

'You know I shan't do that.'

They began to discuss plans, becoming so deeply absorbed that they forgot the time till Rachel said:

'It's late . . . I ought to be going, oughtn't I?'

'I suppose so,' he agreed reluctantly.

They went out to the car and drove along the shadowed lane towards the house where her employer lived.

'Peter . . . if Belle won't divorce you, we could go abroad, couldn't we?'

'Yes . . . Yes, of course we could.'

'I think I'd like to do that. Away from them all. We could start fresh as if – nothing of this had happened. Would you like it?'

'I'd like anything that would make you happy.'

He stopped the car.

'I'd better not go right up to the gate.'

'No. . . . Oh, my dear, won't it be lovely not to have to do this sort of thing, not to be – afraid all the time?'

'I know. . . .'

He looked at her. Her eyes were dark and starry, her lips parted in a tremulous smile. He held her closely, with a sort of desperation, till she stirred in his arms.

'I must go. . . . Peter, you'll let me know at once, won't you? About Belle, I mean. You'll ring me?'

'Yes.'

'She'll be hateful. She won't believe we've never slept together, will she?'

'I'm afraid not.'

As he drove home he braced himself for the interview with Belle, approaching it from various angles, confronting in imagination a Belle who was by turns angry, heart-broken, contemptuous, indifferent . . . finding at the end of each imaginary scene, so vividly did he imagine it, a great relief at having crossed his Rubicon, only to realize with a sinking of the heart that it still lay before him.

* * *

He drew up in the road a few yards from the house to collect his forces. He had promised Rachel not to tell Belle till tomorrow. Tonight he must seem his usual quiet composed self. He leant back in the car and lit a cigarette . . . then noticed someone come out of the house and walk down the road past the car. The light from the street lamp fell full on her face. It was Moyna Pollard. She walked past the car without seeing him. There was a smile of lingering relish on her face. . . . So – Belle knew now. Or did she? Any other succulent piece of gossip might have brought that smile to Moyna's face. And, even if she knew, it only anticipated things by one night.

He stayed in the car till he had finished his cigarette . . . then put the car away in the garage and entered the drawing-room.

Belle was standing by the mantelpiece, and, as soon as he saw her, he realized that she – knew. Her face was a grotesque mask. The red patches that always betrayed her anger stood out on cheeks and neck, her eyes were hard and staring, her lips a tight line.

'Well?' she said venomously. 'Had a good time?'

He closed the door and crossed the room to her. There was a feeling of constriction at his chest and his heart was beating unevenly.

'Moyna told you?'

'Yes.'

'Belle . . . I'm sorry. Rachel and I love each other and – '

She interrupted him with the spate of abuse he had expected, raising her voice almost to a scream, hurling fantastic accusations at him, using words so crude that he wondered dully where she could have heard them. He felt, as always, bruised and battered by the sheer force of her rage.

'Carrying on your filthy intrigues under this very roof!' she shouted. 'Don't think I didn't know, because I did.'

‘There’s been no intrigue, though I don’t suppose you’ll believe that.’

‘No, you’re right. I won’t.’

‘It’s no use talking about it, Belle. I love Rachel and I want to marry her. Will you divorce me?’

She stood there in sudden silence, looking at him, her breast heaving convulsively, her face so distorted as to be almost unrecognizable.

‘So that’s what you want, is it?’ she said at last, her voice little more than a whisper. ‘We’ll see about that!’

He laid his hand on her arm.

‘Belle – ’

She pushed him away and went from the room.

He heard the slamming of her bedroom door, the tinkle of the telephone bell as she took up the receiver, then her voice, high-pitched and hysterical, as she recounted the interview to Moyna Pollard.

CHAPTER ELEVEN

The christening party at Cobham Lodge was in full swing. Josiah Stephen Willoughby, wearing the Fowler family christening robe of Brussels lace, trimmed with tiny bows of white satin ribbon, lay in his nurse's arms, gazing placidly around him. He was a handsome child, with blue eyes, a well-formed chin and already a suspicion of the Willoughby nose.

Mrs. Willoughby, who always constituted herself hostess at any family gathering, no matter where it was held, presided over the tea-table, in the middle of which stood a large three-tiered christening cake. She had sent over to the house earlier in the day the silver tea urn that had been presented to Josiah by the Willoughby employees on the occasion of his marriage. No family gathering was, in Mrs. Willoughby's eyes, complete without Josiah's tea urn. She stood behind it now, manipulating the little handle and filling the cups with practised skill. The tap dripped a little, but as Mrs. Willoughby moved one cup away she caught the drips in the next, so that none had a chance of reaching the shining surface of the tray. When other people tried to do it, the tray became swamped. . . .

Max stood on the hearth-rug, beaming complacently at the assembly. Helen moved about among the guests, receiving compliments on the baby and herself with her usual air of magnificent assurance. The glances she gave her son held something of speculation in them, as if her mind were already busy with the details of his upbringing. She had decided that he was to combine the best traits of both families. He was to be Max without his bombast, Oliver without his irresponsibility, Peter without his weakness. She had no doubts as to her ability to make what she would of the small lace-enshrouded mortal.

The poor relations clustered round, making the little clucking and cooing noises that, in their day, had been the accepted tribute to infancy. The youngest Willoughby stared at them solemnly. 'So like dear Max,' they murmured. 'Such a fine forehead,' said Miss Hatton. 'You can see already that he has a good brain,' and told them yet again how quickly Max had learnt his alphabet. . . .

Cynthia, as godmother, had held Stephen at the font and renounced the devil in his name, but her thoughts had been far away. She wandered about the room now carrying a plate of sandwiches, her cheeks flushed, her eyes starry. Every now and then she put her hand to the pocket where she carried the letter from Mr. Palmer that had arrived that morning. He had bought a cottage in Maybourne, the village just beyond Hurstmede, and he was moving into it next month.

In jocular, half-teasing fashion he offered her the post of secretary. His present secretary was leaving at the end of the month. Would she care to work for a crusty old curmudgeon like himself? All authors, he said, were kittle cattle, needing as much patience as children, but if she would take on the job it would mean a lot to him to have as secretary someone who was a *friend*, not just a hireling. If she decided to take pity on him they could discuss hours of work and salary later. He was sure they would not quarrel over them. . . .

She had read the letter twenty times and knew it by heart. Had he taken the cottage because . . . because . . . ? She dared not put the thought into words even to herself, but her pulses fluttered wildly whenever her mind turned to it. She was so plain and clumsy and unattractive, surely he couldn't . . . And yet . . . she remembered the kindly, almost affectionate light in his eyes as he teased her on the evening of his visit to The Beeches, and a wave of joy swept over her. It was incredible, but incredible things did happen. Shyly, humbly, trembling with ecstasy, she looked into a future whose glory blinded her. . . .

But the letter must be answered, and at the thought of that a panic of nervousness seized her. She didn't know what to say. She never knew what to say. Whenever she wrote to him, she wrote at least ten letters before the one she finally sent, and even then she was never satisfied, lying awake half the next night, going over each word, wishing she hadn't said this, wishing she had said that, afraid that she had seemed stupid or schoolgirlish or presumptuous and that he would never write to her again.

'Wake up, Cynthia,' said Mrs. Willoughby sharply. 'Didn't you hear me tell you to go and see about the hot water?'

'Sorry,' said Cynthia, flushing, glad to hide her confusion by going out of the room.

'He didn't cry once, the lamb!' said Cousin Effie.

'I have a knack with babies,' said George, who had christened him. 'It's wonderful how few of them do cry with me.'

'Willoughbys don't cry in any case, do they, old chap?' said Max, bending down to prod his son in the ribs.

'Don't do that, Max,' said Helen, quietly authoratative.

Florence sat happily munching christening cake and thinking how nice it was to have Jessica safely at boarding school so that she could not disgrace one publicly, as she usually did on these occasions. Bobby, of course, always behaved beautifully. It had been pleasant to hear Mother threatening to send Tim out of the room for pulling Peggy's pigtails.

'Really, Gertrude,' said Florence, 'Tim seems to get rougher every time I see him.'

'Yes,' agreed Gertrude, and added with apparent irrelevance: 'Have you had Jessica's half-term report yet?'

Mrs. Willoughby glanced across to where Mrs. Fowler sat in the further corner of the room. Mrs. Willoughby, as the grandmother of five, had been prepared to patronize Mrs. Fowler on the acquisition of her second grandchild, but Mrs. Fowler had as yet given her no opening. She did not seem to be particularly interested in the child. There was even a faint irony in the glance she threw him now as she said:

'Helen used to look at me like that when she was a baby. It always made me feel that I ought to be apologizing to her for something – I never knew what.'

So that Mrs. Willoughby was still waiting her opportunity to say, 'When you've had as many as I've had, Mrs. Fowler, you won't be quite so thrilled by them.'

But, of course, thought Mrs. Willoughby, watching her, one could hardly expect her to be thrilled by a grandchild or anything else just now, with her son involved in one of the most disgraceful scandals that Bellington had ever known. Really, thought Mrs. Willoughby for the hundredth time, those Fowlers! Hardly had people stopped talking about Anice's secret marriage (why hadn't Anice come this afternoon? She'd had an invitation) when it became known that Peter was carrying on with another woman and wanted his wife to divorce him. A nurse, too, who had been living for months under his roof, so that one naturally took for granted that the affair had been going on all the time.

It was generally agreed that Belle had behaved extremely well in the matter, trying to win Peter back, offering to forgive him, refusing, as any decent woman would, to be dragged through the divorce court. The whole thing was deplorable, and Mrs. Willoughby wondered how Mrs. Fowler could continue to look as calm and detatched as she did.

At the sound of Oliver's laugh, Mrs. Willoughby turned sharply towards the door, where he stood with Judy, and her lips took on a still tighter line. Oliver had disgraced himself in her eyes by refusing to act as Stephen's godfather and was now disgracing himself further by giving all his attention to Judy Fowler and neglecting the other guests. Unfortunately Emmy was taking her annual holiday in Bournemouth with her father and mother, so could not be used as a lever to detach him from Judy. She must have a talk with Helen. Helen, she knew, had plans for Judy but had been too busy as yet with the coming of the baby to do anything about them.

They must find a solid, respectacle husband for Judy and a solid, respectable wife for Oliver. Both needed a steadying influence that the other could not provide.

'Hand the christening cake to Cousin Maggie, Oliver,' said Mrs. Willoughby.

'No, thank you, indeed,' said Cousin Maggie firmly.

'Then bring me Aunt Flo's cup. I'm sure she'd like another cup of tea.'

'No more tea, thank you, dear,' said Aunt Flo.

Oliver gave his mother a glance of quiet triumph and went on talking to Judy.

'Shall I hold the infant and let nurse have her tea in peace?' said Max, who took a childish delight in holding his son and so far had hardly been allowed to touch him.

'Of course not,' said Helen, with a touch of impatience. 'You can manage perfectly well, can't you, nurse?'

'I'm so glad you can feed him, dear,' said Miss Hatton. 'I always believe that the child imbibes good influences with the mother's milk.'

'When can I say my piece, Grandma?' piped up Peggy suddenly.

Oliver drew Judy into the hall and closed the door.

'The whole thing makes you want to vomit, doesn't it,' he said. 'Let's go for a walk.'

* * *

Mrs. Fowler left the christening party early and walked slowly along the country road towards Langley Place. Her heart was heavy with the thought of Peter, but there was room in it for a little nagging anxiety about Anice, too. During the first few months of her marriage Anice had seemed happy and carefree, delighting in the tiny house on the outskirts of Bellington that she and Martin had bought after a short honeymoon in Scotland. But now that she was going to have a baby all her old restlessness was returning and with it her old jealousy of Helen. The prospect of a child seemed to have shattered the fragile walls of the world in which she and Martin had lived so contentedly. Her face was beginning to wear its old look of strain and even, at times, of ill-humour.

'I suppose Helen will expect me to join the camp of the poor relations now,' she had said to Mrs. Fowler with a wry smile, 'and queue up for Stephen's old clothes. Well, she'll be mistaken. I'd rather my child went in rags.'

'Oh, come, darling!' Mrs. Fowler expostulated.

'Well, Mother, it's not going to be very pleasant for me if my children can't do the things that Helen's do or go to the same houses and that sort of thing. I wish Martin weren't so unbusinesslike.'

Yesterday evening Mrs. Fowler had rung her up.

'You're coming to the christening party tomorrow, darling, aren't you?' she had said.

'I don't think so,' Anice had replied shortly. 'The sight of Helen wallowing in the Willoughby lap of luxury is beginning to pall.'

Mrs. Fowler dismissed the thought of Anice with a shrug, and turned to the thought of Peter. Since the day when Moyna Pollard had told Belle that she had seen Peter and Rachel together Belle had inflicted on him a succession of scenes that had worn his endurance almost to breaking point. . . . Belle screaming abuse for all the household and even passers-by to hear. . . . Belle in clinging *négligés* pleading for his love with a theatrical abandon that must have been carefully rehearsed . . . Belle attacking him with fists and nails in a hysteria of rage . . . Belle threatening suicide . . . Belle pretending that she had actually committed suicide, lying rigid and motionless on the floor, an empty bottle in her hand. . . .

And Peter could not steel his heart against pity for her. He knew that, beneath her play-acting and deliberate loosening of her self-control, she suffered acutely – suffered in her pride and even in the bedraggled remnants of her love for him. She had gone over to see Rachel's employer, hoping to have the girl summarily dismissed, but Rachel had by now told her employer the whole story and Belle's journey was wasted. She wrote to Rachel – letters that sent a wave of nausea through Peter when he read them.

She confided, of course, in everyone she knew, not omitting the tradespeople, adding copious embellishments to the story. People looked askance at Peter when they met him in the street. All Belle's friends cut him. She had even tried to turn Gillian against him, telling her that Daddy was a wicked, cruel man, instructing the nurse, who revelled openly in the situation, not to allow him to have anything to do with the child. The situation had become so intolerable that Rachel had written to an uncle who was Professor of English at Leyden University, asking if any post for Peter and herself could be found there. Whether Belle agreed to divorce Peter or not, they had decided to leave England.

* * *

As she approached the front door a feeling of urgency and apprehension took possession of her, and, even before she entered the hall and saw his hat on the chest, she knew that he was there waiting for her. She found him standing at the drawing-room window, looking out over the pleasant old garden, raked now by bars of gold from the westering sun. . . . He turned at the sound of the opening door. The thinness and pallor of his face shocked her.

'Peter darling . . .' she said.

He greeted her with the quick nervous smile that was little more than a lightening of his features.

'I've come to say good-bye,' he said. 'We're going tomorrow. Rachel's heard from her uncle. He's got rooms for us and can find us both work coaching students in English.'

A sense of forboding weighed down her spirit.

'Oh, Peter, must you go so far away?'

'Rachel wants to get – right away from it. And so do I.'

'Couldn't you just stay in England till Matthew comes?'

He shook his head.

'We must go at once. You'll – explain to Matthew, won't you?'

'Yes.'

'And the others. I won't say good-bye to them.' He was silent for a few moments, then spoke in a jerky, unnatural manner as if each word were an effort. 'I'm – terribly sorry not to see Anice's child, not to see them all grow up . . . Helen's children . . . perhaps Judy's. . . .'

'But, Peter, you'll come back?'

'I don't think we shall.'

He turned to the window again and stood with his back to her, so that she could not see his face, speaking still in that jerky, unnatural voice.

'You'll write to me, won't you?'

'Of course, Peter.'

'You'll tell me everything about – ' He stopped. He could not trust himself to say the name.

'Gillian?'

He nodded.

'Yes, I will.'

'I shall want to know – everything. Nothing will be too unimportant to tell me . . .' His voice trailed away.

She looked at him, her heart heavy with misgiving. Peter was not the sort of man who could lightly cut the ties that bound him to his family. Family ties had always meant more to Peter than they mean to most men.

'I wish I could help, Peter,' she said. 'You'll let me know if I can, won't you?'

He wheeled round suddenly, caught her in his arms and kissed her, holding her so tightly that she could feel the trembling of his body, then, releasing her abruptly, strode from the room.

She stood at the window and watched him go down the drive. Though she could hardly see him for her tears, she knew that he did not look back.

CHAPTER TWELVE

Mrs. Fowler walked slowly down the grass path between the herbaceous borders. As autumn came on, the borders generally seemed to be engulfed by a sea of gold and yellow, but now, in mid-July, the rose red of the hollyhocks, the opal blue of the delphinium, with the smaller fry of poppy, columbine and snapdragon, made a brave show of colour. The gardener had mowed the lawn that morning and it lay in straight ribbon-like strips where the mower had passed over it.

A fly-catcher alighted suddenly on the top of a tall stake with the airy grace of a ballet dancer, darted off in pursuit of an insect and returned to the stake in one swift movement. The fly-catchers had visited Langley Place every summer since Mrs. Fowler could remember, nesting in the trellis against the south wall of the house, patching up the same old nest year after year. The children had always awaited them eagerly, and there had been a friendly rivalry as to who should be the first to note their return. 'The fly-catchers are back, Mother,' they would call from the garden, and then – and not till then – the whole family would settle down to the summer.

Mrs. Fowler stood for a moment, taking comfort from the familiar sights and sounds around her. Matthew was coming home today, and beneath her joy at the thought of the re-union was a nervousness that would not let her rest. She had long ago finished her preparations for his coming but she found it impossible to settle to anything, and, taking her gardening scissors, she had wandered out into the garden . . . and there among her flowers something of her usual serenity was returning to her. The borders were edged with catmint, lacy cascades of lavender blue, mist-like, delicate. She bent down to cut some of the slender strands to put into the vases among the sweet peas, then walked back across the lawn to the terrace steps.

At the end of the lawn the cedar tree looked darkly green against the clear sky, the caverns beneath its shelving branches mysteriously dim. . . . As she went up the terrace steps Mrs. Fowler wondered why she felt so nervous. One reason, of course, was that she would have to tell Matthew about Peter. It would be a shock . . . and he would miss Peter.

Belle had gone to stay with friends in London as soon as Peter and Rachel left England, and Mrs. Fowler had only heard indirectly that she was returning to Bellington this week. After much thought she had sent her an invitation to the family dinner that was to be held tonight (for Peter's sake, and at the cost of any humiliation or rebuff Belle chose to inflict on her, she must keep in touch with Gillian) but had received no answer.

It occurred to her suddenly that Matthew probably knew very little of the real story of Peter's marriage. She herself, from a vague sense of loyalty to Peter and a feeling that any confidence of that sort should come from Peter, had refrained from hinting at its unhappiness. She wondered how much Peter had told him and decided that he had told him nothing. Even to her Peter never admitted Belle's defects. She would have to tell the whole story from the beginning. She glanced at her watch. Matthew should be here any time now. He had asked her not to meet his train. He had always disliked being met at the station. The fuss and bustle, the collecting of baggage and tipping of porters marred the peace of homecoming for him. She went up the stone steps and round to the side of the terrace from where she could see the gates through a gap in the trees. Then her heart gave a leap. The car was just turning into the drive.

* * *

She was not prepared for the change in him. Illogically she had expected the boy who had left her, and just at first, in the flush of excitement at his homecoming, he did seem to be that boy. He leapt down from the car and caught her in his arms.

'It's good to be home,' he said.

They went into the house, his arm through hers. In the drawing-room he stood and drew a deep breath.

'Just as I've pictured it all these years,' he said. 'Not a thing changed.'

She smiled.

'Yes, I wouldn't let Helen even get new curtains.'

He wandered about the room, taking up books and photographs, glancing at them and putting them back without comment. An air of abstraction came over him, and his face fell into lines that made it unfamiliar. Thompson brought in tea, and Matthew greeted her cordially but still with that faint hint of abstraction in his manner.

'Sit down and have some tea, dear,' said Mrs. Fowler.

He sat down by her, and they began to talk desultorily, with an undercurrent of constraint against which she fought unavailingly. Gradually, very gradually, she was forced to the realization that the years had turned them into strangers. She had no hand in what had gone to the making of him since he left her. She knew nothing of his background and experiences. Their paths had diverged so far that they could hardly see each other. Even in his physique there was little of his boyhood left. His figure had thickened and matured. His expression was set and rather stern.

She asked him about his plans. He was not going abroad again, he said. He had been offered a post in the London office of the firm for which he had worked in Kenya and he had decided to accept it. Still struggling against the constraint that lay like a paralysis over the atmosphere, she began to retail the family news . . . Helen's baby . . . Anice's marriage . . . Judy. . . . Then she said:

'Matthew, there's something I have to tell you about Peter.'

He sat there, stirring his tea. His mouth took on a firmer, grimmer line. He did not look up.

'I know it,' he said. 'Belle wrote to me.'

She stared at him in surprise.

'Belle wrote to you?'

'He behaved like a swine to her,' said Matthew slowly. 'It's as well for him that he didn't wait till I came home. He'd have had me to deal with if he had done.'

'*Matthew!* You don't understand. . . .'

He looked at her with a faint smile.

'Peter was always your favourite,' he said. He spoke indulgently and without bitterness. 'In any case it's natural in the circumstances that you should see things through his eyes. I don't blame you. I – '

'Matthew,' she interrupted him urgently, 'you don't know how this has happened. You haven't lived near them, watched them all these years as I have. Belle's been a bad wife to him. Right from the beginning. . . .'

His face had hardened again.

'I'd rather not discuss it, Mother. Do you mind?'

She looked at him helplessly. Belle and her mother (who had died during the first year of Belle's marriage) had come to live at Hurstmede a few weeks before Matthew went abroad. He could have met her only two or three times. Had he treasured the memory of that lovely face through the long years of his exile, and treasured with it a – perhaps subconscious – jealousy of Peter?

'Won't you listen to me, Matthew?'

'What does it matter, anyway?' he said impatiently. 'The thing's over and done with.'

'But I want you to be fair to Peter. I want you to know how it happened.'

'I know all I care to know,' he said with an air of finality. He rose from his chair. 'I think I'll go and do a little unpacking before dinner.'

* * *

He was in the drawing-room, pouring himself out a whiskey-and-soda, when she came down. He looked well in evening dress – a handsome, thick-set, rather grim-visaged man. She dared not mention Peter again. Instead, she began to talk of his boyhood, trying desperately to strengthen the frail thread of memory that alone united them. To herself she was saying: I've lost my two sons. First Peter and now Matthew. . . .

'And do you remember the time when . . .?'

He nodded absently, his frowning gaze fixed on his glass, twisting the stem round and round in his fingers. Sometimes he afforded her reminiscences the tribute of a smile, or rather the slight relaxing of his stern features that did duty for a smile, but he made no other response. I'm boring him terribly, she thought. He's not interested in anything I'm saying. He's hardly listening. . . .

She began to ask him questions about his life in Kenya, but those, too, he answered shortly, with an underlying impatience that increased her nervousness. We're both thinking about Peter, she thought. I wish he'd let me talk about it. . . .

'I suppose it's just along the coast that the climate's so unhealthy, is it?' she said.

He was so deeply absorbed by his own thoughts that he did not hear her. There was a long silence, then he said suddenly:

'Who's coming tonight?'

'All of them, Helen, Max, Anice and Martin. I explained about Judy, didn't I? She's staying with a school friend, but she'll be home in time for dinner.'

He nodded again and drained his glass.

‘Is Belle coming?’ he said, as he put it down on the table by his chair.

‘I don’t know. I don’t even know whether she’s home yet. I wrote to ask her to come – ’

Then the door opened suddenly and Belle appeared. She must have come in very quietly and slipped off her cloak in the hall. She looked so lovely that even Mrs. Fowler caught her breath. Her dress of black chiffon, with long wing-like sleeves, enhanced her fairness. Her hair was an aureole round the heart-shaped face, the blue eyes were limpid and appealing, the cherub mouth drooped exquisitely at the corners. . . . She stood there, framed in the doorway – a beautiful, wistful, unhappy child. It was a perfect entrance.

‘Am I – terribly early?’ she said timidly.

Then her eyes went from Mrs. Fowler to Matthew, and she moved swiftly across to him, her arms outstretched.

‘Oh, Matthew!’ she said.

CHAPTER THIRTEEN

Cynthia cycled down the narrow lane that led to Arnold Palmer's cottage. The air was sweet with the scent of new-mown hay, and feathery tufts on the hedges marked the recent passage of the hay wagons. The ditches on either side foamed with the milky blossom of wild parsley, and the song of the cuckoo rang out with sleepy persistence from a neighbouring wood.

Cynthia had been Arnold Palmer's secretary now for six years. Every day she cycled over to Ivy Dene Cottage after an early breakfast and often did not return till dinner-time. Mrs. Willoughby regarded this arrangement with mixed feelings. It irked her that a daughter of hers should be at the beck and call of someone whom she regarded as a useless member of the community, but she realized that girls were now beginning to take up jobs as a matter of course, and this job had the advantage of being close at hand, so that she could keep her eye on her daughter and know exactly where she was at every moment of every day, which was, Mrs. Willoughby considered, one of the primary duties of motherhood.

Cynthia's brows were drawn into an anxious frown as she cycled along the lane. Arnold Palmer was giving a cocktail party this evening and most of the duties in connection with it naturally devolved on Cynthia.

She felt nervous and apprehensive, terrified of forgetting something or making some social blunder. She was still *gauche* and shy and at her worst with strangers. Her mind ran over the preparations. . . . She had stayed up late last night making savoury biscuits. She would bring them over this afternoon together with the glasses and flowers, which were also being provided by the Willoughby household. The bottles of sherry, gin and other drinks had arrived yesterday and were safely stored under the stairs. There was nothing further she could do till after lunch. In any case she must keep her mind clear for Chapter Ten this morning. . . .

And at the thought of Chapter Ten a ray of happiness flooded her heart. *Blue Roses* was going beautifully. There had been no snags at all so far. And Chapter Ten, Cynthia was sure, was going to be one of his really fine pieces of work – moving, dramatic, with those touches of whimsical humour that, as a reviewer had put it, ran like a golden thread through all his stories. She glanced at her watch and, finding that she was in good time, relaxed her speed and allowed her eyes to wander over the countryside. . . .

It reminds me of that description of a June day in Chapter Three, she thought – the one where he describes the fleecy white clouds and says they're like sheep asleep in a blue field. That chapter was so beautiful that I forgot it was being dictated and just listened.

It made him laugh. He said, 'Wake up, Slowcoach'. . . . I wish he was getting better reviews on *Phantom Flames*.

He's so sensitive. He minds so much, though he pretends not to. . . . Oh, dear, I do hope everything will go off all right tonight. I'm always frightened of his London friends. They make me feel so plain and stupid, but then, of course, I am. I'm glad that some of the family are coming . . . Max and Helen . . . Oliver and Judy. . . . Helen's baby shows terribly, but she never seems to mind going about like that. . . . Mr. Palmer asked Oliver to bring that college friend of his who's on a walking tour and staying at the Red Lion. I don't know whether he will or not. Anyway, one more won't make any difference. Matthew and Belle are coming if Matthew gets back from work in time.

People say that Matthew's drinking too much. Perhaps it's because of Belle. She's always been a bit – difficult, but she's as lovely as ever, and that seems to be all men care about. . . . People are talking about her and Tony Westerham. . . . I wonder how Peter and that girl got on? They've never been back to England. . . . I'm rather glad that Anice and Martin can't come. She snaps at him so, it makes one feel quite uncomfortable. It isn't his fault that Newbolt's is doing badly. He just isn't a business man. . . .

The lane turned a sharp bend and brought the cottage into view. Ivy Dene Cottage, on whose sixteenth-century origin the agents were always very insistent, was a picturesque building, with age-mellowed bricks and lichen-encrusted tiles, set back from the road behind a shady old-fashioned garden. The rooms were low and heavily raftered, the windows small, the whole place more picturesque than convenient. It made a good setting, however, for Arnold Palmer, and he was frequently photographed both in the garden, toying with spade or hoe, and in the study, standing before the open brick fireplace or sitting at the desk at the window round which in summer climbing roses were carefully trained.

Cynthia dismounted at the little green gate, wheeled her bicycle round to the side of the house and entered by the back door. Mrs. Richmond, the woman from the village who 'went with' the cottage, was in the kitchen, washing out a tea-cloth at the sink.

''E's jus' started on 'is breakfast,' she volunteered. ''E's in one of 'is funny moods. Crackin' jokes.'

A weight that she had not known was there dropped from Cynthia's heart. There were days when the novelist's mouth was compressed, his brows knit . . . when she had to step carefully, choosing her words, when speech and silence were equally fraught with danger, for Mr. Palmer had moods that in a lesser man would have been described as irritable. In Cynthia's mind the words 'sensitive' and 'highly strung' covered all such manifestations of ill-humour. Sometimes she admitted that she was desperately, hopelessly in love with him, sometimes she tried unsuccessfully to disguise the fact by high-sounding phrases about platonic friendship and mind-affinity . . . higher and more enduring things, she told herself, than mere love.

She took a duster from a drawer in the dresser and a carpet-sweeper from a cupboard and went down the narrow passage. She always began the morning by dusting and sweeping the study. Mrs. Richmond had a tendency to move things, to mislay things, to put things on top of other things, to destroy as 'waste paper' any loose sheets of manuscript that came her way. Never to the end of her life would Cynthia forget the day when Mrs. Richmond had burnt the four opening pages of *Deep Waters*. After that only Cynthia had been allowed to enter the room, for to Cynthia everything in it was sacred.

From the dining-room door came a faint aroma of coffee and bacon.

'That you, Dormouse?' called a pleasant voice as she passed.

Mr. Palmer had a varied selection of nicknames for her – Dormouse, Miss Muffet (because of her aversion to spiders), Sobersides, She Who Must Be Obeyed. Cynthia never called him anything but Mr. Palmer.

'Yes.'

'Come and say good morning to me.'

Her face lit up with delight at the kindness of his tone. Yes, he *was* in a good mood. . . .

She laughed.

'There's a lot to do today,' she said. 'I'll say good morning when you come to the study.'

'All right, you little crosspatch.'

Light-heartedly, singing softly under her breath (for his good moods always made her extravagantly happy), she entered the study, sweeping, dusting, emptying and cleaning his ash-trays, putting clean blotting-paper into his desk pad, sharpening the H.B. pencil with which he liked to make his notes. Then she beat up the cushions on the settee and straightened the rug by the fireplace, moving softly, reverently, like a priestess tending a shrine. That done, she took the little pile of letters that stood on his desk and sorted them into neat piles, personal letters, bills, circulars, press cuttings. . . . At the top of the little pile of personal letters was a pale grey envelope addressed in purple ink. That was Angela Grey. . . .

The thought of his friendship with Angela Grey brought the familiar pang to Cynthia's heart. It stood for that part of his life from which she was excluded – his visits to London and the people he knew there, writers, artists, actors and actresses. Angela Grey was an actress who had the reputation of being the best dressed woman in London. Cynthia had only met her once, and on that occasion had been studiously ignored by her.

She took up the packet of press cuttings and stood a few moments looking at it with an anxious frown before, slowly, almost reluctantly, she tore it open. These small slips of print could disturb the precarious balance of his serenity for weeks. And today, the day of the cocktail party, it was important that nothing should be allowed to upset him. *The Onlooker*. . . . She drew a quick sigh of relief as her eyes sped down the lines. It was all right . . . 'distinguished style' . . . 'sound psychology' . . . 'insight and lucidity' . . . 'exquisite word paintings of nature'.

She placed it open on the desk and turned to the other, reading it with rising colour and tightened lips . . . 'slick' . . . 'verbosity' . . . 'superficial' . . . 'vapid'. . . . How *dared* they say such things about his work! She read it a second time, her heart beating unevenly, then slipped it into her pocket. She didn't care how wicked it was, she wasn't going to let him see it. He was so sensitive and highly strung. Things hurt him so cruelly. To salve her conscience, she said, 'I'll give it him later . . . when he's got over these ticklish few chapters he's working on now' . . . but she knew she wouldn't. She would burn it in her bedroom grate as she had burnt others.

The door opened, and he entered, smiling at her quizzically over his pipe.

'All set for the great jollification?' he said.

'I think so. The savouries from Roberts' are coming this afternoon. I'll bring the biscuits after lunch with the flowers and glasses.'

'You spoil the old man,' he said.

He slipped an arm carelessly round her shoulders and led her to the desk. She tried to control the trembling that seized her.

'Anything interesting in the mail?'

'There's a review from *The Onloooker*.'

His lips twitched nervously as he took it from her, then relaxed into a complacent smile.

'We've had worse, haven't we?' he said.

'It's lovely,' she said.

He leant back in his chair and opened Angela Grey's letter.

Cynthia watched him, her face set and stony.

'Got my engagement calendar?' he said suddenly.

'Yes.' She took it from a drawer in the desk.

'Put down lunch with Angela Grey at the Ritz on the fourteenth.'

'Will you be in London for the weekend?'

‘For the week, I think. Do both of us good to have a holiday.’

She was silent. Another of those long, empty weeks, every moment of which was haunted by tormenting visions of glamourous women flocking round him at dinners, theatres, dances. . . . He glanced up and caught the rigidity of her expression as she noted the engagement.

‘You should look more grateful than that,’ he said.

She smiled unhappily.

‘I never know what to do when I don’t come here. And I want to get on with the book. I’m enjoying every word of it. It reminds me of *Summer Heritage*, and I’ve always loved *Summer Heritage*.’

Though his expression did not alter, she realized that she had said the wrong thing and remembered too late that he disliked to have his earlier books praised. Such praise seemed to him a deliberate depreciation of his later books, and he liked to think that, in the words of one of his friendlier critics, ‘each book marked a definite advance in power and subtlety over the last’.

He took up the next envelope, addressed in a round childish hand, and carefully slit it open with his paper-knife. Cynthia knew the handwriting. It was one of the schoolgirl admirers who wrote to him regularly. He never showed her the letters and always answered them himself. Generally the correspondence petered out after a month or two, but this girl had been writing to him now for more than a year. In the middle drawer of his desk was a photograph that she had sent him a few weeks ago. Some fascination drew Cynthia again and again to open the drawer and look at the pretty empty face.

As he read the letter his lips curved into a smile . . . and a wave of irritation swept over her. Little fool! . . . Writing to people she doesn't know . . . raving about their books! Then it occurred to her that that was the way she herself had come to know him. I can't blame her . . . I can't blame any of them. . . . I wonder if she's as pretty as the photograph . . .? I wonder if he met her when he went to London last month? I'm almost sure I heard him arranging it on the telephone. Perhaps he took her to a theatre or to dinner. . . .

Mr. Palmer had never taken Cynthia to anything beyond a lunch at the George Hotel in Bellington, but sometimes she imagined him asking her if she'd care to come up to London with him for a lunch and matinée . . . and was torn between delight at the prospect and terror at the thought of proving inadequate to the occasion. (I shouldn't know what to say and my clothes would be all wrong. I expect that's why he's never asked me.)

Mr. Palmer put the letter back into its envelope, slipped it into his pocket and sat for a few moments in silence, leaning back in his chair, a lingering reminiscent smile on his lips. . . . Then he roused himself.

'Well,' he said briskly, 'this won't do, will it? About this evening. How many people are coming exactly?'

She handed him the list. He glanced down it.

'Quite a collection of local worthies.'

'Yes.'

'Your brother and Judy, I see. When are they to be married?'

'I don't know. They haven't decided yet.'

'I should imagine the lady will prove an exacting wife.'

'Why?'

He shrugged.

'I should say that she has an unduly high opinion of herself and expects others to share it.'

'Oh, Judy's not like that,' she said.

He was always running Judy down, yet, oddly, he always seemed to want to talk about her.

'Isn't she?' he said. 'Well, I won't quarrel with you. I'll find something more important than a nonentity like little Miss Judy to quarrel with you about when I want to quarrel with you.'

She was ashamed of the secret pleasure that his disparagement of Judy gave her. It's as if I can't bear his liking anyone, she thought despairingly. I'm getting worse and worse. . . . She glanced at the clock and sat down by the desk.

'Shall we go on from where we stopped yesterday?' she said. 'Or do you want to revise Chapter Nine?'

He fixed his eyes on her with a teasing smile.

'Can't I even take a morning off when I'm giving a party?'

'No,' she said with mock severity, falling in with his mood, 'of course you can't.'

'All right, you little slave-driver. Where had we got to?'

* * *

She went home at the end of the morning, collected the things she had got ready for the cocktail party and after a sketchy lunch returned to Ivy Dene Cottage. He entered the study as soon as she had finished arranging the flowers, and she saw at once that his mood had changed. It often changed like that – suddenly and for no apparent cause. It might be merely the reaction from his genial mood of the morning. It might be that he could no longer see his way clearly in the book he was writing. It might be some casual encounter. When he went into the village to post a letter or buy some tobacco he seldom came back in the same mood in which he had set out. He had generally met someone who by a word or even a silence marred his tranquillity or inflated his self-conceit. These were rather hazardous days, too. *Phantom Flames* had only been out a few weeks, and for an acquaintance to meet him and fail to mention the book was in his eyes a deliberate slight.

He greeted her curtly and sat down at his desk. His long mouth was tightly set, his brows drawn closely together. Another ominous sign was that he appeared not to notice her flowers – tall jars of delphiniums, bowls of roses, sweet peas massed in an old Delph soup tureen. He could not have failed to see them, but he studiously refrained from comment. Her heart grew heavy. It was obviously going to be a difficult afternoon.

'Well, let's get on with it,' he said shortly. 'With this tiresome business this evening, we've no time to waste.'

It was a 'tiresome business' now, no longer a 'jollification'. He dictated for about half an hour, then leant back in his chair and relit his pipe.

'Read from the beginning of the chapter,' he said.

She read it – badly, because she was nervous. His long slender fingers drummed impatiently on the desk. The twitching of his lips showed his irritation.

‘How does that last paragraph strike you?’ he said. ‘Is the description a shade too long?’

Occasionally he asked her advice, though he seldom took it unless it coincided with his own opinion. Without thinking she blurted out:

‘Would she have done that? I mean, you’ve made her so dignified and sensible. Would she have done a foolish thing like that? There seems no reason for it.’

‘I don’t think I asked your opinion on that particular point, did I?’ he said frigidly.

She bit her lip and bent her head over her writing-pad. He went on dictating. Occasionally he paused as if inviting comment, but she remained silent, her head still bent over her work. He began to fidget, throwing her furtive glances. Her adoration was as necessary to him as any of the other creature comforts that surrounded him. Having vented his irritation on her, he felt better. But she had withdrawn from him, and he was lost without her eager response. . . . People were always doing that, continuing to sulk after he had vented his irritation on them and was willing to renew friendly relations. He felt ill-used and sorry for himself. He laid a hand on her arm.

‘I’m sorry, Sobersides,’ he said coaxingly and a little querulously. ‘The old man’s a bit of a bear sometimes, isn’t he? He doesn’t mean it, you know. . . .’

Her relief at the ending of the tension was so great that for a moment or two she could only look at him, her eyes bright with tears. Then:

‘It was my fault,’ she gulped. ‘I mean . . . I’m sorry. . . . I do understand.’

'I know you do,' he said. 'You're one of the few people who do. . . . All forgotten and forgiven, eh?'

She gave him a tremulous smile, unable to trust herself to speak. He patted her hand.

'Well, come along. To work once more.'

He was in high good-humour again, both with himself and her. After all, he thought, a distinguished man of letters who could apologize to his secretary for a passing impatience was rather a fine character. It pleased him for the rest of the afternoon to add fuel to the fire of her devotion by the many little devices in which he was expert – a touch, a smile, an inflection of his voice. Then, beginning to feel bored by the situation and not knowing what to do next with his somewhat involved plot, he leant back and said:

'Now we'd both better have a rest before the jollification.' He went to the door, turned back and added: 'Your flowers look wonderful, my dear. I congratulate you.'

Her heart glowing with happiness, Cynthia began to arrange the cheese straws and savouries and to set out the glasses and cigarettes, watched a little sardonically by Mrs. Richmond, who considered preparations for cocktail parties no part of her work. (If people wanted to drink they should go to a pub and do it properly.)

Then she tidied the study, dusted it again, and gave a final polish to the brass candlesticks and horse bits on the mantelpiece, taking so long that she had barely time to hurry back to The Beeches and change into the flowered voile dress that had been made by Cousin Lucy with more than her usual incompetence.

By the time she reached Ivy Dene Cottage Oliver and Judy and Oliver's friend had arrived, and Mr. Palmer, a genial, charming host, was shaking a cocktail. He had put a few deft touches to the room while Cynthia was away, laying in prominent places literary reviews of the more highbrow variety – one open as if he had just put it down – and some recently published books of poetry and philosophy. The light novels which were his usual reading were hidden from sight. Of his own novels there was no trace. Their absence impressed his modesty on people, and Mr. Palmer spent a lot of time and thought impressing his modesty on people. On top of the letter basket lay the cutting from *The Onlooker*, placed as if casually laid down there, but in such a way as to be legible from the middle of the room, where most of the guests would assemble. About him, as about the room, was a carefully careless air. He looked handsome but just not too well groomed.

He smiled at Cynthia as she entered.

'Here's the young woman who's the bane of my life,' he said. 'She keeps my nose to the grindstone day in and day out. If she didn't I don't suppose I'd ever do a stroke of work. I'm the laziest dog in the world by nature.'

'Hallo, Cynthia,' said Judy in her soft, musical voice.

As Cynthia's devotion to Arnold Palmer seemed to have fixed her mental state at adolescence, so Judy seemed to have progressed further into maturity than her years warranted. She looked poised and sophisticated in her well-cut, closely fitting black dress. And she was beautiful . . . eyes violet blue in the transparent pallor of her face, brows delicate as young moons against the smooth white forehead, lips whose exquisitely chiselled curves held a hint of disdain.

'Hallo, Judy,' said Cynthia.

Remembering the fervent friendship of their girlhood, Cynthia always felt ill-at-ease with Judy. That they had once been so close to each other emphasized the gulf that divided them now. Judy, however, seemed unaware of any constraint in the atmosphere. She treated Cynthia with off-hand friendliness as her fiancé's sister.

'You haven't met Denis Gordon, have you, Cynthia?' said Oliver.

Denis Gordon, a gaunt, untidy-looking youth, with rough-hewn features and a pleasant expression, grinned and held her hand in an iron grip.

'How do you do,' said Cynthia, aware of the awkwardness and embarrassment that the most casual social encounter always caused her.

Glancing at the mirror on the further wall, she saw that her face was flushed and shiny, her hair already coming down and that her petticoat showed beneath the uneven hem of the flowered voile dress.

CHAPTER FOURTEEN

'She's his secretary, did you say?' said Denis.

Ever since he left Ivy Dene Cottage with Judy and Oliver he had been talking about Cynthia, and Judy had answered him tersely, in a manner that plainly showed that she wanted to get rid of him. She had even pointed out a short cut across the fields to the inn where he was staying, but Denis, who was rather an obtuse young man, continued to accompany them and to talk about Cynthia.

'Yes, she's his secretary,' said Judy.

'Gosh!' he said resentfully. 'How on earth does she stand the chap? Ordering her about! She might be a housemaid or something.'

'It's supposed to be a very interesting job,' said Judy. 'He's quite a well-known novelist.'

'Never heard of him,' said Denis.

'Perhaps you don't read much,' said Judy.

'No, I don't. Anyway, I thought him a conceited ass. Throwing his weight about! Showing off!'

'He's generally considered charming,' said Judy.

'You've got an odd idea of charm in this part of the world.'

'You're rather uncompromising in your judgments, aren't you?' said Judy. 'He was a very good host.'

The young man blushed.

'Yes. . . . I suppose it's not quite the thing to run him down after drinking his sherry and eating his cheese straws.'

'Cynthia made those.'

'Did she?' said Denis with interest. 'They were jolly good.' Then, his resentment returning: 'But, damn it all, why should she? What does he think she is? Made my blood boil the way he ordered her about.'

'He is her employer, you know,' said Judy, 'and she has a great admiration for him. . . . If you go down that lane it will bring you out just below the Red Lion. You are staying there, aren't you?'

'Yes,' said Denis.

'Perhaps we could fix something up for tomorrow,' said Oliver.

'I'd like to, but there's some old aunt in the neighbourhood I'm supposed to be looking up. . . . I'll give you a ring, anyway. Well, thanks for the party. Good-bye.'

'Need you have been quite as rude as that, Judy?' said Oliver, when Denis had set off with long swinging strides down the lane.

'Evidently,' said Judy. 'It took all the rudeness I was capable of to get rid of him.'

'Why did you want to get rid of him?'

'Because I want to talk to you. . . . Let's go through the wood.'

They walked in silence over the fields and crossed the stile that led into the wood. The rays of the setting sun fell slantwise through the branches of the beeches on to the bracken beneath shedding a light that seemed itself to be green, so vivid was the green of leaf and fronds all round. They followed the path that wound among the trees. Suddenly Judy broke the silence.

'Oliver, you said last night – '

He groaned.

'Good lord, Judy, must we go over all that again?'

'Yes, we must. I meant what I said. I won't marry you if it means living in Bellington or – anywhere round here.'

'My dear girl. I'm as keen as you are to get out of it.'

'You're not. You think you are, but you're not. You're – afraid. You want to go on putting it off. You've got into your rut and you're comfortable in it. You pretend to hate it, but you don't really. It's just a pose. You've even stopped writing.'

'I haven't,' he said sulkily.

'You have. You just play at it now. It's part of the pose. You don't take it seriously any longer. Just because a few things came back – '

'For heaven's sake, Judy, stop nagging. We've talked this over till I'm sick of it.'

'So am I. It's time we did something more than talk.'

'I thought I'd made it clear that I'm fully determined to leave the business and Bellington at the first opportunity. But I'll wait till I'm in a position to make my own terms.'

'Which will be never.'

'It would be if I used your methods. It's no good charging at a thing of this sort like a bull at a gate and putting everyone's back up.'

'In other words, you're frightened of your mother.'

He flushed.

'That's a damned offensive thing to say.'

She threw him a quick glance.

'If it weren't true you wouldn't be so angry. . . . Anyway, why should your mother come into it at all? Max is the head of the business, isn't he? Can't you just tell him you're leaving – and leave?'

'Mother owns most of the shares. She still runs the business.'

'She seems to run the whole lot of you as well. . . . Really, for a man of your age to have to climb into his bedroom window after a dance, because his mother has all the doors locked at eleven!'

'It seemed to amuse you at the time.'

'I pretended to be amused, but it was – humiliating. . . . I'm sorry if I'm being disagreeable, Oliver, but I'm not going on like this any longer. How long *have* we been going on like this? Ever since we got engaged. Saying that we'd leave Bellington as soon as we got married and doing nothing about it. You've stopped wanting to go in your heart, and if you don't do something about it soon, I shall.'

'The place might be a plague spot, the way you talk about it.'

'You used to talk about it in the same way. You've changed.'

'I haven't.'

They had reached the clearing and the fallen log where Peter and Rachel had once sat and confessed their love. Judy sat down, and Oliver stood facing her, his foot on the log.

'You'll get like all the rest in time,' she said. 'You're starting already. They've no eyes for anything but the petty little details of their petty little lives. Mother's the only one who's different. She lives here, but she doesn't belong here. It wouldn't matter where Mother lived, because she carries her own world about with her. When I'm with her I'm – happy, but it's no use staying in a place just because you're happy with your mother. I've got my own life to make, and I want it to *be* a life. I'm not highbrow and literary – I leave that to you – but I mean to *live*, not just exist.'

'Finished?' he sneered.

She stood up and faced him.

'Not quite. I've just one more thing to say, and that is, unless you *do* something by the end of the week, I'm through with you.'

'What do you mean by that?'

'What I say. . . . I shall break off the engagement if you don't do something definite about it by the end of the week.'

'How do you mean, definite?' he said. 'I can't pack up and move to London in two days.'

'You can tell your mother you're going. You've never even done that yet, have you? If you really meant what you say, you'd go straight back and tell her now. . . . Well, that's my last word. I'm through with you if you don't do it. You can marry Emmy. She's been hanging about after you for years. She'll make you a very good wife, too.'

He glowered at her.

'Why not tell me straight out that you don't love me?'

‘I do love you,’ she said. ‘It’s because I love you that I can’t bear to stay here and watch you getting like all the others.’ Her voice broke suddenly. ‘Oh, Oliver, let’s not quarrel . . . I do love you. . . . ’

He took her in his arms, holding her closely.

‘Oliver,’ she whispered, ‘you’ll – do it today, won’t you? I’ve got a horrible feeling that if we don’t do it now we’ll never do it . . . that we’ll come to hate each other, despise each other. . . . You will, won’t you?’

‘Yes.’

‘You promise?’

‘I promise. . . . Judy, I love you so . . . I couldn’t bear to let you go.’

‘Don’t say that,’ she cried. ‘You won’t have to let me go.’

He pressed his lips on hers and they stood for some moments, tense and motionless, then she released herself gently, straightening her hair and looking about her with a little twisted smile.

‘We used to come here for picnics when we were children,’ she said. ‘Mother used to sit on this log and read. Everything seemed so safe then.’

* * *

Mrs. Willoughby had had a difficult day. Directly after breakfast Florence had arrived in a distracted state, saying that Jessica’s headmistress had just rung up to tell her that Jessica had run away from school. Mrs. Willoughby at once took charge of the situation. She put on her hat and coat and was looking out a train to take her to Jessica’s school, when

Gertrude appeared, accompanied by a defiant, dishevelled Jessica and a sullen Tim.

Jessica had run away in the early morning, when it was still dark, caught a train to Bellington, and gone straight to Gertrude's house, where she had stood beneath Tim's window and thrown pebbles at it. Tim had come down at once and had undertaken to conceal her in the coal-shed till they had made more definite plans. The plans had been discussed by the two of them, Tim in his dressing-gown, Jessica in her school uniform, sitting side by side on a heap of coal.

Tim did not wish to be left out of the venture, and they had decided to run away together that evening after Tim was supposed to be in bed, make their way to the coast and travel as stowaways to some foreign country. At this point Tim saw the maid pulling back the window curtains of the drawing-room and, after promising to bring Jessica her breakfast as soon as possible, returned furtively to the house.

The discovery of traces of coal on Tim's dressing-gown puzzled Gertrude, and her mystification increased when, looking out of her bedroom window after breakfast, she saw Tim entering the coal-shed with a plate of bread-and-butter. She followed him and found Jessica already setting to work upon the second piece. Jessica, silent and defiant, refused any explanation. Gertrude had rung up Florence and, finding that she had gone to Mrs. Willoughby's, hurried Jessica, still silent and defiant, and freely streaked with coal, through the streets of Bellington to The Beeches. Tim accompanied them, imitating Jessica's attitude of silent defiance.

As soon as they entered the morning-room at The Beeches

Florence seized upon the culprit and shook her in mingled exasperation and relief. Mrs. Willoughby set her lips grimly, took off her hat and put the time-table back into the bookcase. Gertrude poured out a confused account of what had happened.

'Coal all over his dressing-gown. I shall have to send it to the cleaner's. . . . After giving him that bicycle for his birthday and after him promising faithfully to try to be a better boy! I do think – '

'That will do, Gertrude,' Mrs. Willoughby interrupted her. 'Take him home now and he must go straight to bed as soon as he gets there and have nothing but bread and water for the rest of the day.'

'I won't say I'm sorry, anyway,' said Tim. 'I'm not sorry. I'm glad. I'd do it again – '

Gertrude dragged him from the room before he could finish the sentence. He was heard expostulating passionately as they went down the drive.

Florence sat down on the sofa and began to cry.

'I don't know how you *could*, you naughty girl. I'm nearly *dead* with anxiety. I've got a dreadful headache. . . . I can't think what I'm to do with you. . . .'

'Go upstairs and lie down on my bed, Florence,' said Mrs. Willoughby. 'You'll find some aspirins in the medicine cupboard in the bathroom.'

Florence obeyed mechanically, sniffing dolorously as she went from the room.

'Shut the door, Jessica,' said Mrs. Willoughby.

Jessica hesitated then obeyed.

'Come here.'

Again Jessica hesitated and again obeyed, standing in front of her grandmother – a tall, slender child, with a pale, thin, freckled face, hazel eyes and untidy red-gold hair.

(I won't be frightened, she was saying to herself. I won't. I *won't*. . . .)

Mrs. Willoughby stood and looked at her for some moments in silence. Her mouth was set, her nose an eagle's beak, her eyes piercingly stern beneath gathered brows.

(I'm *not* frightened. She can't kill me. She can't even make me go back. . . .)

'I'm not going to ask you why you ran away from school, Jessica,' said Mrs. Willoughby at last, 'because I'm not interested in why you did it. You're an extremely naughty little girl and you deserve to be severely punished. I'm not going to punish you, however, in any other way than by sending you straight back to school. You'll go back by the next train.'

Jessica gulped and swallowed.

'I won't,' she said clearly.

Mrs. Willoughby's lips took on a tighter line.

'What did you say?' she asked with ominous quietness.

(If I'm not careful, I'm going to be frightened. If I'm not *very* careful. . . .)

Jessica flung back her head, defying her own fear as well as her grandmother.

'I said, I won't,' she repeated clearly.

'Do you want me to have to take you back by force?' said Mrs. Willoughby, 'because, if you refuse to obey me, that's what I shall do.'

Jessica knew that it was no empty threat. The old lady was quite capable of doing it. . . . A feeling of angry helplessness swept over her. The grown-up world was too strong. It would conquer her in the end, however long she defied it. Her anger mounted as she surveyed the forces so relentlessly arrayed against her.

'Well?' said Mrs. Willoughby, omnipotent and aloof.

Suddenly Jessica's anger boiled over in a turgid stream.

'I *won't* go,' she said. 'If you drag me there, I'll fight all the way. I'll scratch and kick and bite you. I *hate* you. When I'm grown-up I'll go right away from you and never speak to you or see you again. You're a horrid, cruel old woman.' (Beneath her rage stirred a sudden feeling of exultation. I'm not frightened of her any more. I shall never be frightened of her again.) 'I wish I had someone else for a grandmother. I wish I had – someone kind like Mrs. Fowler.'

Mrs. Willoughby stood there in silence. A dull flush had crept into her cheeks. She was trying to hide even from herself the hurt she had received. 'Someone kind like Mrs. Fowler. . . .' The dislike and contempt she had always felt for the woman made the hurt the more intolerable.

She turned away, speaking coldly and distantly as if no longer interested in the conversation.

'If you prefer Mrs. Fowler for a grandmother, you'd better go to her.'

Jessica was afraid now – she didn't know why.

'Yes, I will,' she said, bursting into tears and running from the room.

When Florence came down Mrs. Willoughby was sitting at her desk, doing the tradesmen's books.

'Where's Jessica?' said Florence.

'She's gone to Langley Place to see Mrs. Fowler.'

Florence was relieved but bewildered. The crisis was evidently over, however, if Mother had sent Jessica on a message to Langley Place.

'Is she going back to school?'

'Yes.'

'When?'

'As soon as she returns from Langley Place.'

'Oh. . . .' said Florence.

Florence was feeling a little uncomfortable about James, who hadn't been consulted in the matter at all. He hadn't even been told that Jessica had run away from school. He had gone to the office before Jessica's headmistress had rung up, and Florence had gone straight to The Beeches and then Gertrude had arrived with Jessica. The whole thing would need a good deal of explaining to James, who was, as Florence put it to herself, inclined to be 'touchy about Mother'.

'Well, I'd better go and tell James about it now,' she said.

'There's not the slightest need to do so,' said Mrs. Willoughby. 'She'll have gone back to school by the time he comes home. You can tell him then, if you like. . . . Now will you go down to Cluett's for me and ask them why they haven't sent the butter with the other groceries? Tell them I'm very much annoyed about it. And Bobby's shoes should be ready today. Remember to call for them. His others are nearly through, you know, and I don't want him to have to wear his best for school.'

'But, Mother – '

Mrs. Willoughby turned the eagle's beak to her.

'I'm very busy, Florence. Shut the door behind you as you go out.'

Florence hovered for a moment or two then went out and shut the door behind her. She hadn't really been told anything about Jessica, and she didn't know what to do about James. Mother evidently had the matter well in hand, but then Mother wouldn't have to deal with James when he found out about it. He'd be furious. He'd call it 'more of the old woman's damned interference'. Life was very difficult sometimes, thought Florence with a sigh, as she set off to complain about the groceries and call for Bobby's shoes.

* * *

Jessica did not come back till after lunch. It was a long morning for Mrs. Willoughby. She felt hurt and angry and – though she would not have admitted it – a little afraid. She had never before been defied by a child. It was like a tiny crack in the foundations of her house. She was relieved when she saw Jessica pass the window, walking with her usual light swift step, but, when Jessica entered the room, Mrs. Willoughby continued to sit at her desk with her back to the door, as if she had not noticed her entrance.

'Grandma,' said Jessica at last.

Slowly, very slowly, Mrs. Willoughby turned round. The eagle's beak stood out sharply.

'Well?'

Jessica's sulkiness had gone. Her small pale face shone with a sort of exaltation.

'I'm sorry I was so rude to you. I'll go back to school.'

Mrs. Willoughby was silent for some moments, then said:

'Did Mrs. Fowler tell you to say that?'

Jessica's eyes opened wide.

'Oh no. I asked her if I ought to go back, but she wouldn't tell me.'

'How do you mean, wouldn't tell you?'

'She just didn't seem to want to talk about it. We talked about other things. We talked about flowers and books. We like the same sort of books.' There was a note of happy importance in the child's voice. 'We both like poetry. She read me a lovely one called *Nod*. And she took me to the box-room and showed me some old dresses that had belonged to her grandmother. I tried one on. And she showed me some very old photographs. It was lovely.'

'She'd no right to treat you like that when she knew that you were in disgrace,' said Mrs. Willoughby sternly.

'But she didn't seem to know. I mean, I told her, but she didn't seem to – understand. We had a lovely picnic lunch on the terrace – just salad and then raspberries and cream. She always has lunch like that when she's alone. And after lunch we picked some flowers and arranged them together. Then she said I'd better come home.'

'I should think so,' said Mrs. Willoughby through compressed lips.

'Then I asked her if she'd go back to school if she was me, and she said she would but that that was nothing to go by, because everyone must decide things for themselves and not just do what other people would do. And, anyway, she said' – again the note of pleased importance in the childish voice

– 'no one but me knew all the circumstances, so no one but me could really judge. She told me to think it over on my way home. And I did. And I thought I'd go back to school and I thought I'd say I was sorry as well.'

Mrs. Willoughby was too much outraged to speak. That this woman's futility should have brought Jessica to a sense of duty when her own authority had failed!

'There's a train at half past three,' went on Jessica. 'I could catch that. Where's Mother?'

Just then Florence and James came in. After lunch Florence had been to James's office and told him about Jessica, and James had set off for home at once, working himself up into what Florence called a 'state' on the way. Interfering old devil! Who did she think she was? Oh no, he didn't come into it anywhere, did he? He was only the child's father. So the old girl had said that Jessica must go back to school, had she? Well, he was darn well going to say that she mustn't, and he was going to have his own way for once. He was sick of being treated as if he had no rights over his own family.

Reaching home and finding that Jessica had not returned there, he continued to fume at Florence and had the satisfaction of reducing her to tears – a qualified satisfaction, because she was very easily reduced to tears. Then, keeping his anger at white heat, by a recital of his wrongs (because he knew that he could only defy his mother-in-law with his anger at white heat), he hurried to The Beeches, Florence almost running to keep up with him, and into the room where Jessica stood in front of Mrs. Willoughby, looking from the distance like a prisoner in the dock.

Mrs. Willoughby threw them a quick unsmiling glance.

'Jessica's going back to school,' she said.

'She's darn well not,' blustered James. 'If the kid's unhappy there, she's staying at home.'

Mrs. Willoughby's eyes rested coolly on her son-in-law's flushed, perspiring face.

'Your tie's crooked, James,' she said.

James grabbed his tie and pulled it to the other side of his neck. Something of his advantage was, he felt, already slipping from him.

'I've decided myself to go back to school, Father,' said Jessica. The sense of importance still supported her. She was the centre of the little scene. She had run away from school, defied Grandma and had lunch with Mrs. Fowler. 'I'm not really unhappy there. Not as unhappiness goes. Or, if I am,' she added, 'it's of my own making.'

But James wasn't going to give in as easily as that.

'If I say the kid's not going back, she's not going back,' he shouted. 'There's been just about enough interference and – '

'It's still crooked, James,' said Mrs. Willoughby quietly. 'It's the one Cousin Maggie gave you last Christmas, isn't it? I always thought it an unfortunate choice. There's too much purple in it. I'll take Jessica back to school myself. . . . Oh, and, James, the way people are dumping rubbish on that piece of waste ground in Charles Street is a scandal. Everyone's talking about it. . . . Come along, Jessica. You'd better have a good wash and then get something to eat.'

She propelled Jessica gently in front of her out of the

room. James stood staring at the closed door. He looked flushed and angry and defeated.

'Damn the tie!' he said, tugging it back to its original position.

* * *

So that when Oliver approached his mother that evening she was in good fighting trim, unprepared for compromise or surrender. The hint of a crack in the foundations of her house had frightened her, and the curious feeling of resentment against the whole Fowler clan that Jessica's attitude had strengthened made her unlikely to show indulgence to Judy or her 'whims'.

'May I speak to you, Mother?' said Oliver, entering the little sewing-room upstairs, where Mrs. Willoughby sat before a pile of household mending. Mrs. Willoughby turned the eagle's beak to him, unsmiling.

'Yes,' she said shortly.

Judy was right, he thought. I *am* frightened of her. I hadn't realized it till now.

He perched on the bare wooden table among the sheets and pillow-slips.

'Look here, Mother,' he said, 'you know I've never been happy in the business. . . .'

She gave him no help, continuing to draw her needle in and out of a fine damask table napkin. After a short silence he continued: 'I'm not cut out for a business man, you know. I've given it a good trial.'

Still she said nothing.

'I'd like to get right away from Bellington. So would Judy.'

Her mouth hardened at the mention of Judy. Otherwise she gave no sign of having heard him.

'It isn't as if – I mean, I can earn my living by writing. I've had work accepted. If I had more time for it and lived somewhere more – congenial, I know I could make a success of it. We'd like to live in London.'

Mrs. Willoughby raised an expressionless face.

'There's nothing to stop you living in London or anywhere else you choose, Oliver.'

He took up a pillow-slip and began to twist it absently in his hands.

'There's the money . . .'

Mrs. Willoughby broke off a length of cotton.

'I thought you said you could earn your living. Move out of the light, please, Oliver. I want to thread this needle.'

Oliver shifted his seat on the table, knocking over a small pile of linen.

'Pick that up, please,' said Mrs. Willoughby.

'I *can* earn my living,' said Oliver, replacing the pile, 'but naturally it takes time to gain a footing and – get known. I could hardly keep myself and Judy on what I earn at first.'

'What do you suggest, then?' said Mrs. Willoughby.

'Won't you continue my salary as an allowance?'

'You were paid an allowance,' said Mrs. Willoughby slowly, 'while you were being trained for work in the mill, and you are paid a salary now that you have finished your training and are working there with Max. Apart from the mill, I see no reason for paying you either allowance or salary.'

'But, Mother – ' he protested.

She interrupted him.

'Your father founded the business and intended that you and Max should carry it on. He certainly wouldn't have consented to finance you in the nonsensical idea of frittering away your time and money in London. If you want money you must work for it.'

'I suppose you don't consider writing work?'

'No, I don't,' said Mrs. Willoughby simply.

'Palmer makes quite a good thing out of it.'

Mrs. Willoughby shrugged.

'As I said before, there's nothing to stop you going to London and earning your living by writing. You're a free agent. That's a very different thing from frittering away money your father made by the business and intended to be used for the business. He made every penny of that money by hard work. He worked fifteen hours a day and – '

'Thanks. I'm sick of hearing about that,' said Oliver, standing up and thrusting his hands into his trouser pockets.

'I'm not going to dwell on the subject. I'm merely pointing out that the business and Bellington were good enough for your father and me.'

'Well, they're not good enough for Judy and me,' said Oliver.

He was aware that he was losing his temper and conducting the interview badly, but he couldn't help it. He felt sore and humiliated.

'As you've introduced the subject of Judy Fowler,' said Mrs. Willoughby, 'I should like to tell you that I consider her, and always have considered her, a most unsuitable wife for you. With the exception of Helen, I dislike the whole family. They have a bad effect on every one of you they come in contact with. I consider Judy selfish, flighty, conceited and unreliable.'

The colour flamed into Oliver's face.

'I won't have you speaking of her like that,' he said. 'Just because she's – different, because she isn't smug and petty-minded and self-satisfied like the rest of you – '

'Don't shout, Oliver,' said Mrs. Willoughby quietly, 'and pick up that face-towel you've knocked down.'

Oliver picked up the face-towel, threw it on to the table and turned to the door.

'Oliver,' said Mrs. Willoughby.

He wheeled round.

'Yes?'

'I'll allow you three hundred pounds a year for two years. If you aren't earning enough to keep yourself by then you must come back into the business.'

He stared at her.

'Three hundred a year!' he said. 'We can't keep ourselves in London on that. And – two years! That gives me no chance at all.'

'That's my last word,' said Mrs. Willoughby, 'and I must have your final decision by the end of the month.'

He flung himself out of the room, slamming the door.

* * *

Max was just coming in by the front door when Oliver reached the hall. He often called to see his mother on his way home from the mill.

'Hallo! What's the matter?' said Max.

‘I’d like a word with you, please, Max,’ said Oliver shortly.

They went into the morning-room, and Max closed the door. At first he couldn’t make head or tail of the incoherent story that Oliver poured out.

‘Don’t worry, old boy,’ he kept saying reassuringly. ‘You’re shaping quite well on the whole. You’ve not done at all badly. It’s a complicated business to get the hang of. . . .’

When he realized that Oliver was what he thought of as ‘unsettled’, he looked a little more serious but still unperturbed and even faintly amused.

‘I hate it all and so does Judy,’ said Oliver. ‘I must get out of it. I’ve been talking to Mother, and she won’t understand. She offers me three hundred a year for two years. It’s ridiculous. Surely I’ve a right to a share of the money Father left. A moral right, anyway.’

‘I dunno about a moral right,’ said Max. ‘It was left pretty well tied up in the business, you know. No one except Mother can touch much of it.’

‘It was a damned unfair way to leave it,’ said Oliver. ‘Making slaves of us all!’

‘Oh, I dunno,’ said Max vaguely. ‘After all, it was his money.’

‘You won’t back me up, then?’

‘My dear chap, it’s not a question of backing you up. What could I do, anyway?’

‘You could talk to Mother and tell her she’s *got* to be reasonable. After all, you’re the head of the business. She’d listen to you.’

Max smiled.

'She wouldn't take the slightest notice of me. Look here, Oliver, don't be a fool. The work's not too bad. I'll see you get a rise next year. Bellington's a decent little place to live in. Helen and I are quite happy here, anyway. There's quite a decent set of people and there's the tennis club and the dramatic society and – dances and things in the winter. Why don't you take up golf?'

'Oh, hell!' said Oliver between his teeth.

The sound of the slamming of the front door re-echoed through the house.

CHAPTER FIFTEEN

Mrs. Fowler stood at the window of the drawing-room, looking out over the terrace. The rain beat against the panes in quick sharp gusts. A grey cloud hung over the garden, hiding the park and the hills beyond. Through the driving rain even the roses by the terrace balustrade looked blurred and indistinct. It may be only a shower, thought Mrs. Fowler. If it goes on, perhaps none of them will come. . . .

It was Sunday afternoon – the afternoon set apart for the family – but Mrs. Fowler was guiltily conscious that deep down in her heart she hoped that the rain would keep the family away. She had put a little pile of books on the table by her chair and was looking forward to a long quiet afternoon. Peter used to laugh at her habit of selecting a number of her favourite books to 'dip into' whenever she had an afternoon or evening free for reading. Other people, he said, just had a book and read it through till they'd finished it. . . .

'I get the same sort of gloating feeling that misers get, I suppose,' said Mrs. Fowler. 'I think I have all afternoon and evening and I can just – wallow.'

She looked round the room – friendly and gracious, with its faded cretonnes and threadbare damask, fragrant with the scent of roses and pinks and the log fire (a luxury in June) burning in the hearth. It held the suggestion of a fort in a hostile land. Here – till the family came – she could feel secure and at peace. And yet – not even here could she feel quite at peace. There was Peter's last letter. She took it from her writing-table and read it again.

Always in Peter's letters there was something that tore her heart . . . his never ceasing nostalgia for his family, most of all for Gillian . . . his wistful desire for reconciliation with Matthew. He and Rachel loved each other deeply, but they could never quite forgive themselves for what they had done. He's been unfortunate in his women, thought Mrs. Fowler with a wry little smile. Belle was too unlike him, and Rachel's too like him, too sensitive and conscientous, too ready to suffer in his suffering, to exaggerate the wrong her love had done him. And there was Matthew. . . . Mrs. Fowler only dimly understood the dark and obscure forces that had made Matthew hate Peter.

At first, of course, he had believed Belle's stories of Peter's cruelty, had seen him almost as the brutal husband of Victorian melodrama. Later he had modified this view, but continued to cherish his resentment. Mrs. Fowler suspected that Belle deliberately fostered this resentment, rousing his jealousy by means in which she was an adept, for, despite his gradual disillusionment, Matthew was still enslaved to her loveliness and to the beguiling sweetness she could put on and off at will. And he clung to his belief in Peter's unkindness because it excused, to some extent, Belle's instability and unreasonableness. She had suffered so deeply that her nerves were still ajar. All Peter's letters contained messages to Matthew, friendly, casual messages with an undercurrent of pleading, and Matthew ignored them, listening with a stony expression and making no comment when Mrs. Fowler read them to him. Once she said, 'Matthew, mayn't I send some message back to him from you?' and he answered curtly, 'No.'

But in the letter she had received yesterday Peter told her that Rachel was expecting a child. Perhaps the coming of this new life would break the threads that bound them to the past and give them happiness. Peter was doing well at his work and was now in partnership with a Dutch architect. If only they could – forget.

She shrugged as if to dismiss the problem and, sitting down in her chair by the fireplace, took up Philip Sidney's poems.

> With how sad steps, O Moon, thou climbs't the skies,
> How silently, and with how wan a face!

The timeless beauty of the words seemed to flood her whole being with peace. . . . Then, before she had finished the sonnet, she saw a thick-set figure pass the rain-blurred window and knew that Matthew had come. . . .

* * *

He entered the room and went to the fireplace, holding out his hands to the blaze and greeting her without smiling. Matthew seldom smiled. He had a round face that made you see him in retrospect as a chubby baby, but it was set generally in lines of grim discouragement. Mrs. Fowler felt less at ease with him than with any of her children. There were those long years of absence and – there was Belle. She knew that he was unhappy with Belle, but she dared not sympathize. He refused even the silent sympathy that Peter had accepted. . . . And yet he seemed to take some comfort from her presence. He would often visit her, sitting in silence, gazing abstractedly in front of him, answering shortly and a little impatiently when she tried to talk to him.

'How's Belle?' she said.

'Quite well, thanks,' he replied, frowning as if the question were intended to convey pity or demand confidence.

'I suppose she's not coming this afternoon?'

'No. . . . The weather's too bad.'

'I thought Gillian looked rather pale yesterday.'

Now that she had six grandchildren, Mrs. Fowler had followed Mrs. Willoughby's example and confined the Sunday gathering to the grown-up children and in-laws, inviting the children to tea on Saturday.

'She's all right,' said Matthew, 'she never has much colour.'

She took up her tapestry work and began to draw her needle in and out of the small canvas squares. He seemed quite content to sit there, relaxed in his chair, frowning at the fire. Sometimes she wondered if he came to her hoping for some help that he never received. She had this feeling of uncertainty and inadequacy with all her children. She shrank from bringing pressure to bear on them in any way or obtruding on their privacy, and so, she suspected, she often failed them. They wanted help and advice, and she had none to give. . . . Her thoughts went to Mrs. Willoughby. She can always give people advice. I'd be better if I had more of her in me. A little smile twitched her lips. And perhaps she'd be better if she had more of me in her. . . .

'What are you smiling at?' said Matthew suddenly.

'I was thinking of Mrs. Willoughby.'

He gave his quick impatient frown and returned to his reverie.

'Matthew . . .' she said after a short silence.

'Yes.'

'I heard from Peter yesterday.'

The hard look came into his face that always came when she mentioned Peter.

'Rachel's going to have a baby.'

Still he said nothing.

'Won't you let me send him your good wishes?'

He rose from his chair and stood in front of the fire, hands thrust deeply into his pockets, frowning gaze fixed on the hearthrug.

'It's no use discussing it,' he said. 'You don't understand.'

'Do you understand?'

He raised his eyes and looked at her sharply.

'What do you mean by that?'

There was the sound of wheels on the gravel drive and, glancing out of the window, Mrs. Fowler saw Anice and Helen descending from Helen's Daimler.

'Helen picked me up,' said Anice with a harsh little laugh as they entered. '*Such* a treat for the poor shopkeeper's wife to be given a lift by the great Mrs. Willoughby.'

'Don't be silly, Anice,' said Helen in her calm clear voice.

* * *

Mrs. Fowler sat at the tea-table, pouring out tea. Matthew handed round the cups. His abstracted rather morose air had not left him, but Mrs. Fowler still had the feeling that he was glad to be there with them all.

Judy came in, looking flushed and lovely and a little tumbled.

'I was reading in my bedroom,' she said, 'and I nearly went to sleep.'

'You ought to have gone out for a walk,' said Helen.

'On a day like this?'

'Of course. You've got a raincoat and wellingtons, haven't you? A walk in the rain is a tonic.'

'Thanks. I don't need one,' said Judy.

As she took her cup from Matthew she gave him a little *moue* that invited him to join with her in friendly mockery of Helen. The grimness of his face relaxed in answer to it.

'Oliver not come?' said Judy, perching on a shabby Queen Anne stool that had been her favourite seat since she was a little girl.

'No,' said Mrs. Fowler. 'We're a small party today. . . . Is Martin coming, Anice?'

'Martin?' Anice gave the harsh little laugh again. 'Heavens, no! He got a bundle of second-hand book catalogues by last night's post and he's still lost to the world. I had to shout at him to get it into his head that I was coming. He's almost as bad as his uncle.'

‘What about Max, Helen?’

‘He’s had to go up north on business,’ said Helen shortly. ‘The trains are difficult. He won’t be back till tomorrow.’

Helen’s life, on the surface at any rate, was complete without Max. It was she who made the decisions, organized the household and brought up the children. Max’s function was merely to earn the money necessary for these things. The children were like a miniature regiment, living their lives to an undeviating routine and obeying on the word of command. Only Clarissa, the second one, showed signs of restiveness, and these were quelled by Helen so effectively that they never reached open rebellion. Superbly assured, magnificently equal to all occasions, Helen seemed to have met with no check so far in her triumphant career as wife and mother. And yet, thought Mrs. Fowler, watching her closely, there was surely a faint cloud over her serenity today, a suspicion of unhappiness in her clear blue eyes. Mrs. Fowler was surprised by the pain that shot through her heart at the thought of any hurt to Helen. I should have imagined it would have amused me. It would have amused Millicent. Perhaps Millicent’s slowly dying, and soon there will only be Milly left. A pity, thought Mrs. Fowler dispassionately. . . .

‘Are Bruce and Patsy coming to the dancing class next season?’ Helen was saying to Anice.

‘Of course,’ said Anice. ‘I called at Crofton’s yesterday about some new dancing sandals for Patsy.’

‘She could have the ones that Clarissa’s grown out of,’ offered Helen.

‘No, thank you,’ said Anice with a sudden sharpness in her voice.

Mrs. Fowler threw Anice an anxious glance. She looked thin and worn. Her lips were beginning to take on a bitter curve. This senseless rivalry with Helen was exhausting her. Everything Helen's children did, hers must do. Everything Helen's children had, hers must have. Helen's children's friends must be her children's friends. . . . Living in a small semi-detached house in the more unfashionable part of Bellington, she forbade her children to have any dealings with the other children in the neighbourhood, condemning them to constant mockery and petty persecution. She sat up late into the night making elaborate little garments to rival those that Helen bought for her children from expensive outfitters. She skimped herself of food so that her children should attend the same dancing class and riding-school as Helen's. And so fiercely did she resent Helen's offers of help that Helen had long ceased to make them. She nagged incessantly at the children and at Martin. A few days ago Mrs. Fowler had with an effort overcome her usual reserve to remonstrate with her.

'Anice,' she had said, 'Max is a wealthy man and Martin isn't. Why don't you just make the best of things as they are? You'd get far more happiness out of life, and so would Martin and the children, if you'd try to do that.'

Anice's pale cheeks had flushed.

'I don't know what you mean, Mother,' she had replied. 'I naturally want to do the best for my children.'

And Mrs. Fowler had sighed, remembering how far back into their childhood this obscure jealousy of Helen went, how inextricably it was interwoven with the motives of almost everything she did.

Martin had at first responded to her exhortations by zealous application to the business, but get-rich-quick methods were so alien to him that he became discouraged and finally a little resentful, and he had begun of late to take refuge in the interests he had shared with his uncle – first editions, manuscripts, old prints. When Anice's nagging drove him from her he would go to the tall, shabby house and sit with the old man in the study, poring over catalogues. . . . The old man never greeted him or appeared to know that he was there, except that now and then he would silently point out an item in a catalogue or hand him a recently purchased book for his inspection. Living alone in the dark dingy house, seldom going out, he seemed almost to have lost the power of speech . . . and Martin found the silence, the absence of effort and urgency, a grateful change from the atmosphere of his own home.

Of late, Anice's restlessness had invaded the shop, and she had insisted on taking a hand in its management, introducing 'fancy goods' – leather bags, painted trays and games – without much success, for the innovation had alienated old customers and failed to attract fresh ones.

Helen began to describe a new fruit-bottling outfit that she had just bought. She's thinking of something else all the time, thought Mrs. Fowler, watching her. She's worried. . . . She glanced at Anice. Anice was listening intently, a speculative frown between her eyes, and Mrs. Fowler knew that she would give Martin no peace till she had a fruit-bottling outfit like Helen's.

'Here's Oliver,' said Judy, as another figure passed the rain-drenched window.

Her eyes went to him questioningly as he entered, but he avoided her gaze, apologizing at unnecessary length for his lateness and taking his stand on the hearthrug, where he began to discuss the political situation with Matthew in man-to-man fashion, turning his shoulder on Judy and the others. He seemed nervous and ill-at-ease, and, not being particularly interested in politics, showed complete ignorance of Mr. Churchill's de-rating scheme and appeared not to know that there was to be a general election the next year. Judy watched him, her delicate brows drawn into a frown, her slender foot tapping impatiently on the carpet. Suddenly she sprang to her feet.

'Come on, Oliver,' she said. 'The rain's almost stopped. I want a breath of fresh air.'

* * *

They walked in silence till they reached the park. Then:

'Well?' said Judy. 'Have you told your mother yet?'

'Told her what?' said Oliver.

She knew by the sulky look on his face that he was trying to evade the issue, and her lips tightened.

'That you're leaving the business and that we're going to London as soon as we're married.'

'I thought we'd gone over all that. We couldn't possibly live in London on three hundred pounds a year.'

'We could. I could get a job.'

'You don't know what you're talking about. And then – two years! Suppose I still wasn't making enough money to keep us and we had to come back . . .'

'We needn't come back. She can't force us to.'

'What would we live on?'

'Other people manage. Your mother's bullied you, Oliver, but she's made you too comfortable. You've lived too soft. You couldn't bear not to know where your next meal was coming from.'

'Could you?'

'Yes.'

'You think you could.'

'Very well, I think I could.'

'How could we have children if we were living that sort of life?'

'Better have children, living that sort of life, than have them here, where they'd belong to your mother.'

'Now listen, Judy. You want to leave Bellington because it's narrow and commonplace. Don't you see that life in London or life anywhere would be just as narrow and commonplace on three hundred pounds a year? It would be hemmed in by petty worries about bills and food and things.'

'Better that than being hemmed in by petty scandal and tittle-tattle.'

The rain began to fall again in driving gusts, and they took shelter under one of the tall elm trees. Oliver stood there, his shoulders hunched, his hands thrust deep into the pockets of his raincoat, scowling at the rain-sodden landscape.

'Three hundred a year!' he burst out at last. 'Don't you see how impossible it is?'

'Talk to your mother again, then.'

'It's no good. She won't listen.'

'What about Max?'

'That's just as useless. Between mother and Helen, Max can't call his soul his own.'

'Can you?'

He did not answer.

'Well, I'm willing to take the risk if you are,' she went on. 'It's you who're frightened.'

'I'm frightened for you, not myself.'

She threw back her head.

'You needn't be frightened for me.'

He turned to her. There was pleading beneath the sulkiness of his voice.

'Look here, Judy. I've been thinking it over. We can surely – compromise.'

'Compromise?' she flashed. 'I suppose you mean, give in?'

'No, I don't. I mean, live in Bellington but – keep in touch with things. Go up to London for plays and concerts and art exhibitions. Later, we might run to a flat there. Judy darling –'

He slipped his arm round her waist, but she flung him off, her eyes bright with anger.

'I've never despised anyone in all my life as I despise you. I wouldn't marry you now for anything in the world. I don't know how I ever could have thought you loved me. You love your coffee and kidneys for breakfast, your slippers warming by the fire. You're more like a cat than a man. You can talk, but it's about all you can do, and even that means nothing.'

Suddenly he was as angry as she was.

'You've made everything quite clear, haven't you?' he said. 'All I ever meant to you was something to help you get away from Bellington. It's a good thing I've found out in time.

You're as spoilt and selfish as my mother always said you were, and – '

He stopped, frightened by her pallor and the fire of her dark eyes.

'How *dare* you!' she said in a low strangled voice. She tore the ring from her finger and threw it on to the grass. 'There you are! Marry Emmy and have a lot of simpering brats with long noses and no chins. Sit by the fire and get fat. You're starting already. Let your mother run your life for you and tell you when to change your underclothes and where to go for your holidays. I'm sick of it all. I've finished with you.'

And before he realized what was happening, she was running back through the rain towards the house.

His face rigid with anger, he bent down to where the sapphires sparkled at the foot of the tree, slipped the ring into his pocket and strode off across the park in the direction of the main road.

CHAPTER SIXTEEN

Matthew hung up his coat and hat in the hall, smoothed back his hair and entered the drawing-room.

Belle lay on the sofa reading a novel. She turned her head to smile at him lazily as he entered.

'Hello, darling,' she said.

He was conscious of a sense of relief. She was in a good mood, anyway. She had not been brooding over imaginary wrongs ever since he left her, persuading herself that she had been deliberately excluded from his mother's tea-party. The relief was followed by suspicion, and he tried to prevent his eyes from roving round the room in search of evidence that she had not spent the afternoon alone. He was a jealous man. Belle had early discovered this, and had learnt to play on his jealousy from sheer love of tormenting him.

'Come and sit down,' she said, moving her dress to make room for him on the sofa.

He sat by her, looking at her in silence. . . .Putting up her arms, she drew his head slowly down till she could press her lips on his. She took a never-failing delight in her power over him. The secret knowledge that he fought against it and tried to throw off his enslavement lent a subtle savour to her triumph. He was difficult, recalcitrant. Peter, till just at the last, had been too easy. . . . She felt the tremor that ran through his thick-set frame at the touch of her lips and withdrew them, holding him away from her, still smiling up at him. The wide sleeves of her dress fell back, showing the rounded milk-white curve of her forearm.

'Well,' she said, 'did you have a good time in the old home? Tell me about it. Was Helen there?'

'Yes.'

'And I suppose she'd been bottling something or preserving something or running some committee, and you all had to hear about it?'

'She'd been bottling raspberries.'

She threw back her head and laughed.

'Thank heaven I wasn't there! Who else?'

'Anice. . . .'

'Oh, Anice. . . . Still panting after Helen?'

'Yes.'

'Who else?'

'Judy and Oliver.'

'Are they still engaged or aren't they? No one seems to know.'

'I presume they are. She was wearing her engagement ring, and they went out for a walk together after tea.'

'There seems to be a vague idea abroad they've had a tiff. It's high time they got married. They've shilly-shallied for long enough.'

She wondered whether she dared poke a little fun at his

mother and decided not to risk it. She had done it once, and his anger had frightened her.

'Had a lonely afternoon?' he said casually.

Malice invaded her smile.

'No, I had a visitor.'

'Oh, who was it?' he said, trying to keep the suspicion out of his voice.

Her eyes danced teasingly.

'Guess.'

She knew the name that was in his mind, and he knew that she knew it, but he did not say it.

'I've no idea.'

'I won't tell you till you've had three guesses.'

She was trying to force him to say Tony's name, exulting silently over his unsuccessful efforts to conceal his jealousy. Tony Westerham was a good-looking youth, several years younger than Belle, who had conceived an ardent admiration for her and had haunted the house till Matthew's obvious lack of cordiality had discouraged his visits. He had not ceased his visits, but came now only when Matthew was not at home.

'Moyna?'

'No.'

Her eyes still challenged him mockingly. He had to say it.

'Westerham?'

There was triumph in her laugh.

'No. . . . It was Betty Masham. She only stayed a minute or two.'

He wondered if she was telling the truth. He had caught

her out in so many lies that he could never take for granted that she was not lying. Her eyes, over-bright, glancing, slid from his.

'You're growing bald . . . here and there,' she said, putting a hand to either side of his temples and drawing his head down again.

He disengaged himself gently and rose from the sofa.

'Mother heard from Peter yesterday,' he said.

She made no comment.

'He says that Rachel's going to have a baby,' he went on.

In the silence that followed he realized that her mood had changed – suddenly and completely, as it so often did. She sat upright and rigid on the sofa, her hands clenched tightly at her sides, her lips compressed. He sat down by her again and put an arm round her shoulders. She flung it off with a quick angry movement.

'Don't. . . . Don't touch me.'

He leant back wearily against the cushions.

'Oh, for Heaven's sake, Belle,' he said, 'don't start a scene over it.'

She looked at him. Her cheeks were flushed, in her eyes was the hard brilliance that always heralded a storm.

'You don't care how much I suffer as long as there isn't what you call a scene,' she said in a high-pitched choking voice. 'You never have cared. . . . You enjoy hurting me. . . .'

'How have I hurt you?'

'Blurting it out like that. . . . You only did it to torment me because you know how much I loved Peter.'

'If what you've told me about Peter's true,' he said shortly,

'I don't see how you could have possibly loved him. In fact you've often told me that you hated him.'

She was twisting a small lace-trimmed handkerchief round and round in her fingers.

'He was only like that after that woman got hold of him. That wasn't the real Peter . . . I loved the real Peter. He's the only man I ever have loved. Those years with him were the only time in my life I've ever been really happy. . . .'

Her lips were trembling, her eyes were full of tears, but she was not so abandoned to distress that she could not throw him a quick glance to see how far she was goading him into jealousy. His face was set and expressionless.

'He'd have come back to me if it hadn't been for you,' she went on. 'If you hadn't persuaded me to divorce him, he'd have come back to me.' Her voice broke. 'I can't bear it. . . . Peter . . .' She buried her face in the cushions in a sudden tempest of tears. 'It's all your fault. I've been miserable ever since I married you. You knew that Peter would have come back. You rushed me into marrying you. And now you're gloating over me. . . .'

'Belle, do be reasonable,' he pleaded. 'Surely you realized that when Peter and the girl married they'd probably have children. I don't see that it affects you – or me – in any way at all.'

She raised a tear-stained face.

'You wouldn't. . . . You've never understood me. . . . You've never even tried to understand me. Peter's the only person who's ever understood me. . . .' She gave the twisted handkerchief a wrench, tearing the lace from the fragile linen.

His expression had darkened.

'As I said before, if Peter was the swine you've made him out to be – ' he began, but she interrupted him, putting her hands over her ears and starting up from her seat.

'Don't,' she said. 'Don't . . . I won't listen to you.'

Sobbing uncontrollably, she ran from the room.

Her bedroom door closed with a slam, but it did not keep out the sound of the high-pitched staccato sobs.

He crossed the hall to the little room he used as a study and, taking a bottle of whiskey from a cupboard, poured himself out a stiff dose, drained it, then stood listening. . . . The sounds from above were increasing in volume. Belle was deliberately working herself up into an attack of hysterics. He hesitated for a few moments then went upstairs and entered the bedroom. Belle lay on the bed, her hair disordered, her face half buried in the pillow, her slender body shaking convulsively. He closed the door and went over to the bed.

'Stop that, Belle,' he said.

She ignored him.

He bent down and took her by the arms, holding them so tightly that he seemed to be pressing his fingers against bare bone.

She screamed.

'Don't! *Matthew!* . . . You're hurting me.'

'I know I'm hurting you,' he said savagely through clenched teeth, 'and I'm going to hurt you still more if you don't stop that damned play-acting. It's the only way to deal with you. D'you hear me? *Stop* it!'

She gave another sharp cry then lay silent, her eyes closed, her breasts rising and falling.

'You beast!' she panted.

He stood, looking down at her, hating himself for the sensual pleasure the scene had given him, hating her because he knew that she had shared it. He turned to the door.

'Matthew!' she whispered, moving her head in his direction.

He went out without answering. His face was drained of colour, and there were beads of perspiration on his forehead. He walked downstairs to the hall and stood there motionless for a few moments, his hand on the handle of the study door.

For the first time since he entered the house he had remembered Gillian.

* * *

He found her in the nursery, sitting in front of a painting-book. He noticed that the page was blank. She had probably been sitting there, tense and wide-eyed, listening to the scene downstairs and to the sobs and screams from Belle's bedroom. She was a tall, thin child, with a pale, pointed face, dark shadows beneath her eyes and a nervous manner. She went to the High School now, and her reports showed her to be intelligent if somewhat erratic in her progress. At home she was expected to efface herself entirely or take her place as spoilt darling of the household according to Belle's moods. Matthew did what he could, which was not much, to shield her from Belle's uncertain temper and to give her the normal background of childhood. A brusque, irascible man in general, he had always shown an almost womanly tenderness to this child of Peter's. He sat down in the chair by the fireplace and took out his pipe.

'Painting?' he said.

She dipped her brush into the water, as if to hide the fact that she had not yet begun.

'Yes.'

Glancing at her, he saw a tight, closed look on her face. Damn Belle and those hellish scenes she made! It wasn't fair on the kid. His mind went to the household arrangements. It was the housemaid's afternoon out, and, as Belle was not passing through one of her maternal phases, probably no one had given a thought to Gillian all afternoon.

'Had your tea?' he said.

She nodded.

'I went down to the kitchen and had it with Cook.'

'Good.'

'I had cheese and pickled onions.'

He smiled.

'Not so good.'

'I liked it.'

He was conscious of a temptation to ask her who had had tea with Belle, but resisted it. He had not yet descended to pumping her about Belle's affairs. . . . The tight closed look was still on her face. He watched her, wondering what she was thinking of. She began to paint with quick jerky movements, bending her head over her work, pretending to be absorbed in it.

'Bother! I've smudged it.'

She threw the book on to the floor and leant back in her chair.

'Pick that up, young woman,' said Matthew.

She slid her eyes to him with a quick glancing look that had something of Belle in it.

'I needn't do what you tell me,' she said. 'You aren't my real father.'

He was silent. When he married Belle, Gillian had accepted him, first as her 'new Daddy', then as 'Daddy'. She had soon forgotten Peter altogether and looked on Matthew as her real father. He had known of course that, sooner or later, someone would tell her the truth, but he wished it had not happened today.

'You aren't, are you?' she persisted.

'No.'

'So I needn't do what you tell me, need I?'

'Not if you don't want to.'

She sat there, staring in front of her for a few moments, then slipped down from her chair and picked up the book.

'I do want to,' she said.

She approached him slowly, and he held out an arm to draw her to him.

'Tell me about my father,' she said. 'He was your brother, wasn't he?'

'Yes.'

He would have liked to ask who had told her, but decided that it didn't matter. The surprising thing was that she had not discovered the truth till now.

'How long have you known?' he said.

'Only today.'

Perhaps Cook had told her over the cheese and onions. Or she might have gleaned something of the facts from overhearing Belle's outburst downstairs. Anyway, it didn't matter. . . . He thought he heard a sound in the distance and stiffened as he strained his ears to listen.

'It's all right,' said Gillian reassuringly, 'she's stopped crying.'

He felt an unbearable pity for the child, and, with it, a strange sense of guilt towards Peter that he had never known before, as if he were responsible to Peter for the child's happiness and had failed in his trust. But that was ridiculous. Peter himself had deliberately abandoned his child to a woman whom he knew to be neurotic, unbalanced and vindictive.

'Tell me about him,' she said, looking up at him earnestly. 'His name was Peter, wasn't it?'

'Yes.'

'Tell me about when you were little boys together . . . what you did. . . .'

Again he was silent. To think of the boy Peter brought with it all the pain of a dead limb waking to life.

He took her on his knee.

'Not today,' he said. 'I will one day.'

She gave him the quick nervous smile that – like Peter's – was little more than a lightening of the small expressive face.

'You won't forget?'

'No.'

She flung her arms about him and clung to him, her thin body trembling.

‘I don’t want him for a father,’ she said. ‘I want you. . . . I love you. . . . I don’t like having two fathers. . . .’

She burst into tears and he held her closely to him. . . . Suddenly she sat up, smiling tremulously, wiping the tears from her cheeks with the back of her hand.

‘I’m sorry,’ she gulped. ‘I didn’t mean to cry. I won’t do it again.’

* * *

Upstairs Belle lay on her bed, watching the purple bruises slowly forming on her white arms.

A little secret smile curved the corners of her lips.

She would show them to Tony tomorrow.

CHAPTER SEVENTEEN

It was Clarissa's birthday, and Mrs. Willoughby and Helen were in the pantry, engaged on preparations for the party, which was to take place in the afternoon.

'Is your mother coming?' said Mrs. Willoughby, spreading butter over a loaf with a practised sweep of her long-handled knife. She wore a white apron with a bib and a pair of white sleeve protectors.

'I don't think so,' said Helen apologetically. 'She finds these things tiring, you know.'

'Of course,' said Mrs. Willoughby, who knew that Mrs. Fowler found few things tiring and could easily have come if she had wanted to.

'I enclosed a letter to Belle with Gillian's invitation card, asking her to come, but she didn't answer it. . . . I think that's enough bread-and-butter, don't you? They won't eat much with all these jellies and trifles and things. . . . Shall we start on the sandwiches now? Gillian sent an acceptance, very badly worded and spelt abominably. You'd have thought that Belle would have helped her with it.'

'They must begin with bread-and-butter, but – yes, perhaps this is enough. . . . I don't listen to rumours of that sort as a rule, but people are talking a good deal about your sister-in-law.'

'And Tony Westerham,' said Helen. 'I know. . . . I've got the tomatoes here ready sliced. . . . And they're saying that Matthew drinks and knocks her about.'

'There's no truth in that, of course. . . . Don't make them too thin.'

'There may be. Matthew's not a patient man, and I believe he drinks a good deal, though I don't think anyone's ever seen him the worse for it.'

'It's all most unfortunate,' said Mrs. Willoughby, her lips set in a tight line of distaste. 'Don't cut the crusts off. I never do for children. Is Judy coming?'

'No. I believe she's afraid of meeting Oliver.'

'And Oliver never goes anywhere because he's afraid of meeting Judy,' said Mrs. Willoughby, with a flicker of grim amusement on her impassive face. 'These broken engagements are always a little awkward in a small place like this. Just for a time, of course.' She spoke without rancour. Oliver had found himself the object of many unaccustomed indulgencies in his home since the breaking of the engagement. 'They'll soon get over it, and Oliver will settle down to the business. It was only that Judy unsettled him.'

'Yes . . . Judy's the youngest, of course, and she's always been a little spoilt. Mater spoilt her and so did Peter. . . . I made the cheese cakes last night. Cynthia said she'd make them if she had time, but I thought it best to be on the safe side.'

Mrs. Willoughby frowned.

‘She didn’t have time. Mr. Palmer came back yesterday and sent for her and she was working there till late. It’s very annoying. . . . Pass me that knife, will you, dear? . . . He’d been away for a fortnight and must come back the very day we needed her.’

‘I’m glad she’s had a holiday. She’s been looking very tired lately. . . . I’ll put the fruit salad into individual glasses, shall I? Children always like it that way. Anice said she might look in, but she wasn’t sure that she’d be able to manage it.’

‘I hope those reports one hears about Martin’s business aren’t true. Where’s the whipped cream? . . . Thank you.’

‘I’m afraid they are. . . . Oh, dear, I’ve filled this one too full. . . . Max and I are tired of offering to help her. We’ve given it up.’

‘She should never have married him. Everyone in Bellington knew what he was. I’ve no patience with inefficiency. Be careful how you cut that iced cake. The icing looks a bit crumbly.’

They cut the cakes and set out the chocolate biscuits in silence. Stealing an occasional glance at her daughter-in-law, Mrs. Willoughby saw that her brows were drawn together in an anxious frown. All morning she had noticed an air of troubled preoccupation about Helen.

‘Is anything the matter, Helen?’ she said suddenly.

Helen put down her knife.

‘Yes. . . .’

‘Come into the morning-room,’ said Mrs. Willoughby, leading the way.

Helen followed slowly.

'I didn't mean to tell you,' she said as she closed the door. She had gone very pale. 'But – I'm terribly worried.'

'What is it?'

'It's – Max.'

'Max?'

'Max and – that woman.'

'You mean . . . ?'

'Miss Drew, his secretary. She goes away with him on all his business trips, you know. He says they stay at different hotels, and – they may do, but . . .' She turned to the window and stood with her back to Mrs. Willoughby. 'I know there's something between them. I can tell. I called at the office yesterday and she was just typing at her desk, but – I *knew*. I knew as well as if I'd had actual proof. Max is different. I couldn't bear it if – ' She stopped, then, controlling her voice with an effort, went on, 'I keep thinking of what happened to Peter. . . .'

'Have you taxed him with it outright?' asked Mrs. Willoughby, wasting no time in sympathy or conjecture.

'No.'

'Don't,' said Mrs. Willoughby firmly. 'Just keep your eyes and ears open, and if you find out anything definite, come straight to me. There's probably nothing in it, but, if there is,' – her nose became the eagle's beak – 'I'll deal with it.'

Relief swept over Helen. Max's faithfulness seemed secured now that Mrs. Willoughby had taken it in hand.

* * *

Gillian stood in front of the cheval mirror in her mother's bedroom, anxiously surveying her reflection. Everyone in the house but herself had forgotten about the party. . . . Belle had gone to London to have lunch with Tony Westerham, and Matthew was at the office. She could have told Cook and Minnie, the housemaid, of course, and enlisted their help, but her pride prevented her. She shrank from the looks of gloating pity that they would exchange over her head. 'Poor little thing!' Cook would say, and Minnie would tut-tut and murmur, 'Fancy 'er goin' off like that with never a thought to the kid's party.'

At first she had not considered that she would need help. She would just put on her party-frock and walk down to Aunt Helen's. But when she took the party-frock from the drawer at the bottom of the chest, where it was kept, she found that something had happened to it. It wasn't only that it was creased and crumpled. That wouldn't have mattered so much. It was that it had become too short for her to wear. She hadn't worn it since last year, and it had been too short then. It looked so funny now that it would make everyone laugh. Slowly, uncertainly, she took it off and laid it on the bed. The only other possible frock was the navy-blue woollen one, with the white pique collar. She took it from the wardrobe. It was big enough and it looked quite tidy, but it wasn't a party-frock. All the other children would be wearing party-frocks. . . . Again she resisted the temptation to consult Cook or Minnie. She was tired of people being sorry for her. She stood there in her petticoat, considering the situation, then, coming to a sudden decision, slipped her school coat over her petticoat, put the two dresses over her arm and set off for Langley Place.

Cook and Minnie saw her from the kitchen window as she went down the pathway to the gate.

'Well, of all the . . . !' said Cook. 'What's she up to now?'

'Whatever it is, it's not our business,' said Minnie. 'If she wants someone to look after that kid, she should get a nurse or something.'

'She's 'ad enough of nurses,' said Cook darkly. 'It was a nurse what started the trouble.'

Mrs. Fowler, seeing the small figure trudging up the drive, a frock over each arm, came herself to the front door to meet her grandchild.

'Darling!' she said, 'whatever –'

Gillian walked past her into the drawing-room, a purposeful frown between her brows.

'Look, Gran,' she said, spreading out the two frocks over the settee. 'It's Clarissa's party today, and my party-frock's too short.' She slipped off her coat and held the tumbled pink silk frock against her thin body. 'I know it's creased, but, even if it was ironed out, it would be too short. It shows half my petticoat, doesn't it?'

'Yes,' said Mrs. Fowler.

Her heart contracted as she looked at Peter's child. The thin oval face, none too clean, was wax-like in its pallor, the thick straight fair hair was untended, the fringe falling down almost into the blue eyes.

'*This* one's all right,' said Gillian earnestly, taking up the navy-blue frock, 'but it isn't a party one, is it?'

'No,' said Mrs. Fowler.

'Well, which shall I wear? Is it better to wear a party one that's too short or a not-party one that's not too short?'

Mrs. Fowler was a little taken aback. She wasn't used to making sudden decisions. Millicent always stood apart, critical and amused, and watched other people making them, while Milly accepted any decision that anyone made for her.

'I think a good wash first,' she said, temporizing.

'Yes,' agreed Gillian, 'but after that?'

'We'll think while we're having the wash,' said Mrs. Fowler.

It's the sort of situation that Mrs. Willoughby would just take in her stride, she thought, as she moved the sponge gently over the pale cheeks. I wish I knew what to do.

'Now the nails,' she said. 'Come to my bedroom, and I'll get out my manicure set.'

'Your best one in the green case?' said Gillian, feeling pleased and important.

'Of course.'

Yes, Mrs. Willoughby would have known exactly what to do, wouldn't have felt a moment's doubt or uncertainty from the moment the child appeared at the door, carrying her frocks. . . . Perhaps if I pretend to be Mrs. Willoughby, it will come to me, thought Mrs. Fowler. . . . She stood in the middle of her bedroom and pretended to be Mrs. Willoughby . . . thinking herself with desperate intensity into that brisk, efficient personality. She glanced at the mirror on the wall, half expecting to see an eagle's beak in place of her own nose. She didn't, but in that moment she knew what Mrs. Willoughby would have done. . . .

'Put on the blue dress,' she said briskly.

'Am I going to wear that?'

'No. . . . Do up the fastenings while I ring for a taxi.'

'To Crofton's,' she said to the taxi man when he arrived.

Gillian sat entranced while the assistant in Crofton's juvenile department spread out party-frock after party-frock.

'You can choose the one you like best,' said Mrs. Fowler, feeling a little guilty, because she knew that Mrs. Willoughby wouldn't have done that.

Gillian chose a frock of peach-coloured taffeta with a pale blue ribbon belt.

'Not if it's expensive, Gran,' she whispered. 'I like it, but I'd rather have one of the others if it's expensive.'

'That's all right, darling,' said Mrs. Fowler.

'Is it cheap?'

'Terribly cheap,' said Mrs. Fowler.

Recklessly she bought new shoes and socks, a new petticoat with lace insertion and a pair of lace-trimmed drawers. 'Oh *Gran*!' gasped Gillian in ecstasy.

'And a hair-cut, please,' ended Mrs. Fowler, saying to herself, I ought to have thought of that first. Mrs. Willoughby would have. . . .

They arrived at Helen's just as the party was starting. Mrs. Fowler stood in the doorway, her eyes following Gillian in the mazes of Blind Man's Buff, aware of a little lump in her throat and thinking, I wish Peter could see her. . . .

'How sweet Gillian looks!' said Helen. 'Did Belle ask you to bring her?'

'Yes,' said Mrs. Fowler, who had never been a great stickler for truth.

Mrs. Willoughby bore down on her, majestically welcoming.

'This is an unexpected pleasure,' she said. 'I hope you'll stay and have tea with us. . . . Helen, bring that chair for your mother.'

'I can't stay, thank you,' said Mrs. Fowler. 'My taxi's waiting.' She wanted to thank Mrs. Willoughby for dealing so efficiently with the crisis of Gillian's party-frock, but realized that Mrs. Willoughby wouldn't know what she was talking about. 'So nice to see you all,' she murmured, and drifted away in a vague Milly-ish fashion.

* * *

'Now you're ready,' said Anice, putting the final touch to Patsy's hair-ribbon. 'And if you spill anything on that frock at the party I shall be very cross with you.'

'I won't, Mummy,' said Patsy, looking down reverently at the wisp of white organdie that was her party-frock. 'I'll be *very* good.'

'Where's my tie?' called Bruce from his bedroom.

'I put it out for you on the chest of drawers with a clean handkerchief,' said Anice. 'Do be quick, Bruce. The taxi will be here soon.'

'May I go to Bruce?' said Patsy.

'No, he doesn't want you bothering him now,' said Anice.

'She can come if she likes,' called Bruce.

He was a kind and conscientious elder brother, though the standard of conduct he set the five-year-old Patsy was one she often found difficult to live up to.

'Very well,' said Anice, and Patsy trotted off happily to the bedroom that Bruce kept so immaculately tidy, his possessions marshalled in orderly fashion, each in its own place. Patsy's untidiness troubled him, and he made ceaseless if unsuccessful efforts to correct it.

'If I let you stay here,' Anice heard him say as the door closed, 'you must be quiet and not touch anything.'

Anice went downstairs to the sitting-room, where Martin sat at the table, surrounded by papers, wrestling with the almost hopeless entanglement of his affairs.

'You did order the taxi, didn't you, Martin?'

He looked up at her.

'Yes,' he said, and added mildly: 'They could just as well have gone by bus. They'd hardly have had to walk at all.'

Her lips tightened.

'Of course they had to have a taxi.'

When Helen's children came to parties at her house they arrived in a car, driven by a uniformed chauffeur. The least she could do was to send her children to Helen's in a taxi.

She glanced at the piles of papers that surrounded him.

'Getting on all right?'

'Yes, thanks.'

'Do you know exactly where we stand yet?'

He re-lit his pipe before answering evasively:

'Not quite. . . .'

She stood looking at him, tight-lipped and silent. She had been like that ever since they knew that Newbolt's could not weather the storm. Tight-lipped, silent and withdrawn. She had stopped nagging at him. Her eyes returned to the papers on the table, and, seeing a second-hand book-catalogue among them, she took it up and dropped it into the waste-paper basket. He gave no sign of having noticed the action.

'If the worst comes to the worst,' she said, 'I shall get a job.'

'We might pull round,' he said.

'You know we can't,' she said shortly.

She heard the sound of the taxi and went into the hall.

'Come along, children,' she called.

They came downstairs and she gave them a final unsmiling scrutiny.

'Let me see your nails, Bruce. . . . Pull your socks up again, Patsy. . . . Have you both got your handkerchiefs?'

Bruce was a tall good-looking boy, with dark eyes and a small disdainful mouth. Patsy was a plump little roly-poly of a child, her face round and dimpled in its frame of soft brown curls.

'Remember, ladies first, Bruce. See that all the little girls have something to eat before you take anything yourself. Mind you don't get over-excited, Patsy. I shall ask Aunt Helen how you've both behaved. . . . Say good-bye to your father,' she added as an afterthought.

Bruce went into the sitting-room, and his eyes rested on Martin with dispassionate contempt.

'Good-bye, Father,' he said.

Martin looked up at him over his pipe.

'Good-bye, Bruce,' he said pleasantly. 'Have a good time.'

Patsy ran across the room and flung herself into Martin's arms, hugging him tightly. She was aware of the tension in the family atmosphere, and, though she understood little of its cause, her heart was torn by pity for the father she adored.

'Good-bye, darling . . . darling. . . .' she said.

'Good-bye, sweetheart,' said Martin, smiling at her as if to reassure her.

Outside in the hall Anice was helping Bruce into his coat. Her face softened as she watched him fastening up the buttons with that air of serious absorption he gave to everything he did. She was intensely proud of her son and took a secret comfort from the bond of affection between them.

'Look after Patsy,' she said, 'and remember to tell Aunt Helen that I'm afraid I shall be too busy to come, after all.'

Patsy came into the hall.

'You've crumpled your frock already,' said Anice reprovingly as she held out the little coat. 'Now remember "please" and "thank you", and not to have more than one helping of anything.'

She stood at the door and watched them go down to the waiting taxi. A small tousled head appeared over the fence.

'Where you goin'?' said its owner, the youngest child of the family that lived next door.

'Patsy!' said Anice warningly, seeing that Patsy was about to answer.

Bruce could be trusted to resist all overtures from common neighbours as well as to ignore their taunts, but Patsy needed constant watching.

* * *

The poor relations had come in force to the party. Miss Hatton, wearing her pink bow, sat at the piano, nodding and smiling as they played 'Come, Lassies and Lads', for musical chairs. The others sat in a little cluster, watching the children and finding in the new generation all those elusive family likenesses that they had found in the previous one.

'Do you remember that portrait of Grandmama as a child? . . . There's something about Clarissa's mouth . . .'

'And Stephen, of course, is Josiah over again.'

'I think that baby's going to have the Willoughby nose.'

'I hope the next will be a boy.'

Max, red-faced and perspiring, romped about like an overgrown schoolboy, enjoying the game as much as any of the children. He had wanted to perform conjuring tricks, but Helen, remembering his previous efforts (he was so clumsy that no one in his audience was in the least doubt as to how the tricks were performed), had firmly quashed the idea, and a professional conjurer was already unpacking his bags in the morning-room.

Gertrude and Florence hovered about on the outskirts of the game. They wore dresses of foulard silk of the same pattern, except that Gertrude's had a blue ground and Florence's a beige. Mrs. Willoughby had given them the material at Christmas and had paid Cousin Maggie to make them up. The dresses had the bunchy, over-trimmed look that all Cousin Maggie's dresses had. Both sisters were conscious of a vague sense of aggrievement because they had not been asked to come early and help with the preparations.

'Did she ask you to do anything?' said Gertrude.

'No,' said Florence. 'I could have made some of those little chocolate cakes. . . .'

‘And I could have made some of those little toadstool things with bananas and meringues. I asked her to help with Peggy’s last party.’

‘And I asked her to help with Bobby’s. . . . You’d have thought . . .’

There was a silence, during which they watched Helen, lovely, despite her pregnancy, in a dress of rust-coloured *crêpe de chine*, making overtures to a one-year-old guest.

‘I don’t really think red suits her, do you?’ said Florence.

‘No, I don’t . . . and I think a professional conjurer’s overdoing it a bit. We’ve never had one at parties before.’

This slight criticism (they never allowed themselves more than a slight criticism of anyone within the family circle) restored their spirits, and they began to watch the game.

‘Tim’s getting rough again,’ said Florence, with quiet satisfaction.

‘How’s Jessica getting on at school?’ said Gertrude.

Florence thought of the half-term report that she had received that morning – ‘Must try to work harder and not break the rules so frequently’ – and answered vaguely, ‘She seems to be good at games. . . .’

* * *

Bruce trotted decorously round with the others. He considered Uncle Max’s efforts to amuse the guests – clutching at chairs, pretending to fall over them, capering about, giving wild signs to Miss Hatton to stop the music whenever he was in a good position – extremely silly, but he joined dutifully in the laughter they excited. Patsy, of course, was helpless with laughter, but Patsy was only a little girl. His eyes scanned the faces of the grown-ups who stood talking in groups on the outskirts of the game, and he strained his ears as he passed them to find out if they were discussing his father's impending failure.

A sense of angry humiliation smouldered at his heart. He felt a bitter resentment against his father, a fierce protective love for his mother. When he was a man he would win success and give his mother money and luxury and – everything she wanted. He and she would live together (his father had conveniently faded from the picture) in a house like this, and have a car and a chauffeur and a lot of servants. He's a muddler, he thought contemptuously, and he'll never be anything else. Even that washer on the kitchen tap . . . Mummy and I had to do it again. Max was 'out' and left the game, sobbing loudly into his pocket handkerchief. The children screamed with delight. Clarissa and a little girl with red ringlets alone were left.

Cynthia and Mr. Palmer came in and stood in the doorway, watching. Cynthia looked pale and dispirited. She had been correcting proofs all day without even an interval for lunch – eating a sandwich and drinking a cup of coffee over her work.

That, of course, didn't trouble her. What troubled her was the thought of the letter she had written to Mr. Palmer while he was away, a long intimate letter in which, shedding her usual shyness and reserve, she had told him something of what he had come to mean in her life, had even hinted that, feeling as she did, it might perhaps be better if she no longer worked for him. She had written it on impulse, had posted it without stopping to re-read or reconsider it, and had lain awake all night in a cold sweat of terror, thinking about it.

An anguish of apprehension had alternated with heady excitement as she awaited his reply, but no reply had arrived. When he returned yesterday he had sent for her at once to start on the proofs. His manner had been kind but rather formal, and he had still made no reference to her letter. At first she had gone through her work heartsick with shame . . . for she knew that she could not fulfil her threat, could not face the thought of not seeing him, speaking to him every day. . . . Then gradually something of her depression had left her. Perhaps he had not received the letter . . . Letters were often lost in the post.

'Judy and her young man not here?' he said, looking round the room.

'It's been broken off,' said Cynthia. 'Didn't I tell you?'

'Oh yes,' he said casually. 'I believe you did.'

She had told him in the letter. He *had* received it then. . . . But even so her new-found hopefulness refused to be quenched. Standing there with him in the brightly lit room, with its festive atmosphere of music and laughter, the children gay as butterflies in their party-frocks, she felt herself swept up on a wave of exultant happiness. He *did* care. He *must* care. He hadn't written because he was going to speak . . . perhaps this evening . . . perhaps tomorrow . . . Oh, God, let him love me. . . . I'll be good for the rest of my life if You'll let him love me. . . .

Miss Hatton took her hands off the piano abruptly and the

little girl with red ringlets sat down on the only remaining chair. There was a burst of applause. Clarissa broke into tears, stamping a small foot in white silk sock and dancing sandal.

'She *cheated* . . . I was there first. . . . She pushed me. . . .'

What followed was like a conjuring trick. A glance from Mrs. Willoughby, a swift movement from Helen, and Clarissa had vanished as suddenly as the handkerchief was shortly to vanish from the conjurer's hat. . . .

* * *

They had had tea, and the conjurer had finished his performance. The children scuffled about, waiting for the Treasure Hunt. Gillian had felt exuberantly happy all afternoon in her new dress – and the secret consciousness of the new petticoat and drawers – but the novelty of it was beginning to wear off, and her mind had turned to the problem that had haunted it for the past few weeks.

She had learnt that Matthew was not her real father from a conversation that she had overheard between Cook and the girl who brought round the milk, and her thoughts of it had been coloured ever since by the shocked horror that had shown in their voices. It was something to be ashamed of – she didn't know why. At first she had resented Matthew's supplanting her real father . . . then, because she loved Matthew, she had been ashamed of the resentment and had shown him an almost passionate devotion to make up for it.

After that, her attitude to the problem had passed through a bewildering succession of changes. She had felt a great curiosity about Peter . . . had built up in her imagination the figure of an ideal father . . . had adored it . . . then hated it . . . then adored it again. . . .

Gradually these emotions had burnt themselves out, leaving only bewilderment. Perhaps it wasn't anything to be ashamed of, after all. . . . It might even be something to be proud of. . . . Looking at the crowd of children around her, with Clarissa (restored to favour at the price of an apology to the little girl with red ringlets) dancing about on one leg and Patsy convulsed with laughter at Uncle Max's antics, she decided to put it to the test.

'I've got two daddies,' she announced loudly to the group of children nearest her.

'*Gillian!*'

Mrs. Willoughby, Helen and a host of poor relations bore down on the group, hurrying the children away, quickly starting another game before the dreadful import of the words should have time to sink into their minds.

After that, the grown-ups watched her with something of the same shocked horror that had been in Cook's and the milk girl's voices, hastening to break up any group of children in which she found herself.

I'll ask Gran about it, she said to herself. I'll go and ask her tomorrow. . . .

CHAPTER EIGHTEEN

Judy sat on the window-seat of the Chelsea flat, sipping her sherry and looking down at the river. Arnold Palmer stood by the fireplace, one elbow resting on the chimney-piece, watching her. The flat belonged to a friend of Arnold's, who had lent it to him while he was abroad, and Arnold had brought Judy to it several times during the last month after a concert or a matinée.

It was six weeks since Judy had broken off her engagement to Oliver, but she still felt sore and humiliated. That he should have preferred the comfort of his mother's house to her love was a bitter draught for her pride to swallow. She shrank from going into the town for fear of meeting him, or, indeed, of meeting any of her acquaintances, for she was aware that people were still discussing the news with morbid relish. They knew the reason why the engagement had been broken. . . . She had wanted him to leave Bellington and Willoughbys', and he had refused. And who was Judy Fowler, anyway, to think herself too good for Bellington? And what had she got out of it, with all her airs and graces? She was Left. . . . Oh yes, said the gossips, *he* broke it off. She'd give her eyes to get him back, but he'd had enough of her.

Even the manner of her friends held a sympathy that she found almost intolerable. Emmy was now a constant visitor at The Beeches, and rumours of Oliver's engagement to her flew round the town, to be contradicted and, after a few days, repeated. Martin's failure – Newbolt's was being sold to pay his debts – deepened Judy's depression. . . . So that, when Arnold Palmer invited her to spend a day with him in London – lunch at the Savoy, a matinée and then a visit to a friend's flat for cocktails – she had accepted without hesitation. For a day at least she could escape from Bellington and all it had come to mean to her. Other invitations followed quickly.

Between the visits to London were frequent telephone calls and letters. His manner lost its whimsical detachment, became deferential, ardent. . . . And today she knew that he was going to ask her to marry him. Looking down unseeingly at the river, she was trying to decide what her answer should be. Her love for Oliver was dead. She was sure of that. When she thought of him now she felt only anger and contempt. Marriage with Arnold would salve her pride and give her the entry to a new world – a world of movement, of artistic interests, of quick casual contacts.

The inhabitants of this world might lack roots and background, but at least their minds were not centred on their neighbours' affairs. It was the world she had intended to enter with Oliver, and Oliver had failed her. Well, she would enter it in spite of him. Obscurely, half-unconsciously she felt that by entering it with Arnold she was punishing Oliver for the humiliation he had inflicted on her. Arnold, she suspected, lived only on the fringe of this world, but he spoke its language, shared its interests. He knew Paris, Berlin, Vienna almost as well as he knew London. The cottage at Maybourne was only a phase and one of which he was already tiring. And she had almost persuaded herself that she was in love with him. He was tall, handsome, distinguished-looking. . . . It gave her a thrill of pride to enter a crowded restaurant at his side. Often, when he put his hand under her arm to steer her across a street, she experienced – and encouraged – a distinct tingling of the nerves. She didn't feel as she had felt with Oliver, of course, but she didn't want to feel that again. Besides – she had proved that it didn't last. . . .

He sat watching her in silence, noting the lovely line of her averted cheek.

'Judy . . .' he said.

She turned her head to him slowly and as if reluctantly.

'Yes?'

He came and sat on the window-seat by her.

'I've been in love with you from the first moment I saw you. Did you know that?'

Her eyes – deep violet fringed with dark lashes – met his steadily and she spoke without embarrassment or self-consciousness.

'No . . . I knew, of course, that lately – '

'Will you marry me, Judy?'

She moved her eyes back to the river.

'I don't know.'

He took her hand in his. She made no movement to withdraw it.

'Do you love me?'

She looked at him with a faint smile.

'I don't know,' she said again.

He drew her to him and kissed her on the lips. A tremor shot through her. . . . She freed herself gently.

'You do love me, don't you?' he said.

'I think so, but – so many other things come into it.'

He still held her hand in his. He was surprised and – deep down in some secret part of him – a little resentful at his own nervousness and her composure.

'What things, Judy?'

Again she averted her face.

'You're a – way of escape. I could easily persuade myself that I loved you because I want to escape.'

'Escape?'

'From Bellington and all it stands for.'

'Good Lord, I should think so! . . . You're wasted in that mud-flat. Judy, you're splendid. You're starlight and sunshine. I want to shout out to the whole world that you belong to me.'

She thought, I wonder which of his heroes said that . . . and hated herself for the thought.

'I shall never belong to you,' she said. 'However much I loved you, I should belong to myself. I'm that sort of person.'

'I know you are. That's why I love you . . .' He smiled. 'Any other objections?'

She was silent for some moments then said:

'There's Cynthia.'

'What about her?'

'She's in love with you, isn't she?'

He shrugged.

'A schoolgirl infatuation. She won't grow up till she's got rid of it. It's a kindness to free her.'

'Have you ever been in love with her?'

'She's bored me inexpressibly since our first meeting.'

'Poor Cynthia! She'll hate me.'

'Judy . . .' He spoke hoarsely and a little unsteadily. 'Judy, you will marry me, won't you?'

Again she was silent.

'I shouldn't want to live near Bellington, you know,' she said at last.

'Of course not. I was going to leave the cottage anyway. You'd like to live in London?'

'I'd like to travel.'

'We'll go wherever you like . . . Switzerland, Italy, Egypt.'

She stretched out her arms and smiled.

'Oh, lovely. . . .'

Places where she could – forget, where life could begin all over again.

'I've never been abroad,' she went on. 'I've never been anywhere or done anything.'

'Then it's – settled, Judy? You'll marry me?'

'Yes.'

He took her in his arms again and kissed her. . . . I *do* love him, she assured herself . . . but in the moment of assurance a sudden sharp memory of Oliver stabbed her heart, and she stiffened in his embrace. It was as if her thought communicated itself to him. His arms dropped abruptly to his sides.

'What about – ?' He stopped, unable to say the name.

She put up her hands to straighten her hair. They were trembling slightly.

'Oliver?' she said coolly. 'I don't love him, if that's what you mean. I haven't even seen him since we broke off the engagement.'

He laughed a little harshly.

'That's all right, then. . . . Kiss me, Judy.'

He pressed his lips on hers . . . and one hand strayed down to her breast. She thought, I shall have to put up with – being mauled. Oliver didn't maul me, but Oliver didn't love me. Oliver's never loved anyone but himself. Arnold's probably what's known as an 'experienced lover'. I suppose I'm cold-blooded. . . .

'That's enough, Arnold,' she said at last.

Despite the steadiness of her voice, her usually pale cheeks were flushed.

He released her and stood smiling down at her (she *does* love me, he was saying to himself exultantly), then went over to the side table.

'Have another glass of sherry?'

'Thank you.'

He poured out two glasses, and she sat there on the window-seat looking down at the river while he stood by the chimney-piece, watching her. She thought, It's only about five minutes since I was sitting just here and he was standing just there looking at me. . . . We might hardly have moved . . . but in that five minutes I've done something that's going to change my whole life. . . . Have I done something dreadful?

Shall I look back to this moment in years to come and wish it hadn't happened? . . . I don't care . . . I'm going through with it now.

'Judy . . .'

'Yes?'

'Do you know how old I am?'

'No.'

'I'm fifty-three. Old enough to be your father. Are you shocked?'

'No. I thought you were about that age.'

'Are you wondering . . . ? I haven't, of course, been celibate all these years.'

'I could hardly expect that,' she said levelly, her eyes watching the flash of a seagull's wings against the grey stream of the river.

'I'll make a clean breast of it all,' he said.

'Please don't,' she said, with a quick intake of breath.

She felt that she could not bear to hear the dreary sagas of Arnold's amours, with Arnold as hero of each. . . .

'You'd prefer me not to?' he said.

He was disappointed. He had rehearsed the sagas and they were rather effective.

'It doesn't concern me, does it?'

'If you feel like that . . .' he said. 'But, perhaps, when we know each other better . . .'

She glanced at her watch.

'I ought to be going now.'

'Must you? We've a lot to talk about, you know. I'd hoped you'd stay here till the last train.'

An evening of dalliance with Arnold. . . . It was a test she dared not face – yet.

She shook her head.

'What about going out somewhere to celebrate, then?' he persisted.

'I think not. I'd rather go home.'

She got up and went to the mirror on the chimney-piece to renew her make-up. Over her shoulder she could see his reflection in the glass. His face was pale, his eyes hot and a little bloodshot, his lips set in a fatuous smirk. There were beads of perspiration on his forehead. She recognized it as the mask of male desire, and a sudden weariness swept over her.

'Sure you won't change your mind and have a nice cosy evening with me?' he said.

'Quite, thanks,' she said, absorbed apparently in the process of drawing her lipstick across her lips.

'When shall I come and see your mother? Tomorrow?'

'If you like.'

Beneath his passion there stirred again that faint resentment. She made him feel like a blundering schoolboy.

'What about the ring?'

'Oh yes . . . the ring.'

She had a sudden vision of herself and Oliver standing under the elm tree in the park as she tore the ring from her finger and flung it on the grass. She could smell the acrid tang of sodden leaves, hear the monotonous dripping of the rain, see Oliver's face, white and set, as he looked at her. . . .

'What would you like? Diamonds?'

Oliver's had been sapphires. Perhaps it was on Emmy's finger now. At the thought that he would hear of her engagement tomorrow morning, a cold, hard triumph filled her heart.

'May we discuss that later?' she said, drawing on her gloves.

He was conscious of an uneasy sense of frustration. Her remoteness, the odd suggestion of inviolability that she carried with her, even when he held her closely, put spurs to his passion, but he refrained from further attempts at love-making. To restore his self respect (for he was accustomed to easy conquest) he thought, She's – unawakened. I shall have to go slowly with her at first.

On the way to the station he was his old self – gay, whimsical, detached. They talked of trivial matters, made fun of the Bellington worthies, avoiding by tacit consent the Willoughby family, and touched lightly on their future plans.

He found her a corner seat on the train, bought her a selection of illustrated papers and a sheaf of American Beauties. His manner was almost paternally kind and protective. His smile held a wistfulness that touched her. It's going to be all right, she assured herself. . . . I *do* love him. . . .

* * *

Mrs. Fowler was feeling a little weary. Gillian had come to see her in the morning, and they had looked through some old snap-shots, picking out all those that included Peter. Then they had wandered round the kitchen garden, and she had told Gillian the stories of Peter's boyhood that Gillian never tired of hearing.

The day after Clarissa's birthday party Gillian had suddenly appeared at Langley Place, her small face set and earnest, and, without any preliminary, had burst out: 'Please tell me about my father, Gran, my *real* father. And – and 1 don't really *quite* understand about it.'

Mrs. Fowler had explained the situation as gently as she could, aware that no amount of explanation could make it seem a happy or a normal one. But, fortunately, it was Peter's personality that held Gillian's interest rather than the situation itself. The thought of him had a compelling fascination for her, and she was hungry for the slightest detail about his childhood. She would stand under the tree where he used to play, by the wall that used to be his 'fort', a dreamy look in her eyes, as if she actually saw the boy crouching there behind the log of wood that was his 'gun'.

'You musn't talk about this to other people, you know,' Mrs. Fowler had said. 'It must be our secret.'

Now the child's absorption in the 'secret' worried her. I suppose I've made a mess of it, she thought. I ought to have said, 'Wait till you're older.' That's what Mrs. Willoughby would have said. . . .

Hardly a day passed when Gillian did not visit her, eager for fresh stories or a recital of the old ones. Her interest included Matthew, though in a lesser degree. Matthew was a familiar, unromantic figure of her everyday life. About Peter, her real father, whom she could not remember, hung a strange, almost legendary glamour. For Matthew she felt a tenderness that had a touch of the maternal in it. She knew that he was unhappy and had a vague, unformulated idea of the cause of his unhappiness. It belonged to the dark world from which she loved to escape into the bright world of normal childhood where Peter and Matthew had once lived and where she seemed somehow to be living with them now as a playmate. . . .

Mrs. Fowler was aware that this was an unhealthy state of things. She felt that she ought to put a stop to it, but didn't know how to. And, oddly, Gillian seemed to thrive in this strange dream life. She lost her peaky look and listless expression. Unhealthy or not, it brought a sort of radiance into her starved life.

This morning, Mrs. Fowler had told her about the day when Peter, dressed in his best clothes ready for a party, had gone into the garden and fallen into a heap of soot, left for the gardener by the chimney-sweep. Matthew had tried to clean him up, and the result was that two black, almost unrecognizable figures appeared at the door of Mrs. Fowler's bedroom, and from a mask of soot Matthew's voice had issued, suavely apologetic, 'I'm afraid we've met with a slight accident, Mother.'

Gillian had laughed delightedly.

'I wish I'd been there,' she had said. 'I'd have cleaned them both up.'

'You'd only have made a third,' Mrs. Fowler had said, and they had laughed together at the thought.

Gillian had begged to be allowed to take home with her some of the snapshots of Peter.

'Just to look at when I'm in bed . . . to say good night to. . . . *Do* let me, Gran.'

And, reluctantly, Mrs. Fowler had agreed.

She had been aware of a curious sense of foreboding all the afternoon and was not really surprised when Belle burst into the drawing-room at tea-time, her face distorted by anger. She was not really surprised, either, by the things Belle said. She sat there listening as the accumulated hatred of years poured itself out . . . and seemed to be watching a turgid whirlpool from a great distance.

'She shall go to a boarding school now,' said Belle. 'When it comes to her own grandmother poisoning the child's mind with filth like this it's time something was done.'

'I suppose you found the photographs,' said Mrs. Fowler mildly. 'I admit I gave them to her and I admit that I told her about Peter, but there was nothing – filthy about it.'

Belle's answer was another outburst of abuse. Something of Mrs. Fowler's detachment left her as she listened, and her thoughts turned to the scene that would inevitably take place between Belle and Matthew when Matthew came home from his office. Matthew's anger was easily roused, and he would brook no criticism of his mother from Belle.

'. . . and I hope you're ashamed of yourself,' said Belle before she paused for breath.

Mrs. Fowler considered the question dispassionately.

'No,' she said. 'Not in the way you think. But I'm glad you've decided to send Gillian to boarding school.'

'Oh, she shall go, don't you worry,' said Belle with a harsh laugh. 'And I'll take damn' good care that you have nothing more to do with her.' With that she flounced out of the room, slamming the door so violently that the whole house seemed to shake.

Mrs. Fowler sent away her tea untasted and took up her

tapestry work. Sometimes the monotonous work of drawing the thread in and out of the canvas had a steadying effect on her nerves but today her heart remained heavy with anxiety and suspense. Had Matthew come home yet? What was happening in the little Georgian house that looked so pleasant and peaceful from the outside?

Suddenly the telephone bell rang, and, laying down her needlework on the table by her chair, she took up the receiver with an unsteady hand.

'Yes?'

'It's me, Gran,' said Gillian's clear, childish voice. 'I thought you might be worried. It's all right.'

'How do you mean, all right, darling?'

'I mean, it's all over. They've – they've finished. Mummy's stopped crying and gone out, and Daddy's in the study. I'm just going to him. I'll see that he doesn't drink too much. Don't worry.'

The voice was confident and resonant. It occurred to Mrs. Fowler for the first time that this child of Peter's was the only one of them who knew – and knew instinctively – how to manage Matthew.

'Oh,' she said, not knowing what other comment to make, and added: 'You are going to a boarding school, aren't you, darling?'

'Oh yes, that's all fixed. Daddy wants me to go, too. Isn't it lovely?'

It was as if the child were already emerging from the world of doubt and gloom in which she had lived so long.

* * *

Mrs. Fowler took up her tapestry work from the table again, then let it fall on her lap and sat motionless.... Matthew, Peter, Helen, Anice, Judy.... The shadows seemed to be closing round all of them. And I can't do anything to help them, she thought.... All I can do is to sit here and worry. At least it was Millie who sat there worrying. Millicent had been straining at the leash now for some time. Millicent wanted to go abroad. All her life Millicent had wanted to travel, but first there had been Henry (who always liked to spend his holidays in Bournemouth) and then there had been the children.... Well, they're off your hands now. There's only Judy left, and she can easily go to stay with a school friend or one of the others. She'll probably patch up her quarrel with Oliver in a week or two and they'll get married. She's only going about with Arnold Palmer to make Oliver jealous. They're all off your hands.... Yes, agreed Milly, but they need me still.... They don't need you, said Millicent. There's nothing you can do for any of them any longer. If you don't start living your own life now you never will. Forget them.... Shut up the house and go abroad for a year... two years.... See the places you've always longed to see....

She rose, and, going to a drawer in her bureau, took out the travel pamphlets that Millicent kept there to browse over when the wander-fever took her. Why not Norway first...? She saw the fjords deep blue beneath a cloudless sky, with the green pine trees climbing up to the snow-misted heights.... Then Denmark... Copenhagen with the lovely statue of the Little Mermaid and the dream forest of Charlottenlund... then –

She heard the door open and slipped the travel booklets behind her cushion.

It was Judy.

'Well, darling?' said Mrs. Fowler, turning a welcoming smile to her.

Judy didn't speak. She whipped off her hat and, drawing up her stool, sat down on it, leaning her head against Mrs. Fowler's knee.

'Is anything the matter, Judy?' said Mrs. Fowler, laying her hand on the dark hair in a light caress.

'I'm going to marry Arnold Palmer,' said Judy.

'Oh, Judy!' Her hand still moved softly over the shining raven-dark hair. 'Have you thought it over carefully?'

'I know what you mean. . . . Yes, I've thought it over carefully.'

'Do you think you'll be happy?'

'I don't know. . . . How does one know? But – you'll always be here, won't you?'

Mrs. Fowler was silent. Judy looked up at her. There was sudden sharp anxiety in the violet eyes.

'You will, won't you?' she said breathlessly. 'You'll always be here – just like this?'

Mrs. Fowler seemed to see Millicent creeping to the door defeated, her travel booklets under her arm.

'Yes, darling,' she said reassuringly. 'I'll always be here – just like this.'

CHAPTER NINETEEN

Cynthia and Cousin Effie sat at the table in the sewing-room, stitching name tapes on the pile of household linen that Mrs. Willoughby had bought, according to her custom, at the Summer Sales. Mrs. Willoughby was giving one of her periodic family luncheon parties today, and Cousin Effie had, in its honour, put on her whole collection of jewellery, together with a heavily beaded 'modesty vest'. She wheezed rhythmically as she worked, and occasionally made comments on the weather or family affairs which Cynthia received in silence.

Ever since she heard of Judy's engagement Cynthia's spirit had seemed to wander in a fog of misery and despair – a fog so black that it shut out all hope and purpose from life. In order to fill the long, empty days, and to hide her hurt from those around her, she had flung herself into a feverish round of domestic activity. She turned out drawers and cupboards; she went every day to help Gertrude, whose maid was away on holiday; she made jam, pickles, bottled fruit. . . .

Deliberately she neglected her appearance, taking her hair back into an uncompromising 'bun', dispensing with make-up, savagely despising herself for the romantic dream in which she had lived so long. Oliver she avoided, as he avoided her. It was strange, she thought with a wry smile, that they should both go about the same house silent and unhappy because of Judy.

As she devoted herself to housework, Oliver devoted himself to his work at the factory. Mrs. Willoughby was pleased with him. He was, she considered, settling down at last. And Emmy pursued him with quiet, unremitting determination, accepting his snubs, enduring his petulance, crying when he was most unkind, but always, as Helen put it contemptuously, 'coming back for more'. Mrs. Willoughby was pleased about that, too. Marriage with Emmy would bind him to Bellington and the business.

Cynthia had not seen Judy or Arnold since she heard of their engagement. From Arnold she had received only a formal note thanking her for her services and telling her that they would no longer be required. The cottage had been put up for sale and was now occupied by two middle-aged women, who kept hens and ducks and geese in the garden and served 'Teas' in what had once been the study. On the one occasion when Cynthia had had to go into Maybourne she had cycled three miles out of her way to avoid passing it.

And last week Judy and Arnold had been married quietly in London, thus depriving Bellington of the wedding festivities and adding another item to its score against Judy. On the night of the wedding, Cynthia had lain awake till dawn, sobbing noiselessly into her pillow. Helen, who had been to the wedding, told her that Judy looked very beautiful and seemed very happy. It was obvious, she added, that Arnold was very much in love with her. They were going to spend the honeymoon in Italy. . . .

And now, as she drew her needle in and out of the linen, she tried not to think of them, tried not to see Arnold's face looking down at Judy with the smile – half tender, half amused – that she knew so well.

'Listen,' said Cousin Effie suddenly. 'They've come. . . .'

She heard the sound of voices in the hall – Gertrude's, Florence's, Helen's – and laid down her work.

'I'd better go,' she said.

As she crossed the hall the housemaid was just admitting a young man with rough-hewn features, a blunt nose, a long mouth and an expression of almost comical good-humour. A sharp pang shot through her heart. . . . She had seen him last at Arnold's cocktail party a year ago. Arnold, genial and charming, moving about among his guests. . . . The memory hurt almost unbearably and she felt a sudden fierce anger with the man who had summoned it.

His ingenuous young face lit up with pleasure when he saw her.

'I don't suppose you remember me, Miss Willoughby,' he said. 'I'm Denis Gordon.'

'How do you do,' she said stonily. 'Come into the drawing-room.'

The drawing-room was empty. He stood on the hearthrug and beamed down at her.

'It's grand meeting you again like this,' he said.

'I'll tell my mother you're here,' she said and went quickly from the room.

Mrs. Willoughby was in the kitchen, supervising the final arrangements for lunch, and the others had joined her there. Florence was showing her some patterns of gingham that she had got from Crofton's that morning.

'It's for Jessica's summer frocks, you know,' she was saying. 'Which do you think I should have? I rather like the blue.'

'Blue's apt to fade,' said Mrs. Willoughby. 'Have the pink.'

'Yes, of course,' agreed Florence. 'I'll have the pink. I'll order it this afternoon.'

Gertrude was as deeply absorbed in the choice of the gingham as Florence. Helen stood by the window, gazing out at the back garden with an air of abstraction.

'That friend of Oliver's is here,' said Cynthia.

'Oh yes,' said Mrs. Willoughby, 'Oliver said he might be coming for lunch. He's staying with an aunt. . . . Will you see to the table napkins, Cynthia, and make sure the flowers are all right? Cousin Effie's done them, but . . .'

She left the sentence unfinished. Cousin Effie was always hurt if not asked to 'do' the table napkins and flowers, but she made depressed-looking little hats of the table napkins and 'did' the flowers by the simple method of ramming into each vase as many flowers as it would hold.

'Very well,' said Cynthia.

Mrs. Willoughby went slowly to the drawing-room, followed by the others. She had been troubled lately by a painful form of rheumatism in her hip and had come to rely on Cynthia a good deal.

Still with that stony anger at her heart (for to whip up her anger dulled the pain a little), Cynthia refolded the table napkins and rearranged the flowers, removing half the contents from each vase and putting them into a large Chinese bowl on the sideboard.

When she returned to the drawing-room Oliver and Emmy had arrived, and Denis was inviting the whole party to tea at his aunt's on Saturday.

'It's only about six miles,' he was saying, 'and my aunt would love you all to come over.'

'Thanks . . . I'd like to,' said Oliver.

'But, Oliver,' said Emmy timidly, smiling her rabbitty little smile, 'we were going to that concert on Saturday.'

'What concert?' said Oliver, contracting his brows.

'The one at the Town Hall.'

'I don't remember anything about it,' said Oliver shortly.

Emmy's indeterminate little mouth trembled, and her eyes filled with tears.

'You'll come, won't you, Miss Willoughby?' said Denis to Cynthia.

Meeting his eyes, she was aware of something bright and warm trying to penetrate the coldness round her heart, and she shrank from it in sudden panic. No, she couldn't go through *that* again. . . . All she wanted now was to be left alone in this refuge of drab unexacting duties that she had made for herself.

'I'm afraid I can't manage it,' she said.

'We could arrange it for some other day,' persisted Denis. 'What day would suit you?'

'I can't manage any day,' she said with a curtness that made the others turn to her in surprise, and went to sit with

Florence and Gertrude on the settee, pretending to be absorbed in the gingham patterns. A hot, unbecoming flush had flooded her cheeks, and her heart was beating unevenly.

* * *

Lunch was over. Florence and Gertrude had gone into Bellington to buy the gingham, Oliver had set off for the mill, accompanied by Denis, and Emmy, who was always the last guest at any function, because she could never make up her mind to go, wandered disconsolately down the road, uncertain whether to return home and have a good cry or to follow Florence and Gertrude into Bellington. Cynthia had gone back to the sewing-room immediately after lunch, refusing even to join the others for coffee.

Only Helen and Mrs. Willoughby were left in the drawing-room. Mrs. Willoughby looked round at the empty coffee-cups.

'I've told Oliver over and over again not to put ash in his saucer,' she said, 'but both he and that young man did it. It's a disgusting habit. There are plenty of ash-trays about. . . . I was expecting Max to lunch, Helen. Why didn't he come?'

Helen shrugged.

'I suppose he was lunching with that woman.' She took a letter from her handbag and gave it to Mrs. Willoughby. 'I found this last night. It – doesn't leave much room for doubt, does it?'

Mrs. Willoughby read the note in silence.

'No,' she said, handing it back.

'What shall I do?' said Helen.

She looked unhappy and bewildered and unsure of herself. Mrs. Willoughby remembered that once – only once – she had had a little – only a little – trouble with Josiah, and she had felt like that. . . . It was the only time she had felt like that.

'Have you mentioned it to him?'

Helen shook her head.

'Don't, then. . . . Where did you find the letter?'

'In his sports coat pocket. I was looking for the key of the garden shed. I oughtn't to have read it, of course, but –'

'Of course you ought to have read it,' said Mrs. Willoughby.

She hadn't any patience with that sort of thing. If a woman wanted to know what her husband was up to, she had every right to go through his pockets.

'It didn't really tell me anything I didn't know already.'

Mrs. Willoughby looked at her watch.

'He'll be back at the mill now. . . . I'll go there and see him.'

'Oh . . . do you think that's the best thing to do?' said Helen, taken aback.

'Yes,' said Mrs. Willoughby.

'Shall I come with you?'

'No. What were you going to do this afternoon?'

'I was going to see Anice.'

'Then go and see Anice. Put the letter back in his pocket as soon as you get home, and, if he mentions the matter to you, pretend to know nothing about it. Now get me my hat and coat from my bedroom to save me going upstairs.'

Half an hour later, Mrs. Willoughby entered Max's office. Max sat in the swivel chair at his desk, and Miss Drew – a pretty girl, with a weak mouth, china-blue eyes and ash-blonde hair – sat at her typing-table near him. Max rose with a smile of welcome and brought forward the armchair kept for visitors.

'Sit down, Mother,' he said. 'Nice to see you.'

Mrs. Willoughby ignored him and turned to the girl.

'How much does Mr. Willoughby pay you, Miss Drew?' she said in a curt, business-like voice.

Miss Drew, too, had risen to her feet. She stared for a few moments at the visitor, then stammered:

'Three pounds a week.'

Mrs. Willoughby opened her bag and took out some notes.

'Here is your salary for this week and next. You're dismissed.'

The girl stared and blinked, then tossed her head with an attempt at bravado.

'I take my orders from Mr. Willoughby,' she said.

'You'll take this one from me,' said Mrs. Willoughby grimly. 'And now will you go at once or shall I have to have you turned out?'

The girl looked at Mrs. Willoughby, then at Max, then again at Mrs. Willoughby. There was a silence during which the ticking of the ormulu clock on the mantelpiece could be heard.

'Look here, Mother – ' began Max indignantly.

Mrs. Willoughby did not move her eyes from the girl's face. Miss Drew tried to return her stare, but the china-blue eyes dropped in discomfiture, the small mouth began to twitch, the air of pert assurance vanished.

‘Well?’ said Mrs. Willoughby implacably.

Suddenly the girl burst into tears, snatched up her hat and coat and ran from the room.

‘Look here, Mother – ’ began Max again.

Mrs. Willoughby’s eyes wandered round the room.

‘I think those curtains need cleaning, Max,’ she said. ‘I’ll have the others put up next week and send those to the cleaners’. I’m sorry now that I got that colour. It shows the dirt so soon.’

‘Mother, this is outrageous,’ said Max, but he met Mrs. Willoughby’s eyes, and his bluster died away into an angry muttering. He stood there like a small boy caught out in some flagrant misdemeanour.

‘I’ve intended for some time,’ said Mrs. Willoughby, ‘to tell them not to put such a high polish on this floor. It looks well, I know, but it’s dangerous, especially with those mats about.’

‘Listen, Mother – ’

‘I wish you’d call at Durant’s on your way home, Max, and remind them to send to The Beeches for that armchair. The spring’s almost through the seat, and I particularly asked them to send for it yesterday.’ She glanced at her watch. ‘Well, I have several things to do in the town, so I’ll go now. Don’t trouble to see me out.’

She went down the long corridor towards the main entrance. Oliver was coming out of one of the doors with a sheaf of papers in his hand. Mrs. Willoughby stopped.

‘Oliver,’ she said, ‘if there aren’t enough ash-trays at home, I’ll gladly get some more, but will you *please* not put your cigarette ash on the saucer of your coffee-cup? It’s a disgusting habit and gives the maids a lot of unnecessary trouble,' and went on without waiting for him to answer.

He stood there, looking after her, the ill-humoured expression on his face relaxing into a faint smile.

* * *

As soon as Mrs. Willoughby had left him Max went round to the tea-shop where he and Miss Drew occasionally had tea together, to find her sitting alone at a table, staring in front of her with set angry face. He sat down next to her.

'Dorrie . . .' he said.

'Yes, I hoped you'd come,' she said. 'We've quite a bit to talk about, haven't we?'

Her tone was not encouraging.

'I'm sorry, Dorrie. . . . You see – '

'Oh yes, I see all right,' she said with a harsh little laugh. 'I see what all your high-falutin' words mean when it comes down to brass tacks. There you sat and let her insult me.'

'She didn't insult you,' said Max. 'She hardly said anything.'

'She looked it, then. I've never been looked at like that in all my life before.'

Max tried to take her hand, but she snatched it away.

'Leave me alone . . . I always knew there was a yellow streak in you. If you'd had the guts of a louse you'd have stood up for me.'

She had raised her voice, and Max was glad that the tea-shop was almost empty.

'Listen to me, Dorrie,' he began, but she interrupted him.

‘I’ve had enough of listening to you,’ she said. ‘You never loved me. You know you didn’t. We both knew all the time you didn’t. You only took up with me because your wife hadn’t any use for you, and, now I know you better, I don’t wonder. She can have you back and welcome, you dirty coward.’

He had flushed a dull red.

‘All right,’ he said stiffly, ‘if that’s your attitude . . .’

‘It is,’ she said, drawing on the coat that she had thrown over the back of her chair. ‘I’ve finished with you and I’ve finished with Bellington. You can damn’ well get another girl to listen to your mealy-mouthed bunkum and find out what a lousy cur you are. And you’d better ask your mother’s permission before you take her to the pictures or you’ll be getting into trouble.’

Secretly she welcomed the ending of the affair. She had had high hopes of it at first, even believing at one time that she could persuade Max to divorce his wife and marry her, but she had long since realized that it was leading her nowhere. He hadn’t even given her any presents worth speaking of.

‘Good-bye,’ she said, spitting the word out at him viciously, ‘and I hope I never set eyes on you again – or that blasted old she-devil either,’ she added as an afterthought.

With that she swung out of the shop on her stilt-like high heels, *retroussé* nose held high, small mouth pursed in exaggerated disdain.

* * *

He was still seething with anger when he reached home, and all of it was concentrated in his mind on Helen. She must have been spying on him. That last letter. . . . Had he left it in his sports coat pocket? Had Helen found it and shown it to his mother? It was the sort of thing a woman would do. . . . Spying on him . . . going through his pockets. . . . She deserved all she got and he'd tell her so. He'd assert himself at last. 'Coward' . . . 'yellow streak' . . . 'cur'. . . . The memory of the words rankled deeply.

On reaching home, he went straight up to his dressing-room and felt in the pocket of his sports coat. The letter was still there. He took it out and stood staring at it fixedly as if trying to discover whether Helen had read it. Then he tore it into shreds, flung it into the waste-paper basket and went downstairs to the drawing-room. Helen was sitting in an armchair, her feet on a footstool, embroidering a little frock.

'Hello, darling,' she said, smiling a lazy welcome. 'Had a good day?'

He stood looking down at her, his face dark and lowering.

'Helen,' he said, 'did you know that my mother called at the office today?'

'Did she?' said Helen, carefully drawing out a strand of pale blue silk. 'I knew she was going into Bellington. She often does call at the office, doesn't she?'

'You know that she called at the office,' he said sullenly, 'and you know why.'

She gave him a look of innocent surprise.

'Darling, why should I? Something to do with your carpets or dusters or something, I suppose? She always likes to have two spring cleanings a year, you know, and I suppose the second one's about due.'

He was silent. Perhaps Helen didn't know. He'd be a fool to let the cat out of the bag if she didn't. Perhaps someone else had told his mother, and Helen knew nothing. Now that the wave of anger was dying down he realized that the less he said, the better. But – *did* Helen know?

'Had Mother anything to tell you this morning?' he said.

'Let me see,' said Helen, considering. 'No, nothing important. Gertrude had had a letter from Jessica. Gillian seems to be settling down well at school. That friend of Oliver's came to lunch. . . . Max darling, be an angel and pass me my other work-box. It's on the table. I'm too lazy to move.'

He passed her the box in silence. She went on talking unconcernedly as she drew her needle in and out of the white *crêpe de Chine*.

'I went to see Anice this afternoon. Martin still hasn't got a job. Anice says she's going to get one herself. She's learning typing and shorthand and book-keeping. She went up in the air again when I suggested our helping them. I really haven't any patience with her. . . .' She held up the little smock. 'Babs will look sweet in this, won't she?'

He stood there, uncertain, ill-at-ease. His anger had turned to a smouldering resentment. He felt that he'd been cheated, bamboozled – *managed* somehow by the two of them, but he didn't know how. He'd finished with that little slut, Dorrie, anyway. He'd only turned to her because she was young and fresh and gay and, as it had seemed then, in love with him. Wistfulness invaded his spirit. His youth was slipping from him and with it his last hopes of romance. If only Helen weren't so damned self-sufficient!

The telephone bell rang. Helen took up the receiver.

'Yes?'

'That you, Helen?' said Mrs. Willoughby. 'Has everything gone all right?'

'Yes . . . I think so.'

'Well, tell him that Cousin Effie will call with the other curtains tomorrow morning and take those that are up now to the cleaners.'

'Yes, I'll tell him.'

She put back the receiver.

'Who was that?' said Max.

'Mother.'

He looked at her suspiciously.

'What did she want?'

'She wanted me to tell you that Cousin Effie will be calling with the curtains tomorrow.'

'Oh,' said Max.

Something disconsolate in his voice and manner touched Helen despite herself. He seemed for a moment as if he were one of her children asking for help and comfort. And her relief at the ending of the affair (for she knew instinctively that it was ended) revealed to her in an illuminating flash of knowledge how great a part this large, rather foolish man played in her scheme of things; how bleak and empty life would be without him.

She rose and took from her desk a letter that she had received that morning from Stephen's headmaster.

'I wanted to consult you about this, Max,' she said. 'It's from Mr. Randolph. He says that Stephen could be moved up at the end of the term if we like, but he thinks it would be better for him to stay down for another term. He missed a good deal, of course, when he had measles. What do you think? He's well below average age. Do you think it would be good for him to stay down for another term?'

Max cleared his throat.

'Er – yes,' he said judicially. 'Yes, I do.'

'And perhaps it would be as well if you had a little talk with him in the holidays. His half term report wasn't very good.'

Max felt vaguely flattered. Helen didn't usually ask his advice. He had often felt piqued by her telling him of arrangements she had made about which he considered that he should have been consulted. It occurred to him suddenly that perhaps Helen wasn't quite as self-sufficient as she seemed. Perhaps it had been his fault. He had been engrossed in the business, and Helen had not liked to trouble him with domestic details. He must try to pull his weight more in the future.

'Yes, dear,' he said. 'Of course I will.'

* * *

Mrs. Willoughby turned from the telephone to find Oliver standing by her.

'I'm going to London next week, Mother,' he said.

She was silent for a few moments, then said:

'Very well, Oliver.'

'I shall probably take a room there permanently.'

Mrs. Willoughby suddenly realized that she was tired, so tired as to be almost unequal to this fresh complication.

Moreover, the nagging pain in her hip had worsened since her expedition into Bellington. For the first time since she could remember she felt at a loss. . . . She spoke, however, in her usual short authoritative manner.

'I hope you're not starting that nonsense about wanting to leave the business again, Oliver,' she said.

'No. I shall be here as usual during the week. I shall use the London room for occasional holidays and weekends.'

He tried to stop there and was annoyed with himself because he felt impelled to continue with explanations, almost excuses. 'I'm more interested in London plays and concerts and art exhibitions than in any diversions that Bellington has to offer. You see, I don't play golf like Max. . . .'

She threw him a keen glance. He stood there, his hands in his pockets, his mouth set. The sunlight showed up the lines on his thin face. They had deepened in the last few months. He looked irritable, ill-humoured and unhappy. . . . Oliver with rooms in London. It was a startling idea, but, after all, the danger of his marrying Judy was over now, and this small spurt of independence might make him more contented. He would probably tire of it soon enough.

'Very well, Oliver,' she said, as if graciously extending her permission. 'I'm quite willing to agree to that.'

She waited for his thanks, but he looked at her unsmiling and said quietly:

'I should do it whether you agreed or not.'

CHAPTER TWENTY

Mrs. Fowler stood at the door of Anice's house, conscious of that slight sinking of the heart that she always felt before entering it. Martin answered her knock. He held a tin-opener in his hand.

'Oh, come in, Mother,' he said, standing aside. 'I'm just getting the tea.'

She went into the living-room, where tea was laid on the big square table.

'Sit down,' said Martin, drawing up a chair towards the fire. 'I'm expecting the children any minute, and Anice shouldn't be long now.'

'Let me give you a hand,' said Mrs. Fowler.

'No, that's all right,' he said. 'It's well under weigh. I was just opening a tin of sardines.' He looked at the table. 'Have I got everything?'

'Yes, I think so,' said Mrs. Fowler, who found Martin's absorption in his house-keeping duties rather touching.

It was five years now since Newbolt's bankruptcy, and Martin had not yet found another job. His manner was hesitant and diffident, and his name was connected in the neighbourhood with failure and inefficiency. At last, Anice herself had taken a job as secretary to Mr. Creighton, Bellington's leading solicitor. After much persuasion she had allowed Mrs. Fowler to pay the rent of the house, but she still obstinately refused to accept any help from Helen and Max. Martin, while continuing to search for work in a desultory way, looked after the house and children in Anice's absence.

'I've washed one or two things for Anice,' he said, as he set the dish of sardines on the table. 'She does the washing at the weekend generally, and it's rather a lot for her. They're on the line now, but they don't seem to be drying much. Do you think it's any good leaving them there?'

'No, I think I'd bring them in,' said Mrs. Fowler. 'Let me help.'

Together they brought in the washing – tea-cloths, towels, pillow-cases, handkerchiefs – and hung them over the clothes-horse in the kitchen, then Martin opened the oven door and looked anxiously inside.

'I've made a stew for supper,' he said. 'I think it's going on all right. I'll turn the gas down now.'

'You're a very capable housewife, Martin,' said Mrs. Fowler as they returned to the living-room.

His ugly mouth flickered into its rare smile.

'It's quite interesting in a way,' he said. 'I made some pastry last week. It was a bit heavy, but it wasn't bad on the whole.'

There was the sound of the opening of the front door and Patsy ran into the room, flinging herself into her father's arms.

‘I’m not too late to help, am I, darling?’

‘No, of course not,’ he said. ‘Let’s go and put the kettle on.’

Bruce entered more sedately, greeted his grandmother with punctilious politeness, ignored his father, and began to arrange his books on the small writing-table, where he did his homework.

Patsy went into the kitchen with Martin, and they heard her clear, childish laughter as she chattered and ‘helped’. . . . They returned together, Patsy carrying a plate of biscuits, Martin a dish of tinned pineapple.

‘Tinned pineapple, Bruce,’ said Patsy excitedly. ‘Isn’t it lovely!’

‘Yes,’ said Bruce shortly, and Mrs. Fowler caught the look of contempt he shot at Martin as Martin set the dish on the table.

‘Here’s Mummy,’ said Patsy, but it was Bruce who leapt from his seat and ran down to open the gate for Anice. She looked tired and nervy as she came into the room. There were dark shadows beneath her eyes, and her lips were set in a thin tight line. Even her greeting to her mother was curt and unsmiling. Bruce hovered about her, taking her hat and gloves, arranging the cushions in the armchair into which she sank, bringing up a footstool, while Patsy and Martin gave the finishing touches to the tea-table. There was a sympathy and solicitude in Bruce’s manner that was obscurely but unmistakably directed against Martin. At every visit, Mrs. Fowler found the division of the small family into two camps more marked.

'Your hands are filthy, Patsy, and so are yours, Bruce,' said Anice. She turned to Martin, and there was an edged sharpness to her voice as she added, 'You might at least have seen to that, Martin.'

The children ran upstairs, and Martin went into the kitchen to make the tea. Anice lay back in her chair, closing her eyes.

'Well, tell me all the family news,' she said.

'I think you know most of it,' said Mrs. Fowler. 'Peter's going into a sanatorium next week.'

Anice shrugged.

'He worried himself into T.B., wondering whether he ought to have left Belle. I haven't any patience with him. He wanted to eat his cake and have it.'

Mrs. Fowler was silent. The birth of Michael, Peter's son, had seemed to bring him peace, but a year or two ago the signs of tuberculosis began to show themselves and, though he wrote cheerfully, it was clear that the disease was making headway.

'I'd hoped that when he got a child of his own . . .' she said at last, and ended the sentence with a sigh.

'Children of one's own, as you should know, Mother,' said Anice dryly, 'don't often simplify life. . . . Have you heard from Judy?'

'I heard yesterday.'

Judy wrote regularly to her mother – hard, bright, impersonal letters that told her nothing of Judy herself.

'Meals at the Savoy and theatres and concerts, I suppose?' said Anice.

The bitterness in her voice made Mrs. Fowler's heart contract.

'She'd had lunch at the Savoy and been to a concert,' she answered quietly.

'That leaves Matthew and Helen, doesn't it?' said Anice. 'I can probably tell you more about Matthew than you can tell me. Belle came to see Mr. Creighton this morning. It seems that she's at last persuaded Matthew to do the gentlemanly thing and let her divorce him, so that she can marry Tony Westerham. The condition that Matthew made was that he should keep Gillian.'

'I didn't know that,' said Mrs. Fowler. 'Poor Matthew!'

Again Anice shrugged her thin shoulders.

'He's only getting what he asked for. He must have known what Belle was like.'

'I don't think he did.'

'More fool he, then!'

'Anice, my dear!'

'I'm sorry, Mother. I'm afraid I haven't much sympathy to spare for other people's troubles these days. . . . It'll be odd for you to think that both your sons are divorced husbands of Belle's, won't it? That only leaves Helen. Have you seen her lately?'

'I was there yesterday. . . . Anice, she was terribly disappointed that you won't let Patsy and Bruce go to Babs's party. She really wants them – and you.'

'I'm sure she does,' said Anice with a little twisted smile. 'Poor relations are in the Willoughby tradition, aren't they?'

Martin came in with the teapot.

'Tired, darling?' he said solicitously.

'Why trouble to ask that question every time I come in?' said Anice shortly. 'You know that I'm always tired after a day's work.'

'Well, tea's all ready,' said Martin cheerfully. 'Have yours where you are, dear.'

'No, thank you,' said Anice, moving to her seat at the head of the table.

It was an uncomfortable meal. Anice nagged incessantly. She found fault with the tea, the bread-and-butter, the table-cloth. She blamed Martin for putting the jam-jar on the table, ignoring Patsy's timid reminder that she had blamed him the day before for turning it out into a glass dish.

When she had finished her tea she pushed her plate away with a quick, jerky movement.

'Don't forget to chop some firewood before you start your homework, Bruce,' she said.

It was a task she always set him and that he always resented.

He sat there for some moments in silence, a dark scowl on his face, then said slowly:

'Why can't Father do it? He's got nothing to do but loaf about all day.'

Two bright red spots blazed in Anice's pale cheeks.

'How *dare* you say that!' she said. 'Go out of the room!'

Still scowling, he rose from his seat and went out. They heard him go upstairs to his bedroom.

Anice turned to Martin.

'If you were half a man you'd have thrashed him for that,' she said. 'No wonder your own children despise you.'

They had forgotten Patsy. She stood by the door watching them, eyes dilated in her small, anguished face.

'I – I'm going out,' she said in a strangled voice.

'Yes, go out, pet,' said Martin. He spoke in his usual kindly, cheerful voice, and his eyes held hers steadily as if to reassure her. 'Go into the garden and get us some vegetables for supper. Get whatever you like.'

She smiled at him tremulously, keeping her eyes on his . . . while gradually the world became normal and familiar again, losing the nightmare quality that had for a moment invaded it.

'May I get carrots?' she said.

Martin lit his pipe and threw away the match.

'Yes, that's grand. We all like carrots. Find us some nice big ones.'

They saw her running lightly past the window on her way to the vegetable patch.

* * *

Mrs. Fowler followed Anice into the kitchen and closed the door. Anice busied herself at the sink, keeping her back to her mother.

'Anice,' said Mrs. Fowler, gathering her courage, 'do you realize that you're in danger of becoming a shrew?'

Anice wheeled round. Her face was working.

'Yes, I do,' she said. 'You needn't tell me. I know but – I can't stop. I – hate myself for it, but – I can't stop.'

She sat down at the kitchen table, and, burying her head in her arms, burst into tears.

Mrs. Fowler laid a hand on her shoulder, but Anice, still sobbing, shook it off.

'Please go . . .' she said.

Mrs. Fowler went back to the living-room, where Martin was piling the used crockery on to a tray.

'I think I'll be going home now, Martin,' she said.

'Yes . . .' he agreed. 'I'm sorry. I'm afraid it's not been much fun for you.'

'Anice is crying.'

'I know . . . I won't go to her. She'd always rather be alone when she's upset. She gets over-tired, you know.'

He walked with her down the little path to the gate. At the gate he said:

'I think I'm going to emigrate.'

'Emigrate?'

'Yes. I've written to someone I know in Sydney. I don't mind what sort of work I do. . . . Then Anice and the children can come out to me.'

'Have you told Anice?'

'Not yet.' He gave her the same gentle, reassuring smile that he had given Patsy. 'You needn't worry, you know. I love Anice and she loves me. It's going to work out all right in the end.'

* * *

Mrs. Fowler's way to the bus-stop took her past The Beeches, and she stood at the gate for a moment, considering. . . . While shopping in Bellington the day before she had seen Mrs. Willoughby hobbling painfully on two sticks from Crofton's to the car and had been surprised to find how concerned she felt to see her old foe's magnificence thus – ever so slightly, for Mrs. Willoughby's grim countenance wore its usual expression of resolution and authority – dimmed. On a sudden impulse, she decided to call and ask how she was. The visit would, at any rate, shorten a long evening that she knew she was going to spend in worrying about Anice. There were days when she couldn't help worrying about Matthew or Peter or Judy or Anice, and this was one of them.

Cynthia opened the door. She wore an overall and a dust-cap, and there was a smudge across her forehead.

'Oh, do come in,' she said. 'We've had the workmen and I'm just clearing up after them. Did you want to see Mother?'

'Yes, please,' said Mrs. Fowler.

At that moment, Mrs. Willoughby came into the hall, leaning on her two sticks. At sight of Mrs. Fowler, the eagle's beak dwarfed every other feature.

'Good afternoon, Mrs. Fowler,' she said majestically. 'Will you come into the drawing-room?'

Mrs. Fowler entered the drawing-room and took the chair that Mrs. Willoughby offered her, gazing round in awe at the solid phalanxes of photographs that covered chimney-piece, piano and occasional tables. They had increased to formidable proportions with the years, and photographs of Mrs. Willoughby's grandchildren at every stage of infancy now jostled photographs of her children at the same stages.

There was a short silence.

'Very disquieting news from Germany,' said Mrs. Willoughby at last.

‘Yes,’ said Mrs. Fowler vaguely. ‘You mean Hitler and all those dreadful murders. Such an odd name to give it – a purge – isn’t it?’

Mrs. Willoughby ignored this.

‘James says that from now on there’ll be no end to his demands, and Max says that he only wants to be treated decently by other nations and then he’ll respond and behave decently. Time will show which is right.’

‘Yes,’ said Mrs. Fowler.

That seemed to dispose of the subject. There was another long silence. Mrs. Fowler remembered the reason of her call, but now that she was face to face with Mrs. Willoughby she found it impossible to offer sympathy or even ask how she was.

‘I just wondered,’ she said in her gentle, deprecating voice. ‘I just wondered . . . I’m going into Bellington tomorrow and I wondered if there was anything I could do for you there to save you the trouble of going in yourself.’

Mrs. Willoughby looked at her . . . and the eagle’s beak receded.

‘That was kind of you,’ she said. ‘Very kind.’

It occurred to Mrs. Fowler that in all the years of their acquaintance this was the first time she had ever called here casually and as a friend. The same thought occurred to Mrs. Willoughby. There was a sudden constraint in the atmosphere.

‘It wouldn’t be any trouble,’ went on Mrs. Fowler a little nervously. ‘I was going in, anyway, and I have all morning.’

‘No, it’s quite all right,’ said Mrs. Willoughby. ‘Max generally calls in the morning on his way to the office to see if there’s anything I want.’

There was another silence in which Mrs. Fowler suddenly found the courage to say:

'I'm so sorry about your leg. It's arthritis, isn't it?'

'So they say.'

There was a note of encouragement in Mrs. Willoughby's voice, as if, though she did not need the proffered sympathy, she did not actually reject it.

'I'm afraid it's painful,' said Mrs. Fowler.

'A little. Sometimes,' said Mrs. Willoughby. (It was the first time she had admitted that to anyone.) 'But one gets used to it, like everything else.'

There was another silence, but, oddly, the constraint seemed to have vanished.

'I know,' said Mrs. Fowler. She wondered whether her indigestion (she had been rather troubled by indigestion lately) was worthy to be mentioned in this connection and decided that it wasn't.

'How are the others?' she went on.

'Quite well, thank you,' said Mrs. Willoughby. 'At least I'm not sure about Oliver. He had 'flu when last I heard about a fortnight ago.'

'I had a letter from Judy yesterday,' said Mrs. Fowler. 'She said she had tea with him on Tuesday, so he must be all right.'

Mrs. Willoughby threw her a quick glance, then dismissed the subject with a shrug. She disapproved of Oliver's meeting Judy Palmer in London like this, but it wasn't her business. She couldn't have told exactly when she had realized that Oliver wasn't her business. It had been a very gradual process, beginning, of course, on the day when he had quietly announced his intention of taking rooms in London. At first he had gone there for an occasional weekend. Then he had gone there every weekend. As time went on, the weekends became longer and longer . . . till now he only came to Bellington for the directors' meetings of Willoughbys', and not always for those.

Though she would not have acknowledged it even to herself, it had been fear of defeat that made her postpone the battle with Oliver till it was too late, till he was a stranger of whose interests and background she knew nothing. Sometimes she thought it would have been better if she had let him marry Judy. He hadn't married Emmy, after all. Mrs. Willoughby felt a little guilty about Emmy. She had missed George's curate and a quite eligible bank cashier because she was waiting for Oliver, and only last year, having finally given up hope of him, had married a widower with four children. The widower was a kindly, inoffensive man, but the four children were what Emmy called a 'handful'. She was generally in a state of tearful distress when Mrs. Willoughby visited her.

'And you're all quite well, I hope?' said Mrs. Willoughby.

'Yes, thank you,' said Mrs. Fowler. 'All except Peter. He seems to be no better. He's going into a sanatorium.'

'I'm sorry,' said Mrs. Willoughby.

She tried to whip up her old disapproval of the Fowlers, but it was not easy. Peter Fowler had behaved abominably, but she could not forget Max's lapse. The scandal had been better managed (as a Willoughby scandal would naturally be better managed than a Fowler one), but the lapse was the same. Even

Gertrude and Florence were less satisfactory than they used to be. Jessica was now an attractive, spirited girl of twenty, and both Florence and James appeared to be completely under her thumb. They had not even consulted Mrs. Willoughby about this latest shocking plan of letting the girl go to live in London and attend an art school. As to Gertrude and George, they had, to their own and everyone else's surprise, produced another baby last year and they were both behaving extremely foolishly about it. They seemed to have fallen in love with each other for the first time (their marriage had been a very unemotional affair) and to be as much wrapped up in the baby as if it had been the only one they had ever had. They had even called her by the ridiculous name of Chloe, ignoring Mrs. Willoughby's suggestions of Ellen and Mary and Dorothy, as they seemed these days to ignore all her suggestions. They allowed Timothy, now at Oxford, a freedom that seemed outrageous to Mrs. Willoughby, but when she expostulated, Gertrude only said, with a slight impatience in her voice: 'Oh, he's all right, Mother. George says that you can't keep young people under as you used to.'

Only Cynthia gave her no anxiety – Cynthia, silent, docile and hard-working, taking on herself the whole burden of housekeeping, ready always to give a hand to Gertrude and Florence when they were in domestic difficulties. She was over thirty now, and there was a faintly spinsterish air about her. She was inclined to be a little sharp with the maids and a little suspicious of the tradesmen. The others were beginning to refer to her as 'poor old Cynthia', but to Mrs. Willoughby she was the only one of her children who was really satisfactory.

She entered the room now, still wearing her apron.

'I'm getting ready for the workmen tomorrow, Mother,' she said. 'Would you like the best spare room done first?'

'I think so,' said Mrs. Willoughby, and added: 'You've got a smudge across your forehead, dear.'

Cynthia went to the looking-glass and took her handkerchief from her pocket. As she did so, a letter fell out. She picked it up, flushing slightly, and thrust it back. It was from Denis Gordon, and had arrived by that morning's post.

Denis had paid several visits to The Beeches after Oliver had moved to London, and on each occasion Cynthia had treated him with a studied indifference that almost amounted to incivility. Then he had obtained a post in Singapore, and she had received the news with relief, expecting that at last the matter would end. But he wrote to her from Singapore at regular intervals, though she had answered none of his letters, hoping that if she continued to ignore them he would leave her alone. I couldn't go through *that* again, she kept telling herself. I couldn't bear it. . . . I'm happy as I am . . . perfectly happy. . . . I won't answer this letter either.

'I've put up the chenille curtains on the landing, Mother,' she said as she turned aside from the mirror.

'Thank you, my dear,' said Mrs. Willoughby.

The telephone bell rang on the desk by her chair, and she took up the receiver.

'Yes? What a nuisance, Gertrude! . . . Yes, that's the worst of these daily women. . . . I can't lend you Cynthia till the workmen are out, but they'll have finished by the weekend, and you can have her then, but I must have her back as soon as possible, because we're starting spring cleaning.'

Cynthia caught the flicker of amusement in Mrs. Fowler's eyes, and the colour flooded her pale cheeks.

'Gertrude's woman's little boy has got measles,' said Mrs. Willoughby, replacing the receiver. 'She can have you till the beginning of next month, Cynthia, but I must have you back then for the spring cleaning.'

'Here's Helen,' said Cynthia, glad of the interruption.

Helen entered in her usual brisk, business-like fashion. She was still a strikingly handsome woman, but stout and matronly-looking. She now had five children and was expecting another in four months' time. . . .

'Hello, Mater,' she said, raising her eyebrows slightly in surprise at finding her mother in her mother-in-law's house.

'I just called on my way back from Anice's,' explained Mrs. Fowler.

'Is she going to let Patsy and Bruce come to the party?'

'I'm afraid not,' said Mrs. Fowler.

Helen shrugged.

'Well, I can't do anything more about it. If she won't let them come, she won't. I've given up trying to understand her.' She turned to Mrs. Willoughby. 'I called to say that I'm afraid I may not be able to come on Sunday, Mother. Stephen's having a friend over for the weekend and I think I ought to be at home.'

'Very well, dear,' said Mrs. Willoughby, facing the fact that the only guests at next Sunday's gathering would probably be a smattering of the poor relations.

The glory had been departing from the Willoughby Sunday evenings for some time now. Gertrude and George could not come because of the baby. Florence and James seldom came because Jessica had generally made some other engagement for them or was having friends over for the weekend. Even the ranks of the poor relations were thinning. Aunt Flo had died last year. Aunt Bessie was bedridden. Only Miss Hatton seemed unaffected by the passing years. She had lately taken to a bright red tulle neck bow and had reburnished her best hat with a bright red feather, that almost – but not quite – matched it.

'Max will look in if he has time,' said Helen, but Mrs. Willoughby knew that he wouldn't come without Helen. Max was a family man, a child among his own children, who disliked leaving his home circle during the weekend even to visit his mother.

'Very well,' said Mrs. Willoughby again.

'Have your new morning-room chair-covers come?' said Helen, feeling rather guilty about Sunday evening, and anxious to change the subject.

'Yes, they came this morning,' said Mrs. Willoughby, raising herself from her chair, and taking her sticks. 'Would you like to see them? Excuse us a moment, Mrs. Fowler.'

They crossed the hall to the morning-room, leaving Cynthia and Mrs. Fowler alone. Cynthia stood by the fireplace, her eyes fixed unseeingly on the fire, lost in her thoughts.

'Why don't you go, Cynthia?' said Mrs. Fowler suddenly. Cynthia roused herself with a start.

'Go?' she repeated. 'Where?'

'Anywhere,' said Mrs. Fowler.

Cynthia looked bewildered.

'I am going away with Gertrude in August.'

'To help with the baby?'

'Yes.'

'I don't mean that sort of going away. I mean, why don't you – break loose?'

Cynthia stared at her in amazement.

'Break loose,' repeated Mrs. Fowler firmly. 'Go and live on your own somewhere. Enjoy yourself. Take a flat in London. You've been in Bellington long enough. If you don't go away now it will be too late. You never will.'

'But I don't want to go,' protested Cynthia. 'I'm perfectly happy here. And – they need me.'

'They don't need you,' said Mrs. Fowler. 'They just take you for granted. They aren't even grateful.'

A sudden breathless anger seized Cynthia.

'You've no right to say that. You – '

They heard the clip-clop of Mrs. Willoughby's sticks in the hall. Cynthia plunged from the room, brushing past Mrs. Willoughby and Helen as they entered.

'You have enough dust-sheets, Cynthia, haven't you?' called Mrs. Willoughby. 'There are some more in the linen-cupboard, you know.'

Cynthia did not answer.

Mrs. Fowler rose from her chair.

'I must go now,' she said.

'I'll come along with you, Mater,' said Helen. 'I just want to show Mother these patterns for the new dining-room curtains.' She drew a little bundle of patterns from her bag. 'I'm taking them home for Max to choose which he likes best.'

'Oh yes, I noticed those materials in Crofton's yesterday,' said Mrs. Willoughby. 'Personally I like the old-gold one best.'

'Yes . . . I think that's the one Max will choose.'

'But they hadn't much left,' said Mrs. Willoughby. 'It might all be gone by tomorrow.'

'Well, as a matter of fact,' said Helen, looking slightly – only slightly – abashed, 'I have actually ordered it.'

CHAPTER TWENTY-ONE

'I must show you that bit of Chelsea I got yesterday,' said Oliver. 'I think you'll like it.'

He took a delicate piece of china – the figure of a child – from a Sheraton display cabinet and handed it to her.

Judy carried it over to the window to examine it, noticing with secret amusement that his eyes remained fixed on it anxiously.

'It's all right,' she said. 'I won't break it. You hate people touching your things, don't you?'

'No, no, of course not. . . .'

'It's lovely, Oliver.'

She gave it back to him, and he replaced it in the cabinet, taking out his handkerchief to remove an almost imperceptible mark that his fingers had left on the polished surface of the mahogany. She watched him, her lips curved into a faint smile, then sat down on the cushioned window-seat and let her eyes wander over the expanse of chimney-pots – some squat, some thin, some short, some tall, some plain, some elegant, all wearing their soft grey plumes of smoke – that comprised the view from Oliver's sixth-floor flat. A graceful church spire cut sharply into the sky. A block of offices reared itself up in the distance like a giant among pygmies.

‘Your chimneys are charming, Oliver,’ she said. ‘They’re almost worth that ghastly climb.’

He came across the room and stood by her, his hands in his pockets.

‘Yes, they look nice today,’ he said. ‘A blue sky suits them.’

‘I like that cheeky-looking one over there.’

‘I know. It’s terribly inquisitive. It’s always trying to peep into this room, but it’s not quite tall enough. . . . Oh, by the way, Judy. . . .’

‘Yes?’

‘I’ve got those tickets for the concert at the Albert Hall. You are coming, aren’t you?’

‘What date is it?’

‘The sixteenth.’

‘My dear, I can’t. I’ve promised to go to some wretched literary affair with Arnold.’

The tight, closed look came over his face that always came over it when she mentioned Arnold.

‘I thought you said you’d keep the date free.’

‘I told you I might not be able to manage it.’

He went over to the mantelpiece and began to fidget with the ornaments. She saw that he was put out. It took little to upset the precarious balance of Oliver’s serenity.

‘How are you getting on with the book?’ she said after a few moments’ silence.

‘I’ve not had much time for it lately.’

‘I thought you’d got Mr. – who was it? – Wentworth to collaborate with you.’

Oliver seemed to stiffen.

‘I found him a little casual,’ he said. ‘I told him in the end that I’d rather carry on by myself.’

‘Oliver, do come and sit down and stop fidgeting about over there.’

He came and sat by her on the window-seat. The light fell on his keen, narrow face. His hair was already greying, his thin body stooped, fine lines were etched on his brow and round his mouth. He wore the anxious, worried look so often worn by people who take trouble to avoid worries and anxieties.

‘I don’t like that chimney with a cowl,’ she said. ‘It has a sneering expression.’

He smiled, his good-humour returning.

‘It’s a little embittered,’ he said. ‘It used to keep a carriage and a butler and a footman, and now it’s a third-rate lodging-house.’

‘I know. Like that place in Bellington where Martin’s uncle lives. By the way, Martin’s gone to Australia. I heard from Mother yesterday.’

‘Has he got a job out there?’

‘I don’t think so. I think he’s just hoping to find one. . . . There was quite a budget of family news. Peter’s worse, I’m afraid, and Belle’s divorcing Matthew. That’s comical, isn’t it? And Mother – I’m worried about Mother, Oliver.’

‘Why?’

‘The doctor says that her indigestion isn’t indigestion, after all. It’s heart trouble. She had a bad attack last week.’

‘I’m sorry.’

‘She’s all right again now apparently. She’ll just have to be careful. Have you heard from Bellington lately?’

'I had the usual saga of Willoughby news last week. It seems that Willoughbys' is doing well – so well that it's all Max can do to cope with it. The old girl can't hold the reins, of course, as she used to.'

'She's not worrying you to go back into the business, is she?'

His lips flickered into a dry little smile.

'Good Lord, no! I'm no longer of any importance in the Willoughby scheme of things. Bobby and Timmy and the rest of them are coming on. Bobby starts in the mill next month, and Timmy in the New Year. Timmy is proving a little intractable, I gather, but he'll probably settle down in time. Then there are all Max's young hopefuls. Youth is knocking at the door. It will soon be jamming the doorway. . . . No, they pay me my director's salary now chiefly to keep me away from it.'

'Which is just what you wanted.'

'Which is just what I wanted. By the way, I'm expecting Cynthia this evening. Did you know she was staying in London?'

'Yes,' said Judy. 'She came to dinner with us the other night.' She was silent for a few moments, then went on, 'You know, you and Cynthia are rather alike, Oliver.'

He looked surprised and a little affronted.

'My dear, I can't imagine any two people more unlike than Cynthia and me. Cynthia's interests are bounded on all sides by the four walls of the kitchen, and I flatter myself that mine are a little wider than that.'

'You both run away from things. . . .'

He threw her a quick glance.

'I wonder if we fare any worse than people who run into things.'

She flushed slightly and said nothing.

* * *

The Bloomsbury flat had been Oliver's home now for three years. He had ransacked sale-rooms and haunted auctions to get the period pieces that furnished it, and every available surface was covered by his collections of snuff-boxes, miniatures and china. The caretaker of the flats, who lived in the basement, 'did for' the other tenants, but, except for occasional cooking, Oliver had refused her services. He could not bear that anyone except himself should touch his things. He would spend all morning pottering about among his treasures – dusting, polishing, rearranging – and the rest of the day prowling round in little, out-of-the-way junk shops in back streets and alleys, hunting for bargains.

Too sensitive to endure the discouragement of even a few set-backs, and finding a personal humiliation in each rejection of an M.S., he had long since ceased to make more than a pretence of literary work. The book on which he was now ostensibly engaged – an historical novel of the twelfth century – had been at the same stage for the last year. He had collected, and was still collecting, a mass of material – as unwieldy as it was scholarly – but he had lost interest in the story, and the research for it had become an end in itself. He still tried to make the literary and artistic contacts that had been the dream of his youth, and in that he was generally successful, for he was a pleasant, intelligent companion, cultured and critical, with occasional flickers of dry humour. But the friendships never lasted long. His over-sensitiveness made him 'touchy', quick to imagine slights and rebuffs; he was irked and secretly terrified by the claims and responsibilities implicit in any human relationship.

Judy was the one constant factor in the ever-changing kaleidoscope of his friendships. When first she came to London they had avoided each other. Then had followed a friendship with dangerous under-currents that took them perilously near the whirlpool of an 'affair'. But in both of them was an inbred caution, as well as a faint suspicion of the other, that held them back. Judy's affection was tinged with contempt, his with resentment. And so the relationship had settled down into a habit, a humdrum matter of routine. Every week or so, Oliver rang her up and asked her to come to tea with him. They went to concerts and theatres together. To Oliver, Judy stood for the world of beauty and romance into which he had once wandered; to Judy he was a link with the old days when life had been serene and carefree – days to which, through the long disillusionment of her marriage with Arnold, her mind turned with increasing nostalgia.

* * *

Oliver rose from his seat, glancing at the Louis-Seize clock on the mantelpiece.

'I'll leave you with the chimney-pots while I get tea,' he said.

'Let me give you a hand,' said Judy, knowing that he would refuse, for it worried him to have anyone else in the little kitchen, where everything had its place. Even the making of a cup of tea was a sort of ritual.

She stayed there on the window-seat, gazing absently out over the chimney-pots with their plumes of smoke while Oliver pottered about in the kitchen, setting out the Crown Derby tea service, the Georgian silver, the cake from Gunter's, the sandwiches he had made himself. Waiting for the kettle to boil he stood and watched her through the open doorway, delighting in the pure line of her profile, the slender grace of her figure, savouring his delight the more keenly because it was the same impersonal delight he might have taken in a piece of sculpture or a painting, exulting subconsciously, with an exultation that held something of bitterness, in his freedom.

While they had tea they talked of books, plays, music. . . . As long as one stayed in the world he had made for himself, he was an ideal companion. He showed her a water-colour that he had bought in a junk shop and that he was convinced had been painted by Turner.

'I think it's one of those he did for copper-plate engraving,' he said. 'No one but Turner could have done that sky. . . .'

Judy, looking at his happy, absorbed face, thought, He's only at his ease with things. People scare him. . . . And suddenly she admitted the fear against which she had been barring her mind all afternoon . . . and a dark cloud seemed to close down over everything, blotting out the pleasant sunlit room. She thought, Suppose I told Oliver now what's in my mind, that I'm afraid I'm going to have a child, that I hate the thought of bearing Arnold's child, that I feel like something in a trap? . . . Poor Oliver! He'd be panic-stricken. He can't bear being brought up against reality.

'I must go now,' she said, drawing on her gloves. 'Tell Cynthia I'm sorry I missed her. . . . Oh, I nearly forgot! Arnold and I are giving a small cocktail party on Friday. Will you come?'

Again the tight, closed look came over Oliver's face. He wasn't in love with Judy. He couldn't have explained to himself the repugnance he felt for Arnold. It was as if an old wound, whose origin he had forgotten, were set aching by the thought of him.

'Sorry. I'm afraid I can't manage it.'

She was suddenly angry.

'Why won't you ever come to my house, Oliver? It's childish. It – '

She would have liked to say that it increased the smouldering jealousy that Arnold had never ceased to cherish against him.

He flushed.

'I have an engagement on Friday,' he said stiffly.

'You know quite well that you haven't,' she said. Her anger mounted. It was he who gave their friendship the air of an intrigue by refusing to visit her in her home or, if he could avoid it, meet her husband. 'After all, why should I go on coming here, if you never come to my house?'

There was consternation in the glance he threw her. She had been the reason why he had built this refuge against the world, but, oddly, she was part of the refuge. Her visits were woven into the fabric of the life he had made for himself.

‘I don’t know what you mean,’ he said. ‘I – ’

Then Cynthia came in – a Cynthia whom Bellington would hardly have recognized. Her hair was sleekly set and done in the latest style; her face was delicately made up; the expensive simplicity of her dress lent an air of *svelte* gracefulness to her figure. But the glow that should have completed the transformation was absent. Her eyes were lack-lustre, and a suggestion of listlessness hung over her.

‘What a climb!’ she said as she slipped off her cloak and laid it over the back of one of Oliver’s Regency chairs. ‘Why do you live on the top floor, Oliver?’

‘He likes his chimney-pots,’ explained Judy.

‘I think they’re depressing,’ said Cynthia. ‘One might as well live in a graveyard.’

She sat down by Judy on the window-seat and they talked desultorily, while Oliver fussed about with glasses and a cocktail shaker.

‘It’s quite a new departure for you to come to London like this, isn’t it, Cynthia?’ said Judy.

‘Yes.’

‘Are you enjoying it?’

‘Yes, thank you.’

She gets more and more difficult to talk to, thought Judy. Is it because we’ve just naturally drifted apart or because neither of us can quite forget about Arnold?

‘What made you decide to come?’

Cynthia was silent. She might have replied, ‘Your mother . . .’ It was not Mrs. Fowler’s advice – Cynthia considered that an impertinence – that had made her decide to leave home. It was the flicker of amusement in Mrs. Fowler's eyes when she heard Mrs. Willoughby say, 'I'll lend you Cynthia'. She had tried to forget it, but the memory had haunted her so constantly that she had missed an overcharge of twopence on the butcher's bill and made an incorrect entry in the laundry book. She had reasoned the matter out, admitting frankly that she had become a household drudge but assuring herself that the love and gratitude of her family was her reward. Then followed a week of petty annoyances. Gertrude, when told that Cynthia had a bad headache and could not look after Chloe as usual on Nurse's 'afternoon off', expressed only peevish resentment. Helen sent her a curt message one morning telling her to take Clarissa to the dentist in the afternoon, ignoring the fact that Cynthia might have made some engagement of her own. Mrs. Willoughby rated her soundly for no other reason than that the milkman was late. Max, generally kind and considerate, seemed to think it reasonable to 'borrow' her to dust and sweep his office during the week his office cleaner was away.

'I don't want to get a stranger,' he explained. 'There's a lot of stuff lying about.'

'Can't Helen spare one of the maids?' Cynthia had asked.

He looked at her in surprise.

'They've enough to do at home.'

'What about one of your typists?'

He shrugged.

'It's hardly their job, is it? . . . My dear girl, it's only a case of running round each evening. I asked Mother and she said she could easily spare you.'

'Oh, well, if Mother's willing to spare me, I suppose I must be spared.'

The sarcasm in her voice was lost on him.

'That's all right, then,' he said. 'It's only for a week, you know.'

That night she decided definitely to leave Bellington and take a flat in London. Max's brusqueness, Gertrude's unreasonableness, her mother's calm acceptance of her services, the faint tinge of contempt that showed itself in the attitude of all her relations and friends, added fuel to her smouldering resentment. Memories that had lain dormant for years awoke to torment her. ('It's only Cynthia' . . . 'Cynthia doesn't matter' . . . 'Cynthia won't mind staying at home. She's used to it.') She would make a clean break with the old life and start a new one. In London she would find fresh friends, fresh interests. And she must go now before it was too late. The vision of herself growing older and older, a sort of unpaid family servant, filled her with fear and despondency. They did not want her or need her or love her. They weren't even grateful to her. . . . Now that she had realized it she must act at once. The question of expense did not enter into the situation. Her allowance was a generous one and she had saved a good proportion of it for many years.

She had meant to tell Mrs. Willoughby of her decision outright, but at the last minute her courage failed her and she said in her usual deprecating voice,

'I think I'd like to go to London for a holiday, Mother.'

For a moment the eagle's beak stood out on Mrs. Willoughby's countenance, and Cynthia felt the childhood's fear that she had never quite outgrown. Then the eagle's beak receded. There was, after all, nothing unreasonable in the request. Cynthia was old enough to take a holiday alone in London if she wished to. And, in any case, Oliver was there to keep an eye on her.

'When?' was all she said.

'I'd like to go next week.'

Mrs. Willoughby considered.

'Yes, I think I can spare you next week. Helen, of course, will need you for the children in the school holidays, but that's not for a month yet. There's no reason why you shouldn't go next week. You may stay a fortnight, if you like.'

And Cynthia had said, 'Thank you', her heart leaping as though she were a prisoner receiving an order of release. She packed her trunk with trembling hands. . . . She was leaving home for ever. She would go to an hotel and look for a flat, then, when she had found one, she would write and tell her mother of her decision. She would be free at last. So keen a sense of exhilaration seized her at the thought that she felt faint and dizzy. . . .

And, right from the beginning, the thing had been a failure. She was lonely and unhappy and afraid. She was afraid of the commissionaire at the hotel, of the waiters, even of the chambermaid – a saucy young woman who would have been given short shrift at The Beeches. She was afraid of the agents who took her over flats and of the flats they took her over. She was afraid of the bus conductors and the taxi drivers. She was afraid of the people who jostled her in the streets. She did her best to combat her timidity. She went to an expensive hair-dresser and an expensive beauty parlour. She bought expensive new clothes. She even tried to make friends with the other people staying at the hotel, but she lacked courage to make overtures herself, and, when overtures were made to her, was held in such a paralysing grip of shyness that she seemed to be repelling them.

And all the time there was a cold, lonely, unwanted feeling at her heart. Her thoughts turned continually to Bellington. Had anyone remembered to see about the new washer for the scullery tap? Was Babs' cough better? Had Helen got her new curtains up yet?

She felt like an exile, shut out of the warm, familiar world she knew, condemned to wander in an alien world of hostile bus conductors and taxi drivers and hotel attendants, who spoke to her brusquely and didn't care what happened to her. She was no longer Aunt Cynthia or Miss Willoughby of The Beeches, and no fresh identity had come to fill the gap. Sometimes she had a horrible feeling of not existing at all. . . .

She had, of course, got in touch with Oliver, but Oliver's life was self-contained and regimented. He shunned anything that upset the even tenor of his ways. He asked her to the flat once or twice and expected the matter to end there, taking for granted that her time was fully occupied by theatres, cinemas and meetings with old school friends. She went to several cinemas and theatres but did not enjoy them. Her home-sickness became a physical oppression. . . .

Judy asked her to dinner, but that evening, like everything else, had been a dismal failure. The Judy of their girlhood seemed to have vanished behind a hard bright shell of sophistication. Cynthia felt stupid and provincial. She could think of nothing to say.

Arnold was charming, with a charm that would have raised her to heaven in the old days but that left her now unmoved. She failed to respond, and Arnold, always sensitive to atmosphere, became sulky and silent. The only satisfaction that the evening afforded her was the knowledge that her love for Arnold was dead. Before that she had not been quite sure. . . .

Well, I've learnt my lesson, she had said to herself last night as she sat in the lounge of the hotel, wearing one of her new evening dresses, waiting till it was time to go into dinner, feeling bored and lonely and miserable. I'll settle down in Bellington now for the rest of my life. They need me there, and I've found out that that's all I ask of life – to be needed. I'll start on that new smock for Chloe as soon as I get back. I'll take all the children to the fair and give them a good time. I'm sorry I was so short with Max when he asked me to do his office. I'll offer to do it next year without being asked. I'm glad I didn't tell anyone about the flat. I was mad to think of it. I'll stay out the fortnight (her pride upheld her as far as that) then I'll go back. . . .

The dining-room doors were thrown open and she went to sit at the little table that had been assigned to her because it was set in a piercing draught and she looked the sort of person who wouldn't make a fuss. As she sat down she had a sudden vision of the dining-room at The Beeches on Sunday evening, with Gertrude and Florence and Helen and Max. . . . She heard her mother's clear incisive voice, Max's hearty laughter.

. . . Her throat contracted and she pushed away her soup untouched.

* * *

Judy rose slowly from the window-seat. Her pale face looked very beautiful in the soft, dark frame of her furs. Her small tilted hat threw an alluring shadow over her limpid violet eyes.

'Well, it's been nice to see you, Cynthia,' she said. 'Are you free on Friday? Arnold and I are giving a small cocktail party. We'd love you to come.'

'Thank you so much,' said Cynthia. 'I'm not quite sure. . . . May I leave it open?'

She felt that she had had enough of Judy's suave sophistication and Arnold's studied charm.

'Yes, leave it open,' said Judy. 'Just come along if you can.'

The casualness of Judy's invitation and Cynthia's obvious reluctance to accept it showed to both of them how the gulf between them had widened with the years. Cynthia had a sudden vision of Judy sitting on the bed in her bedroom at Langley Place and saying: 'We'll always be friends, won't we? Even if I marry and if you marry.' She smiled a little wryly at the memory.

'What are you smiling at, Cynthia?' said Judy curiously.

'Just something I thought of.'

'Oh, well . . . good-bye. . . . Good-bye, Oliver. You'll be giving me a ring or I'll be giving you one, I suppose, before long. . . . Don't bother to come down with me. I don't want a taxi. I'd rather walk.'

He went down with her to the street door. A passing newspaper boy was calling, 'Mussolini Marching on Adowa'. Oliver bought a paper and glanced at the headlines. Disturbing news, of course, but less important in Oliver's eyes than the enamel snuff-box that he had seen yesterday in a Bond Street window and that he had decided to buy tomorrow.

'What does it say?' said Judy.

'They're invading Abyssinia.'

Judy shrugged. To her, too, it seemed far off and less important than the problems that beset her.

'I thought the League of Nations was going to stop all that,' she said vaguely.

'When shall I see you again, Judy?'

'You won't come on Friday?'

'No. . . . May I ring you next week?'

'Very well. . . . Good-bye.'

'Good-bye.'

He took his leave of her with the old-fashioned courtesy he always showed her. He had not kissed her since the day their engagement had been broken off.

Cynthia turned from the window as he re-entered the flat.

'Oliver, do you ever feel homesick for Bellington?'

'Good Lord, Cynthia! What an idea!'

She gave him an apologetic smile.

'Yes . . . I don't suppose many people do.'

'I expect you're glad of a break,' he said. 'Still having a good time?'

'Oh yes . . . of course.'

'Finding it difficult to crowd it all into two weeks, I suppose?'

'Yes. . . .'

'You must give me a ring if there's anything I can do for you, you know.'

She looked at him gratefully. From Oliver, who hated to have claims made on him, who shirked all responsibilities, the offer was a generous one. It showed that, despite his efforts to conquer it, the Willoughby clan instinct still survived in him.

The telephone bell rang and he took up the receiver. She saw his brows meet in a quick frown.

'Oh yes. . . . Yes, of course. . . . Yes, do. . . . any time. . . .'

'It was Denis Gordon,' he said as he put back the receiver.

'I didn't know he was in England,' said Cynthia.

She had gone very pale.

'It seems he got his leave earlier than he expected and just caught a boat.' He stood there, tapping the fingers of one hand against the palm of the other – a habit of his when he was put out. He hated to have the smallest detail of his arrangements upset. 'It's really very awkward. . . . He said he was coming round and then rang off. I'd made all arrangements for a dinner for two. . . . If he'd let me know earlier. . . . We could go out, of course, but that means altering all my arrangements here. I do dislike having things sprung on me. . . .

Cynthia rose.

'It's all right, Oliver,' she said a little breathlessly. 'You and Denis have dinner here. I can easily come another night. I'd – rather come another night. I've got a headache. I'll go. . . .'

'Of course you mustn't,' said Oliver. 'Perhaps Mrs. Bury

could manage a third, but it's – very awkward. I don't even know where he was ringing from.'

'Please let me go, Oliver,' she pleaded.

'Nonsense! I shouldn't dream of it. He may not even be coming tonight. I couldn't catch what he said very clearly. I'll go down and see Mrs. Bury, anyway.'

When he had gone Cynthia stood gazing out over the chimney-pots, her heart beating unevenly, her thoughts so confused that she was only aware of an agitation more violent than any she had ever known before. Then, coming to a sudden decision, she snatched up her coat and bag and went to the door. It opened before she reached it, and Denis stood on the threshold. His good-humoured, rough-hewn face lit up at the sight of her.

'I say, this is grand,' he said. 'I ran into Oliver downstairs, and he told me to come straight up.'

'Of course. . . . You're just back, aren't you?' said Cynthia. 'Do come in. Will you have a cocktail?'

She tried to speak naturally, but her voice seemed to come from a long way off and a pulse in her throat was throbbing so that it seemed to choke her. He stood watching her. . . . Despite the new style of hairdressing, the rouge and lipstick, the fashionable cut of the new dress, she still wore the air of a lost child that had touched his heart when first he saw her.

'I didn't know you were coming back so soon,' she said as she handed him his cocktail.

'My leave was put earlier. . . . You got my letters?'

She looked away from him.

'Yes . . .'

‘I only arrived last night. I thought I’d get in touch with Oliver and – hear all your news. I didn’t expect to find you here.’

‘I’m – having a holiday in London.’

‘Are you enjoying it?’

‘Yes,’ she said, then, afraid that her voice had sounded a little forlorn, added, ‘tremendously.’

She thought she read a faint amusement behind the kindliness of his grey eyes, and the colour flooded her cheeks.

‘Good!’ he said, then, casually: ‘Are you doing anything tomorrow evening?’

‘Yes, I’m afraid – ’ she began, and stopped.

Mechanically she had gathered her forces to shut out the warm glow that still tried to steal into her heart whenever he was there, but she found suddenly that her forces had deserted her. In the surroundings of her own home the resisting of him had become a habit, but she wasn’t in the surroundings of her own home any longer. She had resisted him there because he threatened to disturb her peace, and now her peace had vanished. She was in a bleak, dark, no-man’s-land, longing for comfort and companionship. She struggled for a few moments then surrendered. The surrender was like the sudden easing of a physical pain. ‘No,’ she said. ‘I’m not doing anything tomorrow evening.’

Then Oliver came in. He looked flushed and harassed, but triumphant.

‘It’s all right,’ he said. ‘Mrs. Bury says she can manage another quite easily.’

CHAPTER TWENTY-TWO

Arnold was writing at his desk when Judy entered the study. He raised his head and looked at her with a smile.

'Oh, it's you, my dear. . . . I expected you back earlier.'

Judy was silent for a moment, trying to gauge his mood. His smile meant nothing, of course. He could always smile. . . .

Despite his sixty-odd years, greying hair and lined face, Arnold was still a handsome man. His tall stooping figure gave him an air of elegance that he was at pains to cultivate, wearing carefully cut suits, generally of pale grey, with a carnation or orchid in the button-hole. Sometimes he appeared in an old-fashioned cravat, and he had of late begun to wear a monocle on a broad, black ribbon round his neck and to carry a rather long, silver-mounted stick.

'I'm a dandy,' he would say. 'Openly and unashamedly a dandy. My spiritual home is the Regency age.'

The pose was a fairly recent one, and Judy suspected that the publicity it gave him compensated in some degree for the decline of his literary reputation. She closed the door and went over to his desk.

'It's not very late. . . . How have you been getting on?'

He leant back in his chair and laid down his pen.

'So-so . . . I shall be glad when Miss Filey returns.'

Miss Filey, his secretary, was away on holiday, and Judy was guiltily aware that she ought to be filling her place – typing, taking notes, discussing the next chapter, as Miss Filey loved to do. In the early days of her marriage, anxious to fulfil her part of the bargain, she had done that, but it had not been a success. Arnold's vanity demanded constant flattery, and Judy was unable to supply it. She knew that he had been as relieved as she was when the arrangement came to an end.

'Is there anything I can do to help?' she said, drawing off her gloves.

He took up a press cutting from his desk and handed it to her.

'Perhaps you wouldn't mind pasting that in the book,' he said. 'It came by this afternoon's post.'

'It's good, isn't it?' she said when she had read it.

'Is it?' he said with a pretence of nonchalance. 'I've hardly had time to look at it.'

She smiled to herself, half amused, half irritated, aware that he must have read it a dozen times and could probably have repeated it by heart. Glancing down at the waste-paper basket, she saw a ball of crumpled press cuttings. The one he had shown her was evidently the only good one of the batch. That explained the faint hint of acerbity that underlay the pleasantness of his manner.

'I'll put it in now,' she said, and went over to Miss Filey's table, where the press-cutting album and pot of glue were kept.

Carefully she added this last addition to the chorus of praise – a chorus that no discordant note was ever allowed to mar.

Arnold wrote in silence for some minutes then laid down his pen again.

'I don't think it quite does justice to the character of Imogen,' he said.

'Perhaps not,' said Judy, trying to instil the right tone of sympathetic interest into her voice.

As Arnold's literary reputation declined, so his appetite for praise increased. His novels were still best sellers, but the creative impulse that had inspired them had long since been exhausted. They were now feats of virtuosity, written to a formula, repeating over and over again the situations and characters that had first won him success. His tricks of style were becoming accentuated, and his work afforded a happy hunting-ground for the parodist.

Judy took the book of press cuttings over to his desk.

'That all right?' she said.

He considered it critically.

'Not absolutely straight, but it will do. . . .'

He turned over the pages, re-reading his earlier reviews. The complacent smile still lingered on his lips when he glanced up at her.

'You look very sweet today, my dear,' he said, laying his hand on hers. She withdrew hers with a quick, instinctive gesture, and his brows came sharply together.

'Let me see . . .' he said in a tone that was elaborately casual, leaning back in his chair and joining the tips of his fingers. 'I've forgotten what you were doing this afternoon. . . . Shopping, wasn't it?'

'I told you at lunch that I was going to have tea with Oliver,' she said shortly.

He was always laying these childish traps for her, trying to catch her out in some lie about her meetings with Oliver.

'Oh yes, of course. . . . I hope you asked him to come on Friday.'

'Yes.'

'Is he coming?'

'No. He has an engagement.'

'I see. . . .'

She tried to sidetrack him away from the subject of Oliver.

'Cynthia was there. I don't think she's enjoying her holiday very much.'

'Was she there all the time?'

'No. She came after tea.'

They're both as jealous as if it were a real affair, she thought impatiently, and I haven't even the satisfaction of a lover. . . .

'And had Oliver anything to say for himself that's worth repeating?' said Arnold after a slight pause.

'Not much. He'd been reading Roper's *Georgian Age*. He said it was excellent.'

The remark served its purpose in turning his attention from Oliver. Praise of any other writer was, in his eyes, a direct challenge to him. He seemed to consider the question with a judicial air.

'I quite agree,' he said at last. 'His style is somewhat laboured and many of his historical facts incorrect, but – yes, excellent, on the whole. . . . By the way, I had a letter by this afternoon's post.'

His burrowing in his letter-basket revealed a pale blue envelope addressed in an unformed, childish hand that brought a wry smile to Judy's lips. She had long since ceased trying to keep track of his schoolgirl admirers, though she realized that Arnold was becoming more and more dependent on the hero-worship they extended to him. I wish I could feel jealous of them, she thought despairingly, even though I know that there's no reason to feel jealous. I know that it never goes any further than a few parental pawings. He's an expert at parental pawings. . . . I wonder if he's reached the stage of telling them that his wife doesn't understand him. He probably reached it long ago. . . .

'Here it is,' he said, taking up a letter. 'It's from the Friday club. They want me to speak at their annual dinner on the seventeenth. You'll come with me, won't you?'

She was silent. The zest had long faded from appearing in public with Arnold – as the zest had faded from most things – but he still disliked going anywhere without her. She was 'Arnold Palmer's beautiful wife', part of his setting, like the monocle and silver-mounted stick. And he was still in love with her. . . . That was part of the trouble.

'But, Arnold,' she protested. 'I'm going with you to that Literary Tea on the 16th and to the Literary Conversazione on the 18th. I – ' She stopped. 'I couldn't stand three days of it,' was what she wanted to say.

'If you feel like that, of course –' he said stiffly.

'These literary gatherings get a little on my nerves,' she said. 'I sometimes wish I'd married a plumber.'

'Even a plumber, my dear,' he said with a constrained twist of his lips, 'would, one imagines, take a certain interest in his work.'

‘Yes, but a plumber finishes his work when he finishes it,’ said Judy. ‘He isn’t always talking and thinking about plumbing. He doesn’t go to plumbing lunches and plumbing teas and plumbing conversaziones. He doesn’t give lectures on plumbing. He – I’m sorry, Arnold, I’m a little peevish today. Yes, I’ll go with you.’

He smiled, his good-humour restored, throwing a quick, fugitive glance at the mirror on the wall and raising his hand to bring forward the hair over his ears in a more Regency fashion.

‘That’s right. Go with the old man. He’s not so necessary to the scheme of things as a plumber, of course, but he has attained a certain standing in his own unimportant calling.’

She set her teeth. She could endure almost anything from Arnold but the exercise on her in private of his famous whimsical charm.

‘I’ll go,’ she said stonily.

She went over to the window and stood looking down unseeingly at the stream of traffic below. A sense of weariness and futility possessed her. She had married Arnold because she wanted life and movement and she had found only frustration.

‘Let’s go abroad, Arnold,’ she said, turning round to him suddenly. ‘We said we’d go to Egypt, you know, and we’ve never been. . . .’

The suggestion dispelled his precarious good-humour, and a querulous note crept into his voice.

‘My dear, do be reasonable. I can’t possibly go anywhere till I’ve finished this novel, and then – ’

‘And then, I suppose, there’ll be the next one.’

He shifted in his chair under her glance.

'I was planning a book of short stories after this,' he said, 'and I want to write them while the ideas are fresh in my mind. In any case I shouldn't want to be out of England when the proofs of the novel came in.'

'Couldn't Miss Filey correct them?'

'You know that I never allow anyone but myself to do that.'

It was becoming more and more difficult to drag Arnold out of his rut of fiction writing and presiding at literary functions. He seemed to feel happy and secure only when in his study, weaving his tenuous, never-changing plots, or as guest of honour at some sort of literary gathering. More and more of late years he had avoided people who did not share his own idea of his importance, and trips abroad brought him into contact with too many such people.

'What about a fortnight in Paris?' she persisted. 'That needn't upset your work much.'

'We'll see,' he said evasively. 'In any case we shall be going to the sea. . . .'

He always spent August at a small hotel in Felixstowe, where the proprietress, who had first approached him through his fan mail, ensured for him the atmosphere of adulation that he found so necessary. For some years now that had been the only holiday he had taken.

Judy's eyes went back to the busy street . . . and suddenly the terror that lay in wait for her leapt out and seized her by the throat. She felt the palms of her hands wet with sweat and saw the street below through a sort of mist. . . . I won't think of it. . . . It mightn't be true . . . I'm not sure yet . . . not really sure. . . . If it's true . . . if – blind panic surged over her. . . . I won't go through with it . . . I can't. . . .

The mist cleared, and she turned again to Arnold, seeing with merciless clarity the weakness and vanity of the regular-featured, good-looking face. I'm beginning to hate him, she thought. I hate everything about him . . . the way he speaks and moves, his selfishness and conceit and – the beastliness that underlies it all. Then, for refuge, her spirit fled to the peace and safety of her old home . . . and she saw her mother sitting in the basket-chair on the terrace . . . the shadow of the cedar tree on the lawn . . . the green sweep of the park. . . . An unbearable homesickness possessed her.

'Arnold,' she said, 'I'm not going with you to Felixstowe this year. You can go alone. It will do both of us good to have a change from each other. I'll go to Bellington. . . .'

The look on his face told her that his smouldering jealousy had flared up again.

'Rather a sudden decision, isn't it?' he said. 'I suppose you arranged it with Willoughby this afternoon.'

She shrugged.

'If I wanted to have an affair with Oliver,' she said, 'I should hardly go to Bellington for it.'

'Why not admit that you are having one?'

'Because I'm not, and you know I'm not. I'm not even particularly fond of him.'

'Aren't you?'

'No.'

'What is he to you, exactly, my dear? I'd be interested to know.'

She considered.

'He's – just a habit.'

'Oh, so it's reached that stage, has it?' he said.

She gathered up her bag and gloves.

'I'll go and take my things off. . . .'

He crossed the room to her.

'I'm sorry, Judy. . . . Don't let's quarrel. . . . Forgive the old man.'

He caught her to him, holding her closely. She turned her head away, but his lips found hers. . . . She had to stiffen herself to endure his caress, standing taut and rigid in his arms, while his lips wandered over her face, her neck, her hair. . . .

'You do love the old man just a little, don't you?' he said, holding her face between his hands. 'He's not a bad old stick, you know. Some women even find him rather attractive.'

His eyes sought the mirror again, and he moved slightly so as to occupy the centre of the frame.

Judy freed herself. She was trembling and waves of nausea were sweeping over her body. . . .

'I must go now, Arnold. I have several things to see to before dinner.'

'Have a rest, my dear,' he said solicitously. 'You look tired.'

She went out and he sat down at his desk again, turning over the pages of his press-cutting album, while his well-cut lips took on again their familiar complacent curves.

CHAPTER TWENTY-THREE

Judy walked up the road from the station towards Langley Place. She walked slowly, her brows drawn together, her lips tightened. The fears she had held at bay for weeks were closing in on her. Through the long sterile years of her marriage with Arnold the thought of her essential freedom had upheld her. I can always pack up and leave him if things get really unbearable, she had told herself. There's nothing to tie me to him. He's no real hold over me. . . . Neither she nor Arnold had wanted children. And now the suspicion that she was going to have a child had become a certainty, and the knowledge brought only anger and revulsion. I won't go through with it, she thought . . . I can't. . . . There are places . . . I'll find out about them. . . . Even the news that Peter had had a relapse and that Matthew had gone out to Switzerland to visit him failed to pierce the dull cold mist that shrouded her spirit. Yesterday she had received a letter from Mrs. Fowler, asking her to go down for the weekend. 'I've had bad news about Peter, darling, and I want you here.'

Judy had explained the situation to Arnold, packed her suitcase and gone into the study to say good-bye to him. She found him seated at his desk among a chaos of papers, deep in the throes of a major literary crisis. The heroine, who should have been sixty in the last chapter, was turning out to be only fifty, and he was going through the earlier chapters in a feverish effort to put things right. Miss Filey, almost in tears, was assisting him and at the same time indulging in an orgy of self-reproach.

'I ought to have noticed,' she said. 'I shall never forgive myself for not noticing. . . . But – everything fits in with fifty so beautifully, Mr. Palmer. Couldn't we leave her at fifty?'

'Hardly,' said Arnold, dryly, 'considering that the book ends with her conversation with a grown-up grandson. And that conversation is one of the best things in the book. I might almost say that I built the book around it.'

'Of course,' said Miss Filey. 'And she must have met Mark first when she was only six. I quite see that.'

Arnold liked his heroes and heroines to meet first in childhood, to cherish the memory of each other through adolescence, then to meet again by chance in maturity with instant recognition on both sides, followed in the next chapter by protestations of undying affection. One of them was generally married, which provided the tension and drama necessary to draw out the story to the requisite three hundred pages.

'I'm going now, Arnold,' said Judy, standing in the doorway.

'Yes, dear,' said Arnold absently. 'You'll be in to lunch, won't you?'

'Couldn't she be twenty-two when she meets Mark that second time in Florence?' suggested Miss Filey.

'She's twenty-two in 1916,' said Arnold a little shortly. 'People didn't meet casually in Florence in 1916.'

'I told you at breakfast, Arnold,' said Judy. 'I'm going home.'

'Oh yes, of course,' said Arnold absently. 'Matthew's ill, didn't you say? I hope you find him better. . . . It's those years of the war that have thrown us out. . . . If they meet in Florence – and I particularly want them to, because that meeting's one of the best things in the book and I can use that old Italian diary of mine – it must be before 1914 or after 1918.'

'No, it's Peter,' said Judy.

'Of course, darling. . . . I find that one invariably gets tied up in actual dates. In my next book I shall ignore the time factor altogether. It's quite legitimate and much easier.'

'Good-bye, Arnold. The taxi's here.'

'Good-bye, my dear. Have a nice time. Now let's start at the very beginning, Miss Filey, and make a detailed time chart. . . .'

* * *

Only Mrs. Fowler was there when Judy arrived, sitting in her wicker chair at the end of the terrace. Thompson was laying the tea and the deck-chairs were set round, showing that the others were expected. . . . Time might not have moved for the last fifteen years, thought Judy dreamily, as her eyes took in the scene.

'Darling, how nice to see you!' said Mrs. Fowler, drawing Judy to her and kissing her.

Judy took a cushion from one of the chairs and sat at her mother's feet, resting her head against the grey silk knee. Thompson smiled at her – the smile of an old and trusted servant, who was more friend than servant.

'It's nice to see you again, Miss Judy,' she said.

Whenever Judy came to Langley Place she seemed to slip back into her childhood, to become again a little girl – guarded, sheltered, beloved. Once that sheltered atmosphere had irked her. . . . Now it was like a haven to a storm-driven ship. Always about her mother was this suggestion of loving, uncritical understanding. One didn't confide in her because there was no need to confide. . . . She was never inquisitive about one's affairs. She was content to give all and demand nothing in return. . . .

And that, thought Judy, made things both easier and more difficult. It made it easy to withhold confidences, because she could be sure that confidences would never be asked . . . but it was hard to deny the love that crept so insidiously through her defences. I won't tell her, thought Judy, and I won't let her – make any difference. . . . I've made up my mind about it . . . I can't bear Arnold's child. . . . I hate him too much. . . .

Mrs. Fowler drew her hand lightly over the smooth, dark hair, and for a moment or two neither of them spoke.

Then Judy looked up and said, 'Peter . . . ?'

'When I asked you to come,' said Mrs. Fowler, 'I only knew that he wasn't expected to live, but I heard from Matthew again last night. . . .'

'He's – dead?'

Mrs. Fowler nodded.

'Was – Matthew with him?' said Judy after a pause.

'Yes.'

Mrs. Fowler's mind went back to the afternoon when she had received Rachel's letter and had sent for Matthew.

He had come, looking, as he generally did these days, tired and worried, a suggestion of suppressed irritation in every word and movement.

'I can't quite tell from Rachel's letter,' Mrs. Fowler had said, 'how ill Peter is, but I think he's very ill indeed. I want you to go to him for me, Matthew. Will you?'

He was silent for so long that she thought he was going to refuse, then he said:

'Yes . . . I'll go.'

As he spoke a curious tranquillity had seemed to descend on him, erasing the lines of weariness and disillusionment from his face, making it for a moment almost the face of the boy she remembered.

She took from her bag the letter she had received from him last night and handed it to Judy. Judy read it in silence.

He seemed glad to have me with him. We didn't talk much. His mind went back to the times when we were all children at Langley Place. He asked about Gillian. He didn't mention Belle. . . .

Judy handed back the letter.

'Poor Peter! He didn't get what he wanted from life, did he? But then, have any of us got what we wanted from life? Except, perhaps, Helen. . . .'

'What did you want, Judy?'

Judy was silent for some moments.

'Freedom,' she said at last.

Mrs. Fowler smiled.

'You can be as much a slave to freedom, you know, darling, as to anything else.'

'I suppose so,' said Judy, turning her head away.

Then she glanced up suddenly. In the sunlight Mrs. Fowler's face looked fragile and transparent, like a piece of delicate porcelain.

'Mummy . . . you're – all right, aren't you?' she said anxiously.

'Yes, dear,' said Mrs. Fowler. 'I'm taking my pills and being horribly lazy, and I'm better than I've been for years.'

'You're certain?' said Judy.

'Certain. I'm enjoying being a semi-invalid, you know. Those Victorian women who took to their sofas knew what they were doing. I'm reading the books I've been trying to read for years. I don't intend ever to return to a state of rude health. Health is so exacting.'

There was a long silence, then Judy said, 'It's – dreadful about Peter. . . .'

'Don't feel like that, Judy. All of him that belonged to us belongs to us still, belongs to us more, because Peter – understands now, and that makes him nearer.'

'Understands what?'

'Why it all had to happen.'

'Do you know why it had to happen?'

'Almost . . . not quite.'

'How do you know that Peter understands?'

'I can feel it. . . . There's a sort of – gladness about the thought of him that there never was when he was alive.'

'I can only remember Peter as unhappy,' said Judy. 'Unhappy and bewildered. . . . How do you remember him, Mummy.'

'I see him most clearly as a little boy,' said Mrs. Fowler dreamily. 'He had a little set of gardening tools and a little gardening apron, and he used to potter about in his garden – watering things and taking them up and planting them again. He was very earnest about it all. . . . He wouldn't pull the weeds up because he said they were pretty. And he used to collect worms from the rest of the garden to put in his own little plot. Once he put out a saucer of milk for them. . . . He used to take them for rides in his wheelbarrow.'

'I don't remember him, then,' said Judy. 'I suppose I wasn't born.'

But suddenly she saw him quite clearly – small and earnest in his little gardening apron, busy with his miniature gardening tools. He was just on the other side of the lawn. . . . Then he laid down his tools and ran across the lawn to her. But he wasn't Peter . . . he was another child. . . . She tightened her lips and turned her head away, putting out her hand in a quick, instinctive gesture to repulse him. She had gone very pale.

'Here's Helen,' said Mrs. Fowler.

* * *

Max and Helen came slowly up the terrace steps. Max was stout and thick-set, Helen magnificently matronly. Both looked a little self-conscious and wore expressions of deep solemnity. Max bent over Mrs. Fowler's chair and kissed her.

'Accept our most sincere sympathy, Mater dear,' he said, tempering his usually loud voice to a hoarse whisper.

'Let's not be gloomy about it,' said Mrs. Fowler lightly. 'If Peter's here – and he may be – it must be so depressing for him.'

Max gave a startled glance around. Helen looked relieved. She was finding it difficult to put on a seemly show of sorrow and was glad to learn that it was not expected of her. So thick and fast had children, duties and responsibilities crowded in on her since last she saw Peter that hearing of his death was like hearing of the death of a stranger.

'Have you definitely decided to go to the Norfolk Broads in September, Helen?' went on Mrs. Fowler.

'I think so,' said Helen. 'A friend of Max's can get us the yacht, and it would be nice for the children. We discussed both that and the cottage in Cornwall, and we've practically decided on the Norfolk Broads, haven't we, Max?'

Since Mrs. Willoughby's discovery of his love affair she and Helen had been careful to accord him his due position as head of the household, treating him, indeed, with almost exaggerated deference. If it sometimes occurred to him that his advice was asked a good deal more often than it was acted upon, he stifled the thought as disloyalty. He had never again since that occasion wandered into the flowery meadows of illicit romance.

The memory was one of intense humiliation, and he had no desire to repeat the experience. He was supremely happy in his home life, fond of Helen and devoted to his brood of healthy, high-spirited children. There was little of the conventional *pater familias* in his dealings with them. Large, genial, essentially childlike, he was playmate rather than despot. It was Helen who supplied the necessary discipline. Though she was forty, she had had another baby last year.

'I suppose this one really will be the last,' she had said regretfully.

'You'll take Nannie, of course?' said Mrs. Fowler.

'Yes, but it's going to be a bit of a nuisance not having Cynthia,' said Helen. 'I'd taken for granted that Cynthia would go with us, as usual.'

Cynthia's engagement had come as a shock to her family. Gertrude, Florence and Helen felt obscurely that for the first time in her life she was showing herself selfish and inconsiderate.

'When is she being married?' said Mrs. Fowler.

'In October. She's going out to Singapore with Denis in the spring.'

Mrs. Fowler remembered Cynthia as she had last seen her, young and radiant, as if all the frozen part of her had melted in the sunlight.

'It's very awkward for Florence, too,' said Helen. 'Her nurse is away on holiday, and she has no one to take Chloe out in the afternoons. Cynthia always used to do that.'

'So now she'll have to do it herself, won't she?' said Mrs. Fowler with quiet satisfaction.

'Yes,' said Helen. 'That's what makes it so awkward. Florence hates trailing round with children in the afternoon.

She likes to lie down. . . . Of course I know that Cynthia's busy getting ready for her wedding, but I do sometimes feel that she might do a little more than she does for the family these days. Florence says that she hasn't even offered to do her mending for her since she got engaged. She used to be so kind and helpful. . . .'

'"Our blessings brighten as they take their flight,"' murmured Mrs. Fowler.

'Seen anything of Oliver lately, Judy?' said Max.

Judy started at hearing her name. She hadn't been listening. She had been watching the child who should have been Peter but wasn't. . . .

'Yes. . . .'

'The boy's as mad as a hatter,' said Max with an indulgent smile. 'The last time I called to see him the young ass was washing a filthy bit of brass that looked only fit for the dustbin.'

'It was an old horse-bit,' said Judy.

'But what does he *want* with all that junk?' said Max in honest bewilderment.

'It's a harmless hobby,' said Mrs. Fowler.

'If he hadn't shirked his obvious duty he wouldn't need a hobby,' said Helen severely, then, remembering that Oliver's shirking of his obvious duty had left the way open for her boys, added more tolerantly: 'Oh, well, I suppose, as you say, it does no harm.'

There was a silence.

'Arnold all right?' said Max, turning to Judy.

The solemnity of the occasion still oppressed him, and he felt that he must help to keep things going.

Again Judy collected her wandering wits.

'Arnold? Oh yes, thanks. Very busy, as usual.'

'Tell him that I saw one of his books in the public library the other day.'

Max was always sending messages of that sort to Arnold in the naïve belief that they would cause him pride and gratification.

'I haven't read any of them, of course,' said Helen. 'I haven't time for reading, but Mrs. Pringle's very keen on them. She says that his heroes are always so charming.'

Judy gave a little twisted smile.

'All Arnold's heroes,' she said, 'are Arnold, thinly disguised and thickly idealized. I live with the original, so naturally they fail to thrill me.'

Mrs. Fowler threw her a quick glance. Something had happened to Judy – something that had destroyed her poise and assurance, though she still clung to the semblance of it. Beneath her show of nonchalance she was troubled and afraid.

'Mrs. Pringle asked me to say,' said Helen, 'that if he had a spare copy of his last one she'd be awfully glad to have it. With his autograph, of course.'

'I'll tell him,' said Judy, 'but he always says – quite rightly – that if you happened to know a draper you wouldn't expect him to give you vests or combinations, so why should you expect an author to give you books?'

'Really, Judy,' said Helen, 'there's no need to be coarse.'

'Hello, everyone,' said Anice, running lightly up the terrace steps.

She bent down to kiss her mother.

‘I meant to come round to you this morning, darling,’ she said, ‘but I was busy.’

Anice looked, as usual, thin and pale, but Mrs. Fowler noticed that there was an air of suppressed excitement about her. She sat down beside Helen and looked round the circle with a faint smile.

‘Your mother’s bearing up wonderfully,’ said Max, reverting to the hoarse whisper.

He was torn between relief that muted voices, glum faces and conversation about the bereavement were not being demanded and an uncomfortable feeling that they ought to be. . . .

‘You don’t want us to wear mourning, do you, Mummy?’ said Judy suddenly.

‘Of course not, dear,’ said Mrs. Fowler.

‘Don’t you?’ said Max, shocked.

‘No, Max,’ said Mrs. Fowler. ‘It doesn’t mean anything, you know.’

‘Perhaps not,’ said Max doubtfully, ‘but – it looks better, don’t you think?’

Nobody answered him. Mrs. Fowler was thinking of Peter, Helen was planning the holiday on the Norfolk Broads, Judy was still watching the child on the lawn and Anice was thinking of Martin. . . .

As soon as she heard of Peter’s death, Anice had felt that it wasn’t Peter but Martin who had died and her whole body had turned ice-cold. It’s only Peter, she kept assuring herself. . . . Yes, but it might have been Martin. . . . Suppose it had been Martin. . . .

When Martin went out to Australia it had been agreed that she and the children should follow him as soon as he found employment. He had found employment almost at once as chief assistant in a Sydney bookshop, whose owner had been in touch with him for some years. But Anice put off joining him. She would wait till he was more settled. She would wait till the children's education was finished. . . .

Martin was inarticulate. His letters were stilted and lifeless. His suggestions that she should join him were, of his very self-distrust, vague and tentative. And Bruce, of course, influenced her more than she would have admitted. He fought unremittingly against the idea. Patsy wanted to go to Martin, but she was shy and sensitive and almost as inarticulate as Martin himself.

So Anice followed the line of least resistance. She was happy enough as she was. Her marriage with Martin had not been a success. Best not add blunder to blunder by trying to patch it up.

Gradually she had come to the decision that the wisest course was to make the separation a permanent one. Her letters became shorter and shorter, written at longer intervals, ignoring the suggestions, which, on his side, became vaguer and more tentative. And yesterday she had received a letter from him written in a tone of unusual firmness, asking her to let him know definitely whether or not she intended to join him. She had answered it at once, telling him as kindly as she could that she had decided not to come out to him, that their marriage had been a failure and that it was better to face that fact than to risk further years of unhappiness together.

She had gone out to post the letter as soon as she had written it and had returned to learn of Peter's death. And then – it had been as if Martin had died. The memory of him which had grown so dim that she could barely recall his features became unbearably vivid. The stooping, clumsy figure, the unshapely mouth, the steadfast, kindly eyes. . . . She saw them more dearly than the faces of the people round her.

And with the memory the old love for him swept over her in a blinding flood, together with a longing that was almost unbearable. She thought with yearning tenderness of the simplicity she had once despised, of the devotion and integrity that had never failed her, thought with shrinking horror of the life of sterile self-sufficiency to which she had almost condemned herself. *We're happy as we are, the children and I,* she had written. And she knew suddenly that she wasn't, that she never could be happy without Martin . . . that, whatever troubles and difficulties her life with him might hold, it would be better than the barrenness of a life without him.

She sent a cable to contradict her letter. She rang up a shipping company to book berths for herself and the children. And all the time her heart was singing as if she were a bride. Her eagerness held a sting of urgency. There wasn't a moment to be lost. She must get to Martin quickly . . . quickly . . . before anything happened to him. She had told the children of her decision last night – casually, as though it hardly concerned them. Patsy's face had brightened as if a light had been lit behind it. Bruce had sulked and grumbled, but she was so far away from him that his anger no longer affected her. He had been nonplussed by her attitude.

'I won't go,' he had stormed.

'You needn't if you don't want to,' she had said indifferently. 'I expect Aunt Helen would take you.'

Quietly, without further protest, he had begun to make a list of the possessions that he wanted to take out to Australia with him.

'Anice,' said Helen, 'could you and the children come to the Norfolk Broads with us?'

Anice looked at her in surprise. It seemed incredible that they didn't know, but, of course, she had only decided last night . . . when she heard about Peter.

'I'm going out to Martin.'

They stared at her.

'To *Martin*? When?'

'At the end of the month.'

'When did you decide to do that?'

'Yesterday.'

'Are you giving up your job?'

'Yes.'

'It's – sudden, isn't it?'

'Is it? Yes . . . I suppose it is.'

'But, Anice,' said Helen, 'have you considered everything? It's a big decision to make so quickly.'

'I've made it,' said Anice.

'I'm so glad, darling,' said Mrs. Fowler.

'Oh, well,' said Helen, dismissing the problem with a shrug, 'I suppose it's your own business.'

'You can always send Bruce back here to Willoughbys', you know,' said Max, 'if he doesn't settle down.'

'Thanks.'

'While you're both here,' said Helen, 'I wish you'd come and look over some junk that's in the attic. It's stuff that used to be in the old nursery, and I want it for a parish jumble sale, so if there's anything either of you want you'd better take it now or you'll never see it again.'

'I hang on to my things like grim death,' said Max, 'when Helen's on the jumble-sale war-path.'

The three sisters went indoors. Max followed them, humming to himself, till he suddenly remembered Peter's death, coughed and became silent.

* * *

Almost as soon as they had gone, Gillian arrived. She was very slender and upright, and she walked with a light springing step, as though there were wings on her small sandalled feet. There was something exquisitely young and confident and eager about her.

'I'm glad I've found you alone, Gran,' she said. 'I thought the others would be here.'

'They are, darling. They've just gone indoors.'

Gillian dropped on to the cushion at Mrs. Fowler's feet.

'I've been thinking about Daddy, Gran.'

'Yes?'

'He's had such a frightful time lately, hasn't he? With Mother's divorce, I mean, and Father dying.'

Gillian had early decided that Matthew should be Daddy and Peter Father.

'Yes, he has, darling.'

‘I’d like to take him away for a holiday. Don’t you think it would be a good idea?’

‘Yes, I think it would, but what about your school?’

‘I’m seventeen, so I think I’ll leave now,’ said Gillian calmly. ‘Daddy needs me at home, anyway. We’ll take the car abroad and just wander. We’d both love that. Then we’ll come back here when the Absolute’s through and – start fresh.’

Mrs. Fowler smiled tenderly. Gillian – and Gillian alone – seemed able to manage Matthew these days. When she scolded him or flung orders at him his large, sombre face would break into a half-reluctant grin – sheepish, tender, amused. He would let her remove the whiskey-decanter when she thought he had had enough (and she kept him, he complained, on damned short commons); at a glance from her he would make an effort to restrain his ill-humour and impatience.

‘It’s a splendid idea,’ said Mrs. Fowler.

Gillian leant her head against her grandmother’s knee.

‘I don’t remember Father,’ she said, ‘so I can’t feel as sad as I suppose I ought to feel, though’ – with a touch of pride – ‘I did cry a bit last night.’

‘He wouldn’t want you to cry, Gilly.’

‘I suppose he wouldn’t. Do you remember when I used to come here and you used to tell me about him? . . . Tell me some more things about him, Gran. Things he used to do and say. I want to – remember him.’

Mrs. Fowler’s reminiscences were all humorous ones, and Gillian’s clear laugh was ringing out when the others returned from the house. Judy carried a battered toy monkey under her arm.

‘I’d forgotten about it,’ she said to Mrs. Fowler. ‘I used to take it to bed with me, didn’t I?’

‘Well, you don’t want it now,’ said Helen a little tartly. ‘I can always get a good price for old toys.’

‘You aren’t going to get a good price for this one,’ said Judy, then to Gillian: ‘Hello, pet.’

‘Hello, Gillian,’ said Helen. ‘Would you like to come to the Norfolk Broads with us?’

‘No, thanks, Aunt Helen,’ said Gillian. ‘I’m going abroad with Daddy.’

They sat down again, and silence fell on them. The westering sun raked the garden with slanting rays. There was a golden hush over everything.

To Mrs. Fowler it seemed that Peter was there with them, his thin face lit by that tremulous smile she remembered so well. . . . Helen’s thoughts had gone back to her holiday plans. Plenty of thick things for the children. Those pullovers that Cynthia had knitted for them last year. . . . It occurred to her suddenly that she ought to be thinking of Peter, so she stopped thinking about the holiday for a moment or two to think of him, then, her duty done, returned to the holiday. . . . Plenty of towels . . . books and games for wet days. . . .

Anice’s thoughts had leapt ahead to the moment when she and Martin would meet again on the quay at Sydney. Nothing else in the world had any reality for her. The days that separated her from it were an arid expanse to be traversed with dogged patience only because it led her to him. Suppose I’m too late, she thought, and her heart contracted anxiously. I’ll ring up again first thing tomorrow. Perhaps I can get an earlier boat. She tried to think of Peter, but when she summoned the memory of his face it turned into Martin's. . . .

Judy sat, relaxed in her chair, the toy monkey in her arms, surrendering herself to the warmth of the sun and the stillness of the summer evening. The feeling of homecoming lay over her like a benison. The child was still playing on the other side of the lawn, and it seemed right and proper that it should be there. . . . She leant her head back wearily and closed her eyes. . . . In the silence all the turmoil of her spirit died away, and with a sudden uprush of joy she welcomed the new life that was coming to her.

CHAPTER TWENTY-FOUR

Mrs. Fowler descended from the bus and made her way down the sunny road towards The Beeches. It was Thursday, and every Thursday she went to have tea with Mrs. Willoughby and to play a game or two of two-handed bridge with her. Mrs. Willoughby was now so lame that she could only go out in the car or in her bathchair, and she looked forward all week to the visit and to the games of two-handed bridge. She generally won the games, because Mrs. Fowler didn't really care whether she won or lost and never could remember what had gone.

Mrs. Fowler was earlier than usual this afternoon. She had an important piece of news to tell Mrs. Willoughby. Ever since the letter arrived she had been feeling so excited that she could not settle to anything. She had rung up Helen as soon as she had received it, and Helen had been kind but, as usual, a little abstracted. 'Yes, dear,' she had said indulgently, as though she were speaking to one of her children, 'it will be very nice for you,' and then rang off because the fish man had come. Nothing outside her own home had much reality for Helen. . . . But not even Helen's detachment had been able to damp Mrs. Fowler's joy.

Rachel and Michael. . . . From the time of Peter's death Mrs. Fowler had been trying to persuade Rachel to bring the child to England, and at last she had succeeded. They would leave Holland at the end of October and come straight to Langley Place. Mrs. Fowler had never seen her grandson, but the photographs and snapshots that Rachel had sent her showed him so like Peter that they made her heart ache. The same thin, dark, sensitive face. . . . Even the quick nervous smile was Peter's. He had been born in 1929. He would be ten years old now. . . . She saw him playing in the garden of Langley Place . . . sitting on the window-seat of the old schoolroom, as Peter loved to, reading Peter's books. He should have Peter's bedroom, with the school groups on the wall and the bookshelves that Peter had made. It had taken four years to break down the barrier of Rachel's pride and the strange unreasoning resentment she bore Peter's family, but the struggle was over now. *Michael is looking forward so much to coming home* . . . she had written. It was July. They would be here in about twelve weeks' time. . . .

A man and woman passed her, their faces tense and anxious. Mrs. Fowler caught the words 'Poland' and 'Nazis'. It brought her back to reality. She had been so much excited about the visit of Rachel and Michael that she had almost forgotten what she thought of as the 'war scare'.

She went into the little post-office at the corner of the road to buy a book of stamps. There were some magazines displayed on the counter. Idly she opened a spiritualist review and glanced at the contents, though she was not interested in spiritualism. A well-known and tested spirit informed the world through a well-known and tested medium that there would be no war. Well, they ought to know, thought Mrs. Fowler, happiness welling up in her again, as she put the book of stamps into her bag and went out into the road. Rachel should have Helen's old bedroom, and she would turn Anice's old bedroom into a sitting-room, so that Rachel could feel that she had a place of her own. . . .

She was so much absorbed by her plans that she walked several yards past the gate of The Beeches and had to retrace her steps.

Mrs. Willoughby was sitting by the fireplace, a large mending-basket on the floor by her chair. She kept Max and all Helen's children in socks and did all Helen's household mending.

'Oh, it's you, is it?' she said as Mrs. Fowler entered. 'I'd forgotten it was Thursday.'

She never liked Mrs. Fowler to realize how much she looked forward to this weekly visit.

'Sit down,' she went on. 'Well, how are you? Gadding about and knocking yourself up, as usual, I suppose?'

Most of Mrs. Fowler's activities were classed as 'gadding' by Mrs. Willoughby.

'No,' said Mrs. Fowler mildly. 'I went to tea at Helen's yesterday and I went into Bellington the day before. I'm really much better. I've had a wonderful piece of news. . . . '

Mrs. Willoughby made a non-committal sound as she drew out a piece of grey wool.

'Rachel and Michael are coming to England in October. They're going to stay at Langley Place.'

‘For how long?’ said Mrs. Willoughby.

‘I don’t know. I hope indefinitely.’

Mrs. Willoughby snorted.

‘You’re only letting yourself in for a lot of worry and trouble. And you’ll knock yourself up, running round after them.’

‘No, I won’t,’ said Mrs. Fowler happily.

Now that she had told Mrs. Willoughby, the whole thing seemed fixed and settled, as if nothing could happen to prevent it. Mrs. Willoughby’s characteristic fashion of receiving the news gave it the final touch of reality.

‘Shall I help you with some of that darning?’ she went on.

‘No, thank you,’ said Mrs. Willoughby.

‘You let me last week,’ Mrs. Fowler reminded her.

‘I know I did,’ said Mrs. Willoughby grimly. ‘I had to unpick the darns afterwards.’

‘Did you?’ said Mrs. Fowler with interest. ‘I’ve never been much good with my needle. I did knit a pair of socks, though, once. I don’t quite remember when.’

‘Did anyone wear them?’ said Mrs. Willoughby.

‘I forget,’ said Mrs. Fowler evasively.

‘You forget most things,’ said Mrs. Willoughby. ‘I hope you won’t forget to come to my party on Wednesday.’

Mrs. Fowler remembered that Mrs. Willoughby was having her seventieth birthday party on Wednesday. The excitement of her own news had driven it out of her mind.

‘Oh, of course,’ she said. ‘I’m looking forward to it. I suppose all the family will be coming?’

Mrs. Willoughby nodded as she folded a pair of socks into a neat ball and took another pair out of the mending-basket.

'Yes . . . Oliver's the one who's making the most fuss about it. You'd think he was coming from the other end of the world instead of just from London. He's been looking out trains and altering his arrangements and working himself up into a state about leaving his flat for one night ever since he heard about it.'

'Yes, he would,' smiled Mrs. Fowler. 'He took Helen's children to Lord's last week, and they were telling me about it yesterday.'

Oliver was fond of his young nieces and nephews. Every winter he took them all to a matinée and every summer to Lord's. The arrangement had to be made several weeks ahead, every item of the preparations worked out to the last detail, every *contretemps* guarded against. He would spend sleepless nights before the event, and generally some small mishap would occur, throwing him into a state of fluster and distress that caused his young guests much amusement. He had taken them back to his flat for tea after the match last week, and Babs had given a very comical imitation of his consternation when he found that the confectioner had sent an orange cake instead of the raspberry cake he had ordered.

'I sometimes think,' said Mrs. Willoughby slowly, 'that I'd have done better to let him marry Judy.'

Mrs. Fowler realized that this was a generous admission.

'They probably wouldn't have been happy,' she said, not to be outdone in generosity.

'Perhaps not,' said Mrs. Willoughby, 'but they're neither of them happy now.'

Mrs. Fowler sighed as she thought of Judy, so wrapped up in her young son that she had little time or interest for anything else. Her life was now completely detached from Arnold's, but Arnold, busy with his forty-fifth novel, did not seem to realize it.

'She's devoted to the child,' she said.

'That doesn't mean she's happy,' said Mrs. Willoughby.

A male laugh and a female titter floated in from the kitchen regions. Mrs. Willoughby pursed her lips.

'Cook's out,' she said, 'and that girl's gossiping with the baker's man again. I can't trust any of them. I still miss Cynthia.' She threw Mrs. Fowler a keen glance. 'I've never asked you, but it was you who made her go off to London like that, wasn't it?'

'It might have been,' admitted Mrs. Fowler. 'I did say something.'

'She'd have come back if she hadn't met Denis Gordon there.'

'Yes, but she did meet Denis Gordon there,' said Mrs. Fowler with quiet triumph. Then, to change the subject, 'And how's all the family?'

Mrs. Willoughby shrugged.

'Pretty much as usual. Clarissa's school reports are very unsatisfactory.'

'Like Jessica.'

'Timothy isn't settling down at all well at the business.'

'Like Oliver.'

'Peggy seems bent on making this improvident match with a man who has no prospects.'

'Like Anice.'

'Bobby's marriage, I'm afraid, isn't turning out very well.'

‘Like Peter. . . . It’s like a sort of roundabout, isn’t it? You get one lot more or less settled and then, before you know where you are, it’s all starting again with the next.’

‘It seems so,’ said Mrs. Willoughby.

‘And you can’t do anything to stop it.’

‘You aren’t even trying to.’

‘How do you mean?’

‘Bringing Rachel and the child over. Asking for trouble.’

Joy flooded Mrs. Fowler’s heart.

‘That’s not trouble.’

‘People always mean trouble. . . . I’m getting too old to cope with it. I did my best to stop Jessica marrying that Communist and going out to Spain, but since then I’ve let them go their own way.’

Mrs. Fowler had a sudden glimpse of loneliness beneath her friend’s detachment.

‘I’ll come round on Tuesday,’ she said, ‘and give a hand with getting ready for the party.’

‘There’s nothing you can do,’ said Mrs. Willoughby. ‘Helen’s arranging everything. But I’d be glad to see you, all the same. . . . Funny,’ she added meditatively, as she rolled up another pair of socks and took a small vest out of the mending-basket. ‘Funny how I used to dislike you.’

‘I know,’ said Mrs. Fowler. ‘I never exactly disliked you, but I found you very difficult to understand. You helped me sometimes, though. You helped me that day Gillian was going to the party.’

Mrs. Willoughby threw her an uncomprehending glance.

‘She’s a capable young woman, Gillian,’ she said. ‘She looks after Matthew very well.’

'Yes,' agreed Mrs. Fowler. 'They're devoted to each other, but they're both inclined to be a little possessive. I mean, Matthew's inclined to freeze other men off Gillian, and Gillian's inclined to freeze other women off Matthew. Still, I expect things will sort themselves out. They generally do.'

'On the whole,' said Mrs. Willoughby after a short pause, 'quite a fair proportion of our families is happy and well settled.'

'Yes,' said Mrs. Fowler, 'but if this war comes . . . I suppose Cynthia would be safe in Singapore and Anice in Australia, but the rest of them . . .'

'No one would be safe anywhere if it came, but it won't come,' said Mrs. Willoughby, breaking off a piece of white mending wool with an air of finality. 'The whole thing's bluff. He wouldn't dare to fight the British Empire – a common little German upstart like that!'

Her nose became the ghost of the eagle's beak as she spoke.

'They're all joining things,' said Mrs. Fowler.

'I know,' said Mrs. Willoughby. 'It does them good. Max has lost over a stone since he joined the Territorials, and all this Red Cross work the girls are doing keeps them out of mischief.'

'If it does come . . .' said Mrs. Fowler.

She had a vision of Oliver torn from his realm of *bric-à-brac* and make-believe . . . Max uprooted from the home that was his whole world . . . Matthew . . . the young people . . . Rachel and Michael. . . . Suppose that Rachel and Michael couldn't come, after all? . . . Suppose she never saw Peter's son? . . . Her heart turned cold at the thought.

‘It won’t come,’ said Mrs. Willoughby again.

There was the old authoritative note in her voice, and Mrs. Fowler felt a great relief, confident now that it wouldn’t come.

‘They say that half those tanks he takes into countries are made of cardboard,’ went on Mrs. Willoughby. ‘We’ve only to be firm and he’ll climb down.’

‘Yes,’ said Mrs. Fowler. ‘Still . . . Matthew met a man last week who’d just come out of Germany, and he said – ’

Mrs. Willoughby cut her short.

‘I never believe those stories,’ she said. ‘They’re all grossly exaggerated.’ She glanced at the clock. ‘We’ve just time for a game before tea.’

‘I’ll get the card-table,’ said Mrs. Fowler.

‘No, I’ll ring,’ said Mrs. Willoughby. ‘It’ll get rid of that man, anyway. I believe he’s still there.’

She put her hand on the bell, and they heard the closing of the kitchen door and heavy steps on the flagged path outside. Soon a trim housemaid, with frilled cap and apron and a pretty, rather saucy face, appeared. Mrs. Willoughby looked at her for a moment in silence, and the eagle’s beak stood out in all its old grandeur.

‘Please put out the card-table,’ she said, ‘and I should be obliged if you would not waste the entire afternoon gossiping with tradesmen at the back door.’

The girl tossed her head and put out the card-table in silence.

‘I don’t know what they’re coming to,’ said Mrs. Willoughby when she had gone. ‘Would you believe it – this girl wanted Sunday afternoon off as well as her afternoon in the week.’

‘Did she get it?’ said Mrs. Fowler.

‘Yes. She held out for it. I don’t know how it is, but they aren’t as easy to get as they used to be. . . . And now I’m afraid she’s making up to the baker’s man.’

‘He’s the nice-looking one, isn’t he?’ said Mrs. Fowler. ‘He comes to Langley Place. I’ve tried making up to him, myself, but he hasn’t given me any encouragement,’ then, meeting Mrs. Willoughby’s blank stare, she said, Now, Millicent, to herself, and added aloud in a vague Milly-ish fashion, ‘Things are very difficult, aren’t they? . . . Where are the cards?’

‘Here,’ said Mrs. Willoughby. ‘Let’s cut. . . . Your deal. . . .’

Mrs. Fowler took the cards, and began to deal.

Persephone Books publishes forgotten fiction and non-fiction by unjustly neglected authors. The following titles are available:

No. 1 William – an Englishman (1919) by Cicely Hamilton

No. 2 Mariana (1940) by Monica Dickens

No. 3 Someone at a Distance (1953) by Dorothy Whipple

No. 4 Fidelity (1915) by Susan Glaspell

No. 5 An Interrupted Life: the Diaries and Letters of Etty Hillesum 1941–43

No. 6 The Victorian Chaise-longue (1953) by Marghanita Laski

No. 7 The Home-Maker (1924) by Dorothy Canfield Fisher

No. 8 Good Evening, Mrs. Craven: the Wartime Stories of Mollie Panter-Downes

No. 9 Few Eggs and No Oranges: the Diaries of Vere Hodgson 1940–45

No. 10 Good Things in England (1932) by Florence White

No. 11 Julian Grenfell (1976) by Nicholas Mosley

No. 12 It's Hard to be Hip over Thirty and Other Tragedies of Married Life (1968) by Judith Viorst

No. 13 Consequences (1919) by E. M. Delafield

No. 14 Farewell Leicester Square (1941) by Betty Miller

No. 15 Tell It to a Stranger: Stories from the 1940s by Elizabeth Berridge

No. 16 Saplings (1945) by Noel Streatfeild

No. 17 Marjory Fleming (1946) by Oriel Malet

No. 18 Every Eye (1956) by Isobel English

No. 19 They Knew Mr. Knight (1934) by Dorothy Whipple

No. 20 A Woman's Place: 1910–1975 by Ruth Adam

No. 21 Miss Pettigrew Lives for a Day (1938) by Winifred Watson

No. 22 Consider the Years 1938–1946 by Virginia Graham